Acclaim for Marion Stein's

Loisaida

A New York Story

"This is noir at its best, a dark tale that explores human frailty among those who pursue justice, as well as among the perpetrators of horrific crimes. In her psychological insight, as well as in the quality of her writing, Stein is a worthy heir to Raymond Chandler . . .She engages the reader's sympathy with the main protagonist, an actor-turned-journalist, and we follow his growing obsession with investigating a macabre murder, his increasing cocaine, heroin and prescription drug use, and the slow disintegration of his personality. Stein writes with candour and a sense of emotional authenticity. Like a singer with perfect pitch, she has a gift for finding the voice for each character and understanding their motivation. She is able to tell a captivating story, and the result is a book that is impossible to put down."

— **Larry Harrison**, author *Glimpses of a Floating World*

"At once lyrical and lewd, heartbreaking and hardboiled, this is a book that operates on many levels and succeeds spectacularly on every one of them, whether it's the power of the storytelling or the raw language, but most of all this is a perfect evocation of a particular time and the things that made it terrifying and exhilarating. This is a thought-provoking nostalgia rush from an author who operates with complete mastery of her material."

— **Dan Holloway**, author *The Company of Fellows*

"Marion Stein tells her story in many voices. As well as Ingrid and Peter, there's the terrifying psychopathic Joe Holiday, there's crazed Lenny, the aging hippy, and many more. To make all these voices harmonise without sacrificing the individuality and the relevance of each is a considerable feat.

There are other voices, too. There's Raymond Chandler, there's Norman Mailer, there's Charles Dickens, there's Fyodor Dostoevsky . . . There are voices of writers I've never read, voices of writers I've never heard of; there are voices of writers Marion Stein has never heard of. It's quite a performance.

In fact . . . Oh, forget it, I can't face any more of this. What did Thackeray say again? "There's no writing against such power as this – one has no chance!"

— **Iain Manson**, author *Jezira*

About the Author

Marion Stein is a New York based fiction writer and blogger. You can catch up with her at Marionstein@twitter.com, and on her blog www.marionstein.net. You may also find her work elsewhere on the web and in print.

Other available books by Marion Stein

The Death Trip
Schrodinger's Telephone
Blood Diva (as VM Gautier)

Loisaida

A New York Story

Marion Stein

Caradeloca Press

New York, NY

www.caradelocapress.com

ISBN 978-0-615-33681-7
2nd Print Edition, 2015

Cover design and photo by Marion Stein & Craig Savel.
Formatting for this edition by RikHall.com.

Acknowledgements

An early draft of this novel was written long ago in cabaña overlooking the Pacific at Shambala/Casa de Gloria in Zipolite, Oaxaca. Belated thanks to Gloria and the Shambala family for providing an inspiring.

Years later parts of a revision were showcased on the Authonomy website. I am grateful for the feedback – both critical and encouraging, provided by readers and writers there. Special thanks to JD Revene for his astute beta-reading skills and unremitting but tactful honesty, and to Bradley Wind for designing the Cara de Loca logo and the first edition cover.

Also thanks go to Dan Holloway for bringing together some immensely talented people and forming the *Year Zero Writers Collective*. Without *Year Zero*, I might never have found the courage to go "indie."

Finally, I must acknowledge the contribution of Craig Savel – my partner in crime and all other things – for his patience, encouragement, and belief.

This book is dedicated to the dead because as someone must have once said, "The dead can only speak through the living." And dear reader, you're about to get an earful ....

Chapter 1

The Stink in 5C – March 1989

Jesus

Jesus Reyes standing by the bed, touches the cheek of his sleeping wife, then places his hand in the air an inch or so above her mouth following her warm even breaths in and out. Ana is snoring softly, as she sometimes does. Never loud enough to wake him, but he likes to tease her about it. He pulls the cover down to reveal her belly, the slight swelling visible beneath her nightgown. She told him they must have started the new one that first night they could after the baby was born. What was it they called that? *Irish twins?* Hadn't his mother said there was an O'Reilly in the family tree? *Some crazy pirate washed up in Ponce once upon a time.*

Next to her, the baby begins to stir. There's a crib in the corner, but Ana is a country girl from Mexico who believes babies should be kept close. She turns, eyes still closed and murmurs in her sleep. Jesus lifts the infant and tries to step softly into the living room.

He walks back and forth holding the boy, concentrating on each step, each breath. *This is what is real*, he tells himself. *This is what's important and worth living for.* He holds his son tight against his chest feeling the quick beating of his tiny heart.

Never before has he felt so much love, or so much desire to protect what he has. How lucky he is now, a beautiful young wife, a family, a home, a job as the super. A life. How easy it would be to blow it all away.

Nearly twenty years since he'd been a teenager in that war. Five years clean. Two without even the medication. But today, all those bad old thoughts coming home because of the smell in 5C.

When you're a super in a building in New York and the tenants start to complain about an odor, and the young man's mailbox is bulging, and no one has seen him in a week, and the last time you saw him you meant to take him with you to a church or a meeting or someplace, or at least to say, "Those marks on your arm. Be careful. So many have died," but you didn't, maybe because you didn't want to seem preachy, or it would have made you think too much about things you shouldn't be thinking about at all, but one thing you're certain about, if you open the door to 5C, it won't be a broken refrigerator causing the stink.

Jesus pictures the day the man moved in. *Was it even a year ago?* Ana said he was a movie star. She'd seen him in something, one of her soaps? He told her he'd given up the acting. He was a writer now. He didn't go out to work every day, but some days Jesus would see him leaving the apartment wearing a suit jacket, looking very smart, professional. And the women he'd bring – beautiful women with straight white teeth and tans like they had nothing better to do than lie in the sun.

Then he started to bring the others. Cheap women and a man with dead eyes hidden behind an easy smile. Neighbors would complain about noises. Pacing all night.

Jesus once asked him about it. "I'm sorry," he said. "I was working on something. Talking to myself, acting out the story. I'll try to keep it down."

Then this afternoon, old lady Sobczak approached Jesus muttering about the smell, and he felt something come up in his gut.

He walked down the corridor keeping his eyes focused straight ahead, afraid if he looked down or out of the corner of his eye, he might catch a glimpse of someone or something he'd left behind on the other side of the world. As he turned the key, he imagined finding not just the body of a single dead junkie, but the jungle itself, the death, the violence, everything he tried so hard to protect

Ana and the baby and himself from ever seeing.

The door wouldn't open. He tried calling the cops, but his hand was shaking when he picked up the receiver, and so he went out. Lit a candle for the young man no one knew for sure was dead. Found a meeting – the first he'd been to in years. After that he walked around the city, past the lost humans begging for change, and then he came home.

What a waste, he thinks. A man like that, handsome, smart, with money. Yet, he could fall so easily, so suddenly and completely. Jesus feels the warmth of the baby's cheek against his own and weeps.

Teri

Outside of 5C, Patrol officer Teri Conner is talking in what her partner Thomas Garcia calls her "loud-soft" voice, trying to coax whoever is inside to answer. Garcia meanwhile pushes the door, which has a little give. Then he takes it – bashing it open with his shoulder once it's clear that whatever is holding it shut isn't very strong. Teri, the junior officer, knows he shouldn't have done that without permission from a sergeant.

They step inside and there's the dead junkie a few feet in front of them. Garcia pulls out his piece, holds it in both hands, points it at the corpse and shouts, "Freeze motherfucker."

He laughs and repeats the phrase, this time clearly for her benefit, "Freeze moth*erfucker*."

Teri snorts, not worth wasting words. The junkie is wearing jeans, no shirt. The belt still around his arm. Syringe on the desk, next to the computer. He must have been sitting on the chair when he shot, then fell over. Teri takes a quick look at the screen, the green letters still glowing. Her days as a secretary are useful. Document names. One is highlighted, titled: *Prologue.* The cursor blinks below the "P" like a beating heart.

The apartment is orderly, more so than the chaos they usually see. *He was someone,* Teri thinks. *He belonged to someone.*

And then despite herself, she's remembering visiting her kid

5

brother, Shawn, in the hospital after he OD'd.

The EMTs cracked a couple of ribs doing CPR. He pointed out the bruises and talked about suing the city. She gave him the look, and he gave her the "just kidding" grin.

"A joke! Really, I'm going into treatment. Swear to God."

And he had. Then dead within a year. He was dealing small amounts of coke in their Queens neighborhood. Pissed off some Colombians, the new kids in Elmhurst, and they blew him away.

Teri was working in an office, thinking about nursing school. But after that, she decided to apply to the academy. Just wanted the chance to get some bad guys.

Her mother between drags of portable oxygen and nicotine rasped, "Honey, I loved your brother to death. But shit, to most people, he *was* the bad guys."

Now here she is, a year and a half later in a strange apartment, standing over another young corpse. Bloated and stinking.

The deceased is around six feet tall, blond and blue. His eyes are open, starting to swell, and Teri wishes she could shut them or at least cover the body.

They radio the station, and wait for their sergeant and EMS.

Garcia pushes up an already open window.

"We're not supposed to touch anything," Teri shouts.

"What? You think you at a fuckin murder scene? This could take time."

"It's procedure."

"Shit." He goes downstairs. She stays with the body. The apartment door is open and the smell is bearable.

Alone with the dead man, she wonders if she could be at a fuckin murder scene. He looks familiar, but she can't place him. The couch is leather and not too shabby, the computer – name brand, state of the art. She notices the books – Stanislavsky, *On Acting*, Kerouac, *On The Road*.

Who was this beautiful white boy with the armful of tracks, the books on the shelf, barely worn Armani jacket draped over a chair?

It doesn't surprise her when the sergeant walks in accompanied by Detective Ouspenski, homicide.

"Did you touch anything?" Ouspenski asks.

"No sir."

"Good girl."

She watches the way he notices things – the small closed suitcase with the airline sticker sitting by the couch, the door bolt now off its hinges thanks to her partner, the latch on the window gate. New York City regulations didn't allow regular gates or bars on fire escape windows, so the gate had a special latch that could be opened from inside the apartment. She heard a skilled burglar could manipulate a latch like that using a wire, open it up from the outside, but it seemed unlikely anyone could have left that way and closed it.

Ouspenski goes into the bathroom. He asks her to follow him. It's a typical tenement bathroom – only a toilet and a sink, the tub in the kitchen. Ouspenski is a large man, tall and heavy, especially around the middle. It feels almost inappropriate, too intimate standing next to him in such a small space.

"Could you fit through there?" he asks, pointing to a narrow window also off the fire escape. It can't be more than nine inches wide.

"I don't think so, sir."

"Yeah, right," he says. There's a little crinkle in the corner of his turned down mouth and something sad in his gray eyes.

The EMS team arrives and pronounces the death. They still have to wait for the medical examiner. Ouspenski steps around the corpse and looks at the computer screen.

"Young lady," he says turning to Teri, "Do you know how to work one of these things?"

"Yeah, I guess. What do you need?"

"Can you get the one called *Prologue*?"

"I think so."

"Can you do it without touching the machine a lot? Just pressing something?"

"The diskette is loaded. It looks like I'd just have to hit the enter key."

He takes a pen out of his pocket. Hands it to her. "Do it with this patrolman."

She hits the key. The machine hums. Then the words appear ghostly green against the black screen:

> This is a story about a revolution that never happened, and the people it never happened to. This is a story about a place - New York's Lower East Side, a.k.a. the East Village, Lo-i-sai-da, a neighborhood of artists, dreamers, hustlers, devil worshipers, anarchists, junkies and yuppies, all competing for breathing space in a city without air. This is a love story about a poor farm boy who meets a beautiful blonde. This is a story about a time - the era of greed, when the poor were objects of scorn not sympathy, and the gentrifiers viewed themselves as urban pioneers. This is a story about sex and drugs and real estate. This is a story about a murder . . .

Chapter 2

The Dead Guy Floating . . .

Peter

Sunset Boulevard always was my favorite film. Scene one – the cops and press descend upon the creepy old house as some dead guy floats in the pool.

Joe Gillis, as deluded as Norma Desmond, thought he could win, come out clean. But he was just another cheap opportunist lulled by the sirens, that glamorous girl group of demons in drag – Success, Ambition, Fame.

Classic line uttered by Joe himself as voice over, "The poor dope. He always wanted a pool."

Me? I was born with one. Had the weird Spanish-style mansion in the Hollywood Hills too. Gone by the time I was seven. But that's what they call the back-story. We'll get to it. We have time.

The story you came for begins much later and won't be found on any floppy diskettes conveniently confiscated by New York City's finest. The action starts on a sweltering summer night when Ingrid Hess asked me for a cigarette, and I almost saved her life.

❖❖❖

Chapter 3

The Night They Never Met

From The Personal Journal and Memoir of Ingrid Hess - a record of her life and her time in New York. Volume I. The Beginning . . .

June 1988

My father was the son of a Nazi officer. This I know. One time when I was staying with my grandparents in Germany, I found a whole trunk full of shit - medals, insignia, official papers from the Reich. My grandmother insisted it was my great uncle's. She also explained to me it's not polite to talk about the war, and then pretended she couldn't understand my German.

My mother was a Dutch whore. This I am not one hundred percent sure about, but she was a stewardess in New York and I have a photo of her with two other women and a man, and I'm sure one of the women is Xaviera Hollander who was of course also a stewardess before becoming a famous prostitute. I've read The Happy Hooker, and there is a woman in it I believe is my mother. My father will only say that she was a model when they met. But then where are the pictures? Where is her portfolio?

Both of them, my parents, kept things from me. When she went into the hospital to die, he would tell me she was getting stronger. He said children were not allowed to visit. Later, he told me that was what she wanted. I believe it. I believe she wanted me to always remember her as looking her best. Why not? She made her living from her beauty. It was the only thing she had of worth. So that's how I remember her - a beautiful accomplished liar who didn't even want to say goodbye to her only daughter if it meant shattering the illusion of her perfection.

My father is in banking. He's worked for all the big firms, Deutsche Bank, Manny Hanny, Chase. When I was a little girl, we lived in New York on Fifth Avenue. We could see Central Park from the living room.

Then they transferred him to Chicago and we moved to a house on the North Shore with a lawn and yard. It was there that she got sick and was gone. My father sent me to Germany to stay with his sister and her husband. It was a mistake to send a long-legged eleven-year-old girl to live with her aunt and the uncle by marriage who had never seen her as a baby.

Daddy tells me he meant well. People can fuck their good intentions. He tells himself that nothing much happened. Jah, jah, Ingrid always the actress.

It doesn't matter anyway. It's all material. I'll make art out of this shitty life. My body is my instrument, my canvas.

When I came back from Germany, I was a mess. I cut myself. You can still see the white marks on my wrist. It was before I learned to use the pills. My father couldn't handle it, put me in a place. Quite an education, it was. I knew that if I got out, I would come to New York and study and dance and everything I was keeping inside me, I would have a way to get it out.

I want to create, to do my own performances. I don't care about Broadway. I saw a play here, downtown. It wasn't really a play - just a man in a flannel shirt and jeans, alone on the stage sitting in a chair with a desk in front of him. There was a notebook and a glass of water on the desk, and he would glance at the notes as he told stories about his life. He was an actor making a film in

Asia about Vietnam. Sometimes he talked about history, but mostly he talked about himself, his experiences. There was a lot about Thai whores.

It was a little funny, but sometimes not so interesting. So self-indulgent. He was pasty and in his forties. Why would the Thai girls want to fuck him if not for the money?

Really, the space was hot and I started to sleep, but I thought yes, this is something I would like to do with dance, to be alone on stage, tell my story with my body, the emotions of it, the experience.

And so it gave me the idea for this journal in which I will record not only the stories of my time in New York, my struggles to create - but more: I will tell my life story. Here will be my words and they will serve two purposes. I will use them to create my story-dances, monologues in movement, yes? And also this journal/memoir will record all that has made me who I am and someday other artists, other dancers will read it and understand Ingrid Hess and how she came to be who she was.

❖ ❖ ❖

Peter

June 1904, *The General Slocum* disaster – one thousand twenty one dead. Most of them children. A ferry taking a group of German immigrants out from Manhattan to Long Island for a church picnic catches fire.

July 1988, all that's left to remember the dead is a faded, urine-stained slab of marble in Tompkins Square Park. I was sitting on a bench across from it. *Ulysses* references the tragedy, so often when I see the worn-out pink monument I think about the semester I wrangled with all things Joyce. But on this summer night, there were other distractions. It was Wigstock – the East Village's annual drag festival. A day when even the straightest of men could try on those red spike heels and channel his inner diva. The event had been happening every summer for years. It was still controlled by the drag queens that started it all, although some said it had become tamer, more "respectable" as the straights and other tourists began showing up. It was a night to hang out, listen to the bands and celebrate fabulousness.

Now after midnight, the festivities were at an end. Some new Cinderella ordinance stopped the music to the great displeasure of the crowd. A kid with purple hair and a face full of safety pins was handing out green garbage bags, advising people to pick up their shit and leave no traces. The homeless, many of whom resided in the park, were doing a job on the beer cans. At five cents apiece, a hundred would get you a meal, or a fix.

The heat and humidity were high. Thousands milled around, breathing in the relatively fresh air of the park – its ten acres the biggest public space on the Lower East Side. Neo-pagans pounded out percussion as a line of expressionless cops stood by, arms crossed. Rumor had it they were going to close down the park. Break up the encampment that developed with the housing crunch.

The park rangers had removed some trash-bag-tents the previous week, leading to a small demo. A few arrests. Now there were all kinds of community meetings going on. Wild stories about secret city plans to concretize the entire space. You could attribute it to paranoia, or even wishful thinking. A lot of the locals liked to believe that they were still being targeted by the city's "Red Squad", and there were plenty of aging activists whose nostalgia for the 60's included tales of protests and arrests. The growing police presence, however, wasn't a fantasy.

Myself – I was just another bright young man looking for the Big Story in the Naked City. It had only been a few months since I moved down from the Upper West Side and started calling myself a writer. Sold a couple of pieces to *The City Eye*. There was something here, an energy to the East Village that didn't exist elsewhere. Nascent, but who knew what kind of creature it would develop into? I still hadn't found the hook, the tale that would be the microcosm through which I would convey this world.

I was working on something, an article, maybe turn it into a series, on the changing dynamics of the neighborhood. I heard there was an anarchist group planning to blow up the Floradora House, a landmark recently renovated for "luxury condos." Started as a hotel in the 1880's. Later a settlement house. Then an apartment building. Torched in the seventies allegedly by the landlord, victim of rising costs and rent control. Home to no one for years, till a developer took an interest. I talked to one guy who'd bought a two-bedroom. Not exactly yuppie scum. He's a teacher with a social worker wife and two kids. They lived down here for years. Had a rent stabilized railroad apartment in a building where the landlord started moving in addicts and goons to clear the place. The Floradora was the most reasonably priced two-bedroom they'd seen in Manhattan. They could barely afford it. Now they get pelted by egg throwing punks who think they're engaged in class warfare.

So I sat in on a meeting of RANT – the Revolutionary Anarchist Action Network. Didn't uncover any plot to bomb anything. Just lots of loose talk.

Nothing I could grab on to. No book deal potential.

Still I believed I'd find my big story, somewhere on the Lower East Side, and a drag festival, in a contested piece of park, on a steamy summer night, with the outer borough cops surrounding like an occupying army, seemed as good a spot as any to look.

I was sitting on a bench, taking in the scene, about to light up a Camel when the most beautiful woman I'd ever seen sat down beside me.

"You have maybe another?" she asked pointing a long hot-pink fingernail at my cigarette.

❖❖❖

From The Personal Journal and Memoir of Ingrid Hess

14 July

I know I must study more. I need to perfect my technique. This means classes and also I must eat. My father won't send more money. He thinks I am "not well" and should move back to Chicago. I won't go back.

I've been dancing at a "gentleman's club." It's not so bad, a way of observing. You watch them watch you.

Sometimes, I really dance for them, but you always need to be careful. They try to grab you and that's why you need the pole. You cannot lose yourself in the dance, which makes it boring. Like any job.

You do stupid things when you get bored. Sometimes I meet men, younger American versions of my father if you want to play that game. Maybe from the Midwest with a stopover in some ivy-league, MBA program. Men like that, they'll give you cocaine and take you out for a good dinner, but you never get what you need.

What I need is a couple of weeks of quiet. Someplace clean where I can sleep. I never seem to get enough money together for my own place. I read the Voice and the Eye and always they have these ads for roommates, but the men want to fuck you and the women don't want their men to want to fuck you, so it doesn't work out.

I got so desperate and tired that I walked into a hospital. (I am here now. They finally felt I was safe enough to give me a pen.) I showed them my wrists. I told them I was in the mood to die. The resident wasn't impressed.

"Those scars look old and superficial," he said.

"Next time maybe I make them deeper, motherfucker. Why don't you check my record? Call Chicago."

I had to wait almost twelve hours in the ER. They think I'm crazy but not too crazy.

I have a roommate. She's not crazy either. Katherine, middle aged, the veteran of many failed suicides. None, serious. The first day she tells me that her family doesn't like her. I am thinking they're just sick of her whining. She's all alone in her beautiful, deluxe apartment on the Upper East Side. Boo fuckin hoo.

I always listen. Sympathetic. It's my nature.

"We are both orphans," she says.

I notice her watching me. Watching while I do my stretches.

"I should do that," she says. Telling me this hurts, that hurts, pointing to her shoulder. Asks me to rub her neck. That's how it starts. You can figure out where it leads.

Soon she's promising me that I can stay with her when we get out. I'm thinking I can probably get her to pay for my classes and I don't even have to eat her pussy, just touch her a little. Like a mercy jerk-off every couple of days.

The cow tells the son.

Big conference including the social worker. After, she tells me the son and his wife will stay with her. No Ingrid.

I hate her. I feel nauseous when I think about touching her. Now, I've got nowhere to go and they're ready to kick me out.

Peter

She had platinum hair, breasts bursting out of her halter-top, blue crystal eyes, long thin legs. In another setting, she might have been taken for a hooker. Here, in a park full of drag queens, I found myself staring at her uncovered throat for signs of an Adam's apple. That kind of perfection just couldn't be real.

She was wearing cut offs and white leather boots that came mid-thigh. The skin between the boots and the shorts was tan and tight and muscular.

"Those must be hell in this heat," I said staring at her footwear as I handed over the cigarette I had just started.

"One must suffer to be beautiful." Her inflection was slightly off, like an accent or a put on. I watched the smoke leave her mouth in circles perfectly timed and executed.

I smiled as though responding to some purposely ironic remark. Her face was completely deadpan and made me remember something I'd once read about Garbo. There's a shot of her, a close-up, at the end of *Queen Christina*. The director had told her to think of "absolutely nothing."

As she inhaled taking deep theatrical drags, I tried to think of something clever to say. But before I had a chance to open my mouth, this crazy park character, the one with the rooster on his shoulder, came up and asked her if she wanted to pet his bird.

❖❖❖

From The Personal Journal and Memoir of Ingrid Hess

16 July 1988

Forced from hospital yesterday. I hate them all, doctors, nurses. They act so noble, but they don't help anyone.

I call the Game-boy. Flabby-assed, forties - he makes computer games for children and has a fat baby face. He once told me he'd do anything to help me. He'd leave his wife and his children if I only said please.

Now I ask him for a few dollars, just to get by and he says, "It's over Ingrid."

"Oh yes? Let me tell that to your wife."

Finally, he agrees to see me.

First he tells me, "This is the last time." Then we go to a cash machine. He gives me a hundred dollars, reminds me that it's "a loan."

"I told you I just got out of the hospital, you asshole."

We walk to the hotel where we used to screw. It's not the best place, but clean. He pays the room for a week.

I'm thinking he'll fuck me once. It'll take five minutes and then he'll leave and I can sleep in soft sheets with air conditioning, and I can watch television and call room service whenever I'd like. I can do what I want. He probably won't come by more than twice and with any luck, he'll come when I'm out.

It's less than five minutes and he starts on the lecture. "Ingrid, you can't keep living this way. I can help you. They need a girl in the office, receptionist."

"I am a dancer."

"Of course you are. But this is New York."

"I'm not going to be your secretary,"

"Receptionist. You just answer the phone. It can't be any worse than shaking your tits at a strip club. I mean, who do you think you are?"

"I'm Ingrid," I tell him. I slap his face. Dress. Take bag. Leave. Fuck him and the room. What I don't even bother to say to him, is that someday when he remembers *the day he pushed me away, the day he lost me forever, I won't even remember his name.*

I take a taxi down to the East Village. There's a painter there. He used to call me his muse. But it looks like his building has burnt down, so I go to a phone booth. His number is disconnected. I walk over to the park where there's a big celebration going on.

I see a man sitting alone on a bench, writing in a little book. It's funny because I'm thinking he could be my brother - blond with blue eyes. But something sad in him. Gentle.

I ask him for a cigarette. He stares at me. Shy? Gay? Intimidated by me? Then another one comes to sit. Not so nice, but not afraid. Beard, long hair. Not combed, dirty, a little bit of a belly. There's a chicken on his shoulder.

He asks, "Do you wanna pet it?"

"What?"

"Do you want to pet the bird?"

I start to laugh. I'm not sure at what. The unmitigated disaster that is my life? I pet the bird. The handsome man just sits there statue silent, but listening.

Birdy rolls joint. He takes the cigarette out of my mouth and steps on it. "These things will kill you," he says. He places the joint between my lips. Touches them and then licks his fingers.

"Strawberry," he says.

I can't help smiling.

His teeth are yellow, but something about him isn't so bad if you combed his hair and gave him a shower. I'm thinking it wouldn't be terrible to fuck him.

He tells me that he's Lenny, from Texas.

"You are a cowboy? John Wayne?"

"No ma'am."

"Ma'am. Yah. Texas."

I'm slipping into my accent. It's how my mother spoke.

The pot is very good. He tells me that he's studying to be a warlock, and asks if I'm interested in magics. That's how he says it. With the "s".

"Men have called me a witch." The statue man is

looking at his shoes, but still listening. Like me, he is an observer. I think Birdy also passed him the marijuana. I wish he would say something. I'm suddenly feeling hungry and horny and imagining both of them fucking me at once and then all of us going out for a good meal and dancing and I'm wondering if anyone has any coke.

"The bird is my familiar," Birdy says. "I can call forth demons."

Many beautiful women passing, some men too in gowns, also beautiful like women. Floating. But I am the most beautiful.

"I'm hungry," I tell him. Put head on his shoulder.

"I can cook," he says. "We can go to my apartment and I can make you anything you want."

Birdy takes my hand and we get up. I turn and look at the statue man still sitting. I am trying to will him to speak, but he only looks down and I look away.

Birdy's building is east of the park. Between B and C. They say it's changing, the area, but still it's not so nice. The hallway is narrow and has a pissy smell. Inside the apartment there is an old couch and chair, like from the street. Bedroom, only a smelly mattress on floor. (At least there is a sheet!) No air conditioner, just a fan next to the bed. We fuck. It's too fast. His breath stinks.

Later, more pot. Grinning idiot. Touches my hair.

"Stop. I'm hungry. Get me something."

He bites my lip. Not really hard, but still.

I push him off me. "Who the fuck do you think you are?" Angry, I start to curse him in German.

He looks frightened. "Tongues! Demon talk!"

"Yes, I am demon! Satan has sent me to torment you. Now get me some food before I curse your balls to fall off."

He goes to the kitchen. He's there cooking now. Singing to himself. Moron! But the food smells good and the fan isn't too bad. I can stay here a few days. Get some rest. Unbelievable the things one must do to survive this life!

❖❖❖

Chapter 4

Summer in the City – 1988

Kyra

Ya like these tits? Got them in '68. Same surgeon Edie went to. You know, Edie *Sedgwick*? I was like the *prototypical* Chelsea girl, okay? I shoulda been in that movie. Hung at the Factory. Knew everybody. Andy, Ultra Violet, Holly Woodlawn. I fuckin *shot up* with Lou Reed.

I know there's all this shit coming out now about the silicone. But thank God for these. The rest of me could fall apart and they'd still have a life of their own. Nice size, too. Not like they're freaky or anything.

Considering everything, I don't look too bad now. But twenty years ago, when I was nineteen, I could make like a thousand dollars a night, just dancing. I mean I didn't even have to *fuck* anyone.

Glory days.

Followed by the lost years. Lost my son for one thing. After I got out of jail (long story) him and his father disappeared. And that my friends is the tragedy because if I'd a had my boy, I never woulda picked up again.

Woulda, shoulda, bullshit.

So I wound up back in NYC. Thought I was set up down here on the Lower East Side, but then I got a little behind in the rent and my roommate's boyfriend made it clear there wasn't enough room for the three of us no matter what the sleeping arrangements, which is how I wound up couch-surfing the good nights and sleeping *al fresco* the bad ones.

One day I'm in Tompkins. Found a half pack of Camels on a bench. Sitting, smoking one after the other. Lenny comes up, tells me these things are gonna give me cancer and offers me the world's fattest joint. I knew he was kind of whacked out. But he was the first person in so long just to be *kind* to me. Look, I'm sure he wouldn't a kicked me out of bed, but it wasn't even a sex thing. It was like hippie shit, y'know? Like hey, you need a place to stay, you need a meal? Hey, I got a place for you. I got some food.

I had bronchitis or something. He fixed me tea, grilled cheese sandwiches with tomato soup. *Homemade* soup.

The apartment wasn't a palace, but I had my own room to crash in, and a bathroom, with a tub.

He was scraping together a hundred a week rent. I started paying half after I was able to work again. See, there was a rent-controlled tenant paying like a hundred a month. She died. Lenny found out and offered the super some key money. It's not like it was going to last forever, but Lenny's not too, what do ya call it, *future oriented*?

For me it was fine. A chance to get my shit together. Which I was doing. Working three nights a week at a club in Jersey. In maintenance. Okay, sometimes I'd shoot a little on top, but who doesn't?

Then her royal Ingridness comes onto the scene. I mean there's Lenny in the park like every day trying to make time with the ladies. It's all he does. But everyone knows he's crazy. Talking about the forces of Satan, talking about killing the mayor. He doesn't exactly get "lucky" a lot. I come home and see her in the kitchen, writing in her little notebook, looking like the Queen of her castle, treating Lenny like the hired help. I could tell this was *not* going to have a happy ending.

❖ ❖ ❖

Joe Holiday

Joe working his shift at *Arcana Books*, specializing in fantasy, science fiction and occult science. Minimum wage, but they paid him off the books, and besides he liked talking to the customers. All types came in. After five men in suits, he wondered what oracles they consulted before making investments. The Hell's Angels who had a club over on 5th – a lot of them and their women were into this shit. He listened, picked things up. As with many of his interests, he appeared more knowledgeable than he was, actual reading being too time consuming. Besides, he considered most writers idiots. Joe liked the term "occult science." Sounded more serious than "new age." More accurate too, considering there was a whole body of esoteric knowledge going back to ancient times. He disliked the stuff that talked about women as the keepers of all wisdom. Historically, the great magicians were men. Women weren't even allowed to study *kabala*. Joe hadn't actually studied it himself, but he knew a lot of those English guys like Crowley and Regarde were into it. Crowley, he liked. Guy looked like a warlock. *Society of the Golden Dawn*. Those were some serious motherfuckers. Joe had heard the stuff in the books, even the books with titles like *The Real Secrets of the Golden Dawn*, was just pap for the public. He was sure the real deal must have involved blood rituals, human sacrifice, that kind of thing. *Do what thou wilt*. Those guys didn't get caught up in terms like "good" and "evil". They didn't make racist distinctions about "black" and "white" magic. They knew what they wanted: *power*. And they were prepared to get it by any means necessary.

That the means to power might involve the wearing of ceremonial robes, the drawing of pentacles, and the right words recited in the correct order with the proper intonation – this did not sound implausible to Joe. Again, historical precedents. All the world leaders from Ramses to Hitler and even Reagan had had astrologers. He'd heard the Israeli army had checked with a kabalistic scholar before the first strike in '67. It made sense to him that success at magic would take years of practice and discipline. It was the same formula for success with anything. Joe did not consider himself a successful man. But he understood the formula.

Success in magic, from what he heard, was a subtle thing. The best magic appeared to fit into the natural order. Like say a drug lord outlives his rivals who all kill each other. What role do the birth dates play? Or the homage paid to the local voodoo priestess?

Just look what happened down in Mexico, Matamoros. Marijuana dealers had been making human sacrifices for years until they got stupid, snatched some gringo college kid whose disappearance brought down heat from El Norte. But how long had they run a safe and successful operation before that mistake?

His girl, Moira probably knew about that. Girl was deep. She'd lived with Robby (the Acid King) Assad from the time she was fifteen till the feds caught up with him. She never asked Joe about his past. Didn't say much about her own. But he sensed a strength, a loyalty. Joe would bet that if Robby had asked her, she would have gone out and found him a virgin. Yeah, he could imagine Moira scouting the clubs for some sweet young thing, enticing him or her home, slipping them some kind of tranq. He could see her wearing a red robe, or maybe naked, out in a stone temple in the middle of the desert, with the full moon lighting up her back as she plunged a knife into the chest of the writhing victim laid out before her. There she was drinking the vic's blood from a golden chalice. He'd have to ask her about it sometime, but he didn't think she'd tell.

His reverie was interrupted when he noticed Lenny had walked into the store. Joe was glad the manager wasn't around to give him a hard time. Lenny's hygiene wasn't the greatest, and he never bought anything though he'd spend hours reading the comics and talking to customers. Joe liked Lenny. He was pretty generous with his pot. Grass wasn't Joe's drug of choice, but he appreciated Lenny wasn't out for anything. He was with a Puerto Rican guy Joe knew vaguely – Johnny.

Joe went over to say hello. They were looking at the latest issue of the *Laksdale* series, a fantasy comic book whose storyline took place on a distant planet where the women all wore cone shaped hats with veils and cinched at the waist dresses that spilled out their bosoms, and the men had even bigger chests and everybody said "thou," but they could "jaunt" and "gallivant" around the galaxy.

The drawing on the cover, a princess astride a horse, sword raised, reminded Joe of Moira. Same beauty queen corn-color hair waving in the wind. Only the cover girl was busty whereas Moira was flat. Lenny who'd also been admiring the artwork said, "My girlfriend looks like that."

Joe and Johnny made eye contact on that one. Even by the standards of the Lower East Side, Lenny was thought to be delusional.

"Wow!" Johnny said. "She's hot. Where'd you meet a girl like that?"

"In the park. She's living over at my place. She's real pretty. But man, she can sure be mean sometimes!"

"I hear that," Joe put in for conversation, not too sure whether or not they were discussing a hallucination.

Lenny invited them over to meet her. He offered to whip up omelets if they'd stake him on beer. Joe was about to get off shift and figured what the hell. Johnny was set to go too, but then his beeper went off.

"Duty calls, man."

Johnny worked for El Rey de Reefer, a.k.a. the King of Cannabis, a.k.a. the Mogul of Marijuana. Guy ran a pot delivery service. Johnny was one of his boys. Talked like he was some big time drug dealer, but it didn't sound any different to Joe than delivering pizzas, except that pizza boys were less likely to get their teeth bashed in. Johnny, Joe thought, was the perfect example of a man failing due to lack of discipline. The boy was good looking, wavy black hair, well proportioned. Dressed well. Looked like a preppy with a really great tan. Talked like one, too. Even had some college. But what was he, twenty-five or something? Already getting a gut and with a droopy ass. An hour a day of free weights, and he could get some fine piece to take care of him. No way he'd need that stupid delivery thing. Joe only wished he had Johnny's natural assets.

Johnny left to answer his call. Joe and Lenny walked east over to Lenny's. Lenny was rambling about Ingrid. Joe asked if Lenny's neighbor, Jacques was around. Maybe they could invite him too. Jacques was big time into black magic. Had a look that would've freaked out Crowley. Six five at least. Bone thin. Old Ukrainian women crossed themselves and crossed the street when he'd pass by.

Lenny claimed Jacques had made him his apprentice, was teaching him stuff, rituals and the like.

When they got to the apartment, they heard definitive moans and pounding coming from Lenny's room.

Lenny dropped his six-pack and went to the bedroom door. Opened it. Saw his lady boffing someone and then *apologized*.

Joe didn't make assumptions. He and Moira had an open relationship although there was a clear understanding you didn't bring someone else home unless your lover was also involved. Maybe it was a money thing. But he saw the stricken look on Lenny's face.

They talked it out. Seemed like not only was Ingrid giving it away to someone else, she wasn't giving it to Lenny at all.

"Is it okay with you, man?"

"I just wish she'd be nice to me. Like she was that first day. Even if she doesn't wanna fuck me. I just wish she'd be, you know, *nice*."

Joe led Lenny to Ingrid's door. Told him what to say and how to say it. The other guy got up and left. Ingrid came out. Naked. Lenny was right. Straight off the comic book cover. Real haughty too. Telling Lenny he had no right to talk to her like that. She was every bitch who'd ever spit at a panhandler, every Euro-trash *artiste* moving into the neighborhood and paying more for a month's rent than a working man would see in a year. He recognized immediately she was not the Princess Heroine of the fantasy strip, but the Evil Sorceress. And Joe knew she would eat Lenny alive unless someone stepped in to stop her.

From The Personal Journal and Memoir of Ingrid Hess

26 July 1988

No phone in this shithole. I go down to the corner and call Katherine. Leave message.

"So are you happy, darling? You abandoned me and now I'm in the gutter. Thank you and drop dead."

Try again later. Plan to say, "Fuck you, fuck you, fuck you." Second "fuck," she picks up.

"Oh Ingrid, I'm so sorry. Please come see me."

"I don't even have taxi fare."

She tells me just come and the doorman will take care of it. Her son and his wife are in the Hamptons.

Her apartment is hideous. Bourgeois. Too many things. Photos in glitzy frames. Porcelain cows, china cows, stuffed cows. Cows everywhere, for this cow! Her collection!

Katherine, almost crying just to see me. Wearing auburn wig, pageboy. (Did I tell you she pulls out her hair?) Stomach popping from pants suit. Fat gold earrings, so heavy her lobes droop. Lipstick over dry bitten lips. Licking lips with her tongue. The way her jaw sticks out, she's a beagle.

Never notice before how loose her neck is. Why doesn't she take care of this? Dear God, take me while I am young and beautiful!

"You look wonderful," she says.

Kettle whistles. We go to what she calls the "sun room." Tiny closet-like space, but has window on two sides and a skylight. Plants, glass table, little cakes and tea. AC blasting. We drink hot tea to stay warm in New York in July.

"How have you been?" touching my hand.

"How can you ask me that? You live here in this beautiful place while I have nothing. How can you be so insensitive?"

"You hate me," she says - always making it about her. "Why did you come?"

"You asked me to." Shove cake in mouth. "Besides, I'm hungry."

"Oh Ingrid, I'm so sorry."

"Fuck sorry, cunt." I hold back these words and the desire to smash one of her dollhouse plates over her stupid head. Want to tear up everything. Start crying. Cannot stop. Nothing is working. Thinking, even if she offers to let me stay here, I can't live in this boring Upper East Side with her always here. If only I had a place. Even the shithole, I could fix with money.

"There, there," she says. "There, there." Her arms around me. "Maybe you need to lie down for a bit."

I let her lead me to bedroom.

Heavy dark woods, a "set" like out of a store display. Too cheap to hire decorator?

Rubs my shoulders. "You used to do this for me in the hospital," she says. "Now it's my turn to do it for you."

I did more than rub her shoulders. She wants me to do everything, then pretend nothing happened. We are just girls! Yeah, yeah sixty-year old girl. Too tired for this. Want her to work. Want her to know she is doing these things.

My back to her. Feel cold dry hands under shirt.

"Does this feel okay?"

She keeps going, unhooks my bra. I turn, lay on back.

She stares. Not moving. I put her hand to my breast. It's so rough. Why doesn't she use lotion?

"Feels good," I tell her.

"I missed you."

Hug her. "Me too."

Kissing me. All over face. Put my mouth, tongue in her mouth.

Two of us rolling, rolling.

I push tit into her mouth. Put my hand on her, then inside. Here is the wetness, the life. Surprises me always she is this way. Moaning sounds. Touches me too - just outside.

The first time in hospital she told me she'd never been with a woman before. Later, she laughed and said, maybe in college. Yeah, she probably fucks the maid.

I work down her body. She moans. Knows what is coming. Kiss her belly, stretch marks, decay. Want to yell, "Go to a gym! Do something about this! How could you let *this happen to your body?"*

Pussy tastes strange, with smell, like, what? Fruit? She has used something, maybe? Knew we would be like this, planned it.

After, still in bed, tears running down her cheeks. "I want to be with you. I wish you could stay here."

"Why not?"

"My son wouldn't understand. He's coming back tonight. He'd try to lock me up."

"What are you, a baby? Because you love a woman? He cannot do this to you."

She tells me one time she gave money to someone, "a very bad man." Now everything is in her son's name. She has an allowance.

"This is awful to let him control your life!"

"But what can I do?"

"Give me money. I'll get a place. You can see me there. We can be together there."

"How much would you need?"

Heart beating, very fast. Now I want to kiss her.

"A small place, maybe $1,500 a month, plus the deposit."

"Oh no," she says, "I couldn't. He'd know."

"But that's what it costs."

"No, I'm sorry, dear. I can't."

"Are you stupid? Don't you understand Katherine? I'm on the street. I have no place."

Whining. "But what do you want from me?"

"I want you to help me, damn it!"

"He'll know."

"You use me. You bring me here and then throw me away!"

"I love you." *Goes to take something from dresser.* "Ingrid, please. Please, take this watch. It must be worth at least three thousand."

Gold. Swiss. Better than nothing.

She gives me papers so they will know it isn't stolen.

I tell her I must go.

"Yes," she says. "My son will be home soon. You should

leave."

Stop at first jewelers. Get only sixteen hundred. Enough for rent deposit, maybe?

There's a restaurant I used to go to with Game-boy. Half diner, half steak house. I'm hungry and want some meat so I stop in.

The steak, bloody, squirting like something still alive, struggling. Yes, in New York even the food must fight.

Waiters watching me. Still early for dinner and everyone away at beach. One other customer, a man - of course, staring. Good features, hazel eyes, reminds me of a boy from school in Germany. Leather jacket, helmet by side.

"It's nice to see a woman with a healthy appetite," he calls loud from his table.

I lick my lips. Raise glass to him. "Do you have a cigarette, darling?"

He comes over. Dave. Advertising. We chat and he orders more wine for us both. Maybe not so exciting as I had thought, but I need to get the taste of Cowthrine out of my brain. He sees me see the ring on his finger.

I catch his hand in my own. Touch ring. "It's okay."

He strokes my hand, thumb moving back and forth across wrist. Sip wine. "Maybe we go someplace?"

"Great. I can give you a ride. My bike."

"The place I am staying is not very nice. Perhaps we go to a hotel?"

His cheeks red. "I'm sorry. Really, I'm just a ... I mean, I didn't realize... I don't have that kind of money."

Spit out my wine. "You think I am for money? Oh no, I just thought we would be more comfortable."

"Can you forgive me?"

"Yah. But at least we must stop someplace. You have enough money for us to get a little something? For the mood?"

It feels good to ride downtown on the bike. Old times. Stop, pick up whiskey, then on the street some blow. Tells me he used to live "in the neighborhood." Now, Brooklyn.

"I would never leave Manhattan," I tell him.

He starts to tell me how someday Brooklyn will be like Manhattan. He tells me about the property he bought.

"Please shut up," I tell him.

Inside apartment, he says, "Ah! Great space."

Always in Manhattan, they say this.

No one is home. Good. He's pushing against me before we even get to room.

"Slow down. Drink first."

He puts coke on my body. Snorting from my stomach. Licking it from my clit. Puts me on the edge. Almost, almost. Then fucking. Still shaking from his mouth. Lucky woman this wife.

I hear something, pushing on the door and the little bolt comes right off and there's Birdy with his stupid crazy face staring.

"Get the fuck out!" I yell.

"I'm sorry. I heard screaming." Closes door.

"Who was that?" Dave, wilting.

Don't want to lose feeling. "He's nobody. Forget it." Start to moving more.

Voices from living room. Can hear them, Birdy, other man. Can't hear all, but other man is saying something like, "You take that shit from her?"

Birdy opens door again. "What the fuck do you think you're doing, bitch?" I can see the side of the other man. Telling him what words to say.

Dave pulls away. "Sorry man, I didn't know." Grabs pants.

"I don't believe it," I say. "You're letting him throw you out!"

"I don't want trouble," he says and leaves.

I go to living room. Birdy is sitting, rolling joint. Looks at me and his hands start to shake. Why not? I am magnificent in my anger, my nakedness.

"Who the fuck do you think you are? What business is it of yours? Huh?"

"Don't yell at me!"

Such a baby.

"I thought you'd be my girlfriend. I thought you'd be

31

nice."

"Oh yah. Now I see it. You act like you rescue me in the park. You invite me to your home. How nice he is! Such a sweetheart. You're like the others. All you want is this!" I slap hand to my crotch.

"Well, you're not paying rent."

"You son of a bitch." I go to the room, and get five twenties from the jeweler money. I tear them up in front of him. "Here is your rent, you swine."

I turn around, notice the other one sitting in corner.

Small ridiculous man wearing glasses held together with a band-aid at his nose. Messy, overgrown hair. Arms strong, not bad. Big shoulders like some small men. He says nothing.

Suddenly, feel strange. Maybe up from bed too quick. Don't want him to know. It's like with an animal - never good to show weakness, fear. Put hands to hips. "And who the fuck are you?"

He waits. Staring. Maybe this one also thinks he is warlock. Soft, almost a whisper, he says, "Joe. Joe Holiday."

Joe Holiday

Joe Holiday was not the name he was born with, but he had it for a long time and it fit. Taken from a book, sort of. He picked it up in Ohio of all places from a woman who taught writing at a community college. He'd gotten a GED in prison. After, he wanted to better himself, so he took a class.

The woman, Emily, was sweet. Not stupid exactly, but naive. Twenty-six year old virgin when they met. Five foot nothing. Weighed in somewhere over two hundred.

Like him she was mixed. In her case Samoan, Japanese Polish. His mother was part Polish, a commonality he used to his advantage.

He still thought of Emily now and then because strange as it seemed, it was the most physically satisfying relationship he ever had with a female.

He was twenty-four then. Spent most of his adolescence in juvenile centers, followed by a prison stint. He hadn't been with a lot of women. Wasn't even sure he liked them. She was his first virgin too, unless you counted a couple of boys taken by force inside.

He loved her oversized breasts and her softness, but mostly he loved how absolutely crazy she got when he ate her pussy. The first time he did it, she scissored her legs shut. No one had ever even touched her down there, she told him.

He tried using his hands. Couldn't convince her it was for her own pleasure, but she was willing to tolerate it for his. Then when she was loose and gooey, he went back with his mouth. No resistance, but after a while she was saying, "Okay, that's enough now." He kept going. It must have taken an hour that first time, but when it happened it was the biggest thing he'd seen. She screamed and screamed. He put his dick in, and could feel her whole insides contracting. She even lost control and peed on the bed.

He'd heard men talking about this shit in prison. But he hadn't really believed their stories. Now he understood that a man who could do this to a woman, could own her completely.

He moved in a week later. He liked her things – the books he could browse through while she was at work, the TV and stereo. Even the way the light came through the bay windows made him feel good about himself. The refrigerator was always full. Every night she cooked for him, usually steak or salmon. He always picked the wine. He'd had a cellmate in for insurance fraud who was something of a connoisseur. Joe tried to pass some of his acquired knowledge on to Emily, but she didn't have a head for it.

He was working some bullshit convenience store job in the mornings. She taught at night. They'd have an early dinner together, sometimes fuck, then she'd leave for work and he'd "hang with the guys." Sometimes he'd get home with just enough time to put on a fresh shirt for work. Emily would still be asleep. She slept like the dead, and didn't ask what she didn't want to know.

Most of those nights he spent with Tina. Tina of the nineteen-inch waist and five inch fuck-me stiletto heels. Latina features, straight blonde hair. Butt like a ten-year-old boy's. Beautiful pre-op transsexual. She kept talking about the operation, but Joe thought she was fine the way she was.

It was a sweet set-up. Emily and the apartment, the food, no demands. Tina and the things he could do with her. They'd get an eight ball. Invite her girlfriends. He could play games with her. Bondage, water sports. Things he'd never think of doing with Emily.

Tina got on him sometimes about money.

"What about that guy in New York, robbed a bank so that his girlfriend could get the operation?"

"What about it? The asshole's in jail now. That's what about it."

Then she got on a kick about Emily. He should kill Emily, and then they'd split the money.

Joe laughed. "What money? She's a fuckin school teacher."

Tina would spin out fantasies. Joe could marry Emily. Take out life insurance. "There's all kinds a ways a person could be worth more dead," she'd say.

Sometimes when she went on too long, he'd have to slap her to shut her up.

Then she stopped talking about the operation, stopped talking about Emily. Started in on all the things she and Joe could do if only they had the money. No bullshit jobs. Travel to some island where the sun was hot, the blow was cheap and they could hire servants to wipe their asses.

She worked as a manicurist. Debts for student loans to cosmetology school, maxed out credit cards. One day Joe noticed a fine new stereo.

"Where's this from? You got yourself a sugar daddy?"

She giggled. "No, it's from my cousin, Mickey. Fell off the truck. He does security in a warehouse. Sometimes, he can get stuff."

Mickey's name started coming up a lot.

"He's kind of a what you call it? *Underachiever*. Real intelligent. Knows about electrical stuff. He told me he could disable the whole security system."

"Yeah, why doesn't he?"

"You know us PR's, no initiative."

"You're first cousins, right?"

"Yeah, he's my Tia Lucy's baby boy. Only guy in the family not giving me a hard time about you know."

"I don't have to worry about this guy?"

She started to unzip him. Puckered her fat lips and blew a kiss. "I don't know Papi. You know how they say. Incest is best."

One day, he was twirling his fingers around her pubic hair. Thinking how amazing it was, her blondeness down there. No roots. She started talking. "I got it all planned out," she said. "Mickey stops the alarm. He helps you load the stuff on the truck. They got those lifting machines."

"Forklift?"

"Yeah. Then you leave Mickey tied up. There's another guard too, but he won't make no trouble."

"You got somebody to sell this shit to?"

"Yeah, as a matter of fact. I know a guy."

"Uh-huh."

"I'm serious."

"So I drive the truck. What do you do?"

"I don't do nothing. I'm the brains."

"Well, Doctor Einstein, I got one problem with that plan."

"What's that?"

"I don't know how to drive."

The places he grew up didn't have driver's ed. He didn't mind not having a license. It was a good excuse when Emily would get on him about finding a better job. Besides, he figured if he did drive, for sure one night he'd be fucked up out of his head and crash. Kept him out of all sorts of trouble, like the kind Tina was suggesting.

Tina was shocked. She'd lost her car after her last boyfriend stopped making payments. Along with not having the money for the operation, she considered this a major tragedy.

"How could you not know how to drive? What are you, a retard?"

He hit her. Bruised her cheek. She cried, which made him feel so bad that Emily be damned, he spent the whole night, holding her, apologizing. Promising he'd learn if it would make her feel better. Sometimes Joe flew off, when someone said something like that – even though he knew she didn't mean it. But the truth is, he liked to keep them smiling. It bothered him though that *he had* to keep them happy. That if it ever blew up with Emily, he'd need to move in with Tina. It made him feel like it was some kind of job. Like all these people were always demanding so much of him, so naturally when she said something insulting like that, he just lost it.

The next morning Emily asked him what time he'd gotten home.

"Late."

She didn't ask more. Just sipped her coffee slow.

He realized she wasn't accusing him. In fact, it was an opportunity. "I was at Eddie's. I told you about him, right?"

"Right," she said absently. "Your friend, Eddie."

"Yeah. What happened was, we had a few beers too many. He couldn't drive me home. I wound up crashed out on his sofa."

"Uh-huh."

"You know I'm thinking, I wasn't too drunk to drive. I mean, if I knew how. If I had a car. I coulda come home early enough, spent the night snuggling next to you."

"Oh that's sweet. You want more pancakes, sausages?"

"No honey." He grabbed her ass as she swung back to the kitchen. "Maybe some more of you."

She kissed him. "You know I'll teach you driving if you want. You never seemed interested before."

"I know. I'm a slow thinking guy. It's so much work for you. But I been thinking how it would make it easier, find a better job."

"I don't mind. I'm happy, baby. I've been thinking about getting myself a better car. I doubt I'd even get $500 for this one. I'd give it to you if you got the license."

"You're wonderful," he said.

Soon he was spending a lot of time with Emily practicing the driving. They'd go out to the country, stop for dinner at little places. She was very patient with him. He felt closer to her, yet knew if they ever did pull the job, he'd leave. Maybe go off someplace with Tina, but then he'd leave her too. Both of them, talking plans. Emily imagining kids, buying a house. Tina and her "after the operation blah, blah blah." Sometimes Joe felt like he'd blow up if he stayed. He wanted to travel, see stuff, not get tied down. He'd even tried to tell them, but they never listened. Just kept talking their dreams. Made him feel used, like he was a blank screen they were making movies on.

What he liked most about Emily was how she appreciated his mind. Tina, on the other hand, was so stupid she *thought* she was smarter than he was.

Emily thought he could do better, be better. At times, he felt it was "nag, nag." But he liked that she cared. That she thought him capable of being *somebody*. She was always trying to encourage him – read, try again at the community college. He read some science fiction and fantasy, a little history – wars and kings. Mostly, he liked listening to Emily talk about what she was reading.

That day on the way to the test for the license, she was telling him how they were going to let her teach a more advanced composition course the next semester. They'd be reading Faulkner.

"You ever read Faulkner?" she asked him.

He hadn't even heard of him.

"You remind me of a character in one of his books."

"Yeah?" He asked, interested.

"Joe Christmas. He comes out of nowhere. Lot of anger buried deep inside."

"He a good guy, this Joe Christmas?"

Emily blushed. "No, he's a killer."

Joe teased her, "So thanks a lot for the high opinion."

But it stuck in his mind. Joe Christmas. From nowhere.

He passed the test. She signed over her Datsun, and they did the paperwork. He wanted to celebrate with her, but she was teaching that night, so he went to see Tina instead.

"Finally," Tina said when he showed her the temporary. "Things are set for Friday."

"That soon?"

"Got to be, honey. Got to be."

On Friday afternoon, Mrs. Burnham came in to get a trim, have her roots touched up and get a manicure. While Mrs. B. sat under the dryer, Tina sneaked into the coatroom, took the VISA card and driver's license out of the wallet and walked the three blocks to the U-Haul center. She was wearing a tasteful scarf and sunglasses – the kind like Jackie O. She parked the vehicle several blocks away and walked back to work just in time to do Mrs. Burnham's nails.

Joe went out to the truck at nine-thirty. Emily didn't work Friday nights, so he had to pick a fight with her to get out.

He'd never driven anything but the Datsun before, so he managed to sideswipe a parked station wagon as he pulled out of the space. Making a right, he brushed a streetlight. Another driver gave him a look. He gave the driver the finger and hoped that the cops were all busy harassing youth.

He drove to the warehouse. Tina and Miguel had driven out with him before in Miguel's car, so he wouldn't get lost. He parked, put a stocking over his head and opened the gate with the key Mickey had given him. Once inside, he headed for the coffee room where he knew Mickey and the other guard would be taking a break.

Per Mickey, the other guard, a fat old white guy, didn't know anything. When Joe entered the room waving the gun he'd borrowed off of Tina's fence, and telling them to drop their weapons, the old man's face first drained of color and then suddenly went beet red. Mickey told his coworker to be cool and gave Joe a look that Joe interpreted as "don't play with him or he might catch a heart attack."

Joe tied the old guy up, then left the room with Mickey, making a point to shove the gun into Mickey's back and lead him out with the words, "You gonna help me load."

It took them a couple of hours. Before he left, he tied up Mickey as they had planned.

Tina's fence, Artie Pontucci, had a place about twenty miles further out. Quiet country road. Driving along, listening to the country station – the only one with reception – Joe was thinking about his meeting with Artie a couple of weeks before, back when the whole thing was still theoretical. Artie had taught shop at the high school till they fired him for being too close to some of the boys. Joe was watching the way he let Tina sit in his lap, all kissy faced. Artie saying how he'd known her for so long, back when she was Carlito.

"Don't worry yourself. She's not my type. I don't eat fish," he said, catching Joe's look.

Tina laughed. "What you talking about Uncle Artie? I still got all my equipment."

Artie kissed her cheek. "Yeah, but you're just too pretty for me, darling. I like it a little rough. Now your boyfriend there, I could go for some of that. Hey, just a joke, man."

"Yeah," Tina added, "He got himself a honey a lot hotter than you."

Later that night he'd started slapping Tina. Telling her never to say shit like that about him in public. At first, it was almost like a game. He knew Artie was really the one he was pissed at, but he was getting more into it and he couldn't stop. He apologized, but things hadn't been quite right with them since.

Maybe when he got the money, he'd just run off.

He turned onto a dirt road and pulled the truck into Artie's driveway. Artie lived in an old farmhouse with a big empty barn for storage.

Tina was waiting. Joe, Artie and some boy who looked maybe fifteen started unloading. Then Artie gave Joe his cut. Tina was holding Mickey's. Joe returned the gun.

Joe let Tina drive the U-haul back to the center. They dropped the keys in the box.

"I can't believe we did it," he said.

"Biggest thing to hit this town. Shit."

They walked to her house and fucked around just like old times, but even better, high off what they'd done. After, he couldn't imagine anything better than spending the money with her.

"So where are we going?" she asked.

"Wherever you want."

"Jamaica. Then New York. I want to buy a condo."

"We don't have enough for that. Not even if you took your cousin's."

She laughed. "That's right. We gotta drop it off for him before we leave."

"Look," he said, "I gotta go pick up some things at Emily's."

"We can buy new things."

"I got to talk to her."

"What you gonna tell her?"

"The truth. I met somebody else."

"You gonna break her heart."

"I know. She's a nice lady. I hope she meets somebody someday."

Tina kissed him closed mouth on the lips. There was something *demure* about it. He had a vision of the two of them, well dressed, eating in some fancy New York restaurant. He'd order the wine and the waiter would compliment him on his choice. They had money now. It could happen.

He put on his pants and picked up the brown paper bag with his cut.

"Why you taking that with you? Don't you trust me?"

"Why not take it? Don't you trust *me*?"

She grabbed his arm. "No, no I don't."

"Thanks a lot."

"It's just, I don't want to see nothing go wrong. I love you. But I seen how money burns a hole in your pocket. Maybe you'll leave here and wind up spending a grand on coke. The police'll pick you up buying a new suit. We just so close, baby. I don't wanna blow it."

He knew she was right. He could see himself giving something to Emily. He owed her. Then if she suspected the money was dirty, who knew what she might do?

They kissed again. "I'll see you later," he said. He left the bag.

When he got to the apartment, Emily was in bed. Not asleep. "Hi lover," she said. She pulled down the blanket so he could see her breasts.

"Emily," he said absently squeezing a tit, "We gotta talk about something."

Her eyes went wide. "No, no you don't have to talk to me."

"Em…"

She wrapped her arms around his neck and pulled him down to her, enveloping him. Her mouth over his. He couldn't say a word, but managed to pull himself up and away.

"I'm sorry," he said.

"Please don't."

"Emily, it's not right. It's not working for me here."

"We can go someplace else."

"I didn't want to have to tell you. I met somebody. I was with somebody else last night."

"You like her more than me?"

"It's not that."

"I understand. Just don't do it again, okay?"

"Emily, I'm going to do it again. And it's a man. I told you I could be that way."

She started crying. She looked very young. Like a big fat kid. The kind other kids beat up. He felt bad.

"I thought you meant in prison. I thought . . . Okay, look, if that's what you need, I can deal with it. Just don't leave me, baby."

Her nose was red. Her face swollen. He brought her a tissue.

"You'll meet a nice guy. You'll see. It'll be okay."

"But I love *you*."

He packed up his things. There wasn't much. She kept crying. Got herself out of bed. Threw her arms around him from behind his back.

"I love you so much," she said.

"Look, it's not going to work." He pushed her away.

She whined, "I taught you how to drive. I gave you a car."

He'd had enough. "So I'm supposed to be grateful for the rest of my life. I'm supposed to marry you or something?"

"I'm sorry. Whatever I did wrong, I'm sorry."

He ignored her. She started to yell. "You used me! You took my money. Now you found somebody else and you're leaving. How could you? How could you do this to me?"

She started toward him and he hit her. She wiped her bloody nose with an arm and kept coming, still sobbing, still begging him to stay as he walked out the door. He couldn't believe her lack of dignity.

He returned to Tina's. The door was open. Empty. Nothing in the closets. Not even a sheet on the bed.

He wanted to kill her. The tenants in the building kept stuff in the garage, which was never locked. He looked around. Picked up a baseball bat then grabbed a canister of gasoline.

Tina had a friend, Suzie. Kind of pretty, long-legged, light skinned black girl, but with some acne scars. One time the three of them had been drinking, doing some coke. She'd said something to him, some kind of joke he didn't like. So then he told her she'd be pretty if it wasn't for her face. After that she was always bad mouthing him to Tina.

He knew where she lived and drove over. Grabbed the bat from the backseat, used it to crack the glass in her door. Crept into her room. The shade was down but there was a streetlight right by the window, so it wasn't too dark. He went up to her bed. Put the bat across her neck and then cupped her mouth with his hand.

Her eyes opened wide.

"Just tell me where she is."

He kept the bat down, but lifted the hand on her mouth.

"I don't know."

"I know you do," he said, softly. "Don't make me hurt you. Just tell me, now."

Nothing.

He pushed the bat against her throat, then lifted it.

She gasped.

"Tell me what you know."

"I know she's scared of you. She thinks you're crazy. She's going away with Mickey."

He hit her. Stuffed a sock in her mouth and tied her hands behind her with a scarf. Turned her over and sat on top of her butt. Angry as he was, he was aware of her shape and his excitement.

He pulled her up by the hair. "Where is she?"

He took out the sock. She screamed. He pushed her head into the pillow. She was trying to wriggle free. He pulled her hair picking her head up, stuffed the sock back in, pushed down her panties and fucked her up the ass.

"You like it this way? Don't you bitch? All of you, the same."

He didn't come, but stopped after a while. He took the sock out again. "Just tell me where she is and it'll be okay."

She gave him two addresses, one for Mickey and one for Tina's mother. He stuffed her mouth one more time and tore the phone line from the wall. He was going to leave her, but then he thought she might get free and call the police or Tina before he had a chance to do whatever it was he was going to do. So he took the phone cord, got back on top of her and pulled it around her throat. It made him hard again, so he pushed inside her thighs a couple of times. Then she was still.

He went to Tina's mom's first. Sneaked around the side of the house and looked into a kitchen. An older Hispanic woman was making breakfast. Tina and Mickey were drinking coffee. He didn't see the money, but Artie's gun was between them. Tina must have taken it after he'd given it back to Artie. He was probably in on this too. There was also a rifle on the table.

Joe thought about his options.

The sun was coming up. Even if he could find a weapon, they might be gone before he got back. Mickey was twice his size. No way he was going in with just the bat. The money didn't even seem that important. He never believed he was going to get it, and if he had gotten it, he would have blown it in a week. It was the way they'd used him that was making him so crazy. Suzie was a bitch, but she'd never hurt him. He'd just been angry and killing her had relieved some of that. But it was stupid. Probably left prints in the apartment. Besides, for all he knew Mickey and Tina might have some plan to rat him out before they left town. His life was fucked. He couldn't go back to Emily's as if nothing had happened. He'd cashed his last paycheck Friday afternoon. Had a big $125 on him. Probably a good idea to leave the car too.

He got the canister out of the car, poured the gasoline around the wood framed house and lit a match. Watched the flames from his rear view as he drove away.

He parked near enough to Emily's so she'd notice the car. He left it unlocked, the keys above the visor, the papers in the glove compartment. He took out the canister and the bat and threw them in a dumpster. He walked to the station and got on a bus.

For a long time he didn't know whether or not the police were looking for him. The first time somebody asked him his name, he told them it was "Joe." Almost said "Joe Christmas" thinking about Emily's book, but then he played it around in his mind till he came up with something a little different.

"Joe Holiday." he called himself.

Ten years later, he was still Joe Holiday, from nowhere. Still felt white-hot anger when he thought about Tina and Mickey, which he tried not to do very often. He'd vowed never to let anybody take him for a fool ever again. So far nobody had.

Chapter 5

A New Lease

From The Personal Journal and Memoir of Ingrid Hess

3 August 1988

    This morning began with the usual upheaval. Birdy, at the door, whimpering. Not yet even 11. Tells me he has to come into the room.

    I've spent some money from the watch. A new mattress and spring box, a used dresser. Some sheets and towels. It's my room now. He said I could stay till I find a place and he'd take the living room or sleep in Kyra's when she's out. "I need something from the closet," he whines.

    Every time he opens the damn closet, you can smell the mold, dirty socks, dried cum. I let him in and go to use the bathroom. Then I come back and Kyra is there with him.

    Sarcastic she says, "What a great dresser! How much did it cost?"

    "Gift from a friend."

    "Can your friend give you some cash for the rent?"

    He'd taped together the twenties. They can go fuck themselves if they think they're getting more from me. They should pay me to live here. I'm watching every penny now, trying to get enough together for something decent. Last time I tried Katherine, the number had changed to unlisted.

"I can't pay you more and then have the money to leave? What do you want from me?"

I start talking about the hospital and maybe I should kill myself in front of them, maybe that's what they want. Lenny goes soft. He's also been there.

"Then you know," I said. "I can't deal with this."

He tells me he understands. Kisses top of my head which almost makes me vomit, but he sees only my smile.

Lenny and the crackwhore both leave and I'm alone in the apartment getting ready for my class.

The toilet won't flush. Stupid toilet, but God bless the stupid toilet. Thank you for the fucked up toilet because that's what leads me downstairs to talk to the super. I could see him from the window, out on the steps where he seems to live, drinking from a bottle in a brown paper bag.

I go out and tell him. He takes the cigar from his mouth, "Plunja inda basement."

He points to the basement door.

"It is not my job to fix the toilet. You are the super."

"Missy, ain't my job ta fix yo toilet."

"Do I need to go to the landlord?"

"Lemme set you straight, li'l girl. None of you all ain't even supposed to be in that place. You talk to the landlord, he gonna throw you out."

I call him a liar. Lenny pays rent.

He shakes his head. "He ain't pay rent. He pay 'don't mess with me' money. He pay that direct to your truly."

I sit down on the stoop. Take out this book, you, precious journal, my thoughts. Put on it a little cocaine left over from motorcycle man. Cut lines. Roll dollar bill. Snort line, offer to Mr. James who's happy to take it and passes the paper bag with the bottle to me.

"Oh yah. Now I remember. Lenny told me you were the important man around here. I don't know what I was thinking. But could you maybe help me out with the toilet?"

He comes upstairs with me stopping to grab the plunger and a toilet snake. I walk ahead of him on the steps. Give him a chance to watch my ass.

"I can't remember exactly, what Lenny said. What is this deal you have?"

We're upstairs now, and I'm rolling him a joint from Lenny's stash. He puts a hand on my thigh and says, "You want me to explain it to you?"

I take his hand off but gently. "Mr. James, you don't want Lenny to get jealous, do you?"

He removes his hand, sips his whisky, takes the joint to his lips and laughs till he starts coughing. Hacking cough, like maybe he's going to drop dead in front of me. Then he says, "I see what you do. You don't give a rat's titty about Lenny."

He goes into the bathroom. It only takes him a minute to fix.

He's talking the whole time, like he's so smart and he wants me to understand his little scheme. He starts to explain about the rent laws. The old woman who used to live in the apartment, paid only $105 a month with rent control. Cash always. Mr. James collected. She died. He never told landlord. Lenny gives him $400 a month and some pot. James gives $105 to the landlord. Keeps the rest.

If the landlord finds out, he'll raise the rent. There's still a limit because of the housing law, but he'll find a way around it. James tells me apartments like this are going for $1,000, more maybe.

"But he will find out, the landlord?"

"They got a lot of buildings. Don't pay much mind to every apartment, but sure I watch out. They get suspicious, I'll throw you all out."

I ask the name of landlord.

"What you wanna know that for?"

"Curiosity."

"Meow. Meow. Better watch out." Raises arm, makes like claw with hand.

On my way out, I see a sign in the hall. Building inspection. There is a stamp with the name and address of the landlord.

I can tell from the address it's east of Astor Place where I have to go to catch the train. Not too far. I walk past the park. Many policemen. Helmets, dark plastic visors covering faces. Welcome to Berlin, USA-style. I observe their bodies. I understand the language of the bodies. What is it they are afraid of? What is it they are guarding? Inside there are people living in the park. They have tents and build fires. Piss at trees. Beg for change.

Pathetic, these creatures. But can they really make so much trouble for all these police?

(Someday I will create a dance with masked-police figures behind me. I am homeless, defenseless fawn, running as they come after me.)

I reach office. Basement of building. Sign outside: Co-ops for sale. The pictures look like Lenny's apartment with new floors and shiny paint.

"I am here to see Mr. Veroni," I tell some woman sitting behind a desk.

"Which one?"

"Whichever one is most important."

"What's it about?"

"It concerns a building of his."

"We don't got no vacancies. You can fill out a form."

"My name is Ingrid Hess. I have some important information..."

A man comes out from door behind her desk. Comb over, sweat on the forehead. I smile at him.

"Young lady, you wanna see me, come on in my office." He adds to the woman, "Hold my calls."

His office! Please. I think back as a child playing in my father's office.

Veroni's office. Tiny. Black spots on the ceiling. No window.

Tell him I know about activity in one of his buildings. Costing him money. I pause (actress, yes?) explain more.

He smiles. Big space between teeth. "Yeah, I knew that James was running some kind of scam. So what is it you want?"

"I have been staying in the apartment. The people there are involved in drugs. One sells marijuana."

"So what is it you want me to do?"

"I would like the lease on the apartment."

He takes a paper from a filing cabinet. I see him making calculations. He tells me rent is $1,200 a month.

"That's not right. You can't raise it so high with the stabilization."

"Look, you're not even there legally, so don't tell me about the law. Besides we gotta renovate. It needs new fixtures. We can raise for that."

We negotiate. $1,000.

"But this is still more than double what we pay Mr. James."

"Honey, from what you said, Mr. James is history. It's a two bedroom, maybe convertible to three. A nice girl like you shouldn't have no trouble finding someone to split the rent."

Veroni wants $2,000 for first month rent and security deposit, but tells me he'll give me a break and accept $1,600. I only have $1,100 left from the Cow. I leave him $600 and sign a paper saying I will have the rest before September 1, or he will keep all, void lease.

"Maybe we can be friends. I wouldn't need so much from a friend."

"I will have it." I sign everything. "So you call someone now, to get them out?"

"Oh baby doll, that's your problem."

He explains how difficult it is to evict in New York. Police do nothing.

"But you must know people."

"Just because I got an Italian name, don't make me Frank fucking Sinatra."

Tells me it's my name on the lease. My job to get them out.

Always the same. All men. "You will not help me unless I sleep with you." I say it loud for the secretary to hear.

He whispers, "That's my sister-in-law out there." Louder he says, "What the hell are you talking about?" Then he

49

tells me to give them a week and change the locks. If it's still a problem call him and maybe he'll come up with something."

It's too late to go to make my class. Instead I go to a café near his office. Writing all from a table in the shade in the garden. There is a fountain here and statues like from old churches all around. On the wall, paintings and photos by local artists. Mixing of forms, old and modern. I so love this city.

Much to do, but now, finally, I have hope. A place of my own! Must find roommate, perhaps dancer too. I've got to get the rest of that money. Need Lenny-Birdyman-birdybrain and whore out. Veroni, no help. Nobody helps me. I am alone. Must be hard, the way of New York, turn heart into stone. Do what I have to do to survive, to triumph.

Chapter 6

August 13, 1988 – Before the Riot

Peter

Back when I was a kid, during those awkward weeks between prep school and summer camp, I'd spend time at my father's place in West Hampton. It was a haven for theater people then. The painters went to Sag Harbor. Old money WASPs had inhabited South Hampton for centuries. The gays had the Pines on Fire Island. Only the tourists and the poor stayed in town.

These days West Hampton is full of Yups, mostly Jewish, the striving sons and daughters of City College graduates who themselves summered in the Catskills (if not where they wintered.) A lot of the old timers in West Hampton have already taken the money and run to the next great place – lamenting how the "new people" have changed everything, while in their hearts they are thrilled, amazed at the prices paid for glorified shacks perched on shifting sands.

I didn't have a share, a weekend place, a get away, but I was enjoying my summer in the city. A quarter of the people gone and not missed. Short movie lines. Available parking. Restaurants with empty tables and blasting AC.

I can imagine my friend Johnny Ramirez, chiding me, telling me I enjoyed it only because it was my *choice* to be here, reminding me that for many the price of even a movie ticket was beyond reach and the waiters not so welcoming. But on that particular August day, Johnny and I had not yet become friends although we were about to be acquainted.

I was slightly involved with an attorney I'd met shooting pool at a bar. Turned out we'd gone to the same college – that one in New Haven. She was a couple of years ahead of me and we hadn't known many of the same people. She was from Queens, but had lived in "New Yawk," the Upper East Side for years.

She had a summer share in the Hamptons – only a couple of houses down the beach from my father's, which was also occupied by renters. When I told her I hadn't actually been to my Dad's place in years, she invited me out to see "the old neighborhood." She even managed to get Thursday and Friday off, the idea being we'd have some private time before her whole gang arrived for the weekend.

Only it wasn't going especially well. I kept getting the feeling she was mistaking me for someone else. Specifically, and this surprised me because she *was* a lawyer and smart, she apparently thought I was Dr. Brent Harrison, the upstanding young intern I played for six months over a year ago on *The Wild and the Innocent*. Or maybe she mistook me for Brent's bad boy twin, Travis, also portrayed by yours truly.

"They shoulda just killed you off. I mean the guy they replaced you with, he's such a nebbish."

"I don't know. I mean, I haven't been watching."

"I tape. Fast forward to the good parts. Julie's pregnant! And I think they may be setting up some kind of lesbian thing with Diana and this new nurse."

"Maybe they're really long lost sisters."

"You think?"

On she went as we walked along the beach. I was starting to feel a familiar sense of panic. What in God's name did this woman *want* from me? Did she think I was *the guy*? The smooth, slightly unattainable kind they're always after. I admit to sharing with him a certain hesitancy about commitment, and I have gotten myself out of more than one awkward situation by muttering the old stand-by,

"I'll call." Still, in my heart, I have always remained the gangly thirteen year old unsure of his ability to even unhook a bra.

The sun was in full SPF proof intensity, the sand too hot for bare feet, the salt air piercing my tobacco coated lungs. Her babbling was becoming almost incomprehensible. I'd slept with her three times including that first drunken night, but suddenly any achieved intimacy seemed illusory. I was remembering those childhood summers, how I would stay at the house, usually with some young woman, often a not overly talented or attractive aspiring actress my father had hired for the role of my companion. Dad mostly stayed in the city. Came down for weekends with his friends.

Now I was back, surrounded by the same dunes, the same wooden houses looking so fragile on their stilts, maybe a foot or so closer to being wiped out by the next hurricane than they were when I was a boy. Here I was hand in hand with a woman completely incapable of ever understanding anything about me.

Should I have told her being on a soap was the most depressing and anxiety provoking experience of my life? That having grown up in a household where the Dewhurst-Scotts might drop in for dinner, I found my own mediocrity worse than failure?

That the pinnacle of my acting career was playing this nonsense, and being well paid for it while my more talented classmates were waiting tables and driving cabs to support their acting addictions, that my agent had told me with my looks I could play these parts for years to come – that all this made me feel a weight descending on my soul as heavy as the burden felt by the tragic heroes I'd once aspired to portray – how could I possibly relate this to a woman for whom Erica Kane was a role model?

Would she have understood when they still hadn't fired me after months of missing rehearsals and slurring my lines from all the Valium I needed just to get myself on the set, I began to come on to every actress, *actor*, assistant and extra, until finally my obnoxiousness caused the producer to replace me and advise me to "seek help"?

So I went back to see my shrink, Dr. Leider – the kindly soul to whom I had related my troubles for several years before I discovered he had lost his entire family by the age of ten when he was sent from Austria to England to stay with a spinster great aunt, only days before the *Anschluss*.

I'd started seeing him, at my father's insistence, during a bad time in college. Just your typical nineteen year old identity crisis stuff, with the added stress of too many all night study sessions and a reading list heavy on philosophy and literature. I'd gotten to the point where I felt Nietzsche was talking especially to me. In fact, they were all talking to me. I *was* young Werther, and Stephen Dedalus as well.

Back then, Dr. Leider had diagnosed a mild chemical imbalance. He'd given me some stuff to calm me down. Suggested I get out more and read less. Encouraged me to change my major to acting which we both thought might provide me with the outlet I needed. I'd seen him from time to time after that, mostly to get refills on my prescriptions.

After the soap debacle, I went back into therapy on my father's dime. It helped me come to certain conclusions. The first one being if I ever acted again, I would kill myself. I chose journalism, because writing wasn't a performance where I would be judged better than my peers because I *looked* right for the part. If I stayed away from theater criticism and the arts, my father's name wasn't going to open any doors.

It was my last chance to be a man, a fully functioning adult, or as Dr. Leider might have said, "a *mensch*."

Of course, in a conversation on this topic I had months later with Johnny Ramirez, he argued I was born with so many keys to so many doors that my father's name was irrelevant. My looks, race, class, and ivy-education – all that would give me an in to whatever field I chose – an unfair advantage over poor dark-skinned boys like himself, however facile they were with words.

By the time her fellow Hamptonites arrived on Saturday morning, whatever connection had existed between the lawyer and myself was rapidly dissipating. Her friends were all first generation Ivy League. Lawyers or in "financial services." Raised on

Lawn*guy*land or in the outermost parts of the outer boroughs, now living on the Upper East Side. They found my living situation amusing. A walk-up, the East Village, no doorman. With their sixty-hour plus working weeks, they couldn't imagine life without someone to hail their cabs and guard their deliveries.

"But he grew up in *Manhattan*," she said, her whiny accent emphasizing the word as though it were a foreign country. "He was raised in the *Nebraska*."

At this they actually gasped and proceeded to ask me if I knew so and so or such and such, naming with fascination the various celebrity habitués of my well-known, if not notorious, childhood home and digressing into stories of their own close encounters with greatness.

Suddenly, an obese woman who had earlier introduced herself as a stock analyst, shouted, "Didn't you used to be Dr. Brent Harrison?"

Having heard this straight line before, I quickly replied, "No, but I played him on TV."

I made an excuse about having to get back to town. Using the acting angle, I told them I had an audition – with Scorsese, and would be reading with DeNiro. They asked more questions and I found myself describing the plot of the film, which involved my character, an aspiring journalist, tracking down the dark past of a mysterious minister – a modern day Rasputin who had become the confidant of the First Lady when her son became ill. (It was a screenplay I had once almost written, started and stopped sometime during my college troubles.) As I spun my tale, my lawyer friend watched – her mouth slightly agape, as though she were reappraising my talents.

I drove the hundred and ten miles back to Manhattan as quickly as I could. My car's an old yellow- Beetle – no AC, but cool enough on the highway with the windows rolled down. Once I passed the Nassau County line and got to Queens the temperature shot up. It was much worse when I emerged from the Mid-Town Tunnel onto the city streets. Then came the five flights of stairs up to my apartment. I've been to the Brazilian rainforest, and let me tell you, in terms of the sweat factor, New York City in August has it beat.

I entered my apartment turned on the air, startled the roaches in my sink when I went to fill a water glass, took a Percocet (left over from some dental work) for my splitting headache, then discovered to my horror I was out of cigarettes. Or rather, I'd left the pack in my car.

The thought of stepping back out into the airless hallway, then down and up the five flights was not appealing. I washed down a couple of Valium anticipating the nicotine withdrawal.

I bought time by gathering my butts from the ashtrays and cleverly rolling myself a final smoke. My brain was then cleared enough for me to come up with a plan. *Delivery*.

I thought of getting pizza or Chinese delivered and asking for a pack with my order, but I'd had breakfast in West Hampton, and it was too hot for more food. Then inspiration struck. Someone had told me about a pot delivery service. I even remembered the phone number, *4-REEFER*. I'd wanted to call anyway, for the journalistic possibilities, if nothing else. I figured it wouldn't be too much to ask for a pack of Camels with my order.

A man with a mild Spanish accent answered the phone.

"Hola. Royal Messenger Service. This is El Rey speaking."

I hesitated. "I heard that . . . Is this . . ."

"This is the Marijuana Hotline," he said. "Pot is what we got. Can I take your order?"

I ordered the minimum. $25 for a quarter ounce, allegedly organic and domestic. "Humboldt," he told me. "None of that Agent Orange pesticide shit."

I asked if the delivery person could bring me a pack of Camels as well.

"I don't know. That crap'll kill you man." He finally agreed he would *tell* the "messenger" about my request, but couldn't guarantee it would be honored. "I can't speak for somebody else's consciousness. You know what I'm saying?"

After I got off the phone, I regretted not asking for a video as well. The apartment was cooling down. I was beginning to look forward to spending the whole weekend inside and alone when suddenly a bullet like blast came from the air conditioner, followed by silence. I noticed the clock on my VCR had also gone dead. Two minutes later everything was on again and a minute after that there was a knock on my door.

It was the super's wife. Despite being in what looked like the tenth month of pregnancy, she had waddled up the five flights. Sweet lady, but another one who always looks like she's about to address me as Dr. Harrison. She told me there was a problem with the electricity and would I mind not using the air or any major appliance, at least for a couple of hours.

I opened the windows and turned on the fan. Street noises came through as clearly as if I'd been one floor up instead of five. A while later the buzzer rang. My messenger had arrived.

It wasn't the kind of transaction one completes in the hallway, besides I wanted to get some information, so I let the man in. He looked to be around my age – mid-twenties. Tall, Latino, handsome in a dimpled chin, chiseled featured kind of way. He wore a Panama hat, long sleeved peach colored, tailored shirt with the sleeves rolled up between his wrists and elbows. He had on a tie and a satin paisley vest, slightly worn black 501's, and despite the heat, motorcycle boots. I was surprised, as I'd heard the service used bicycles, and he wasn't dressed like any bike boy I'd ever seen.

"Those are some stairs, man," he gasped.

I got him a glass of water.

"Mind if I sit a minute?" He took out a cigarette and caught my look, "I got your smokes." He threw me the already opened pack.

"Thanks. I'm Peter," I said.

"Johnny. I've seen you around."

I nodded. I'd noticed him before too. In the park, at a café, on the street, usually making time with an attractive woman.

"Aren't you a bit overdressed to be riding a bike in this weather?"

"I don't ride a bike."

"Oh? I had the impression you guys did a lot of deliveries and . . ."

"What are you a fucking reporter?"

"Yeah, I'm a writer."

"Oh really?" His smile would have been worth money if his teeth hadn't been so stained. "I thought you were an actor."

"What gave you that idea?" I asked. I was wondering the same thing about him. He looked like he could have played the troubled but good-hearted poor boy on a soap, and his voice was deep, resonant like an easy listening DJ.

"I was talking to this girl, once," he said taking a deep drag off his cigarette, "Not doing too bad either. Then you walk by. She almost came on the spot. Starts saying how hot you were in some movie, *Sophomore Break* or something."

"*Freshman Summer.*"

"Right. So she was about to go up to you. Buy an autograph with a blow job or something and I told her I knew your lover and it was a real shame about him having the virus."

"So things worked out?"

"They would've. But unfortunately at a crucial moment another girl I used to know started yelling from across the street how I'd knocked her up and dumped her."

"Did you?"

"Hey, how do I even know the kid was mine?"

I told him about my career change.

"You'll do okay," he said. "You look like a journalist. I mean, if they ever made a movie about your life, you could play yourself."

I asked him how long he'd been in his line of work.

"You mean for *El Rey*?"

Elray?

"El Rrrey," he said rolling the "r". "The king. Only been a couple of months. Really I'm a student. NYU. I was thinking of majoring in journalism myself. Used to write for the school paper. I got laid off from my job and I couldn't make my loans. Soon as I save some bread, I'll go back. I got plans. El Rey figures I could be his university connection."

"So you like it?"

"Pays okay. Got its drawbacks – last week I went to two

deliveries turned out to be set ups. Had some product ripped off."

"You get hurt?"

"No man, I gave it up. It's the boss's not mine. Besides he's kind of a pacifist. Doesn't want anyone getting killed over product."

He took out my purchase. Asked me if I wanted to sample it. I declined. The truth is, I find marijuana relaxing if I'm alone, but it makes me paranoid with other people. He asked to use the john. When he came out, his pager went off and I let him use my phone to call in. It was another delivery in the neighborhood.

"Well nice meeting you," he said and offered me his hand. I shook it and then slipped him enough for the dope, the cigarettes and a generous tip.

We talked a bit about my doing a story on the operation. He took my card and told me he'd run it by his boss.

"So maybe I'll see you tonight?" he asked.

"Huh?"

"At the demo, man." He caught my blank expression. "Where you been? The Hamptons?"

"Yeah, as a matter of fact."

He laughed. Shook his head as though we'd been sharing inside jokes for years. "Some journalist. They're closing the park down. Last few nights they been stopping people, asking them where they're going and shit. It's all supposed to be a big secret, but everyone knows. They're going to start by imposing a curfew. There's like a thousand cops in riot gear on Avenue A. Vehicles that look like tanks. You haven't seen them? Right down your block, man. The demo's to keep the park open and support the homeless."

He dug into his pocket and found a couple of flyers. "Here, take a look."

The first one was pretty straightforward. It talked about the park as a community resource and "historical treasure." Mentioned gentrification and the need to find appropriate community alternatives for the homeless.

The second flyer theorized that closing the park was part of a bigger city plan to turn the Lower East Side into an Upper East Side clone. It warned of a federal program to turn abandoned military barracks into concentration camps for the poor. *Unless the people act to reclaim the park, the dispersal and disappearance of the park squatters will only serve to herald a new age of Nuremberg laws and the eradication of poverty through genocidal government policy.*

I thanked him for the info. Told him I'd check it out, and we said good-bye. I walked over to my window and started rolling a joint. I watched as Johnny emerged from my building engrossed in conversation with the pretty punk rocker from the third floor. They both sat down on the stoop. I wondered about his other delivery. He looked like a man who owned time.

After a few tokes, I started to have a bad reaction. I could visualize little points of anxiety like sickle cells running through my blood. I thought about my two uncles on my father's side that had dropped dead of heart attacks. The heat was stifling, but I remembered I wasn't supposed to use the AC, so I stripped down to my shorts, turned up the fan, and took a nap. I had a dream about the blonde I'd seen in the park. I'd taken her home and we'd gone to bed. When I looked down my cock had turned into a rooster and she kept laughing, saying, "Let me pet your little bird."

I woke up, sweaty and thirsty. Even with the fan on and the open window, I could hardly breathe. I figured I might as well go down to the park. The truth is if I'd been able to use the AC, I would have stayed home.

❖❖❖

Joe Holiday

Joe and his girl Moira enjoying a summer afternoon. Leaving Tompkins where they'd gone to cop, they ran into Lenny and Pirate Don.

Pirate Don, or PD so called because he always covered the bald spot on his head with a pirate-style bandana, was planning to stop by Lenny's and sample some shrooms. PD asked Joe and Moira if they'd like to join him.

Something of a hallucinogenic connoisseur, he had known and worshiped Moira since back in the Robby days. The guy stood maybe five six and spoke with a squeek-squawk voice like that smart-aleck time traveling dog in the Rocky cartoons. As Joe and Moira were crashing at his space in the squat, they figured it would be impolite to turn down the invitation.

When they got there, Lenny's roommate Kyra was around. Joe thought she was okay. He'd even boffed her a couple of times. But she had a big mouth.

Joe and Moira declined the shrooms which they didn't think would go well with the numbness they were seeking. Lenny gave them all iced lemonade he'd made. He'd added some mint leaf and was pleased when Moira complimented him on the flavor.

PD was more animated than usual, talking about the demo planned for that night. How it would be just like the sixties – peace and love would change the world, all that old-time hippy shit which struck Joe as ridiculous b.s.

"You wanna fuckin revolution?" Joe asked. "I tell you what I'd do. If I had the money, I'd buy an Uzi and spray the lobby of the Floradora. Take out as many of those Wall Street motherfuckers as I could."

Kyra laughed. "Joe, if you had the money, you'd buy an eight ball and get a room at the Plaza."

Even Moira was smiling. He went along, but figured he'd talk to Moira later about that shit.

Lenny was muttering to himself. More agitated than usual.

Joe asked him what was wrong.

Kyra answered for him. It was the Ingrid-bitch. She'd gotten a lease on the place and was kicking them out.

"First she threatened to get the cops. I told Lenny not to worry. They're not gonna do shit. But then she brings this big bodybuilding Rasta guy home. Tells us that's her new boyfriend and he's gonna break Lenny's neck if we're not out in two weeks."

"That cunt," Joe said. "That fuckin cunt."

Lenny turned to Moira. "Can I come live with you. I can cook."

She patted his hand. "I'm sorry. Joe and I are staying with PD and as it is, the squat collective says it's against the rules."

Joe hated to see Lenny so down. He felt bad he couldn't offer him space. "You gotta stand up to her," Joe said. "Don't be a pussy."

"I want to kill her," Lenny said. "I want to break her up."

"That's right," Joe said. "You gotta protect what's yours. It's like my man here was saying about the park. It's the people's, not the pigs'. You show her. Show everybody like her they can't come down here and fuck with us. *That's* the revolution, man."

"Then it's okay to kill her, Joe?"

"Yeah. It's okay. But you gotta be smart about it. Now, how are you gonna kill her?"

Lenny took some time to think that one over. Meantime, Moira had lit a candle and was cooking up the dope they'd bought in the park. Using her rope bracelet as a tourniquet, she pulled it tight on Joe's upper arm, tapped a vein and shot. Then in a quick and graceful motion, she had the bracelet around her own arm and booted. Joe watched as blood swirled in the syringe.

He felt so lucky to have found her.

Lenny was starting to get excited. "I'm gonna stab her," he announced. "Like this and this." He stood up, acting it out.

Joe was watching Moira. She'd noticed a drop of blood on her arm, swiped it with a finger, then licked it off. She was watching Lenny.

"You don't want to stab her," she said. "There'll be blood everywhere. It'll be very hard to clean up from a wooden floor. Unless you can spread out plastic and get her to stand on it you don't want to do that."

He asked her what he should do.

Moira met Joe's stare. For a moment Joe felt they were communicating telepathically. He was telling her, *"You and me are the same. We think the same and got the same secrets inside."*

"It would be a good idea to hit her from behind. Something blunt, no sharp edges, but heavy," Moira said. "Then when she's down, you tie a plastic bag around her head to make sure she dies."

Joe respected his lady's plan, but he wanted her to know he could think of stuff too. "What about shooting some bad shit into her, ODing her?"

Moira shook her head, then lit a cigarette. "She OD's and then what? Do you call the cops? Leave the body somewhere? You never want to do that. You always make the body disappear, so why waste dope? If anyone asks about her, you just say she went off with some guy. She won't be missed."

PD was humming, listening to music playing in his head. Kyra had been in and out of the room, getting dressed. Joe wasn't sure how much she'd heard.

"I don't know why you're even talking about this shit," Kyra said. "Even if Ingrid did disappear, she signed a lease. They're gonna come around for the money. We're fucked no matter what."

"There's a principle here," Joe said. "We got to show all those rich bastards we're not pussies."

Lenny's beeper went off which startled PD into awareness. They all decided to go over to the park. Lenny could call in and the rest of them could check out the demo.

El Rey

El Rey smoking his special stock, rolled in brown paper, fat as a *Cohiba*, waiting by the phone for incoming orders. As owner and chief operating officer of the Royal Messenger Service, he considered this task beneath him and dreamed of the day when a bevy of youthful doe-eyed Asian assistants – no females please – would administer to his every need out of a fancy back office.

His dispatcher had disappeared. Biker guy from Florida. Good with people, but El Rey had never trusted him. Who knew what kind of shit he'd been involved with down South? Now snap, gone faster than his sponging family that time he got busted and needed to make bail. El Rey just hoped the son of a bitch hadn't been an agent.

Still the biker had known how to get shit done. Not being a capitalist by nature, El Rey was finding the whole entrepreneur trip a tremendous pain. Renting space, dealing with the phone company, making the payoffs, hiring and firing. Twelve-hour days. He needed a vacation.

A call came through.

"Hola. Royal Messengers. We deliver."

Giggles in the background. "Is this the Pot Hotline? Do you sell pot?" More laughter and a click.

Word was getting out, but half the incoming calls were still cranks. Such a simple idea. Home and office delivery of high quality product. Why was this funny? Why so hard to believe? What they needed, he thought, was more publicity. He'd wanted to run an ad in *The Eye* but his partners advised against it.

"What can they do to me?" he'd protested. "I'm El Rey de Reefer. The King of Cannabis. The Mogul of Marijuana." Even in his days as a street dealer he'd had panache. He worked out of Washington Square back then – wore a flowing purple cape and on occasion a tiara. It wasn't that he was smarter or even more ambitious than the other dealers; what he was, was more *convinced*. He believed great changes were happening on the planet, in the universe. He believed in the new Aquarian age, and he knew herb would have a major part to play. He had a mission. He was the missionary.

In this he differed from his current partners, a consortium of elderly Italian gentlemen who were in it strictly for the cash.

His friend and colleague, Sean McFarland had warned him not to think of himself as invincible, even suggested perhaps their moment in history had passed. Cheap cocaine, no doubt brought in by the CIA, was flooding the streets, while hard working marijuana farmers throughout the nation lived in fear of the dreaded RICO. Plus this crack thing! People turned into automatons. The perfect drug for the overlords' plans according to Sean. Even heroin was more available and less expensive than it had been in years. El Rey did not consider himself "political," but it just seemed like common sense that the white powders were being pushed in black and Latino neighborhoods as part of a wider conspiracy. A conspiracy which El Rey was convinced could be overcome by spreading the gospel to which he subscribed: Herb alone could bring the world together. It had the potential to destroy racism, sexism, homophobia and war.

He remembered his youth, when he'd travel the globe with just a backpack and a small stash. He boarded trains from Oslo to Marrakesh to Nepal, always finding fellow travelers with whom to share, always making friends and lovers along the way. The sex had been so much better too. Pre-AIDS. Now *that* really had to be a conspiracy.

One of his boys, Johnny Ramirez stopped in to cash out.

"Johnny, you get yourself a bike yet?"

"Next week, sorry man."

"My name is El Rey. If you think that's a little funny, you can call me Federico. Freddy even. *Pero* my name is not 'sorry' or 'sorry man' which is lately all I hear coming outa your mouth."

El Rey had hired Johnny weeks before. It was the now disappeared dispatcher who'd brought him in. Johnny told El Rey he was a student at the university, ran into some financial difficulties. He was a good-looking boy. Well-spoken, except he didn't speak Spanish which El Rey thought was a shame. El Rey had hoped once Johnny got back to school he could be his man on the inside, the major connection to the college crowd.

But Johnny was still making fewer deliveries than anyone else. Taking longer to respond to a page. Full of stories about not being able to find a working pay phone. Going on foot or subway. Saying, "Next pay day," whenever El Rey asked him about getting a bike. Sometimes El Rey wondered whether or not the boy could even *ride* a bike.

"Ain't you hot in that shirt?" El Rey asked.

"Well, you're always saying we got to make a good impression. Be professional."

El Rey saw he had upset him. He looked at Johnny's big brown eyes, slightly moist like the tears were going to flow, the full lips pushed out in a little pout. The kid reminded him of those sponsor a third world child ads in the magazines. El Rey was hit with a feeling of tenderness that he didn't even think of as sexual.

He relit his joint and offered Johnny a toke.

"I didn't mean to get on you, I'm sorry. It's just the business. I got a lot on my mind since Snake left."

"Maybe I could help you out with that. I got a friend, a

reporter. He's interested in doing a piece on us. Maybe for *The Eye*."

"You trust him, this reporter?"

"Yeah, I checked him out. Besides he can change names and stuff. Whatever you want."

"I'll think it over."

"Should I tell him to call?"

"Yeah, why not?"

They settled up for the day and El Rey watched Johnny's slow saunter out of the office. Maybe there was hope for him. That reporter thing was sharp. So what if he wasn't the greatest delivery boy in the world, that didn't mean El Rey's instincts had been totally off. Could be he was more the right-hand type. Might do well as a dispatcher. Still, something was bothering him. He'd never seen Johnny in short sleeves and was beginning to suspect he was a junkie, in which case all personal feelings aside, he'd fire his ass. He believed everyone was entitled to a private life, but he'd gone to Catholic school where he'd learned that no man could serve two masters, and El Rey understood that once enslaved by the white powders, no other master was stronger.

The phone rang. He'd been smoking so much he almost missed it, not sure if the ringing was in his head or in his office. Not sure if there was even a difference. That is, if the ringing only existed in his head, and he answered the phone, who would be on the other end?

The ringing reminded him of something. Music? Tinkling? The sound you made when your piss hit the toilet water. Was there a word for that? God he was thirsty. He took a Snapple out of the fridge and picked up the receiver.

"Royal Messengers."

"This is the potline, right?"

"We deliver. How can I help you?"

"Name's Dave. Dave Gould. Got a little radio show here on B RCK. Mind going on the air for a chat?"

"Okay."

"So I hear you sell reefer?"

"Yeah, I'm the king, man. El Rey."

"So you're telling me I can order marijuana by phone, and

you'll send a bike messenger to deliver it?"

"Pot is what we got. Where you located and what you want?"

"You know you're on the radio, right?"

"Shit, I'm on the *radio*." El Rey started to laugh, "No man, I'm in my office!"

"So could I get say an ounce delivered to the station?" He gave El Rey the address.

"Okay, that's in mid-town. I guarantee delivery in half an hour."

He took the address. The man thanked him and told him it was a pleasure doing business. El Rey beeped Lobo, one of his more dependable and presentable boys. He happened to be uptown anyway and had enough product on him to do the job without having to come back down.

The phone rang again. Small job, local. His regular boys were all off or busy, so El Rey was forced to beep Lenny – the crazy hippie.

Suddenly the office phones got very busy, ringing and ringing. El Rey liked to keep regular hours and was supposed to go to his mother's for dinner, so he unhooked the lines.

Lenny showed up about fifteen minutes later. The guy was always happy to get work from him. He shared El Rey's pot redemption philosophy, but Lenny also thought that acid and all other forms of hallucinogen man-made or organic had magical properties. Whenever Sean organized a demo or smoke-in, Lenny could be depended upon to put up posters and hand out fliers. Still, he wasn't the type who could inconspicuously walk around north of 14th street, so El Rey only used him for downtown delivery, and even then, only as a last resort. The job that came through was perfect for him. A lid to some punks hanging out in Tompkins.

The hippie entered with his rooster on his shoulder smelling like he hadn't showered in a while which was baseline. But El Rey noticed something different. Crazy was Lenny's normal, but Lenny seemed insane even for Lenny. Wide-eyed and moving his hands around like he was having a fight with the air.

"Anything wrong?" El Rey asked, immediately regretting his

curiosity.

Lenny sat down and started to cry. El Rey handed him a Kleenex.

"She's so mean to me. I'm gonna have to kill her. I can't go out on the streets again."

Lenny was looking at the rooster while he was talking, so El Rey thought he was referring to the bird. He told Lenny he was sorry to hear about his troubles. He gave him the lid. Lenny kept muttering there was no other way.

"She's gonna get me *evicted*, man."

"Yeah, landlords are pricks. They don't like you keeping pets. Especially livestock."

Three weeks later, Lenny would come into the office offering to sell El Rey a jade ring. When El Rey asked to see it, Lenny pulled it out of a pocket complete with Ingrid's finger. That was when El Rey would realize Lenny hadn't been talking about his bird.

Chapter 7

Dancing in the Streets

Johnny

For years to come, Johnny Ramirez always had wonderful stories to tell about the riot. Like how he was standing next to a drunk, watching him wind up his arm to throw an empty 40-ouncer, *the very one* that would hit the side of a cop's head and set things off.

Then there were the two elderly Ukrainian ladies who'd been gossiping on a bench when the demo turned. He helped them through the mayhem and delivered them to a cop, who raised his face shield and assured Johnny he would "take care of them."

As for the police officer leading them to safety, Johnny described it being "like something out of the First World War, when the Germans and the French would go out drinking together, fuck the same whores and act like blood brothers before slaughtering each other the next morning on the battlefield."

The stories he told were true. But he had witnessed none of it. Lobo was the one standing next to the man who'd thrown the bottle. Johnny *read* the story about the old ladies somewhere. He attracted these tales easily and found himself repeating what he'd heard, with a few embellishments, often over dinner, always on somebody else's dime.

He had not set out to appropriate these experiences. But he'd get so caught up in the telling that instead of saying "he," the word

"I" would pop out of his mouth. Eventually he came to believe these events had, in fact, happened to *him*. But the truth was, he'd missed the demo and subsequent riot entirely.

He had every intention of going. First, he had to cash out at El Rey's office on Bleecker. On the way, as he crossed Washington Square, he noticed a girl sitting on a bench with a bunch of books. Their eyes met and he nodded and tipped his hat to her. He would've loved to have sat down for awhile just to pass the time, see how things might go, but his boss wasn't too thrilled with his work performance, and the job was the best thing he had going, so he was trying hard not to fuck it up.

Fortunately, she was still there when he returned, and this time it was she who said "hello" to him. She wasn't especially pretty, but she was thin with light brown, hippie-long hair. He figured nineteen or twenty. He noticed her books, *The Second Sex, Sexual Politics,* and *The Female Eunuch,* among others.

"Oh, you must be taking Bronmiller's feminism class," he said more statement than question.

"Summer session, yeah," she said smiling. "You're a student?"

"I'm taking some time off right now, but I'm majoring in philosophy."

It was easy from there. He suggested coffee, someplace air-conditioned. He was glad to have the NYU connection, without which he was certain he wouldn't have gotten that far. Since he just got paid, he grabbed the bill. She invited him to her dorm room and they stopped to buy a bottle of wine.

He felt uncomfortable passing the lobby security guard. He'd been pretty pissed off the year before when he'd had to leave school. He owed the money, but felt it was only bad luck he'd gotten laid-off, and what was a poor boy with no family support supposed to do? The student loan program, he'd concluded, was a government con, propaganda to make things look like equal opportunity existed. Now he was in default and owed the banks who'd be hounding him, if they ever managed to find him. He'd never be able to pay everything off and come up with more tuition. The year and a half he'd had was the end of his college career. It was like that novel he'd read for his nineteenth century Brit lit class; the one about the man who only dreamed of getting an education, but was poor and had terrible things happen to him.

"You look so serious," the girl said. "What are you thinking?"

"Oh, nothing. You ever read *Jude the Obscure*?"

She had, and went into a mini-lecture on the over-determinism of Hardy's work that sounded like something she memorized from notes.

Waiting for the elevator, she was talking while he, pretending to listen, was thinking about his life and how it had taken a serious downhill slide after NYU. He'd wound up on the street, then in a squat where he was always on the verge of being kicked out because the place was run by a collective that demanded that everyone help rehab the building, and he didn't have those kinds of skills.

He took a deep breath, fearing that the security guard would recognize his outsiderness, demand his ID, tell him, like that landlord who'd once thrown him out of some space he was staying at in the Polish part of Brooklyn, "No Spics allowed."

He needed something to get him out of his head and felt relieved when they got to her room. Her roommate wasn't around and wasn't expected for several hours. She put on a tape. Jazz, which Johnny didn't know a lot about, but he took a chance and guessed, "Miles?"

She smiled and he knew he'd hit. They smoked some pot and drank the wine. He talked about working for El Rey. He knew her well enough now to know he could afford to seem a little "dangerous," that she would like that.

She told him she thought he looked "hot" the first time he'd passed by. She'd felt almost insulted when he hadn't spoken to her.

"Really? But you must have guys coming on to you all the time!"

She noticed the scar on Johnny's wrist. Some messed up drunken act of desperation.

"It was stupid. I did it a long time ago."

She opened up and told him about *her* "suicides." She'd OD'd

71

several times on Tylenol p.m., but then got "some really good counseling." He nodded. She took his hand and started to kiss his wrist. It seemed silly to him, so he brought her head to his and kissed her lips. She ran up and put a stolen hotel "Do not disturb" sign on the outside doorknob, a signal to her roommate, "Only *she* uses it a lot more than I do."

They sucked and fucked and then they did it some more. Johnny was in no hurry to leave. She had air-conditioning and even a little refrigerator with Entermann's fudge cake and a quart of Frusen Gladje stuffed into the tiny freezer section.

She was talking a lot now, telling him about her life, growing up in Massapequa or Matzah-Pizza as she called it for the mixed ethnicity of the residents. She went on about her fucked up drug addict brother and her parent's divorce.

"Things are relative," Johnny said, "It doesn't seem like you had it too bad. He started telling her about *his* childhood, how when he was four his mother had left him in their one room apartment in East Harlem, and even though she often left him alone, he remembered this one time, she seemed to be gone very long, and there wasn't any food in the house and then it got dark and he couldn't reach the light switches, and he was too afraid to even sleep on his little bed in the living room, so he took his blanket and laid down in front of the door – "like a dog."

Eventually she had returned – drunk and with a man. The man lifted him up in the blanket and threw him down on his little bed. Then the man and his mother started fucking, not even bothering to pull the curtains that separated his mother's bed from his cot.

The way the girl was looking at him, he could tell he'd given her something to think about, but imagined that by the next morning she'd be back tripping off her own self-pity.

"I'm sorry," she said, "You're right. At least it wasn't like that."

Now she was asking him questions about his life, and because he loved to talk, and was a little drunk, and didn't want to get out of bed or leave the nice cool room, he started to tell her about the tragic history of his *familia*.

"My people came from a small village in Honduras," Johnny

began taking a deep drag of a cigarette. He made sure to drop the "H" when he pronounced Honduras, the extent of his Spanish. "They worked on the land for many years, a *finca*, what we'd call a plantation and thought of the land as their own, but of course it wasn't. My great-grandmother was light-skinned with delicate features even though her people were Mestizos close to being Indians. Probably she was the child of one of the finca owners, some son of a bitch who could trace his lineage to Spain and regularly took the prettiest girls by force or bribe. Her parents married her off when she was young, I guess partly hoping her husband would protect her, and she stayed beautiful even as she popped out babies.

"So one day she's out in the field while her husband was someplace else, and the young *patron* comes up on a horse. Grabs her, takes her into the woods, rapes her. That evening her man goes after the guy and beats him to death.

"Wow," the NYU girl said.

"My great-grandfather knows he's fucked. So he runs away and is living in the woods, but the old *patron* (dead guy's dad) is threatening retribution on the whole village. A week later, my great-grandparents' shack burns down. My grandmother, a little girl, was the only survivor though her legs still have the burn scars. The people in the village were afraid to take her in and somehow she made it to a cousin's of her father who lived on an island off the coast. Fisherman. They had a lot of kids. A lot of hungry mouths. So when she was about fourteen, and as beautiful as her mother had been, a man sees her in the town square. Leon. He was a stranger. Jamaican. British civil servant father, his mother also the daughter of a Jamaican woman and a white man which made him a second generation bastard."

"And makes you, black?" the NYU girl said and then added, "That explains a lot."

"Leon's father laid a small settlement on him. Now he was around forty, trying to establish himself as a coffee buyer.

"He decided he was going to marry Rosalita, my grandmother."

"Forty," said the NYU girl. "That's gross."

"Yeah. Well her cousins were happy about it. He gave the family some money. Rosalita had a sweetheart, Humberto. But her family didn't give her a choice. Humberto wound up marrying one of her cousins. Rosalita had a baby, little girl, Bianca, before she was even fifteen."

"Your mother?" the NYU girl asked offering him a plate of cake a la mode.

Johnny nodded pausing to take a drag off his cigarette. "Leon would beat her, drink, whore around. The usual macho shit. Maybe more so because she was so young and never stood up to him.

"Sometimes she'd run into Humberto."

"Her lost love," said the NYU girl.

"He felt bad, to see her like that. So he came up with an idea. See, he had a brother, Manny, living in America. He wanted Rosalita to run away with Bianca. Marry Manny for the citizenship. Humberto was a policeman, even had a little money saved. He was willing to loan it to her for this worthy cause.

"Leon must have got suspicious because before she had a chance to escape, he took Bianca and left town."

The NYU girl's eyes went wide. She sat up in the bed and held her pillow against her chest.

"Rosalita got too depressed to even leave her house. Humberto began to visit her there, just bringing her food at first. It became a scandal. Later, she and Humberto had a son. Kid died of malaria. She was convinced it was God's punishment for the adultery. She told Humberto it was over. This time she took up his offer and moved to the city where his brother lived and married him, although he had a woman, and she just slept on the couch. That was in Newburgh, upstate."

"I've heard of it. It's a pit," the NYU girl said.

"Yeah. Manny helped her find a factory job. But after a while she got work as a housekeeper for this rich American family – living in. She leaves her 'husband.' Years go by and one day he calls her."

"What about Manny?" the girl asked. "Did they have a thing for each other?"

"I think she's been celibate since her son died."

"Oh my God," the girl said gulping down more cake.

"Manny got a letter from Humberto who'd run into a sailor who'd known Leon. They started talking and the guy told him Bianca was living in Newark, New Jersey with Leon's mother. They had the mother's name and Manny checked the telephone information. He called the number and asked for Bianca. The woman who answered had a West Indies accent and told him the girl wasn't home.

"It took Rosalita a few days to decide what to do. My grandmother hadn't seen her daughter in fourteen years."

"Wait a sec," the NYU girl said, "She was only fifteen when she had the kid, and she lost her three years later, and now that's plus fourteen. She wasn't even that old. Like thirty-something."

"Thirty-two," Johnny said. "So first she wrote a letter to her daughter. Then Bianca came to Newburgh for a visit. The first thing she noticed was Bianca had full lips like Leon's. But on her they were already turned down in a scowl, and her voice was very flat. My grandmother told me she almost thought it wasn't really Bianca. Maybe some other kid of Leon's trying to pass herself off. She'd lived different places with different girlfriends of her dad's before he finally put her with his mother. She told my grandmother the old woman was senile and Leon had left her there to take care of her.

"They stay in touch. Couple of years later the old woman dies. My grandmother wanted Bianca to come live with her. But my mother had other ideas. Now that she was free, she wanted to move to New York City. She was going to find a job. She had a high school diploma and was thinking she could go to City College part time."

Johnny stopped for a moment.

The NYU girl asked him what was wrong.

"I was just remembering," he said. "Sometimes she'd go on, tell me about how she had all these hopes and dreams. Before she got stuck with me."

The girl put her arms around him.

"She got herself a little place in East Harlem. She never found the fancy office job she wanted. Maybe, her skin was a little too dark, or those *nice* lips didn't fit in downtown."

The NYU girl was staring into Johnny's eyes like they were an ocean and she was all set to dive in.

"She wound up a receptionist at some auto repair place. She'd go out drinking, date some of the guys that worked there.

"She started to spend a lot of time in bars. She met a man, Puerto Rican, older, Victor Ramirez. Tall, silver hair. *Muy mujeriego*, that's Spanish for. . ."

The girl interrupted, "I know what it's for. I told you I spent a semester in Barcelona. Maybe he reminded her of Leon. Women are really fucked up that way."

"He disappeared. She called Rosalita, wanted money for an abortion. She knew a woman who could do it. My grandmother told her she'd help her but not like that. Moved in. Kept the house clean, kept the men away. Tried to keep my mother sober.

"She stayed till after I was born. She wanted Bianca to move to Newburgh with her. But my mother kicked her out. Went on welfare."

"Then when I was four she met my step-dad. We didn't hit if off so good," Johnny said pointing to his slightly crooked nose. "One day my mom put me on a bus to visit grandma, and I just stayed."

The NYU girl had more questions. Johnny told her about the Easter when he and Rosalita came down on the bus to visit Bianca. It turned out Leon was paying her a surprise visit from Jamaica. He even asked Rosalita to forgive him.

"Did she?" The girl asked.

"Of course she did," he said, "A few weeks later, he sent her a check for $25 with a note telling her to buy something nice for his grandson."

Johnny and the girl were both tired. Johnny wanted to spend the night, but the girl was worried about her roommate.

"So what? Her bed's across the room. I'll just be *sleeping*."

She didn't like the idea, so Johnny imagined a three-way would have been out of the question. They fell asleep anyway, and then were awakened by a pounding at the door.

He was slipping on his pants as the girl undid the bolt for her roommate. She had black hair cut all choppy, and several silver hoops hanging from each ear. She looked at Johnny for a moment as he buttoned his pants, and he thought, "Not bad."

Then he noticed it wasn't a headband wrapped around her hair, but a bandage, and just below it, above her eye, a little spot caked with dried blood.

"Jesus, you wouldn't believe what's been going on at Tompkins Square!" she said.

She told them all about how cops were going crazy, attacking people and hiding their badge numbers.

Johnny and the NYU girl stayed up the rest of the night listening to her stories.

Peter

I finally forced myself into the hallway, down the steps, and out onto the street. Unlike the saying, it *wasn't* the humidity that night, but the heat itself. You could see it radiating off the pavement.

My block, East 7th is quiet, residential. Usually the loudest noise comes from the laughter and conversation of a group of elderly Ukrainian ladies who bring down a bridge table and play cards till the early morning. On that particular night, their spot was empty.

When I got down to the corner by 1st Avenue, wooden police barricades were set up blocking the sidewalks as well as the street. There were two cops standing guard.

"This street is closed," an officer told me.

He and his partner both wore helmets with shaded plastic shields down, covering their faces. It was twilight and I wondered how well they could even see. I noticed there was a piece of tape above his breast pocket. It didn't hit me at that moment that the tape was hiding his badge number.

"I live on this block, sir. I was just going home."

He turned toward the other one who nodded.

"Okay, go ahead." The shield muffled his voice in a strange way reminding me of some science fiction movie where the aliens could be detected by the metallic distortion of their voices.

I walked through a narrow space between the barricades. I was afraid to look back. I was trying to imagine the cop's features behind the mask. He sounded young. Was he afraid? Of *me*? Was it hard to breathe with that plastic down in front of you? Those might be good questions for a reporter to ask, but I wasn't going back for an interview.

As I walked down toward Avenue A and the park, I heard the familiar sounds of a protesting crowd – drum beats, chanting, shouting. Then, suddenly something else. A whistle. Police megaphones telling people to clear the area immediately. My view of the park was still limited to a few feet of iron gate and some bushes. Suddenly people were running out to the other side of the gate. Others were jumping over the fence. I wondered if the exits were blocked, or there was a fire, or who knew what?

A crowd was now rushing toward and past me. Someone shouting some kind of warning. Then I was face to face with another shielded cop. He started to hit me with his nightstick, howling like a drunken frat boy.

The first blow grazed the side of my forehead. Then my arm went up to protect myself. He hit me another three or four times before his partner shouted for him to move on.

I rose to my feet, still shielding myself, not quite sure what had just occurred or whether it would happen again. Everything was louder now, continuous screams, sirens, car horns. I was standing in front of a new bar. An art deco place with lots of chrome. There was a glass wall. The patrons, who all seemed to be wearing black, stared out at the scene, glasses in hand. I went to the door, but it was locked. I noticed blood on my hand from my forehead. I didn't know how bad it was. I was pounding on the bar door, shouting for help. The pony-tailed bouncer behind the glass was shaking his head and mouthing, "no."

I looked down at the corner and watched as two cops beat a skinny young man with a video camera. A third was hitting the camera with his stick, striking it forcefully, as though it were a dangerous animal that might be feigning death. Then they saw a biker pedaling by and like bored pit bulls decided to go after new prey.

Behind me a shouted whisper, "Quick, over here."

I turned. A woman was holding open the door to her building, inviting me into safety. She was wearing a white tee shirt and shorts. Some trick of the light made me see a golden light bouncing off her brown curly hair.

I hesitated for a second, feeling as a journalist I had some obligation to be on the street, to get to the park itself. A new wave of civilians began to roll up the block, followed by more shielded cops. A kid in a Mohawk running by caught their attention as I ducked inside the building.

"It's 4B," she said. "I'm going to stay down here."

I stared at her for a moment, still seeing the light off her hair, wondering if I had a concussion.

"My boyfriend's a medic. He can fix you up."

I nodded and headed up the stairs. When I entered her apartment, I discovered I was not the first refugee she had rescued.

A man was sitting on a rocking chair, clutching a dishtowel full of ice to his bandaged head. He had brown hair going to gray and a bald spot on top but the hair growing down from behind was tied in a ponytail. He wore old jeans and a tie-dyed tee shirt. He was moaning and muttering something about losing his "lucky bandana."

On the couch a couple were sharing a cigarette, passing it between them like a joint.

"Where's the doc?"

"In the can," the man on the couch said.

The woman was holding the cigarette, so I offered one to the man as I got one for myself out of the pack.

He took it. Gestured his thanks. He was a small guy with glasses and curly hair, looked maybe Latino or Italian, even light-skinned African American.

The woman had looked at my face as I'd handed him the

smoke, but when our eyes met, she looked away quickly. She had long blonde hair, was wearing a baseball cap, no make-up. For a moment, I thought it was the same woman I'd seen that night at Wigstock. But this one was like a scaled-down version – more delicate, more real. Thinner lips, smaller eyes, not even polish on her nails, yet in an understated way, breathtaking.

The man in the rocking chair was crying, his voice a high-pitched whine, "I was getting up, man. They didn't have to hit me."

The woman went over to comfort him.

The man on the couch said, "Fuckin pigs. Animals. They all deserve to die."

I was about to ask him what had happened when the toilet flushed and the medic stepped out. He was a large man though he walked with a certain grace. He looked like he could pull a swimmer from a riptide, carry a fat lady down five flights of stairs and follow it up with a marathon.

"Another patient?" he asked.

He examined my forehead, announced I had a minor abrasion and a small bump. He asked about dizziness, told me he didn't think I had a concussion but should stay awake and head for an ER if I got nauseous or even had a headache. He cleaned the wound and put a small band-aid on the cut. He was more concerned about my arm. He told me the good news was it wasn't broken, but I'd be bruised for a while. He went to get some ice.

"I'm Peter," I announced to the others in the room.

No one said anything.

I looked at the man on the couch. "So what happened to your friend tonight?"

"You were there. You know the scene."

The woman went over to the window. She stuck out her head.

"There's still lots of action on A, but this street looks quiet." She turned to the man in the rocking chair. "Do you feel well enough to go home?"

"I guess," he said.

The man on the couch got up. He and the woman helped the rocking chair guy, and the three of them were out the door by the time the medic emerged from the kitchen with the ice.

He looked around the room taking inventory. "Fuckin junkies," he said. "I hope they didn't take anything."

"How could you tell?"

"Drive an ambulance in this town and you figure it out. Not the hippie. But the other two for sure."

His girlfriend came back. Introductions were made. We decided to go up to the roof for a better view.

I walked across the roofs of several connected buildings to the one on the corner. A group of people had been having a barbecue and saw everything.

"The people on the periphery just inside the gate were sitting, listening to the speakers and then there was a scream and the next thing the cops were shouting for people to leave. Only before they even had a chance to get up, the cops were on them with their sticks," one told me.

I finally found someone who'd actually been there when it happened. "What I heard was some punk threw a bottle at a cop and then they all went crazy. But nobody seen that."

The park, or what we could see of it through the trees, was empty except for those guarding it. Avenue A was blocked off. The only cars coming down were ambulances for the wounded. There must have been a couple of hundred diehard protesters shouting the whole world was watching. They were almost outnumbered by the harsh lights of the TV news crews. There were police lining the sidewalk as well, still faceless behind their masks, but more cautious in front of the press.

A blue and white helicopter swooped down close enough for us to feel wind off the propellers. A voice warned us, "Evacuate the roof immediately. There will be no further warnings!"

The medic and his girlfriend offered me their couch, but I decided to chance the one block walk home and stayed up till dawn recording all I'd seen and heard and thought. But the truth is, I didn't know what to think. *Something* had happened that night – a justification for years of paranoia. It hadn't mattered if you were a punk rock anarchist or a slumming Republican. If you were caught in the park, you were a target. And it did seem like the whole thing was planned – the riot gear in place, the massive number of police and vehicles.

I wondered whether the next day's papers would contain angry editorials about police brutality. I doubted it, but was still surprised the next day, the next week, when even after all the articles about the "excessive police violence," most people who hadn't been there didn't grasp what had happened.

But why would they? Maybe the old paranoids were right about the mainstream media and government being aligned with big real estate. Maybe that's where the real story was, the one I should have been after, but I was too caught up to see it.

I admit the whole thing set me off on a high. I proudly showed off my bruised arm as I gave an eyewitness account. I felt like a spy when, dressed in Yuppie drag, I interviewed the police department spokeswoman – the older sister of a college friend. I was a foreign correspondent in the heart of a war zone writing my dispatches from the front.

I sensed I was getting close to finding the big story I had come down here for. I didn't know the events that would lead me to that story were already in motion, being played out piece by piece every day.

Chapter 8

Crazed Cannibal Kilz Cutie

From The Personal Journal and Memoir of Ingrid Hess

28 August 1988

Did I move in illegally and make some stupid deal with the drunk super?

No.

So how is this my fault?

He's crazy and she's a whoring addict. I want them OUT, but at this point, if they could come up with a decent rent share like $700 a month, they could stay in her room. That's FAIR! I get my own tiny room for $300 and they each pay $350 to share the big room. She could even have the living room if she wants. It's not like this wouldn't have happened eventually. Why are they acting like it's my fault?

Andre was supposed to move in next week, but now he's saying he won't pay to sleep in the living room, and besides he thinks Lenny is nuts. I told him sure, but harmless.

Veroni doesn't return calls. He's going to be looking for his money. And I will NOT fuck him. NO! So I have to get them out and get in someone who can pay the rent.

Yesterday, I bring the locksmith. Medico lock. Tells me

it's "the best." I put their things out in the hall. Leave for dance class. Come back, big hole punched in door.

Birdy is different, quiet since chicken incident. I was taking a pee when it happened. Andre was moving some stuff around to see how things would look and he didn't know the bird had gone behind a dresser and WAP. Flat like pancakes.

How many times can I apologize?

I tried to give Lenny money. "Go out buy a parakeet," I said. Then, I even offered him my Nikon. It's the only thing I have left of value. I tell him sell it, keep the money for moving. He banged it against the wall and smashed the lens.

He tells me he will kill me, spread my body to four winds so I can never come back. Let him hit me then. Let him try. Then maybe I could get the cops in and finally end this.

❖ ❖ ❖

Raven

These days she called herself Raven and her hair was black. She was sweet fifteen, but her ID said different. Five-three, ninety pounds the last time she got on a scale. Blue-lensed round wire-rimmed glasses, very sixties from a flea market, black lycra top with a feather collar from Canal Jeans, the tightest jeans she could find and boots from the seventies with big glam-rock platforms. But what she really wanted was a kick-ass pair of Doc Martens which was why she was going to the city – to shop.

Shop and cop.

There weren't any seats on the PATH train, so she took hold of the pole, reminding her of work.

Couple of homeboys got on. Scanning the car for potential victims. She flashed a smile. They moved on. She had $300 in her boot. Pay plus tips from the club where she stripped.

She lived in Union City with an old guy in his thirties. He was cool. She didn't have to do much to stay there and he even let her bring her friends. Still, she dreamed of living in the city, *Loisaida*.

Sometimes she could spend a whole day and night at Tompkins Square. People talked. It was a community. Not like home. She used to be Jill and had red hair and played the cello in the high school band, but nobody liked her. The boys thought she was a brainiac and the girls were jealous, and she was daddy's favorite which meant her mother hated her, and it was all so boring she wanted to puke just thinking about it.

She got off the train in the West Village. It was raining, so she found a cab. She thought she'd drop by Kyra's. Maybe Kyra was holding or they could make some calls from the house.

Out on East 11th. The downstairs building door was open. A guy she knew from the park as Lobo, followed as always by his blue-eyed, shepherd-husky mix, Shaman, was coming down the stairs holding a filled up black plastic garbage bag. Which she might have thought was strange, if she'd thought about it, because he didn't live in the building.

"Hey, how's it going?"

"Okay." He looked like he was about to say something else. She started up the stairs. Turned around, saw him staring.

"You got a problem?"

"You going to Lenny's?"

"Yeah, so?"

"Nothing, man. Nothing."

Weird. She passed the second floor, then onto the third. Somebody cooking something. Heavy smell. Some kind of meat.

There was a hole punched right through Kyra's apartment door. Raven reached through and turned the lock not bothering to knock. The first one she saw was Lenny, joint in hand, sitting on the couch, muttering. An old hippie looking guy with a bandanna wrapped around his head was also sitting, staring off into space. She closed the door behind her and saw the others in the kitchen.

"Shit. It's like Grand Central in here," a light-skinned black man said. She'd seen him around. Didn't know his name. Not much taller than she was, kind of nerdy looking, glasses, but solid, muscular, something scary about him, the way he was coming toward her.

"She's cool, Joe," Kyra said standing in her bedroom door. Cigarette in mouth. Looking like she'd been through some kind of scene.

Raven checked out the blonde at the kitchen table. For a moment, she thought it was Ingrid who'd been living there the past few weeks, but then realized this woman was even prettier, softer looking. The guy sitting next to the woman, she'd noticed before. He lived in the building. Thin like from AIDS. Dressed all in black, except sometimes when he'd wear a theatrical red cape. Called himself the Magus and looked like the decrepit older brother of the image from the Ryder deck.

"What are you cooking?"

"Soup for the people in the park," the blonde said.

"Cool." Everyone felt solidarity with the homeless. The pigs trying to throw them out of Tompkins Square, especially since the riots.

Lenny said, "I fuckin killed her, little girl. I fuckin killed her and chopped her up."

She looked at Kyra, the way she sometimes did for a translation of Lenny talk.

Kyra let out a deep drag. "Ingrid's dead."

"I got her body in the bathtub. Some of it. Wanna see?"

"Yeah, okay."

She could feel the others watching as she followed him to the bathroom.

What was left in the tub was hardly identifiable as human. The head was in a bucket. Lenny lifted it out by the hair so she could get a good look.

"I strangulated her. Joe says we gotta clean it up. Wanna help?"

"No."

Joe came up behind her. "You know you say anything to anybody you dead."

"Yeah," she said. Maybe the first time in years she answered somebody in authority without mouthing off.

Kyra said, "Let's get the fuck outa here."

"Minute." Raven headed toward Ingrid's room. "I wanna check

out her shoes. It's not like she'll miss them, right?"

Peter

Sometimes, sitting on the same bench in Tompkins Square where I first saw that perfect woman, I'd imagine running into her and replay the scene in my head. Rewrite it so I wasn't hesitant. Joke with her, flirt. The stories would flow. We'd leave together.

More than once, she visited me in dreams, which always involved a search – deserted buildings, holes in the floor, stairways leading nowhere.

Late September, there she was. This time, it was in a photo that graced the front page of *The New York Post*, under the headline, **Beauty and the Beast**. Lenny Matthews, "the rooster man," was the beast. The tabloids described him as a kind of latter day Manson. Beautiful European ballet dancer killed by acid crazed boyfriend. Even by New York standards it was pretty *Grand Guignol*. He'd been boasting about the murder. Showing off little trophies. The cops were being accused of ignoring numerous phone calls from concerned neighbors. When they did investigate, he'd readily confessed and told them where they could find her head. It had been left in a bucket filled with concrete in a Port Authority locker, other bits and pieces found in various locations, rumors Lenny had cooked her bones and ladled out the broth with carrots and rice to the homeless who to the city's dismay still haunted the park, at least during daylight hours. A headline, quoting some graffiti allegedly left on Lenny's battered apartment door read, *"Is it soup, yet?"*

Allegedly, because the door no longer existed. Someone had torched the building shortly before the arrest.

As I read the stories, my mind kept spinning back to that day in the park. What would have happened if I had opened my mouth? What if she'd come home with *me*?

I felt I had to find out what had happened to her and why. It was too late to save her, but we were connected somehow. I would speak for her from beyond the grave. And maybe in her story, I'd find that bigger story I'd been searching for.

When I explained all this to Dr. Lieder, whom I still checked in with from time to time for refills of my anti-anxiety medications, he pointed out the obvious – a beautiful blonde I couldn't rescue. When had *that* happened before?

He was alluding to my mother of course, and being a shrink probably knew just what memories he'd triggered. There I was, six years old, watching her shave her legs the day she'd left the bathroom door ajar. She was wearing a tee shirt and satin panties, one foot resting on a closed toilet seat. The toes were perfectly polished the shade matching the pink lingerie she favored. She spritzed lemon-scented shaving cream on a shapely calf. She laughed when she saw me lurking in the doorway. High pitched laugh, like a little girl's. The kind of laugh that always made me turn around. She put some cream on her palm and blew it at me like she was blowing me a kiss.

She was an actress and dancer when Dad found her in some review off-off Broadway. Successful middle-aged producer, beautiful girl. Old story. I don't know why he actually left his first wife to marry her.

They moved west before I was born. Maybe Dad wanted to conquer Hollywood, or she did.

"Rub my feet, Peeper," she'd say after her dancing teacher came out to give her private lessons. I don't know where she got Peeper from. Maybe that time I was watching her shave.

I loved rubbing her feet. She got a pedicure once a week. It's strange. I've never been with a woman whose feet were as smooth as my mother's.

I can remember seeing her drunk. I can remember her fucked up on pills. Sometimes she had that heavy lidded look, like you see in later pictures of Marilyn Monroe. It's from the barbiturates. Officially, it was suicide. There was a note.

Years later a bit before my little college crisis, Dad took me to see *A Chorus Line*. There's a number, a dancer lamenting how she couldn't really sing. He poked me, "That was Bea's problem," he said, and then he added as though I wouldn't have known, "Your mother."

Afterwards things got heated and I made him show me the note, hidden away in a file cabinet.

I'm sorry. I can't do it anymore. You'll all do just fine. I mean it.

"How do you know she wasn't just going to leave? There's nothing in it about suicide. How do you even know when she wrote it?"

He didn't answer. He hadn't been there when it happened, one of his frequent trips back to New York.

We spent the morning by the pool. She was sunning herself, wearing a white bathing suit, the kind with a little skirt, like Grace Kelly in *High Society*. Not that she needed to cover anything. Refreshing herself with Tanqueray and tonics. Mixing them was a skill I'd perfected to please her. She announced it was time for a nap. I followed her upstairs into that big round bed.

"Rub my feet, Peeper."

I remember they were cold. We fell asleep in each other's arms. When I woke up she was making a snoring sound. It was starting to get dark. She wouldn't wake up. I was frightened. The snoring stopped.

I thought I'd made it stop. I thought I'd killed her. I started to scream. There was no one else in the house. It must have been the maid's day off. I guess I called the operator eventually or a neighbor did. I don't remember a lot about the next few weeks. Dad flying in. The funeral. Moving east to start my new life.

Back in the present, Dr. Leider – that Austrian mind reader – was looking at me with more paternal warmth than I'd ever received from my father.

"So, Peter, do you think there is perhaps a connection?"

I was wishing he had not long ago prohibited smoking in his office. "No, I don't see it."

Forty-nine minutes on the clock and someone sitting in the waiting room. He handed me a new script with an increase in my Klonopin and suggested (not for the first time) a "trial" of Lithium.

Johnny

Johnny and PD sitting in Tompkins Square one crisp autumn day, grooving on the falling leaves. The park had been closed nights since the riot. Word was soon it would be closed altogether for "renovations." There was a constant police presence. They watched as the rangers took apart a makeshift cardboard condo that some resourceful soul had managed to piece together. But Johnny wasn't bothered by it right then. He was feeling pretty mellow having swallowed three Klonopin before he'd fixed that morning.

It was funny about the Klonopin. He'd seen a whole bottle in some guy's medicine chest back during the summer when he was making a delivery. He grabbed a few. Stuffed them in his back jeans pocket and forgot about it. Then *voila*, there they were!

First he'd managed to get that great space through El Rey and now this. His luck, he felt, was definitely changing.

"Too bad about Lenny, huh?" he said just to make conversation.

"Yeah," PD said.

"I heard they're closing the park partly cause of that soup story. They think the whole thing is out of control."

PD just looked down at his hands.

"You know I saw him, I guess a couple of days before he got arrested," Johnny went on. "He told me he killed her. He felt bad about it. Wanted to confess."

PD suddenly looked up.

Johnny continued, "He was saying how she was gonna get him kicked out and all, and I said, 'Man, you gotta book! Join the Dead tour or something.' I even offered $5 toward bus fare."

"She *was* gonna get him evicted," The old hippie said, "I'm not saying it was right, what happened, but man. . ."

The conversation died out for a moment. Then PD started talking about a couple of his friends, Joe and Moira. They'd been staying with him, but now the collective had asked them to move on. PD attributed this to some sympathetic statements Joe was making about Lenny.

Johnny remembered meeting Joe a couple of times.

"He works at Arcana, right?"

PD nodded.

Johnny thought for a moment. The place where he was staying had two bedrooms and no rent. It was a safe house for El Rey's stash. It was supposed to be him and Lobo living there, but Lobo had left town a few weeks before. Quit work and took off for Florida with his lady and his dog. Very sudden. Now it was just Johnny and the sixteen year-old punk rocker girl he recently moved in. Might not be a bad idea, getting a couple more people to help out with the groceries and such.

"They can crash at my place," he said.

Dr. Sharon

Doctor Sharon Horowitz found nothing particularly out of the ordinary about her newest "patient," Leonard James Matthews, better known in the tabloids as "The Beast of East 11th, Street."

Her mother, skimming those same newspapers and seeing Sharon's name mentioned as the court appointed psychiatrist, had called to express concern.

"He's in restraints, isn't he? And they've got guards. Please God, tell me they've got guards."

"They have guards, Ma."

What she didn't tell her mother, because really she was passed the age of baiting her, was she actually found Lenny endearing.

She worked on a locked unit in a public hospital with the chronically mentally ill. Most were homeless. She knew this was not the way it had to be. Other countries, other *states* even, did much better with their chronics. She saw the editorials in the paper. If Lenny wasn't crazy, then he deserved to fry. If he was, it was yet another example of the "failure" of deinstitutionalization.

The truth was most schizophrenics weren't going to harm anyone. Housing *all* of them in supportive home environments, was not only more humane, it was less expensive than warehousing them in institutions, and if Lenny had been housed, medicated and managed, then maybe this whole mess never would have happened.

If not for the constraints of confidentiality, Sharon thought, she would write an editorial or at least a letter to *The Times* about the subject.

Except for the heinousness of his crime, Lenny was pretty typical. Confused, delusional, afraid. Her contract work doing court evaluations usually brought her into contact with another type of patient, sociopaths feigning psychosis. Jerks who told her they were werewolves or started to talk in baby voices faking multiple personality like a bad TV movie. The worst were the smart ones who'd actually read the DSM and cherry-picked their symptoms.

Lenny, however, was the real deal.

His thinking was disorganized and paranoid, which made him what those in Sharon's trade, called "a poor historian." She didn't really need to know a lot about his past to do her job – which was to determine whether or not he was fit to stand trial. But she wanted to be thorough, so she called his father who provided some details.

Lenny was a military brat, growing up on several bases in the US and abroad, only child. Age ten, his father retired and the family settled in a small town in East Texas where both parents had grown up. No documented anti-social behavior.

Sharon asked about cruelty to animals.

The Major laughed, "Lenny's got a spot in his heart for critters." He told her a story about one Thanksgiving when Lenny had set free the turkey they were raising to butcher.

"I didn't have it in me to fight with the boy, specially with his ma being so sick."

He'd never been a great student, and after his mother's death his grades went down. Still, the Major insisted, "He was a normal boy back then. Hell, I even found *Playboy* magazines hid in his room."

Then came Lenny's "religious phase." He started telling people he was a preacher, talking in tongues.

"Did you seek psychiatric help for your son at that time?" Sharon asked.

"Didn't seem strange. His mother's people are snake handlers."

Then when Lenny was about sixteen it changed. He stopped

going to church. When the Major asked him about it, he explained, "You're either with God or the Devil and Satan has selected me."

The first definitive psychotic break came at age seventeen. Lenny took some acid and fifteen years later still had not come down.

"He was talking all kinds of nonsense for days. Then he burned down the barn and started dancing around the flames. That's when I took him to the hospital."

Thus beginning Lenny's career as a mental patient.

"They gave him the Haldol, but as far as I could figure, he came out worse than he went in."

She asked if there were any history of violence.

"Not really. That's why this thing's such a mystery to me."

"What about threats?"

"He was *always* making threats. He never *did* anything."

The Major became involved with a family support network. Learned the system. Managed to get his son into a supervised group home in Austin.

Lenny seemed to stabilize, until he disappeared for a few days and came back psychotic. Drugs suspected. Lost his bed at the home.

He lasted a few days back on the farm. Hitchhiked out. A month later, the Major got a call from an ER in Denver. He'd come in hungry and confused. The hospital wouldn't admit him because he wasn't suicidal or homicidal. They'd given him a referral to a shelter. Dad flew in. Searched. Didn't find him. A couple of months later, he got a similar call, some other town, some other state.

In the five or so years he'd been living in New York, Lenny had called his father collect maybe six times. Always asking for money. Back in Texas, he'd had social security coming in. The county mental health agency had acted as his payee. The Major knew Lenny had been cut off at some point, but wasn't sure about his current benefits.

Sharon thanked the Major for talking to her. She found the background helpful, although it had very little relevance as far as her task went which was assessing Lenny's competency to understand the charges against him and assist in his defense.

She read the police report shaking her head. He told the cops he dropped acid almost every day. It seemed plausible.

When he and Sharon met for their first interview, he readily confessed. She asked him what made him kill.

"She was sent by our father to torment me," he said.

"She was sent by *your* father?"

"*Our* father who art in heaven," he said crossing himself.

She noticed he crossed himself upside down.

She asked him if he understood most people would have considered killing Ingrid wrong.

"They told me it was right. They told me she had to die."

"Who told you, Lenny?"

His eyes widened. He leaned forward, staring at her intensely. He was not restrained, but Sharon was thankful at that moment for the burly guards standing by.

"I prayed for guidance to Satan. I performed the proper rituals and he sent his emissaries to advise me."

"How did these emissaries communicate with you?"

"They talked to me."

"So you heard their voices?"

"Of course I heard them. I may be crazy, but I ain't deaf."

From what Sharon could piece together, he and Ingrid had been lovers. Ingrid, perhaps realizing how sick Lenny was, tried to break it off. Lenny felt the same rejection anyone would feel, but being a schizophrenic, he couldn't filter through his "demons" – the anger and rejection he must have felt. He ascribed great powers to Ingrid. His paranoia increased. Lenny was convinced Ingrid was out to destroy him, trying to send him, "out to the wasteland to wander." He continually referred to his fantasies of the "frozen hell," she was condemning him to, a place where he would starve or be killed. So he called forth his demons. The voices – his command hallucinations had told him what he wished to hear: kill her. He told Sharon he resisted the voices at first, but they goaded him. He was afraid if he didn't listen to the emissaries, they would turn on him. They instructed him on getting rid of the body. He felt remorse and wanted to go to the police, but they dissuaded him.

While Sharon concluded he did understand the charges against him, she did not believe he was competent to assist in his own defense. As a result of her evaluation, at least until that assessment changed, he would remain on the locked ward for violent acutely psychotic patients, which meant he would be assigned a doctor from her team. She might even request to treat him. Within ninety days, he'd be reevaluated and then again after a longer interval. She didn't expect much improvement, but eventually he would be deemed competent. The DA and legal aid lawyer would cut a deal for an insanity plea, and he would stay in the hospital until the doctors decided he was no longer dangerous. Given the extremity of the crime, not to mention the publicity, Sharon knew no judge would ever risk releasing him. Her only hope for Lenny was that someday, away from the street drugs and with the appropriate medications, he would at least be free from his demons.

Johnny

Johnny sitting at the kitchen table, smoking a cigarette and feeling sorry for himself. He knew things were going better than they had been, maybe ever, but that's how it always went before it fell apart.

El Rey had made him dispatcher, which meant he didn't get robbed for dope anymore, but now he was stuck in the office. Sometimes the phones all rang at once and he couldn't get to them. It was hard work keeping the orders straight. He was worried El Rey might fire him and kick him out of the space.

Plus his girl, Karma, had just taken off. She had musical aspirations and met a guy at the park with a van and left with him for Seattle.

"You could come too," she'd offered.

Maybe he should've and could've if not for the daily habit he recently reacquired.

Moira walked into the kitchen. She started to make coffee and asked him if he wanted any.

"Please," he said.

She put a paperback on the table. Johnny noticed the 48 cent sticker from The Strand. Stendhal, Le Rouge et Le Noir.

She caught him looking at it.

"You've read it?" she asked.

"In English," he said thinking he probably hadn't.

He realized in the two weeks since she and Joe had been staying there, he'd never been alone with her in the apartment. He found himself wondering what it would be like with her and how long Joe was going to be gone.

"Joe went to get his check at work," she said as though she were reading his thoughts.

PD had filled him in on her story. Sometimes she'd refer to her old life, talk about places she'd been, Algeria, Istanbul, Paris.

He'd never met anyone like her before, and for the life of him he couldn't figure out why she was with Joe. The guy was a stone psychopath, which was another reason why Karma left. She and Joe didn't get along, and the final straw had been with her kittens.

She'd adopted a stray cat about to give birth, made a nice box for it in the corner of their bedroom. The cat had two kittens. They were getting old enough to be running around the apartment. One of them jumped on Joe's lap while he was in the middle of telling some story. It dug in with its claws the way kittens do.

Joe said, "Fuck!" then casually picked it up by its neck and tossed it down the airshaft window as he went on with what he'd been saying.

The apartment was on the sixth floor.

Karma had taken the mother and surviving kitten with her to Seattle.

"Moira?" Johnny said like a question.

"Yes?" she said.

"Well, it's none of my business, but you and Joe?"

"Yeah. I guess it must seem a little strange," she said. She spoke slowly staring into his eyes. "Look, Robby's going to be free in a few years. When that happens, we'll figure out something, some way to get me out of the country, but right now, there's Joe."

"Moira, he's not the only guy out there."

"Listen, it's the sex. Robby did a lot of speed. He was impotent most of the time. He liked to watch me with other girls. Joe is, it's like he woke me up."

"Whatever he's doing . . ."

He put his hand on hers and they just looked at each other for a moment. Johnny felt more in those seconds than he usually felt in a month. Then they heard the apartment door opening and she pulled away.

Joe came into the kitchen. He looked at Moira. "We gotta leave," he said, "Now."

"What happened?" Johnny asked.

Joe kept his eyes on Moira while he answered. "Go to get my check. They tell me the police came yesterday, wanted to ask me questions about the Lenny Matthews thing."

Moira got up leaving her coffee. "I'll get our things," she said, heading for the bedroom.

"Wait a second," Johnny said, "Why do they want to question you about Lenny?" He was watching Joe's face and seeing that kitten going out the window, so he thought about how to phrase the next part. "I mean you didn't have anything to do with it."

"That's right," Joe said, "but I was there, man. I saw it. You know how crazy Lenny is. I couldn't stop him. He threatened to chop me up if I said anything."

Johnny knew that last part had to be bullshit. No way he could imagine Lenny threatening Joe. Besides, why had Joe been making those sympathetic statements about Lenny if the guy was holding a knife to his throat?

Johnny kept his mouth shut and watched them head out the door. Moira turned around for a second and waved. Johnny waved back, sorry to see her go.

Peter

When I proposed writing a piece on Ingrid Hess's murder,

Bernstein, the editor of *The City Eye*, had been skeptical.

"What can you say that hasn't been reported?"

The tabloids had printed the "facts" weeks before. Fact number one, pieces of a girl's body are turning up in various East Village locations as well as other parts of the city. Fact two, the man with whom she had been living, who'd be a prime suspect in any case, happens to be a lunatic. Fact three, the lunatic says he did it and was seen walking around the city with said body parts.

"There's a lot we don't know," I told Bernstein.

He told me I could do it on spec.

I talked to the detective involved, Ouspenski. Asked about the alleged delay in the investigation, reports that people had contacted the police with stories of Lenny's confessing, even showing off bits of Ingrid, days before the police did anything.

"The investigation started as soon as the stories got to me," he said. He blamed the rumors of police inaction on the general hostility toward the cops which had always existed in the community and had been worsened by the riot as well as the ongoing brutality hearings.

"Listen, I'm here. Anyone's got anything to say about this, they can call me direct."

"What do you think made Lenny do it?"

"He's nuts."

"Is that enough of a reason?"

"I got the evidence. I got the confession. I'll leave the psychology to the shrinks."

I asked him if there were any loose ends. There was one thing that bothered him. Off the record – he was supposed to interview a guy named Joe Holiday, find out what Lenny had been saying to him, see if there could have been premeditation. It wasn't critical. It was just that Joe's name had been mentioned by some of the park "regulars" as a particular friend of Lenny's. Ouspenski had gone to the bookstore where Joe worked, but he wasn't around that day and they didn't have an address. When he went back, they told him Joe had come in for his check, and never returned. Ouspenski couldn't find him.

"You think this Joe Holliday could have been involved?"

"I wish I'da had a chance to find out."

There was also the matter of the fire. Shortly after Lenny's arrest, someone had torched the building. I asked Ouspenski if he thought there was a connection.

"I'm not arson."

"You know what I mean, detective."

"Look Teller, a lot of buildings around here get torched. If you're talking about the rumors, that's bullshit."

I didn't know which rumors he meant, but my heart was racing, and I hoped I'd be able to bluff.

"But what about those 'rumors?'" I asked in my best tough reporter voice.

"I don't think there was any occult activity. Just a simple murder. The only people saying otherwise aren't saying it to me. Yeah, that creepy, magick guy lives in the building, but this is America for Christ sakes. A guy's got a right to be a crackpot. Besides, like I said, no one knows anything when I ask. You find out different, Teller, I'd love to know."

"Maybe we can help each other," I said.

"I've heard that one from you guys before," he said. He did tell me where to find Kyra Vanovowich, the other roommate. She'd told the police she'd been away when the murder happened, and Lenny had told her afterwards. She hadn't seen anything strange in the apartment.

"She told us she thought maybe Ingrid had just left, that Lenny was having a hallucination," Ouspenski said.

That night, I stopped by the club out in New Jersey where Kyra worked. The girls wore tassels on string over their nipples so they were allowed to serve alcohol. But there was a room for "private parties" where the rules were more lax. In addition to the waitresses there were a couple of women in G-strings, dancing continuously in cages. Kyra was one of them. I talked to her during a break.

I'd never been to a strip club before, not even back in college. I guess I expected the women to all be young and perfect. Kyra looked at least forty. Tired circles underneath her eyes. Her legs were thin, but the flesh shook when she danced, and her stomach had stretch marks. Her breasts, however, were phenomenal. Large and upright. When she talked, she'd look at them from time to time as though she were checking to see that this one asset, natural or not, still remained.

I tried not to stare at the glittering daisy petals she had painted around her nipples. As she wiped off her sweat with a towel, I noticed she had pancake make-up on her arms and thighs, and small dark marks as well as some bruises visible where the make-up had run.

"Look, like I told the cops. I wasn't even there."

"Well, you knew Lenny, right? Did he ever hurt you, threaten you in any way?"

"Lenny would never hurt me."

"He chopped up a woman, Kyra. What do you think would make him do something like that?"

She looked away for a moment. Then she noticed her arms and started to put more make-up on them.

"She wasn't a woman. She was a Nazi she-devil."

I took a breath. "That's not the story in the papers."

"She'd bring in guys. She'd be fucking them, like right in front of Lenny."

"So you think he was jealous?"

"What difference does it make? She's dead. I don't need this shit. I gotta work."

She started to get up. I caught her arm. "Listen, I know you're a friend of Lenny's. He's got a side to this. You're the only one who can tell it. C'mon, Kyra, I'm not the police. You can talk to me."

"No I can't. I tell you anything I haven't already told the cops, they're gonna be right on my ass again."

"What haven't you told them?"

She held up her hand like she was swearing in court. "I told them everything," she said.

I offered to buy her breakfast after work, but she refused. She did wind up telling me how Ingrid had secured the lease and was trying to evict them, claimed it was Ingrid making threats. Kyra stuck by what she'd told the police about not being around when it happened or when he was cutting up the body. I asked her if she thought anyone else could have been involved.

"I wasn't there, remember?"

I mentioned Joe Holiday, only because of what the detective had said, and because the name had stayed in my mind. I asked her if she knew where to find him.

"Joe? What do you want Joe for?"

"He's a friend of Lenny's too. Maybe he knows something."

"I don't know where Joe is," she said.

I felt she was holding something back, but I didn't know how I was going to get any more out of her. At least the eviction angle was new, a motive, however, warped.

But I had doubts about her reliability. Could Ingrid really have been so ruthless? Whose word did I have besides a junkie stripper's? I wasn't going to crucify a dead girl based on Kyra's opinions.

The next day I visited the American School of Classical and Modern Dance. None of Ingrid's teachers or classmates had much to say. "Full of life and promise," – that kind of stuff. One of the instructors mentioned something that hadn't been in the papers yet. Ingrid had had some kind of a breakdown, or suicide attempt and had been hospitalized at the Eastside Psychiatric Hospital.

The hospital records were sealed, but I knew someone who knew a resident, and I got the name of Ingrid's hospital roommate, Katherine Helman. I looked her up in the phone book and called. A recording informed me the number had been changed to an unlisted. I took a chance and went over to the address. One of those white brick buildings in the East 80's. The doorman let me call up to her apartment on the intercom.

Her voice was soft, as though she were afraid someone in the next room might be listening. "I'd love to tell you about Ingrid," she whispered. "Ingrid was a wonderful girl."

She didn't want me coming up, but finally agreed to meet me at a coffee shop down the block. I knew it had to be her when she walked in – middle aged woman with a scarf covering her head and

Norma Desmond sunglasses, too much rouge, but not enough to label her psychotic, black pants suit, tasteful jewelry. She scanned the room as though she were on a secret mission. I waved to her and she mouthed my name. I nodded and she smiled.

She stopped at the cashier's and bought a pack of cigarettes. Then she walked over to my table. There was a bounciness to her walk. She was almost skipping.

"My son doesn't let me smoke at home," she said lighting up. She took off her glasses and waited for me to ask her something. She told me she and Ingrid had become friends in the hospital.

"She was an artiste. Very serious about her dancing. So many people had used her! Oh Peter, I tried to help."

She started going on about her son. He wouldn't let her have any friends, and she thought he might be trying to kill her to get her apartment.

"He won't let me smoke," she repeated, and then she pulled up her sleeve and showed me an arm filled with small cuts and cigarette burns. "He's afraid of what I'll do."

I tried to refocus her on Ingrid. She hadn't seen her since sometime in August.

"She visited me in my apartment."

Until she read the paper, Katherine hadn't known anything about Lenny. She thought Ingrid had been "on the streets." She'd given her some money to put down on a place, but hadn't heard from her after that.

"It's my son's fault. If only he'd let her stay with me. I know she would have been safe up here. She could have gone to her classes and auditions. It would have been so wonderful for both of us. She was like a dau, a sister to me. It's because I'm weak and can't stand up to him."

She was crying. People around us were looking at their menus, their watches, each other. I gave her my napkin, which she dipped in her water glass and used to dab her face. Then she began asking me questions about myself.

When I said good-bye, she made sure I got her phone number and asked if we'd be seeing each other again. I told her I thought I had everything I needed and then added, "Of course I'll call you if I think of something else you can help me with."

She wanted my card, in case she thought of anything important. As I'm a freelancer, my card has my home number. I've given that number to prostitutes and junkies, but I hesitated before I gave it to her.

Back downtown, I found Jacques Lanoir, another tenant in Lenny's building, the man Ouspenski had referred to as the "magick guy". He billed himself as a magician, but he didn't pull rabbits out of hats. People paid him to perform ceremonies and teach them archaic rites. He did séances as well though he called them something else, and he was known for his hexes and curses. It didn't seem to be much of a living. I tracked him down at an abandoned building on Avenue C where he'd been staying. He looked sick. I had heard he had the virus.

He told me I could ask all I wanted, but he wouldn't answer any of my questions.

I asked about the fire – if he had set it, if he knew who had. He stared into my eyes. Didn't blink – it was a move I remembered as an exercise in acting class. I stared back, but lost the contest.

Finally I said, "Okay, just tell me one thing. Are you the one who wrote, 'Is it soup yet?' on the door?"

He smirked, then replied in his Pepé Le Pew accent, "You should be very careful, Meester Reporter. What is it you say your name?"

"Peter. Peter Teller."

"Ah a Teller," he said. "This is what you are, or what you wish to be, no? A teller of tales."

He said nothing after that.

Bernstein was pressuring me to finish the piece. It was old news. I told him about my suspicion there was more there, maybe some other people involved. Who set the fire? What about the way the body was cut up? Could Lenny really have been organized enough to do it all on his own?

Bernstein wouldn't give me more time, so they ran the piece in The Eye with what I had. I was already planning a follow-up.

Lenny

Stan was back

Stan the man.

"I brought you some lentil soup, from Veselka's," he said.

Stan was nice for a cop. That very first time he'd talked to him, when the other ones were yelling, Stan had been very soft spoken. He introduced himself as Detective Ouspenski. "But you can call me, Stan."

He'd talk about himself sometimes. Tell Lenny how he'd grown up right down on the Lower East Side, Polish dad, Ukrainian mom. He'd ask Lenny about Texas. Lenny knew that Stan was pumping him. But still, he'd never expected a cop to be so decent.

Too bad Stan couldn't bring him some herb. The meds they gave him sucked. But he had to be careful not to let them know. When he first came to the hospital, they'd wanted to give him shots. He made a big deal about how scared he was of needles. Then he was worried they'd give him liquid, but they gave him pills, which were pretty easy to cheek. Sometimes they'd check. The nurse would make him open his mouth and she'd put her fingers in to feel around. But he was psychic and could tell when she was going to do that, so he'd take the medicine about half the time, but not everyday, because that would just turn you into the living dead.

He sometimes saw the living dead on his walls if he stared too long.

Stan was asking him about the fire again.

"Man, that's stupid. You know I was here. I'm not that advanced that I could be two places at once." He slurped his soup. It was much better than the hospital stuff. Not as good as what he could make himself. He suddenly felt embarrassed, remembering making the soup from Ingrid's meat. He had said something about wanting to feed her bones to the homeless, and then Moira and Jacques had decided it would be a really good idea, but he felt bad about it now. He was sorry Ingrid was dead. She was so pretty.

He'd only tasted the soup but once when he was cooking it.

He put down his bowl. He looked at Stan. He wondered if Stan knew what he was thinking.

"Do you think Jacques might have set the fire?" Stan asked.

"I don't know. What's he say?"

"What about that friend of yours, Joe?"

Lenny knew the cop was playing with him now, guessing. He knew he better be careful. If he ever got out of the hospital, he surely did not want to piss off Joe Holiday.

"I don't know."

"Who do you think would do something like that?"

"I told you, man. It was the emissaries of Satan. They purified it with the fires of hell."

"Lenny, I know I asked you this before, but just to get it straight, did anybody help you chop up Ingrid?"

He gave the answer he always gave. "I prayed to Satan for guidance, and his emissaries told me what to do."

"Yeah," said Stan the man. "I hear that."

Lenny wondered if they were ever going to ask him the right question. It was a riddle. He could give them an answer if only they'd ask the right question.

Then Stan left and Lenny went over to the day room. There were some magazines there. Nothing very good like with pictures of naked ladies, but one time he'd found one with a picture of a woman in a bra and panties. Usually they cut them out, but someone must have fucked up. It could happen again. He didn't mind the hospital too much. Three hots and a cot, like they said, and a lot safer than the shelters. It was getting cold out, and he was glad to have the space. The nurses were friendly too, and there were always people around, so you could sit in the day room and jaw away. But he missed his herb and didn't want to be inside when the weather got nice.

Chapter 9

The Start of a Beautiful Friendship

Peter

For all its anarchist pretensions, the streets of the East Village are laid out in an orderly fashion – with a few notable exceptions. Off of 9th street and 3rd avenue, there's a small side street, Hunter's Court, that runs diagonally down to the corner of 10th and 2nd. The houses are older than most of the stock in the neighborhood – brick homes, three stories high with shuttered windows and wrought iron gates. An elegant but translucent lady with a parasol is said to be seen on sunny days from a certain angle. Squint and she's gone, or not, depending on what chemicals you have on board.

The ghost I always saw on that block was of the boy I knew who lived and died in number 12.

Chico McFarland was not yet fourteen when we first met at prep school. But he already possessed a jaded worldliness unequaled by even the other young cynics who made up our small circle of friends.

Chic started mid-semester and was assigned to my room as my old roommate had gotten sacked for selling cocaine. Probably would never have been caught if he'd stuck to the rules and sold exclusively to fellow members of the academy. Unfortunately, he gave some to a fetching local girl whose father was the chief of police and active in Republican politics. It didn't help that his mom was an outspokenly liberal member of Congress.

When I heard my new roommate had arrived, I ran to meet him to prevent an invasion of my closet space. His back was to me. I said, "Hello." He didn't turn around. I said, "Hello," again. He grunted. He was small and thin. More than a year younger than I was, but he'd skipped a grade along the way. Blond hair down to his shoulders. From the back, he could easily have been taken for a girl.

"I'm Peter," I said aiming for firmness in the tone of my voice.

He turned slowly, cigarette dangling from his mouth.

"Pleased man," he said. "Chic." He put out his hand.

His face was still soft, childlike. But there was something hard and old in his hazel eyes. His mouth curled into a perpetual smirk as though he were privy to some inside information the rest of us couldn't even imagine.

It was disconcerting. I was older than he. Bigger. Yet completely from that first moment intimidated.

"Chic? What kind of name is that?"

He took a deep drag, then pulled out the smoke holding it between his thumb and forefinger. "Chico," he said. He enunciated slowly as though each syllable was precious. "Like the Marx brother? One of the old man's jokes."

The old man, I was soon to learn, was Sean McFarland – Yippy prankster, activist, occasional publisher, and at that time rumored to be the largest marijuana importer in North America.

If I were to tell you there was always a note of sorrow in his voice, a tone of regret and loss, would you think it must be my own distortion? That a pubescent boy could not have been the combination of Jack Nicholson, James Dean and Gatsby I remember? Would you doubt my reliability? Would you decide I was about as objective on the subject of Chic, as was that displaced European professor writing on the true and hidden nature of his young stepdaughter?

Would you be correct in doubting me?

Maybe you would be. Because I'll tell you something only distance and perhaps his death have made me unafraid to say, I loved him better than anyone.

Although I didn't know it at the time. What I did understand was my lust. But I'd just turned fifteen, and fifteen year olds are pretty horny. I just whacked off a lot and lived in denial that my upsurge in hormonal activity had anything to do with the young god sleeping two feet away. Occasionally, like when he'd cross the room naked, reality would set in, and I would think. "Damn it! I'm gay. Another cross to bear."

But then I'd rationalize that if I really were queer, given the context in which I lived, I wouldn't be suppressing it. Most of the girls were reading Colette and openly declaring their bisexuality. There were a couple of boys who'd come out at no great cost to their popularity. (I know one of them is now a practicing heterosexual and attorney. The other died at the beginning of the epidemic.)

I understood enough to realize all adolescents had doubts about their sexuality, and I had no real desire to test out my fantasies with boys. My feelings for Chic only made me much more anxious to lose my virginity. By the standards of Breverton, at fifteen, I was already developmentally delayed in that regard.

In fact, I was turning into one of those "nice" boys, the unthreatening, yet straight, type with whom girls like to be "just friends." I even managed to become best friends with Delia Danburger, an overdeveloped fourteen year old, reportedly one of the most skilled and easiest lays at school.

Delia of the black curly hair and emerald eyes. Delia always wriggling her legs slightly when she was sitting. Once, when drunk, she confessed to me she could get off that way, anytime, anywhere. Afterwards, I'd stare at her at parties, in restaurants, watching those luscious legs, moving together ever so gently, the faintest rustle of nylon.

Delia soon developed a "thing" for Chic. They "did it" a couple of times, in Delia's room, not mine, thank God. Then Chic told her it was going to screw up their friendship, so they stopped. Chic could have whomever he wanted, and generally he didn't want anyone for very long.

Delia, Chic and I became a platonic threesome, spending hours in the woods, smoking cigarettes and dope, swearing oaths of eternal loyalty.

Then Delia got knocked up by some Exeter boy. She finally told her mother whom she reported was very understanding. She was going to the city to get it taken care of.

After classes on Thursday, we walked her to the bus stop. Her appointment was for Friday morning. Although we knew we'd see her again by Sunday night, we kept hugging each other, holding on as though we were parting forever.

"You guys are the best," she said. "I wish you were coming."

"Why not?" said Chic.

We couldn't actually join her for the operation as we had a chemistry test that day. But we'd be able to leave by the afternoon. Chic didn't think there'd be a problem staying at his dad's.

I called my father for permission. Turned out he was conveniently going to be out of town that weekend and thus we avoided yet another awkward reunion.

On previous visits to New York, I'd always taken the train, but Chic insisted it would be easier to just catch the Trailways bus as it passed through town.

It was a new world for me. The smell of stale food and farts embedded in the seats. A group of black men were accompanying their elderly mother who'd brought along a basket full of food. I remember their loud talk and how when I tried to follow it, it was as though I was listening to a strange language with which I only had a passing familiarity. It must sound awful, how sheltered I was, but for me the bus ride was as exotic as a trip to Asia.

We were left off at the Port Authority, a place I'd never been, though it was only a block west of the theater district where my father had made his name. The station was filled with the homeless – only back then the men were called bums while the women were given the respectful sobriquet, shopping bag ladies. There were runaways as well, and at points the police eyed us suspiciously. I was a little paranoid, as we'd smoked some pot before we got on the bus, and Chic was holding. I started to walk to the exit sign to get a cab, Chic stopped me.

"We're taking the subway," he announced.

Of course I'd been on the subway before, but rarely. The backseat of taxicabs was much more familiar to me. The subway was the mode of transportation used and often cursed by tardy cleaning ladies and nannies with West Indian lilts.

Chico noticed the way I was taking it all in. He grinned and patted my back. "You're such a tourist, Peter," he said.

It was getting dark by the time we arrived at Chic's house. He rang the bell. A woman answered, short, and Asian. She hugged Chic and told him how happy his father would be to see him. I figured she was the housekeeper. It turned out she was Judith, a semi-famous Filipina artist, his father's girlfriend.

His father, whom he referred to as Sean, was out, but expected back for dinner. We sat down in the living room. Judith was making some kind of spicy soup with a lot of vegetables. Every so often, she'd go into the kitchen to stir the pot. We both had the munchies and were grooving on the smell. Sean walked in. He was well over six feet tall, with long reddish gold hair, large blue eyes, and the beginning of a paunch. His voice boomed to match his frame.

But if you had asked me just then what he looked or sounded like, I wouldn't have had a clue. I was too busy staring at the friends he'd brought with him, John Lennon and Yoko Ono. They hugged Chic and asked him about school. Then Sean rolled a joint for all of us and Judith and Yoko talked about their work. The Lennon's didn't stay for dinner though they left a coffee cake purchased at some Upper West Side bakery with a Hungarian name.

Later we called Delia. Her mother started to tell us she was resting, but we could hear her trying to grab the phone, which she finally managed to do. She reported she felt fine, but couldn't join us that night.

We decided to check out a place in midtown where Chic hadn't been before. It wasn't in, the way the downtown clubs were. But Chic was curious, and besides he told me, dancing to disco music could be fun too, and he always got a kick out of those outer borough girls.

We got there around mid-night. There was a line and a bouncer inspecting the crowd, but he seemed to be letting just about everyone in. I saw him proof a group in front of us, but as Chic had told me, he only had to announce himself as, "Sean's kid," and we were let through.

We headed for the bar. Me, stoned, nursing a drink, drifting in my own little universe, taking in the scene as Chic played it. He brought a couple of girls over. Older women, they looked at least sixteen. He introduced them and got me out dancing with one. Her name was Lourdes, and she was the taller of the two, with wavy black hair, a little too much at the hips, not as pretty as her friend Maria, who was small and delicate and danced well with Chic. They had come in from Brooklyn.

We danced with different girls, but it was Lourdes and Maria we left with. Lourdes suggested we get some breakfast. Chic said we could go to his house. The girls seemed impressed his parents would let him.

Maria told us in the cab we took downtown that her parents were "real old-fashion." She and Lourdes had lied, telling their folks they were spending the night at each other's houses.

Wasted, in the way only teenagers can be and remain standing, we giggled making a large omelet with everything we could find. Then the four of us went up to Chic's room which was L-shaped and as large as some Manhattan studios. First we continued laughing and talking by candlelight. On one side there was a futon on the floor along with some furniture. At the other end of the L there was a desk and above that a loft with another futon, a lamp, and some shelves. He and Maria climbed up to the top and shut a curtain while Lourdes and I stayed down below.

"Well, I guess this is it," she said. She got onto the futon and took off her top and pants, but left on her underwear. I followed her lead. We started to kiss and somehow lost our remaining clothes. She climbed on top of me and grabbed my cock.

"It's okay," she announced. "I'm on the pill."

I was nervous. She guided me in and moved around. It felt wonderful but terrifying, like an amusement park ride that might at any second go out of control. I came and knew she didn't, though she was making little moaning sounds and between our sounds, we could hear Maria and Chic pounding away above us.

"I'm sorry," I whispered.

"It's okay," she said. We fell asleep in each other's arms. When I woke up it was Maria beside me, smoking a joint. She passed it to me. I looked at her.

"We switched," she said.

I wasn't sure what she expected. She started playing with my prick, just casually, and then she put her mouth over it. She rubbed herself on my leg and I could feel her heat and wetness. She climbed on top of me and put me inside somehow managing to turn my body over at the same time so that I was on top. I still came too soon, but it was sweet, so sweet.

I fell asleep again and Chic woke me up hours later. He was already dressed. It was two in the afternoon. The girls were long gone.

He never said anything to me about what role he might have played in getting Maria into my bed. I never asked.

He left Breverton at the end of the school year, complaining it was too regimented. He'd gotten into an experimental public high school that sent students out to internships. We wrote and I even visited a couple of weekends, but then he became distant. Cut me off. Delia too. A few months later he hung himself. There was no note.

I spoke to Judith at the service. "He was just depressed," she said.

I wrote something to read at the funeral, a slightly censored version of that weekend in fact. Sean came up afterward and thanked me. He bent down, lowering his massive head on to my shoulder; I could feel the wetness of his tears. He told me I could always stop by to see him. It wasn't an invitation I took advantage of often, but I had been by from time to time over the years.

Judith was dead, some kind of cancer. Sean lived alone in his old brick house.

He was still an active character in the East Village, organizing smoke-ins and putting out pamphlets. Community meetings were sometimes held in his home which seemed to be open to everyone. But he had changed after Chic's death.

He'd developed some kind of condition that caused all his hair to fall out, convinced it was something the CIA or DEA had done to get him. He had suspicions about Judith's death as well, but never said anything to me about Chic's. He would no longer eat any food he had not prepared himself.

Despite his eccentricities, he was the one I thought of seeing for help with my questions about the Matthews case. He knew everyone. He would have heard something, and he'd be able to track down from whom he'd heard it.

So I walked up the steps to number 12 and rang the bell. It was quite a surprise when Johnny Ramirez answered the door.

I'd seen him on the street a couple of times since he'd sold me the pot. We always nodded to each other.

"Yeah?" he said.

"Is Sean around?"

"You know Sean?"

"Yes, I know Sean. You know Sean?"

"Of course I know Sean. He's not here."

"When's he coming back?"

"Could be a while."

I let myself in and we stepped away from the door. "What are you doing here?"

"He wrote this up before he left," he said, waving around a few typewritten pages. "He asked me if I'd stop by and take it to the printer. He wants to distribute it."

I took a look at the papers he was holding. It was a short manifesto charging the government with encouraging heroin and crack addiction. It went on to make some claims about a plant, a hallucinogen, used by the Ibo people of Africa which could completely curb the desire for opiates.

"Ibo?" I said.

"Sure, he's in Africa now. Gonna get some of the stuff and bring it back."

"How'd you get in?"

"Key."

"You've got a key to Sean's house?"

"He's really tight with my boss. El Rey lent me the key."

Suddenly the connections were shooting through my brain. Sean knew El Rey for whom Johnny worked. I'd heard Lenny also dealt a little pot, maybe even for El Rey. Johnny knew Sean, and of course El Rey, maybe Lenny too. I realized he might know a lot of things.

"Look," I said. "I'm working on a follow-up story about the Lenny Matthews thing. You wouldn't happen to know anything?"

Johnny flashed his Hollywood grin. "Yeah, Peter," he said, "I might be able to help you with that."

Mark Hoffman

Mark Hoffman was raking leaves in front of his cabin. He'd been busy and hadn't been to the weekend place since the beginning of the summer, though he liked to pop by right until the end of fall. For years, he planned to winterize, but he'd waited too long. Beams were rotting, the floor caved and the roof leaked. It would be more work than it was worth.

"Burn it," his ex-wife Deedee had advised when he offered it to her during their settlement. He knew as far as she was concerned, the cabin was one example among many of something he loved, but had been completely unable to take care of or protect. Other examples included herself, and most spectacularly their daughter, Moira.

Was it so terrible to give your only baby girl whatever she wanted? What had she asked for anyway? Lessons, not things. Piano lessons. Riding lessons. She had had her own horse and a tutor to teach her French because she loved the way it sounded.

But Deedee always blamed him for what happened. For not "setting limits." Besides, it was through him she had met Robby Assad.

As he scooped the leaves from a large pile into plastic bags, he was replaying the past, trying to figure out how far back he'd have to go to get a different outcome.

He'd become a lawyer because of certain ideals. He went to work for the public defender's office after law school because he believed that while many of his clients were guilty, the system was not a fair one and they deserved the best representation he could give them. He never really burnt out, but when a friend decided to go into private practice, he went with him. It was more out of boredom, and maybe a little pressure from Deedee as well.

Of course, a criminal lawyer defends criminals. And if he wants to do some *pro bono* work and pay a mortgage, then he needs to defend successful criminals. Usually that meant people involved with organized crime and drugs.

He didn't always like these clients, but he had no problem defending them. The government *did* overstep and act illegally in gathering evidence. It was important to stop civil liberties from eroding. As for drugs, the state had no business criminalizing them to begin with. If drugs had been legal, men like Robby would have been admired and respected as successful entrepreneurs.

Robby was dubbed "The Acid King," but Mark knew he was also involved in the distribution of speed, as well as other things. The first time he defended him, it was on a weapons charge. The feds hadn't been able to find Robby's lab, but they had found his arsenal. Assad himself had taken the stand, (against Mark's advice) telling some crazy story about how the weapons actually belonged to a man named "Steve" who told him he was warehousing collectible comic books.

The jury came in not guilty. Mark believed this was due to the sloppy arrogance of the government attorneys and the general unpredictability of the system. But Robby was convinced Mark won by the skeptical tone he took with the police witnesses, and his impassioned remarks about reasonable doubt.

Afterwards, Robby would sometimes stop by the office to consult on various legal matters. Occasionally, he would give Mark a few pills which the lawyer was not averse to using to mellow out on a weekend.

One day, Robby happened to come by at the same time Moira

was there. Moira had wanted to go on a teen tour to Europe that summer. Deedee felt it was too expensive. Mark had negotiated a compromise. Moira would first spend some time working at the office, doing filing, running errands, earn her trip.

He understood the world could be a dangerous place for a teenage girl, but he hadn't realized his office would be the most dangerous spot of all.

Robby looked at her that first day, and Mark saw what he was seeing. "My daughter," he said, then added, "Fifteen."

"Very nice," said Robby.

Robby hadn't talked to her that day. Mark was sure of that. He must have called later. He must have convinced her to meet him.

Moira told her parents she had changed her mind about going away. It surprised them, but they figured it was just some adolescent thing.

At the end of the summer, she announced she would be moving in with Robby.

"You are not!" Deedee said.

"I'm not going to quit school or anything! I just want to be with him."

"Princess," Mark said, trying to retain his composure, "That's a big decision and . . ."

"Look, I'm already sleeping with him. It's okay. He's had a vasectomy."

He tried to speak to her, but she put his own words in his face. She talked about honesty and integrity and the need to make her own mistakes.

He told her what Robby did was dangerous. She could get hurt.

"He'd never let anything bad happen to me, Daddy."

Deedee kept yelling which didn't help. Finally, Moira said, "I'm going to do it. I can either runaway and do it, or I can still be your daughter. It's up to you guys."

Neither he nor Deedee spoke for a moment and then Moira looked him in the eyes and said, "Daddy, it's what I want."

Later when they were alone, his wife asked, "What are we going to do to stop this?"

"We can't do anything."

"This is crazy! Your fifteen year old daughter is going to live with a drug dealer."

"He's not such a bad guy."

"Mark, we've got to stop him. It's statutory rape."

"I don't think he'd be afraid of the police."

"Oh my God, you've sold her. You've sold our daughter to a thug."

Mark had now gathered four large plastic bags of leaves. He buttoned his jacket and sat on the porch.

It really wasn't so terrible at first, the thing between Robby and Moira. She did finish high school, and she would come home for a meal now and then, at Deedee's insistence always alone. Robby took her to Europe and she came back with presents.

He wondered if she was using, if Robby was keeping her with drugs, but it wasn't something they talked about. He noticed she was thin, looked a little drawn sometimes, but it was fashionable to be thin, and she was still the same sweet girl he'd always known. He didn't ask a lot of questions about their life together.

From what Mark could see, he always took care of her. She never went to college or got a job. Sometimes Mark would express his concern about that.

"Oh Dad!" she'd say, "I could always go to school."

The bust had come in eighty-three. She'd been with him ten years by then. The feds had raided Robby's lab, and there was a warrant for her as well. She was visiting friends in California. The police didn't know where. He got a phone number from Robby.

He was afraid to even call from a booth, convinced the feds were watching. His secretary got the message to Moira.

Once, before Robby's trial, Moira had called his office. He tried to talk her into turning herself in. He wasn't Robby's lawyer anymore, so he told her she should cooperate, give evidence, maybe even get immunity. She told him she still loved Robby and would never betray him.

Assad got twenty-years. The warrant was still out on Moira. He'd seen the indictment. She was considered a full partner in a criminal enterprise.

He was convinced the feds were still watching, too many clicks on his home phone, and mail that looked already opened. Despite the risks, over the years, he and Moira managed to communicate. He'd even seen her from time to time, helped her out with money.

The last time had been in July. She was staying in some dive on the Lower East Side. The man she was with had hardly said a word. She seemed even more frail than usual though she didn't complain about anything and thanked him for the cash.

He went back there a couple of months later, but they were gone. He'd just have to wait until she needed him again. It was getting chilly, so he went inside the cabin, noticed the saucer full of ashes on the table and the empty cans in the trash.

He wondered if it had been his daughter, stopping off to rest on the way to God knows where. He checked the shelves and saw some soup cans were missing.

Even if it hadn't been she, he decided, it was someone else weary and on the road, some mysterious traveler or travelers, searching for a warm place to rest and eat. Whoever they were, wherever they were going, he wished them well.

Johnny

I went over to Sean's to water the plants, pick up some papers. Helping him out on his latest project. He was in West Africa, researching iboga, planning to bring back some plant samples.

You ever hear about Ibogaine? It's from a flowering plant grown by the Ibo people in Africa. They're part of the Yoruba. You know about Yoruba, right? That's where a lot of the slaves in Cuba and the West Indies came from. All those Santeria practices, voodoo as well, that's out of the Yoruba traditions. The plant, it's a major hallucinogen, used in coming of age ceremonies, healing ceremonies. Sacred.

Through the years, there's always been some brave or foolish white guy, usually an American, goes out meets the local holy man and tries this stuff. Writes an article in *High Times*.

That would be some way to see the world, huh? Think I'll pop some of these shrooms and write about it. Journalism. Some racket.

This friend of Sean's, guy named David Rousseau, French guy, biggest player in the pot trade in Amsterdam, owns coffee houses, also exports, he hears about the stuff. Rousseau, he's got everything. Rich, beautiful women, lives on a yacht. Country house in Provence. Happy man? You'd think so, right? Wrong. Cause he's got this major heroin habit. Can't kick. Tried everything. Gone cold turkey dozens a times. Always picks up again. Tried meditation. Had an audience with the Dalai Lama. Filipino psychic surgeons. Nothing works.

Got a theory. Convinced that what he's getting, that rush, that feeling of safety, that if he can get beyond his fears, beyond his need for the feeling, if he can pass that block, he won't use again. See, he's like the recovery groups, he believes the addiction is a spiritual thang. He's also decided he is absolutely not ever going to try to kick cold again, but cutting back hasn't worked either. So he's looking for something that's gonna psychologically and spiritually balance him so that he won't need to use, won't even feel the craving, the dope-sickness which has gotten worse every time he's quit, and at this point, he'd rather die than have to go through again.

One day he's at one of his places. There's this Brit, holding court. Skinny guy, tall, graying beard, forties. Something about him. A vibe. All these younger locals and backpacker types, they're just eating up every word. Rousseau is intrigued. He goes over to the table. The English guy is telling a story about going out into the jungle with a shaman or witch doctor, whatever they call them over there, and how they had to collect lion cub crap for a ritual and the medicine man just walks right past this lioness like she was a sleeping housecat and collects the scat.

Rousseau sits down at the table and introduces himself. The Brit was Roland Mercer. He's a university trained botanist and anthropologist. Oxford man. But he's also a practicing pagan. The prototype alternative-culture-great-white-adventurer, and he's known to have dropped every organic psychotropic on the planet.

He's in Amsterdam for an academic conference, but he also likes to kick back, so Rousseau invites him to some parties. They go out to his place in the country, spend time on the boat.

Roland senses Rousseau is a troubled man. He asks his friend to confide. Rousseau tells him about the dope. On the one hand, it's not like he can't afford it. It doesn't really affect his functioning. It's an inconvenience more than anything. But it's the idea of it that eats at him. He's given up coffee and cigarettes. He doesn't drink alcohol. Why can't he drop this attachment?

Roland tells him about the magical plant. It's just a hunch he has. But he thinks the experience of the high is so much more intense than an opiate high, so beyond it, that maybe even using it just once would cure him of his craving. Reset his brain. In addition it's known to have certain euphoric qualities that last days, so it might alleviate the withdrawal as well.

Of course this fits in perfectly with Rousseau's own theories about his addiction, his belief in a perfect high that's going to make him feel whatever it is he imagines normal is.

He offers Roland an enormous "grant" to procure some of this stuff. Roland then talks Rousseau into accompanying him to Africa, where Rousseau visits the lion-taming medicine guy. Some tribute is given. The herb is prepared. Rituals are performed. Rousseau gets his dose.

He comes back to Amsterdam a true believer. No throwing up, no chills, no sweat. No craving. He's like the Hair Club president; he uses the stuff himself. He's on a mission. Sets up a lab where they turn the extract out in pill form. Contacts doctors, health ministers. Not only does he have the vision of curing opiate addiction worldwide, but he has the idea if they're going to medicalize this stuff, he's getting in on the ground floor, and it's gonna be bigger than Valium.

He tells Sean. Sean's heard of some Ibo plant before but only as a legendary hallucinogen. He becomes an investor. He starts writing the FDA, contacts some doctors who are researching alternative therapies for opiate addicts. People are starting to get interested. So to up the ante a little, Sean takes his own trip to Africa.

And that's how I came to be watching the house when I ran into Peter.

My take on him back in August was he was another rich white guy who doesn't really know the scene.

But it threw me he knew Sean. It wasn't like he knew him as a source. He was protective of him. Checking me out, like "What the fuck are you doing here?"

Then he asks me about the Matthews thing. First instinct, keep your mouth shut. I don't owe Joe Holiday, but I've got nothing against him, and Moira's a hell of a lady. I don't want to complicate her life, or my own. But I read his article, and there was stuff bothering me too. Like I kept thinking what Joe had told me about Lenny threatening him, couldn't have been the way it really went down. And Moira, she just knew, as soon as Joe walked in the door. What if she was there too?

Another thing that didn't make much sense, the way Lobo left. He was making good money for El Rey. You don't just walk out on a gig like that. I remember telling him about seeing Lenny after the murder, and he kind of looked at me, and kept asking, "What else did he say?" "Was that all he said?" And later that night he tells me, him and his old lady are hitching down to Miami, with the dog. Before the weather changes. The weather? Giving up a free apartment and a job because you might need a jacket?

So I figured what I knew had to be worth something to Peter. A lunch and a twenty at least. He told me he wouldn't give me cash for information. Besides its being against his principles, he insisted he didn't actually have a trust fund. I told him I'd checked out his meds when I made the delivery and would be happy with some pills. He was surprised I wanted them.

"You get high on those?"

"Yeah. What do you get?"

"It's medication. Just makes me better able to function."

"C'mon man, you're telling me all the time you've had this shit, you've never realized that two is better than one, and you double the effects with a couple of beers?"

"It's not a barbiturate or anything," he said. "I mean, it's a prescription."

"Oh that's right. Benzodiazepines aren't drugs, and if a doctor writes, it's medication."

I told him a little about my own history with doctors. When I was a kid, I knew just which ones to visit. Who'd write and who wouldn't. They were pretty happy to accommodate me, until I turned eighteen and Grandma took me off her health plan.

"I don't think they're all like that," he said.

"Yeah," I said. "I'm sure your shrink would see you for free. I'll bet after a session, he tells you, 'Oh Peter, that was so good, I should be paying you."

We debated the lunch. I thought it should be at Lutece, maybe Tavern on the Green, or the Russian Tearoom – not having been to any of those places I imagined he frequented. We settled for the Ukrainian Parlor, two days following, one o'clock.

Peter

I was looking forward to meeting with Johnny. I was tired of hearing from my editor how the Matthews case had already been overexposed. I had the feeling Johnny would at least understand my enthusiasm for the story.

Still, he hadn't told me much when we'd met at Sean's, and I suspected he could've just been stringing me along to get the pills.

He was late, but not very, and pretty forthcoming from the moment he sat down. He knew Lenny from the park as well as various meetings and demonstrations, both worked for El Rey. He'd seen him a few days before his arrest.

"He wasn't boasting. He was upset. Scared."

Johnny had questions of his own. Thought there might be a connection to a friend of his taking off around the time of the murder. Then he dropped the bombshell about Joe and his girlfriend being his former roommates, and what Joe said to him about being at Lenny's when the murder occurred.

All this before we'd even ordered lunch.

As he described Joe and Moira, I remembered something.

"Does she look a little like Ingrid?"

"It's the type. Slash model."

"What?'

"You meet a beautiful woman and ask what she does and maybe she's an actress or a waitress or a nuclear physicist, but she also does some modeling on the side. Like waitress slash model."

Our waitress slash waitress, a matronly type with rosy cheeks and a thick Eastern European accent came over. I ordered coffee and a sandwich. Johnny studied the menu as carefully as a tourist enjoying his first experience in a Parisian bistro. He decided on steak and eggs with a side of fries, and a German beer. Probably the most expensive entre he could piece together.

I told him about the threesome I'd encountered at the Samaritan's apartment the night of the riot.

"It sounds like them. I know PD got banged up."

"Is he still in town?"

"Haven't seen him. I can tell you where his squat is if you want to check."

He filled me in on Moira's background as well as describing what had almost happened between them before she left.

"An hour, man," he said. "If I had an hour with her, maybe she wouldn't have gone with him. Then again, maybe he would've killed me."

"You think so?"

"They said they had an open relationship, but Joe seemed possessive. I did see him with someone else a couple of times."

"That could be useful. You know her?"

"Not really. Drag queen. Mirabella. I think she works by the Holland tunnel. I remember running into them at Wigstock. She looked like she might have seen better days."

"Interesting."

"I know Joe did time. No surprise he likes chicks with dicks."

I asked Johnny more questions about what Mirabella looked like and how he thought I might find him slash her. Then, we got back on to Joe.

"What else do you know about him?"

"Not much. I once asked him if he were Latino. You know he looks like he's something. He told me his daddy was a brother. I don't think he was too into the culture."

"Uh-huh," I said jotting it down.

"The name's kind of strange. It reminds me of something, but I can't place it," I said.

"Yeah. I asked him about it once. Said his real name was Jerome. Jerome Comb or Combs maybe? When he left Ohio he thought they might be looking for him. So he's been calling himself Joe Holiday for years. The cops pick him up for a fight in a shelter. They take his prints and come back, 'You're Jerome Comb.' Turns out there's nothing they wanna ask him. After, he changed it legally. He figured he'd been Joe Holiday so long, he might as well make it official."

"He tell you why it was he thought they were looking for him?"

"I never asked." He took the last swig of his beer and deftly motioned the waitress for another.

Watching Johnny eat was like watching some kind of sleight of hand. He never stopped talking, but the food just disappeared off his plate.

Once he told me all he knew, we talked about what I knew. He'd never met Kyra or Ingrid for that matter, had never actually been to Lenny's place. Knew Jacques to say hello to, and by reputation.

"So what you're thinking is," Johnny said chewing on his steak, "Kyra, Joe and maybe Moira, Lobo and PD too, they were all what? Helping to dismember the corpse?"

"Yeah, at least. I mean look, there's a lot Kyra isn't saying. From what you know about Joe, don't you think he had something to do with it?"

"Well maybe, but Lenny says he did it."

"Okay, what if Lenny did it, but Joe was telling him what to do?"

"Yeah, I could see that. And Joe said a lot of shit to me about Ingrid. He hated her."

"Okay, so let's say that Kyra, Joe, Moira and Lobo are in the apartment when Lenny kills her, and then PD walks in for something."

"Nah, it wouldn't've gone down like that. I don't think Lobo even knew any of them except Lenny. Maybe, Lobo walking in . . ."

"Fine. Lobo walks in. Ingrid's dead and . . ."

"He'd have to go along. Help them out. Joe would kill him otherwise."

"Now they're all sitting around the apartment, right? They've got to come up with a plan for getting rid of the body. Who do they ask for help?"

Johnny was chewing his food, but I could see by his eyes, he was thinking. He swallowed and answered. "First of all, I don't know how much help they'd need. I'm willing to bet Joe's killed someone along the way. And Moira must have seen a lot when she was with Robby."

"Let me put it another way. Who would Lenny want there?"

Johnny put down his fork. "Lenny was always talking about Jacques. He thought the guy had power, could teach him things. He probably thought he could manifest demons to disappear the body."

"All right. So they call in Jacques."

"Jesus, Peter. You're putting half the neighborhood in that apartment."

"How do we know it wasn't?"

Johnny smiled. "How you gonna prove it was?"

The waitress came by and took Johnny's plate. He ordered a cappuccino and an apple pie a la mode for dessert.

I was talking about Kyra, how I wished I could get her to open up, to trust me. I thought she could be the key to the whole thing.

"Why should she trust you, man?" he said. What's your angle on this anyway? You've already written your article."

"Maybe it's a book," I said. I was nervous when I said it. It was the first time I admitted out loud what I was thinking of doing. It seemed arrogant, maybe bad luck, like telling someone you're going to get a part, but the more I learned, the more I was convinced this was the ultimate Loisaida story. It had everything, sex, violence, drugs, real estate.

Johnny leaned back in his chair. "Oh, I get it," he said, "All Ingrid wanted was a lease. All Lenny wanted, when he met her, was some pussy, and then to hold on to what he had. Me, I just wanted some pills and this fine meal. But you Peter, you're amazing. You want fame, fortune and a movie option."

I shook my head. "Oh man, it's not like that. It's the story. Lenny, he's not just some low life psycho. He's driven to desperation. It's the whole society, the shelters, the real estate speculation. I mean, I thought, you could appreciate that."

Johnny scraped the plate, looking longingly at its emptiness. "Lenny is not Raskolnikov." he said.

"I know that. But he's stuck in the hospital and Ingrid is dead. Someone has to tell their story."

"Yeah, yeah, the dead can only speak through the living and you wouldn't mind getting a couple of mill' for the paperback rights."

"I'll be lucky if I can get it published."

Johnny lit a cigarette.

After a moment I asked, "You don't like it, my writing a book?"

"It's not that, man. You can do what you want. I'm just saying everybody down here is down here for something. But why would someone like Kyra wanna talk to you? She's got maybe her life at stake, and you're some guy from like the Upper East . . ."

"West . . ."

"West Side, down here, trying to make your bones."

"What do you suggest I do to win her over?"

Johnny shook his head. Then he leaned back and laughed. "I don't know. You'd probably have to shoot dope with her at the least."

Chapter 10

Working the Story

Peter

By the end of our lunch, Johnny had agreed to tell me anything he might see or hear related to the Matthew's case. In return, I'd give him a thousand dollars should my book become a bestseller, and lay at least a couple of hundred on him if it ever got published. I offered to give him an acknowledgment, but he told me to leave his name out.

His little bombshell about Joe's being at the murder scene was the most valuable piece of information I possessed – and more than the police had. I figured it would give me some leverage with Kyra. I now knew more than she thought I knew. The trick would be convincing her I knew more than I did.

But first I wanted to find PD. From Johnny's description, I figured he had to be the guy I saw with Joe and Moira the night of the riot. Joe hadn't directly placed him or anyone else at the apartment, but even if he wasn't there, Moira might have told him something. Maybe he knew where they were.

So the day after our lunch, I walked a few blocks east to the squat where he'd been living. It was an old tenement, five stories, probably ten railroad apartments in the past, but now if they renovated a smart landlord would gut it and turn it into twenty dollhouse-sized studios. Like most of the squats, the building had been abandoned by its landlord years ago, then deserted by the tenants after the electricity and water had stopped. The night before, I'd looked through some old articles I'd saved and come across one written by a colleague and published in *The Eye* a few months earlier. It was about the resourcefulness of the squatters in that particular building. They connected into power lines, reinforced floors and staircases, subdivided with sheet rock and made other renovations. The water was a problem though. They couldn't tap into the city's line. In addition to using fire hydrants, a sympathetic homeowner nearby charged $200 a month to allow them access to his basement sink where the "members" would fill buckets to be used for their plumbing, washing and cooking needs.

The building was run as a direct democracy. Everyone who lived there was supposed to be a voting member of the collective, but not just anyone could move in. This had probably been one cause of the tension with Joe and Moira. Members were not supposed to have long-term guests, and if Joe and Moira had asked for membership, they would have been voted down. The squat could afford to be choosy, looking for new members with skills in carpentry or wiring. Most managed to hold down jobs, maintain relationships, even raise children while also considering themselves housing activists. They were not in favor of hard drug use or other criminal activity.

As I approached the building, I walked past a small man carrying two large covered buckets each suspended from a pole draped across his back. It looked like a pretty heavy load. I offered to take a bucket. This required some maneuvering so as not to spill all he had.

"I'm Tom," he said.

"Peter."

As we headed toward the entrance, he asked, "Who are you visiting?"

"PD."

He looked at me like he wasn't sure.

"Don something. Pirate Don he goes by."

We started walking up the stairs. Tom was managing the load

better than I was, despite his small frame. I hoped we weren't going to the top floor.

He told me Don was gone. He'd left a while back. Told him he was going to hit the road for a while and would give up the space. He'd left some of his stuff as well as his cat.

"That's weird. His taking off like that. Did he say where he was going?"

"Nope. Just said he wanted to travel. I guess he was going out west."

"Yeah, doesn't he have family or something out there?"

"He's from there, man. Didn't he ever tell you about the farm?" Tom was looking at me carefully now. "What is this? You're not a cop?"

"No, I'm a reporter. *The Eye*. I met him the night of the riot. When he got beat up. I was going to talk to him about it, for a follow up."

"Oh yeah. That was fucked. Well, I think he might've gone out to Oregon. There's a commune there. He owns a share or something."

"You have an address or anything, a phone?"

"No. Like I said I'm not sure. I think it's near Portland. It's called Blissdale, no Blythedale, maybe?"

"He wasn't by any chance with his friends, Joe and Moira when he left? "

"Moira? You mean Maureen? The blonde? "

"Yeah."

"She was helping him carry some of his stuff. Didn't see the guy though."

"Listen, in case I try to contact him out there, you happen to know his last name?"

"No idea."

We had made it up to the fifth floor. I stopped to catch my breath and thanked him for his time. He offered to introduce me to some other riot victims, but I declined. I was on my way out the door when I heard someone call my name.

I turned around and saw Laura Micciela, the reporter who'd

written the article on the building. We knew each other from college. She was a year behind me then, but hadn't taken any detours in her journalistic career. She was full time at *The Eye*.

She put her arms out to hug me and I returned the gesture. We'd actually slept together a couple of times back in college. As I remembered it, both episodes had involved alcohol and morning awkwardness.

We ran into each other occasionally. We were always exchanging numbers, talking about meeting for lunch, but somehow never connecting.

"Laura. Hi. You working?"

"No, I made some friends when I was doing the story. I was just visiting. What are you doing down here?"

Her tone reminded me there'd always been this antagonism, sense of competition, maybe, which I think she thought was sexual between us. I reminded her I now lived "down here," only a couple of blocks west. I knew she thought I was a prep school dilettante, not the serious journalist she was, though from what I knew of her background, we weren't so dissimilar. I was pretty excited about my embryonic project, so I offered to tell her about it if she had time to sit for a cup of coffee.

We walked over to the Ukrainian Parlor. In what I thought was a brilliant monologue performance, complete with quotes in character, I told her what I had.

"You're thinking this is a book?" She asked scrunching her face like she just saw a suspicious dot on her pierogi and hadn't quite figured out yet whether it was black pepper or mouse feces.

"Why not? It's a great story."

"But what are you trying to say? What's the point?"

I was suddenly distracted by all the clattering plates and conversations. I thought of Johnny's comments about my being "out for something," and gave her some of the same answers I'd given him. I tried to use words that would impress her – homelessness, dispossession, social justice.

"Don't bullshit me, Teller. You just want to write some trashy true crime thing. Something people can read for entertainment."

"What's wrong with that?" I asked.

"I don't think Ingrid Hess's murder and dismemberment is a laugh-a-thon. Besides how does it change things down here? Whom does it serve? If this is the image you show of the Lower East Side, who's going to care about tenants' rights if they're all portrayed as killers, crazies, addicts . . ."

"So you're saying I shouldn't expose the truth because politically it might be harmful?"

"It's speculation. I don't think you have any truth to expose. Besides, there are a lot of true stories down here that need to be told, stories that would help. Look at the people at the squat. They've rehabilitated a building, provided living spaces for families, brought in members from shelters, given workshops on renovation and bringing buildings up to code. All that work, and the city's still planning on evicting them. What about telling their story?"

I paid the bill and we went our separate ways. Her self-righteousness put me in a sour mood. I found myself continuing our discussion in my head. Wasn't I doing exactly what we'd been trained to do? Pursuing the facts wherever they might lead. I wasn't exploiting Ingrid's death. I was investigating it, searching for answers that would reveal some even bigger truth.

I had a lot of work ahead of me. I went home and looked over my notes. Left some phone messages with people I knew in Oregon and Washington, figuring somebody would know somebody who'd heard of Blythedale. I thought about how I might try to find Mirabella, Joe Holiday's transvestite "girlfriend."

Johnny had had the impression Mirabella worked on the West side, near the tunnel. A lot of men going to and from Jersey in cars stop there to get blow jobs from hookers. They either don't know or don't care whether the girls have something extra. One of these "ladies" had been killed about a year before – beaten to death, the body found in the Hudson. I remembered reading an article about it in *The Eye*, sharp description of the whole scene including interviews with others who worked the area. I stopped by *The Eye* office to get a copy of the piece. The reporter had used pseudonyms, so I couldn't tell whether or not Mirabella might have been interviewed. Unfortunately it was written by Laura, and I didn't feel like asking for her help.

I decided to go over and see if I could find Mirabella myself based on Johnny's description.

There were a lot of hookers near the tunnel entrance. A few obviously men in drag. They all looked tired and sick, and I couldn't imagine what self destructive impulses motivated their customers.

"Wanna date, hon?" It was a man, dark-skinned, black, early twenties. He had on eye shadow, a little mascara. Tight blouse and jeans. Androgynous, but not full out drag. He introduced himself as Sugar.

I told him I was looking for Mirabella. He said he hadn't seen her lately. I gave him ten dollars. "When does she work?" I asked.

He laughed. "She don't work. She's like our guardian angel. Comes around with sandwiches sometimes, condoms. Talks to us."

"She live around here?"

"She want you to know where she live, she tell you herself. Why don't you give me your number, hon? I'll give her the message."

I did. Went home, took a shower and a nap. Tried to think of my next move. I wanted to talk to Kyra again, figured I could find her at the club. About midnight, I got into my bug and took off for Jersey City.

Kyra was dancing in her little cage when I got there. I ordered a scotch, because it seemed like the kind of place where a man alone on a mission like mine, would order scotch. Then I ordered another one. She took a break, and I headed for her dressing room.

"Remember me?" I asked.

"I read your article."

"I hope I didn't say anything that offended you."

"No, it was fair."

"I'd like to do a follow-up. I could use some help."

"I don't have more to tell you."

"Sure you do," I said. "You can tell me about Lenny, what you know about his background. You can tell me lots of things, Kyra. Why don't we go out and get some breakfast when you're done here?"

"You got a car?"

"Parked in the lot."

"Would you take me to the city?"

I think Kyra might have been expecting a fancier vehicle, but she didn't say anything. When we came out of the tunnel, she asked me to make a stop, on Rivington Street.

"I've got to see someone. It'll just be a minute."

"You sure they'll be awake?"

"Oh yeah. They're night people."

It was a pretty rough block but well lit thanks to the high-intensity streetlights. You could read a newspaper while getting stabbed. I pulled up to a hydrant and offered to accompany her. She said it would be better if she went in alone. She ran up the front steps of the building, and pressed a buzzer inside. While I was waiting a man knocked on my car window, and offered to sell me some heroin. I shook my head no, and he walked away.

I was feeling like a kid sent out by his parents to buy popcorn during a nude scene in a movie. But more than that, I felt like I was being excluded from a part of her world, a world I'd need to know to write my book.

When she got back in the car, I asked, "Feel better?"

"Yeah."

"Hungry?"

"I could eat," she laughed. She didn't look out of it or anything. Just relaxed. Very relaxed. We decided to go to a new place on Avenue A. Diner-Diner, retro, but not overdone.

I ordered coffee and scrambled eggs. She asked for pancakes, and when they came she put a couple of teaspoons of sugar on them, then smothered them with syrup, though after that she just picked a little and sipped her coke.

I wanted to take things slow, not confront her too quickly with what Johnny had told me about Joe. We talked about Lenny. She'd seen him in the hospital, thought he looked better than he had in a while. Too bad he was never getting out. She found his father's telephone number for me in her address book. Then she started telling me about all the addresses – places she'd stayed or lived.

I was about to ask her about Joe when she said, "Can I ask you something?"

"Sure."

"You live down here, right?

"Yeah."

"Listen man, I got an appointment in the city this afternoon. Do you think I could crash out at your place a few hours?"

It was already light. When we got to my building, the super was sweeping the stoop. He said "hello." Checked out Kyra and then looked at me as though he had something to say, but didn't.

"I think I used to live in this building," she said.

She told me what a great apartment I had. I made us some coffee.

"Kyra," I said, "I've heard Joe Holiday was there when the murder happened."

"You hear that from the police?"

"No, a friend of his. Joe told him."

She didn't say anything. So, I continued, "You know anything about that?"

"How would I know? I told you I wasn't there."

"I know. I thought maybe Lenny said something to you."

"I'm so tired. Does that couch pull out?"

I moved my coffee table and pulled out the couch for her. I went to get her clean sheets. When I came back, she was in her bra and panties. She took the sheets and started to arrange them. While I'd tried not to stare at her exposed breasts at the club, I couldn't help looking at them in my living room.

She noticed where my eyes were drawn to, looked at them herself and smiled.

We sat down on the now pulled out couch and each had another cigarette.

"I wish you'd trust me, Kyra."

"Christ, Peter. I don't wanna talk about it, okay?" She placed a hand on my thigh. I was thinking about the needle marks on her arms, thinking about the virus, her breasts, professional ethics and a million other things. She started to unzip my fly. I pushed her hand away and took it in my own. We sat holding hands at the edge of the bed.

"Kyra, I like you. But this isn't a good idea. We need to keep things professional. Maybe after the work is done."

"It's no big deal to me," she said.

"I'm sorry."

"You don't have to be so dramatic. I had a feeling you weren't into women."

I wasn't sure whether she had just said that to challenge me, whether she believed I was gay or whether she was just trying to save face.

"It's not that. It's just not a good time for me."

"Whatever," she said. She was lying down by then. Her eyes were closed. I went into my bedroom. I was feeling a little edgy, self-conscious maybe about her being there, so I took a couple of Klonopin to get to sleep.

When I got up it was after one. She was gone, though nothing else seemed to be. I reheated old coffee and found half a bagel still toastable, took a quick shower and dressed. No messages from Mirabella, so I thought I'd head back out and see if I could find him slash her.

I didn't see Sugar again. I started to talk to a couple of the women, actual women as it turned out, who told me about a small park nearby where "the girls" sometimes hung out.

I walked over and found a group, including Sugar who remembered me.

Someone commented on my wardrobe. "College drag. Something for every taste." Another asked, "You working, honey?"

Sugar took me aside and told me he hadn't seen Mirabella, but he'd let me know, and could I lend him twenty? I told him I was sorry, but I couldn't.

I left the park and started walking east, back toward the subway. Someone tapped my arm. I turned around. I was looking at a man with long orange hair tied back in a ponytail. He was about five foot five, a little on the chubby side. Mid-forties maybe. Not flamboyantly dressed, wearing jeans with a studded black belt and an off-white silk blouse like something a secretary might wear to work on Wall Street. His skin had a yellowish tone I thought could have been illness or a bad fake tan. No makeup.

The man looked at me like he was about to say something, but then his face changed, registering surprise. He gasped and cried out, "Oh my! Aren't you Dr. Brent Harrison?"

"That was another lifetime," I said.

"Oh no. It was The Wild and the Innocent." Then after a moment he asked, "Why are you looking for Mirabella?"

"I'd like to explain that to Mirabella."

"Well, I'm not exactly Mirabella today. I'm just a Mira."

I laughed, although I hadn't quite gotten the joke. I told him I was no longer Dr. Harrison. I was a writer doing a follow-up piece on the Matthew's case. Mirabella's brow creased like a Shar-pei puppy's.

"I don't know anything about that."

"I know," I said gently. "But I thought you might have heard something about it. From Joe."

"You talked to Joe?"

"He's gone. Probably, the west coast. I don't think he's coming back."

"Well I don't know anything."

"I'd like to buy you lunch," I said. "Someplace quiet where we can talk."

"I'm not hungry," he started to walk away.

I followed. "Listen, I don't want to hurt you in any way. I'm not the police. I don't have to tell them my sources. I'm just trying to follow up on a story. Sometimes it does some good to tell what you know. Not to have to hold on to the bad stuff. I thought we could help each other."

"You were good on that show," he said.

I was into the scene, playing a role, imagining how a cooler character, someone like Johnny might handle it. "Thank you," I said remembering to smile.

"I thought of acting when I was younger. I had a friend, an agent. He was always encouraging me. But the auditions, the rejection. You wouldn't believe it, honey but I used to be so beautiful. I could make so much doing so little, it just wasn't worth it, the work."

"I can imagine."

"Is it only a story, you're after? I get the feeling it means something more to you. I can tune in sometimes."

"You're right," I said. "I think it could be very important."

I suggested getting some food at a Cuban-Chinese place I knew nearby. Mirabella insisted we get take-out and go up to his place. He, and at this point, I was thinking of him as "he" even though I only knew his drag name, lived in one of those old Chelsea apartment houses. The kind built in the twenties with an ornate lobby, casement windows and other deco touches. The studio was tiny, cluttered with the remnants of a lifetime. Fortunately, there was a separate eat-in kitchen.

"Nice," I said and it was, except for the smell of a not very clean cat litter box.

He'd had the place over twenty years. Rent control. Eighty-five dollars a month. He'd gone through some bad times. But no matter how bad things got, he always made the rent.

"Honey, I'd kill if I had to, to hold on to this."

"People have," I said.

We sat down at the metallic kitchen table, red marble pattern with matching chairs. He brought out the dishes and transferred the contents of the cardboard take out boxes.

Two hungry cats came in to see what we had.

"Tell me about Joe," I said.

"You're pretty direct," he said, and then after a moment added, "Joe was a sadistic son of a bitch."

"I thought you two were close."

"We were for a time." He crossed his arms in front of his chest and started to casually caress his own shoulder. "Isn't it strange how we're always attracted to the people who can do us the most harm?"

I nodded.

Mirabella told me about their life together. Joe had lived there for a while and then the fights started. He'd get violent. Mirabella wanted him to leave, but every time he brought it up, Joe would start making threats, remind Mirabella he was paying half the rent, and talk about other housing opportunities he might have had if he'd left earlier. This went on for months. Mirabella became convinced there was no way out. Then one night, Joe beat him so badly he wound up in the hospital. Afterward he stayed with a friend. The friend insisted on accompanying him to court where they got a restraining order. A group of friends had come to the apartment to serve it on him. Joe had looked at the paper, gotten his things and walked out without saying a word.

A few months later, Mirabella had run into him on the street. Joe said he had no hard feelings. He was working at a bookstore. Living with Moira by then in PD's squat.

"I know how stupid it sounds, but I wanted him back," Mirabella said. He mimed playing the violin. "I guess wisdom doesn't always come with age."

They started to see each other again though not often, and he didn't move back in. The violence returned.

"See, at first, after he'd beat me, he'd seem really contrite, you know? He'd tell me he was sorry I had pushed him into it. I bought into that crap. It took me a long time to realize he enjoyed it."

"Did he tell you anything, about what happened at Lenny's?"

"Oh, Peter," he put his hand on my arm. "This is so hard to talk about. You're not going to give the police my name?"

"Mirabella, I promise you. I'll change the details to protect you. If they find you, it won't be through me."

"Thank you Peter," he squinted a little. I couldn't tell whether he was trying to cry or trying to keep himself from crying. "He told me he killed her."

"*He* killed her?"

"That's what he said. He did it and if I told anyone, he'd kill me too."

"Did he tell you how he did it?"

"No, but he must have strangled her. He liked to do that sometimes. During sex."

"But what about Lenny? Lenny says he did it."

"Look, we were having a fight and he punched me, here." He pointed to his throat. "I couldn't breathe. It was awful. I started to hit him back. He told me he killed Ingrid Hess and if I didn't shut up, he could kill me too. I didn't ask for details. Anyway, I changed the lock again and never saw him after that."

I was sure Mirabella wasn't lying. But I also didn't know whether Joe had been lying, boasting maybe, or trying to frighten him. Despite the fact that they'd spent over a year in an on and off again relationship, Mirabella didn't know a lot about Joe Holiday.

"Did you know that wasn't his real name?" I asked.

"We never talked about his name."

We finished our food. I got up to leave.

"Wait a minute. I'd like to show you something."

He brought out a photo. At first I saw a beautiful young woman with long wavy red hair and large round eyes, posed like Botticelli's Venus – a white sheet draped over one breast, covering her genitals. I looked at the chest and realized the person was a man.

"It's you."

He nodded. "A lifetime ago. Time. Don't waste it."

"You've still got it, Mirabella."

He raised an arm and touched my neck. "That's a sweet thing to say." He put a hand on my shoulder. "Why don't you stay a while? Sometimes experience can make up for what time has taken."

"I'm sorry, if I gave you the wrong impression. I'm straight."

"You wouldn't have said that if you'd seen me then, honey."

Chapter 11

Autumn in New York – 1988

Raven

On a bench outside of Tompkins Square, closed now for "renovations" and guarded like a prison by New York's finest, Raven sat smoking her umpteenth cigarette and waiting for a guy who might or might not have taken off for Seattle weeks ago and owed her $20.

She was about to turn sweet sixteen and secretly fantasizing about the party she'd be having if she'd never left home.

The wind was blowing through her coat which was more decorative than warm as she sipped now lukewarm coffee from a nearby bodega, listening to the last leaves, crinkly brown, shaking off the trees in the park behind her. She heard the city was going to cut down all the trees and put up lots of fences. It reminded her of an old Joni Mitchell song her father liked. Lately she was thinking maybe her dad wasn't so bad.

Not that she would ever go back.

But she wasn't having a good time like when she first ran away. Finding safe space was a constant hassle. The guy she used to stay with in Union City was a freak. It didn't bother her in the beginning. But then it was getting to her the way he wanted her to bring home other girls so he could watch them together and take pictures.

She thought he might have been selling them on the side and that really crept her out because she wasn't even getting a cut.

Now she was staying in a studio off Avenue B. There was nothing but a bunch of mattresses on the floor and people always coming and going. Some guy whose name she didn't even know was there a lot. It was allegedly his place and she had to pay him to let her stay. She'd offered him a blowjob one time when she didn't have any cash. He said that was fine with him, "But I still need the money, honey."

Plus she was getting hassles at work. She had a fake driver's license she'd bought off some asshole from motor vehicles. $250 and she had to fuck him. Had her name and everything right except three years added onto her age. But her boss kept saying she really didn't look eighteen and he should fire her before he lost his license.

A couple of weeks back, some quasi-friends left in an old van, following the sun and heading for the Rainbow gathering. She thought about joining them, but had lately developed a physical addiction to heroin and couldn't imagine going cross-country dope sick.

So instead she was powering her brain with nicotine and coffee trying to think her way out of the mess that was her life. She could get a GED and then go to the City College. She could save money and travel someplace nice to kick. But the more she thought about it, the more she reminded herself of Kyra who was always going to do some cool thing that never happened.

She hardly saw Kyra anymore except at work. After that time at her apartment, Raven always felt funny around her. She didn't like to think about it. Sometimes she'd see it in dreams, which was weird because at the time it hadn't bothered her. She knew she had to act cool or she'd get hurt, so that was how she played it. But there was a moment after she went into Ingrid's room, and she was looking at Ingrid's things, thinking how strange it was that not only was the person who owned all this dead, but she didn't even have a body anymore, really.

She grabbed some bracelets from on top of the dresser. There was also a small wooden box with designs carved in. She opened it and found a book. It was one of those writing books you could find in a stationary store, had a cover with a flowery design. Meantime, Kyra was calling for her, so she just stuffed the book in her bag with the box and the jewelry. She tried on some of Ingrid's shoes, including the Doc Martens, but they were way too big.

Later Kyra told her to dump the jewelry, but she hadn't. It wasn't engraved or anything. She sold some of it. Gave some to friends. She still wore one of the earrings. As for the diary, she only looked at it once. The handwriting was hard to decipher, so she didn't get past the first page.

She still had it in the box with some other stuff she was keeping in the creepy Union City guy's house. Even though they had "broken up," he still liked her, came to the club once a week or so.

The remaining liquid in her coffee cup was cold, bitter and weak. She buttoned the top button of the coat. She was thinking how the guy who owed her money was probably long gone and maybe she should go to a diner or see what was happening back at the apartment. She noticed a man reading a newspaper on the next bench. He looked familiar. She thought she'd seen him before with a couple of people she knew. He was a little old, mid-twenties maybe, but very cute. Puerto Rican.

He looked up from his paper and into her eyes. He smiled. She thought he had a very nice smile, and his eyes were yummy like big melting chocolates. He came over to her bench, asked her for a cigarette and they started to talk.

Johnny

So there was this girl at the park. Cute, but she had on a coat and was sitting down so I couldn't tell for sure about the body. From what I could see it was fine. Gothic look, black hair, dark eyeliner against pale skin. I thought she would have been prettier as a blonde. She asked to see my newspaper. It was funny cause I'd only sat down a minute before, and there was a perfectly intact copy of *The New York Times* waiting on the bench. I'd taken this as a good omen.

It impressed me she was interested in the news. Knew something about the world. We started talking about that war in Africa between the tall and the short people, which she thought was pretty "bogus." We both agreed things weren't a whole lot different here. I told her about my past housing problems. She told me about her present ones. I mentioned my job with El Rey. She thought she should get a bike and work for him. I said if I were a pretty girl with a body like hers and could make good money taking off my clothes, I wouldn't trade it for getting sideswiped in New York City traffic and beaten by assholes trying to rip off product.

It was cold out and annoying to sit there watching the cops walk the perimeter of the park like they were guarding their sisters' honor, so we went over to my apartment. She couldn't believe the space. Started spinning around like a little kid. Her tits bouncing. It was a sight. She couldn't believe no one else was living there. I invited her to move in. She could help out with food, maybe clean it up a little.

We smoked some pot, started to fool around. It turned out she had a great body. Strong, flexible, firm but kind of fleshy around the ass and the boobs. Not a blemish, but I did notice some tracks which wasn't exactly a problem for me. She'd never shaved her legs and had the smoothest white down on them and the tops of her arms as well. I told her the hair on her skin smelled, felt and tasted like a special silk spun by worms fed only on the juices of ovulating women.

I started going down on her and was totally into it, but at the same time a part of me was thinking, "Jesus a fifteen year old stripper! Maybe I'll even be able to quit that stupid job."

I was feeling like I must've done something right, like the fates were looking down saying, "Let's give one John Humberto Ramirez a break."

So we agreed while I was at work, she'd get her stuff. I gave her my key and told her to make a copy, which could have gotten me fired because there were a couple of kilos of El Rey's stash in the fridge, but what the fuck? Laid a little cash on her too and asked her to pick something up so we could both fix when I got home.

When I got back, she had candles lit. There were plates of Chinese food spread out on one of those Indian cloths. After dinner, we put organic oil on each other's bodies, and gave each other massages before we fucked. Then after all that, I still wanted to impress her, to win her heart so to speak, so I was telling her how I'm helping out this journalist, working on a book.

"About El Rey?" she asked.

"No, it's about the Lenny Matthews thing." Then just to be entertaining, and maybe to shock her I said, "Yeah, my previous roommates were part of it." I told her all about Joe Holiday and Moira, about Peter's ideas too. At some point, I realized the look she was giving me, was familiar. It was the same look I'd seen on PD's face when I mentioned Lenny.

When I finally shut my mouth, she said, "You've got to promise you won't tell anyone what I tell you."

I raised my hand like an oath. She told me how she knew Kyra from work, how she was there when the body was being dismembered.

I was thinking, "This can't be. Surely it is not my destiny to wind up living with everyone connected with Ingrid Hess's death." I asked her specifics – dates, times, names – which mostly she didn't know. Part of me thought she could be lying, hustling me, basing everything she was saying on what I'd already told her. I didn't want to bring her to Peter and have him think it was me trying to bullshit him.

It was one of those times when I really wished I'd had a phone cause I would've called Peter right away. But it was forty-five degrees outside, and I was naked. I wasn't gonna look for a working pay phone at two in the morning.

I talked to her about talking to him. Convinced her she could trust him, and besides there might even be something in it for her. I left phone messages for Peter the next couple of days. He tried to call me at work, but we kept missing each other.

Finally, he stopped by my place, but Raven was out, and he couldn't wait the whole day, so we set up a time for her to go see him.

❖ ❖ ❖

Peter

Johnny Ramirez believed his life was ruled by luck – an ever changing, uncontrollable phenomenon, not unlike weather. Sometimes it rained, sometimes it snowed, sometimes Vesuvius blew and the best you could hope for would be to get out of Pompeii alive.

When I dropped by his sparsely furnished place, he was reading his Tarot cards, which he consulted daily like a weather report. He looked at the cards spread out before him and announced, "*C'est la fuckin guerre.*"

"What's it mean?" I asked.

He pointed to a card. The image was of a burning castle, people jumping out of high windows escaping the flames. I thought for a second of Lenny's building.

"It's The Tower. It portends disaster, ruin. The destruction of all existing forms. It probably means I'm getting fired and I'll lose this place."

We were in the living room of his apartment on St. Marks off of 3rd Avenue, a location which he considered, "The center of the fuckin universe."

He'd come to inhabit that space by being in the right place at the right moment, and began the story of how it wouldn't have happened, if we had never met.

He knew he was not the swiftest delivery boy working for El Rey. It was, he said, because he was terrible with money and never had enough to buy a bike, which slowed him down so he couldn't make as many deliveries.

I told him that didn't make sense. There were always guys selling hot bikes cheap in the park. I even bought my own back once same day it got stolen.

The more serious problem, he admitted, was that he did not, in fact, know how to ride a bike. He was scared El Rey would discover this discrepancy in his resume and fire him. So Johnny was always trying to make up for his deficits by being helpful to his boss in whatever way he could think of, short of having sex with him, which Johnny was convinced El Rey wanted, although he'd never said or done anything overt.

"Believe me he likes me. His pupils dilate whenever we talk."

"Johnny, the man is a professional weed head. His pupils always dilate."

When we met, and I'd expressed an interest in doing a story about the operation, he figured he could set himself up as a go between. He mentioned it to his boss on a day when El Rey had been very busy and was smoking some unusually strong pot. Coincidentally, only a few minutes later, Dave Gould, the obnoxious, FCC flouting, talk radio host of B-RCK decided it would be a fun stunt to call El Rey and ask for on air delivery. In his buzzed state, he must have thought the radio guy was me and admitted running the service on the air. Fortunately, neither the DEA nor NYPD could come up with a recording of the broadcast. El Rey later denied making the statements. His silent partners smoothed some stuff over, but were not pleased. His friend, Sean McFarland convinced them he was still the right man to run the operation, but of course changes had to be made.

First off, they decided El Rey's habit of keeping several pounds of herb in a locked desk draw and traveling home with the stash at night, across state lines to New Jersey, was not a good idea. They wanted to use a safe house nearby. One of them owned a small apartment building on St. Marks. El Rey was asked to find a reliable man to move into a soon to be vacated apartment. He chose Lobo, his ace messenger. Since the idea was to have someone there twenty-four hours a day, it was no problem when Lobo suggested his girlfriend move in with him, as well as Johnny and his girl.

Meantime the dispatcher had disappeared. After the radio debacle, El Rey didn't want to be handling the phones himself, so he gave Johnny the job. El Rey never was mad at Johnny for the mix up with the press because the way he remembered it, Lenny had been the one who told him to expect a call from a reporter.

"So see, if I never had that conversation with you, and hadn't told my boss, then he wouldn't've screwed up with Dave Gould, and I'd still be living in a squat."

"But isn't it possible it's not only accidents and coincidence, but our actions that determine the outcome?"

"It was my actions, man! See I was thinking positively, 'How can I help my employer?' That's why I mentioned you to him. That led to the events that got me the space."

"Okay, but you believe what that card is telling you?"

"Yeah, so?"

"Can't you put out something positive now, so that you don't get fired?

"Oh man, I'm always trying. But it's fate. See this card?"

He pointed to two cards in the center of the spread. They were laid out one crossing on top of the other. The one on top showed some kind of spinning wheel. The one on bottom was obvious, The Devil – holding a pitchfork, surrounded by the fires of hell and suffering minions.

"What's it mean?" I asked.

"In this position, it represents where I am. It means that I'm a captive to my impulses, my lusts, self-delusion, all that shit."

"Yeah, but if you have the information, and you believe in it, then why don't you treat it like a warning? Why don't you do something to change the situation?"

"Peter," he said, "If my grandma had balls, she'd be my grandpa. This is who I am in the space I'm in. Whatever happens, that's fate."

I told him he was full of crap.

He laughed, said we saw things differently. "Maybe if I'd gone to Yale, I wouldn't be such a fatalist."

I changed the subject and asked him why he'd been trying to reach me. He told me about the girl, Raven. At first, I tried not too seem too interested, wondering about his angle. But Johnny never was that way with me. Sure, he was always looking out for himself, but it was basic, of the moment. Could I lend him ten dollars? Did I happen to have any Valium?

We were feeding each other. We both got off on the story, imagining the details of how it might have happened. Johnny seemed as interested in it as I was. The more I came up with, the more he gave back to me.

It never hit me that it was, in fact, the occasional small loan he never paid back, the pack of cigarettes, the cappuccinos or beers I sprang for that fed the flame behind his eyes when he'd mirror my passion. It wasn't that he didn't believe in my project, but he was always aware it was mine, and one day I'd leave him behind and take it with me, so he had to protect himself, get whatever he could out of it before the tower caught fire and he'd need to jump out to escape the flames.

Raven

The only other time she'd been interviewed was by a freakazoid who used to come to the club before the boss barred him for weirdness.

That guy also called himself a reporter and wanted to talk to girls. He gave her $100 up front. Mostly he asked her how she liked to masturbate and to describe it speaking into a microphone as he sat playing with himself.

This time she was nervous. Even with Lenny locked up and Joe gone who knew where, she didn't see any reason to tell anyone anything, but Johnny was letting her stay at his space and she didn't want to piss him off.

She asked him to go with her.

"I wish I could, but I've got to go to work. If only I didn't have this job. Wouldn't that be great? I could go with you to the club every night. Make sure you got home okay, none of the guys hassling you. We'd have so much time together."

She called him on his shit and they both had a good laugh. He was sweet, smart, good-looking, and ate pussy like nobody's business, but she'd figured out that first night he could be a manipulative prick.

The reporter's place was only a couple of blocks away. She rang the buzzer and he beeped her up. Fifth fuckin floor of course. When he answered, she smiled. Johnny hadn't told her he'd be so cute.

She couldn't quite place where she'd seen him before. He put out his hand to shake hers.

"Wow, this is a cool space," She sat on the leather sofa.

He took the chair across from her. He turned on a tape recorder, and she started to giggle.

"What's so funny?"

"Nothing. It just reminded me of something."

"Are you nervous? Would you like some water?"

"Yes, please."

He got up and she watched him go into the kitchen. She shouted after him, "and a cigarette."

He returned placing the water beside her. He lit a cigarette and started it, then handed it to her.

"Do you live here alone?"

"Yeah," he said.

"Do you have a girlfriend?"

"Now, Raven, I thought I was doing the interview."

"Do you?"

"Not right now."

She opened her eyes wide and smiled. "Do you want one?"

"I think we should get to work," he said.

"Can I use your bathroom?" He pointed it out. She took a piss. She could feel her clit as she wiped herself. She pulled up her pants and checked the medicine cabinet. Grabbed some Valium. They were only 5 mg, so she took four and swallowed them before returning to the living room.

He was still sitting on the stupid chair, so she asked him if he could get her a real drink. They went through what he had. She decided on vodka and orange juice. He got up and she sat on the chair, so he had to take the couch. Then she moved over and sat down next to him.

"How did you get to be a reporter?" she asked sipping her drink.

He reminded her again she was the one being interviewed. He told her he knew she was frightened. He assured her he would never tell the police his sources. She was still trying to work out where she knew him from.

"I just wish I could relax, you know?" She took off her shoes and socks. She caught Peter looking at her feet. They were a perfect size five. She knew that could be a turn on. She was pretty vain about them too, always making sure her toenails were trimmed and clean. They were polished, the same dark violet almost black like on her fingernails and lipstick.

"Oh, look, my damn shoes are too big. They're screwing up my toes. Could you rub them, Peter?"

She watched him blush. It was beginning to be fun. The Valium was hitting too. It was like a dream.

Creamy, dreamy, steamy.

Peter stood up. He turned off the recorder. He looked at her seriously. "Do you even know anything about Ingrid's death?"

"Oh Christ. I'll tell you, okay. Do you really need that thing on? My voice always sounds so babyish."

He smiled. "I guess we don't need it."

"Peter, really could you just massage my feet a little? Please. They hurt. Man, I was dancing all night."

He started to. His hands were large and strong, a little sweaty. She told him about knowing Kyra from the club. He interrupted to ask her questions. *How long had she known her? When did she first meet Lenny? He stopped and asked her about her old life too. Why did she run away? What was it like at home?*

"That's good," she said about his touch. "Could you do my shoulders a little? I won't bite you. I'll keep talking. I was just getting to the good part."

He agreed. She took off her blouse and her bra. She watched him trying not to look at her breasts. He looked like he was about to say something, but didn't. She got on the floor. He came over to her side and started to rub her back.

"You're good," she said. She went on telling him about going downtown to Kyra's that day. He asked more questions. *Who was there? What did they look like? Who did she see first? What was she thinking? Was she afraid?* She could feel her muscles tensing and mostly he was just touching her, the warmth of his hands helping

153

her through the hard parts.

She turned around and pulled his hands down to her boobs.

"What about Johnny?" Peter asked.

"I only met him last week."

"But the two of you. . . ."

"It's okay. We got that straight the first night."

She stood up and pulled down her jeans slowly, wriggling her body like she'd do at the club. She sat back down on the floor. Peter was standing, still clothed. She lay on her back and raised her legs against his crotch. She rubbed him with her feet, feeling his erection. Then she leaned over and undid his zipper and pulled down his jeans. She started to lick his prick while working her fingers around his balls and asshole.

"Christ," he muttered. His eyes were closed.

She led him back to the leather chair. There was room enough for her to rub her twat against his thigh while blowing him. His thigh was hard. He had a good body, not like Johnny who actually looked better with clothes. She was almost coming. She wanted to get on top of him.

"You got any condoms?" she asked.

"In the bedroom."

"Too far." Keeping one hand on his joint, she reached down to her jeans and pulled one from a pocket. "I want to show you something fun," she said. She expertly opened the packet, put the rubber in her mouth and then onto him. She pushed him down, and climbed on top.

He came in seconds, which was okay with her because she was ready too and let herself go and screamed.

They just sat in the chair for a couple of minutes. Then he got up to take a piss. She was on the floor when he came back.

"Let's do some more," she said.

He lay down next to her. She got on top. He wasn't hard, but she knew she could get him there.

Afterward they were both quiet for a minute, holding each other. Finally he said, "Raven, how do I know it happened the way you're telling me?"

"Fuck you, Peter. You don't believe me?"

"Can you prove anything?"

She told him about going into Ingrid's room, about the little wooden box and the diary inside.

"Can you show it to me?"

She sat up and looked at him. His eyes were colder than she had thought. She didn't like that he didn't trust her. She wondered what kind of house he'd grown up in, if it had even been as nice as hers. She wondered if he had ever learned to play the cello, or been salutatorian in middle school. If he was going to treat her like a piece of trash, she'd play it that way.

"It's going to cost," she said.

"How much?"

She asked a thousand, cash. He said he'd only be able to get $200 out of his ATM. They dressed, not saying anything. She waited in his car while he went to the machine. They drove through the tunnel into Jersey City and the creep's house. She pointed it out to him, but there wasn't a space, so he double-parked.

"Money, now," she said.

He gave it to her.

When she got out of the car, Raven had the strangest feeling she was being watched, but she didn't see anyone on the block.

The creep lived on the top floor of a two family, in a row of two families. She rang the bell but didn't get an answer, so she used the key.

She wandered around the apartment looking for signs of new girls. She didn't see any, which was a good thing in case it didn't work out with Johnny.

She brought a kitchen chair into the bedroom and put it by the closet. She stood on it and reached for the cardboard liquor store box on top. She brought it down and looked inside. Photos including several of the cat she'd left behind at her parents'. Some jewelry she didn't wear much. Letters from her best girlfriend who had died two years before at summer camp, some stupid archery accident. At the bottom, the wooden box. She opened it. The diary was still there.

She figured she might as well take everything. She picked up the box and went outside. She was heading toward the car. Peter was smiling at her, and she smiled back, thinking maybe, despite the earlier tension, things could work out between them. He was good looking, even if he couldn't do it like Johnny. She turned around to close the gate in front of the house. Suddenly she felt someone grabbing her from under her shoulders. The box fell to the ground. A woman picked it up. She recognized the bleached blonde with the sunglasses and Miami tan.

"Mother!" she screamed.

She looked at the two men holding her as she struggled to free herself – beefy white guys in suits.

Peter got out of the car. Ran to the scene.

The men were telling her to be a good girl. Come along quietly. She bit one on the shoulder.

"Bitch," he yelled.

Her mother then yelled at him, telling him not to talk to her daughter that way.

She kept screaming hoping it would bring out the neighbors.

Now her mother was shouting at Peter who was trying to get the box.

"We were across the street in that van. I saw you giving her money, you bastard! That's a crime in this state, mister." She slapped him in the face, then turned to Raven and said, "These men aren't police, honey. They're here to take you to the hospital. I'm going to get you help."

One of the men cuffed her hands behind her back. The other one held her tight, his huge arms encircling her body. The man who'd cuffed her opened the door to the van. Peter was yelling, talking about the box and constitutional rights. The man punched him in the jaw and down he went. Then they threw her in the back and took off.

Peter

Down, but not completely out, I could hear the van pulling

away as some kindly Italian matrons, putting aside their Thanksgiving filled granny carts, helped me to my feet.

At prep, I went out for tennis. We didn't have boxing, so I'd never realized before I had a glass jaw. I began to laugh. Then I said in my best Brando, "I'll never be a contender."

My saviors, who by that point were looking at me with grave concern, asked if I needed the cops. I explained it was a private matter and got back in the Beetle. When the dizziness had passed, I waved to them and drove off.

I was thinking I should call Ouspenski, tell him about the diary, but I'd already told Raven I wouldn't involve the police. Maybe I could track down Raven's parents, but how would I explain things?

"Oh by the way, the *money* wasn't for sex. I'd already *fucked* your fifteen year-old daughter. The money was to buy a journal she stole from a girl who'd been sliced and diced by a group of lunatics."

What I really wanted to do was wallow in self-contempt for a few years. First, I considered Johnny a friend, and it did not seem particularly cool to screw your friend's girlfriend even if that was okay with him. Besides, what I'd just done had violated professional ethics, and was a crime in most states.

But merciful God, it had been wonderful, which led to my fourth reason for hating myself. I recognized that I was feeling guilty about *not feeling guilty* about my first three reasons for feeling guilty. In fact, despite my bruised chin, I was feeling better than I had in a long time. I imagined amusing Dr. Leider with the story and wondered what his reaction would be.

I got back to my building and was relieved that at least Johnny wasn't waiting on the stoop asking where Raven was.

I passed the super's wife in the hallway. She looked at my swollen jaw. "What happen? You was robbed?"

I told her it was nothing. She offered to get me some ice.

Johnny had left a message on my answering machine. He hoped things were going well with the interview.

I washed down some Valium with vodka throwing in a couple of aspirin for the pain. Then I stepped into the tub. Her sweet smell was still on me. I felt a sense of loss as I watched the soapsuds drift down the drain. I thought about calling a lawyer to find out if what her mother had done was legal. She was young, but she seemed capable of making her own decisions.

I was toweling off when I heard the buzzer and went over to the intercom. It was Ouspenski. Just passing by, could he stop up? I thought of saying no. But then again, maybe he had something I could use, so I buzzed him through and put on my pants. The way the day was going, it wouldn't have surprised me if he showed up with Raven's mom and a warrant for my arrest for statutory rape.

He looked around. "I'm sorry to bother you at home. I thought this was your office."

"It's that too," I said. I asked him to sit down and offered him a drink.

"Water'd be fine."

He was looking at my face. He asked me if I was still looking into "that Matthews thing."

I told him I was. It was slow going. Mostly trying to get background.

Did I have anything he might be interested in?

It reminded me of a scene I'd once played as Dr. Brent Harrison.

I told Ouspenski I had nothing and asked if he had anything for me.

"I wish I did," he said. He told me that Joe Holiday still hadn't been found. They knew he'd been living with some blonde named Maureen. Did I know anything about that?

I was planning to tell him about Joe and Blythedale, but I wanted to research it a little first. Maybe even go out there myself. Besides, it wasn't clear to me what role, other than bystander or possibly forced accomplice, Moira had played in Ingrid's death. She was facing a long prison term on drug charges and I didn't want to be the one responsible for sending her up. I was wondering if I might be able to figure out some way to warn her before the cops came.

I told Ouspenski the girlfriend was news to me. "There are a couple of things I'm working on, but it's probably just loose talk, and I can't tell you my sources. If I have anything solid, I'll give you a call."

He got up to leave and I walked him to the door. He smiled at me. It was the first time I really noticed his face. He's a big man with small features, gray-green eyes that dart around.

"Don't work too hard now," he said.

I watched him from the door as he started down the stairs. I was wondering about that remark, whether he knew things I hadn't told him. When I closed the door, I noticed for the first time, the state of my living room – a used condom on the floor, a full ashtray, a glass with a bit of orange juice and a smudge of lipstick, and a silver earring. The place was rank with the smell of sex.

I decided I might as well go over to El Rey's office and give Johnny the news about Raven's getting snatched. Given his outlook on life, I had the feeling it wouldn't be too much of a shock. I figured we could go out and drink like men. I'd buy him a pizza or something. Under the circumstances, it was the least I could do.

Chapter 12

Down the Rabbit Hole

Johnny

Johnny sitting by the phones at Royal Messengers, buzzes Peter through the door. There's a look in Peter's eyes that signals bad news. They nod "hello" but before Peter can open his mouth, two phone lines are ringing. Johnny answers one. Tells them to hold. Goes to the second. Puts them on hold. Returns to the first. Gets interrupted by a third call. It's the seven-thirty rush. They stop taking orders at eight, which makes no sense to anyone but El Rey. Johnny motions for Peter to sit, calls out to a couple of beeper numbers, and waits for the call backs.

Peter tells him about Raven's abduction.

"Nothing lasts forever." Johnny says.

"I was worried you'd be pissed."

"It's not your fault." He wonders from the way that Peter is acting whether or not he boffed Raven before she got grabbed. It wouldn't surprise him. Wouldn't particularly please him either. But the point is moot.

Peter wants to take him to dinner. Will spring for pizza and beer. Wants to talk about the book of course.

Johnny is tired. He'd screwed up a couple of orders. The boss hadn't yelled at him or anything, talked real soft in fact – which might have been worse. Scary, with the apartment at stake if he loses the gig. Part of him just wants to go home. Isolate. Maybe go out and find another girl. But he's not going to refuse a free dinner, besides he doesn't want to insult Peter. Peter is someone who can help him.

They share a joint in the office before Johnny locks up for the night. As they walk toward the pizza place, Peter is telling him what happened in Jersey. Johnny can't help feeling resentment. He recognizes it's the pot screwing up his mind, making him ultra-sensitive, aware of the underneath. He's thinking about Peter's education, his money, how *easy* everything is for him. Yeah, Raven probably fucked him, and for him, it would've just been good sex with a teenage girl, and not a possible way out of a dead-end job – not something on which to pin one's hopes.

Peter suggests Rossellini's. It's the best (and most expensive) pizza in the East Village. Got the brick oven smoky crust that Johnny can already feel crunching in his mouth. They walk over to 2nd Avenue. There's a small group of protesters outside the pizza place. A middle-aged dyke with thick Buddy Holly glasses and gray hair shooting out like Einstein's, thrusts a petition in Johnny's face. She explains that Rossellini's is going out of business at the end of the month. After twenty years, they've lost the lease and Banana Republic is moving in.

Her speech is getting more rapid as she yells, "Banana fuckin Republic. Have they no shame! Naming a store as though colonialism and the oppression of third-world peoples is a big joke. The world is one huge safari-theme park. What's next? What's *fuckin* next? Will they be shooting the natives for sport?"

The petition states the signers are residents of the community concerned because Rossellini's is a neighborhood institution. The undersigned pledge never to shop at Banana Republic or any other business that may open in its spot.

Peter and Johnny both put down their names. As they go in, Johnny mutters, "Yeah, I'm sure this'll just scare the landlord to death."

Inside it's packed, but they grab a table as some people are leaving and place their order. It's mostly NYU students and struggling artist types, with a smattering of the better-dressed newcomers as well.

Peter mentions the cop, Ouspenski, dropped by his apartment.

"This guy does not have my name, correct?"

"Definitely. It's not even in my notes."

"Keep it that way."

Peter says a friend in Portland found a book on "alternative communities of the Pacific Northwest," which had a chapter on Blythedale. He's thinking of flying out there at some point, maybe telling Ouspenski about the possibility of Joe's being there.

". . . But I don't know that Moira really *did* anything," Peter says, "I don't want to get her in trouble. Do you think there's any way to get a message to her?"

Johnny remembers she mentioned getting money from her father. Also seemed to have a way of getting messages from Robby. But he doesn't know details.

"Robby?" Peter says, "Yeah, that makes sense. Maybe I'll head over to the library tomorrow. See what I can find about his case from the newspapers."

"Then you're gonna warn her?"

"Yeah, she could get away from Joe before I talk to Ouspenski."

"Why tell him anything?"

"Why? Because the guy might have actually killed Ingrid. Lenny could rot in the hospital, and he might not even be guilty."

"But you don't know that for sure."

Peter counts out on his fingers. "He told you he was there. Raven saw him at the scene. Mirabella says he killed her."

"I'm not a lawyer, but Mirabella wasn't there. It's hearsay."

"I can't just let him get away with it."

"*You* can't? That's right. I forgot. It's your story. Gonna look good for the book if you solve the case. Yeah, I can see it, you and your man Ouspenski be standing over Joe's body like J. Edgar and Clyde Tolson on top of Dillinger."

"Come on. It's justice. But okay. It might be good for the book. An interesting angle."

"Yeah. But you want it on your terms. You don't like Joe, so you turn him over to the cops. But Moira, she's just too beautiful to be guilty. Too genteel. So you tip her off. How you gonna explain that one to the police?"

"Look you said yourself, that if someone walked in, they would've had to go along with Joe. Like with Raven. You knew Moira. You think she could have . . ."

"I didn't know the lady that well. But like I told you, she spent a long time with Assad. It wasn't her first dance. Despite her polish, she was a stone junkie and a fugitive. I think she would've done whatever she had to do to save her ass."

"I don't know. I only saw her that one time. But there was something about her. I'm not out to get her."

"But Joe's a different story?"

"Joe's dangerous."

"Because he's not white and he's from the street?"

"Because he throws kittens out windows and chops up young women."

"While his girlfriend stands by and . . ."

"Look it's my call."

"Of course."

The pizza comes, brought by a cute girl with short black hair in a flapper bob, long legs, short skirt, fishnet stockings. Johnny gives her a meaningful, "Thank you," but notices she is looking at Peter, which does not improve his mood.

Johnny's thinking no matter what actually occurred at Lenny's, it doesn't justify turning Joe over to the cops. He can understand how Peter feels about protecting Moira, but what Peter doesn't get, and what Johnny doesn't want to bother explaining, is that ratting out *anybody* is wrong. That Peter cannot comprehend this simple fact, doesn't even seem aware of it, is, in Johnny's mind, the very heart of his problem and the reason he will never get Kyra or anyone else down here to trust him.

They finish their food – hot dripping cheese, onions, garlic, three kinds of spicy meat. Polish off several Dos Equis. Smoke many Camels. The cute waitress comes over with the check and reminds them people are waiting for tables.

Peter asks Johnny if he wants to go somewhere else, maybe get coffee or more beer. They decide on Sidestreet Grill, where Johnny can order one of those sweet dessert drinks with Crème de Menthe and maybe wash it down with a nice scotch. Why not if Peter is paying the bill? But as they walk, Johnny is thinking that what he really wants to do is lose all the bad thoughts pinballing around his brain. The worry about the job, the petty resentment he is feeling toward Peter, the anger at losing Raven.

Every good thing that ever comes his way turns to dust and slips through his fingers. This is the way it's always been. Even before he'd gotten thrown out of the university, there were missed opportunities. Back when he was a kid, there'd been a high school counselor who'd visited him at his grandma's after he stopped showing up. Talked about a program for sending "promising" poor boys to prep school. The counselor had been one of those boys himself. Arranged for an interview.

The night before the big day, Johnny was trying to impress a girl, and when she saw a handbag in the window of a store and started admiring it, Johnny smashed the window. Unfortunately, a patrol car was cruising the block at that very moment. When the officer jumped on top of the not especially fleet footed youth, he didn't want to get hauled off to juvey, so he acted crazy, and they took him to the hospital which was how he missed his chance to go to fancy boarding school. Probably would've gotten a scholarship to college as well. Shit, if not for that one thing, he might've been a lawyer by now. One of those good looking yuppies walking down the street, with enough salary coming in to buy many grams of coke every week and go to the Hamptons weekends. But his life is always one fuck up after the other. It was like something he once read Abba Eban said about the Palestinians, "They never missed a chance to lose an opportunity."

Sidestreet is on the same block as the Hell's Angels headquarters and is filled with the usual mix of bikers, yuppies, students and punk rockers. The waitress comes to take their order. This one smiles at Johnny.

"Hey, Ramirez, how you been?"

"Fine, and yourself."

"I'm fine, sweetie. What's my name?"

He reads the tag. "Jeanette," he says stretching it out so she's not too aware of the pause until it comes to him, "Weinberg."

"Weiner," she says smiling, surprised he got that close.

"I can't believe you thought I could forget. Jesus, I lost your number. I had a feeling you worked here."

She writes it down on a napkin. He pockets it looking like this was indeed the plan. She takes the order and walks. He can tell by the bounce in her butt that she's happy, but he doesn't remember a damn thing about whatever happened between them or when. *Sotto voce* he tells Peter, "If you learn the last name, it's a lot easier to remember."

Peter goes back to babbling about "the case" like he thinks the two of them are the Bobsey twins. Johnny is checking out the scene across the room. There's a table right by a big glass window looking out onto 5th Street off of Avenue A, filled with a group of college students – a couple of frat boys, two pretty girls. One is a strawberry blonde, petite, delicate baby-doll features. Some crazy looking homeless guy on the other side of the glass is staring at her. First he points a finger to his open mouth like he's asking for food. Johnny watches the girl focus her eyes on the boy across from her, like she doesn't even see the bum, but of course she does. Then he points to his crotch. She keeps talking. She's more animated now. Johnny can't hear her, but imagines she's telling her friends what's going on. The man starts rubbing his crotch, opens his fly, and strokes his dick. The girl gets up and trades places with one of the frat boys. She's behind a brick pillar now. The bum can't see her. The students are all giggling. The man on the street is still working it, but he looks pissed off. Johnny wonders if he'll finish up by throwing his cum at the window, or maybe he'll throw a bottle instead. The waitress comes over to the students' table and says loud enough for Johnny to hear, "Shit. Is he out there again?"

A minute later, the bartender is on the street yelling at the bum who's back to pointing at his mouth. The bartender gives him a couple of dollars and he walks away.

Johnny wonders if he's seeing his future.

Jeanette comes back with their drinks. She leans down putting them on the table and Johnny gets a good view of her cleavage, which of course was her idea, but she's still a blank to him. Peter is saying something about PD's squat and their policy against hard drug use.

Johnny chimes in that it's all hypocrisy. He'd been to a meeting once, some AIDS group, mostly middle-class gay men and feminist health collective girls. They were talking about needle exchanges. The friend who had brought him warned him to be careful how he phrased his questions. Even in that "non-judgmental environment" you couldn't admit to using.

"A representative from the North American Man-Boy Love Association, would've had his rights defended, but you should've heard all the shit they were saying about needle users. It was so patronizing. How the exchange wouldn't only help prevent the spread of AIDS, but would encourage treatment. Bring the junkies in line."

"And you think that's a bad thing?" Peter asks.

"How many cigarettes have we smoked tonight? We've smoked pot. We've drunk different forms of alcohol. You tell me what's so special, what's so different, *immoral*, if after all this, I want something more and it happens to be a white powder, shot not snorted. Explain to me how that makes me scum. It's bullshit. I use IV drugs sometimes. I hold a job. I'm a decent guy – not out with a knife to someone's throat. Tell me how discrimination against users, how my not being able to buy clean works in a pharmacy, protects society. Make me understand how discrimination against IV users is different from hating Jews or gays or blacks."

"How much do you use?"

Johnny realizes he and Peter have never discussed his use before. He's alluded to it, but Peter didn't know, and now he is going to have to explain himself.

"Look, I'm not physically addicted or anything. But I like it once in a while."

"How often?"

"I don't know. Maybe a couple times a week," Johnny says though his habit has been an everyday thing for months.

Peter asks him more questions. *Was he ever physically addicted? How hard was it to kick?*

He tells Peter about back when he'd been at NYU. He was working nights as a security guard in an office building down on Wall Street. His supervisor sold a little blow to the brokers, and they did it at work to stay awake. He was making good money, so days off *occasionally* he would mellow out with heroin. It didn't affect his schoolwork. Then the company lost the contract. They didn't fire him outright. They offered him another job, but it was way out on Staten Island and there was no way to get out there by mass transit. Being a poor boy without a car, he couldn't take the transfer. But because they made the offer, his unemployment was rejected. His money ran out. He got dopesick. Probably wasn't as bad as a lot of people got it, but bad enough his bones ached, and he couldn't hold down food. Tried to see if he could get anything out of the empty plastic bags or the bottle caps he used to cook. Some other people he knew on the scene were going to break into cars and steal the radios to get money. They asked him to join them.

"I told them I couldn't. I didn't feel up to it. It was too much work. Just stayed in my room puking until I could hold down broth. They told me I wasn't a real junkie. If I'd really had a habit, I'd of gone to the cars. I didn't use again for more than a year, not heroin anyway."

"Why'd you go back?"

"I had money. Besides, it's the marijuana. El Rey's always sticking a joint in my face. It makes me paranoid. Starts me thinking about getting robbed on the job, getting the crap beaten out of me. I need something to bring that down. Smack helps me function in the workplace."

"But if the pot is making you anxious, couldn't you just not smoke it?"

"Man, it's El Rey. Like he's not going to trust me if I don't smoke. No, this is the best way to handle it. Besides, like I said, who does it hurt?"

Peter asks him if he's planning to use that night. Johnny admits he was thinking of getting something. With Raven gone and all, he feels like he needs a treat to get himself through.

"Can I go with you, for the buy?"

"Why?"

"For the story. It's something I need to understand."

"You paying?"

"I can handle it."

They leave the bar and Johnny goes to see a guy he knows on Avenue A. The guy is checking out Peter, but it's cool. Then they have to go to Avenue B, to another guy that sells works because Johnny's set is broke. After, it's over to Johnny's apartment where he does a whole demonstration.

Peter asks a lot of questions. *Why do you do it that way? What is this for? How do you know that needle is clean?*

"What happens now?"

"Now, I sit back."

Peter is sitting back as well. Smoking a joint and drinking, by Johnny's count, his fifth beer of the evening. He takes out a notepad, and starts writing. Whatever resentment Johnny had been feeling earlier, is gone. He feels nothing but love for this man who has listened to his stories, bought him food, paid for his high. An insight about Peter hits him suddenly and he laughs.

Peter gives him a look like *"Huh? What?"*

Johnny smiles. "You're such a tourist, Peter."

Peter puts down the beer. There's a far away look in his eyes and for a second Johnny isn't sure if his friend is about to laugh or to cry.

"I've heard that before," he says.

Peter

While I am certain that Johnny thought otherwise, I am not rich. My father's glory days were back in the fifties. When he left his previous wife to marry my mother, the settlement nearly broke him. Add in the investment in her career and the backing of a few flop plays, he was lucky to hold on to his apartment and the house in the Hamptons.

He's helped me out. Paid my medical bills. My last birthday, he bought me a thousand dollar IRA which I immediately cashed in. His kindness is not exactly a reliable source of income.

When I moved down to the East Village, I had money saved from playing doctor on TV. $625 a month for a small one bedroom was less than what I'd been paying for my matchbox studio on the Upper West Side. But the last time I checked, my savings account was just about played. Journalism was not providing much income. Between the research and the writing, I figured a book on Ingrid Hess's murder would take a year to complete. If I could get a proposal together and press on some connections, I might be able to get an advance from a publisher. But even with my clippings and my charm, I still didn't have any previous books to my credit, and it would take a lot of hustling. I was trying to get freelance work, but concentrating on anything outside of the Matthews case was becoming more and more difficult.

In the past, between acting gigs, I'd worked as a temporary proofreader at law firms, usually graveyard shift. The big firms go twenty-four hours. The lawyers and the paralegals do the brainwork. Word processors provide skilled labor –- typing speed of at least seventy words per minute required – though you don't have to actually understand what you type. Proofreaders make less, twelve dollars an hour to start. You don't have to know much – just the symbols, but they want college graduates – literate, well-spoken types, or as Johnny might more cynically put it, "white people." They like actors and moonlighting teachers.

Late fall through mid-January tends to be "the busy season." The firms need to file certain papers for tax purposes. It wasn't a surprise when the AccuProof Agency called asking if I could use the work.

It was my old friend, Delia Danburger on the line. I hadn't heard from her since the end of summer. We have one of those friendships where we might not speak to each other too often, but we always pick up where we left off. I recognized her sexy little squeak on the other end of the phone. It was easy to picture her too, imagine her on the swivel chair in her office, those thin thighs rubbing together slightly. Her business suits were tailored tight. Her skirts always a little shorter than whatever was in fashion.

After college, Delia had toyed with various career options. She'd gotten onto proofreading to pay the rent, became a dispatcher, and then jumped ship with a few friends to form her own agency.

She was offering me a gig at Finchley, Lamb, Helm, a large firm where I'd worked before.

"What about Black Monday?" I asked. "Surely, the days of car services and catering are gone."

"We're not doing too badly. It's mostly the little agencies that folded. We ate some of them. Just don't expect a wage increase."

"Darwinian capitalism at it's best."

"Please, Peter, don't start going all political on me like after the riot. One catch about the job, sweetie."

"Which is?"

"It's graveyard, Monday through Friday. They want people who can stick it out. Probably through the end of January. It's fourteen per with car service there and free deli lunch. They'll give you a ten percent bonus after the season's done. We'll also throw in an extra hundred. But I need people who absolutely won't fink out."

"That's nuts. The point of temping is non-commitment. What if someone were offered a movie or something?"

"Exactly darling. That's one of the reasons you'd be ideal. You're not acting anymore, right?"

"Yeah but I'm working on something."

"Put it on hold."

I agreed to take the job, figuring if I cut back on sleep, my days would be free for my own research and writing.

Once we'd gotten past business, I started to tell her about the Ingrid project.

"You did that already. I read it."

"There's more," I said and began to go into it.

She interrupted to invite me to a party, mentioned it could be a good place to make some contacts.

"Baby needs a date?"

"Baby has a babe, babe. But this is mostly a business connection crowd and you know Jade. She can be *extreme* even for Soho."

"Yeah, but don't you usually have someone in reserve?"

"Not really. There's this lawyer I've been fucking on the side, but his wife keeps a tight leash."

"Delia, Delia. When are you going to settle down?

"What about you baby? God Peter, you're so damn beautiful. Where's *your* girlfriend?"

"Well, there was this fifteen year old stripper, in my apartment the other day . . ."

I could hear her laughing. I know she thinks I'm repressed, maybe some kind of closet case. It wasn't that I wanted to boast about Raven, but I felt so excited about the story I couldn't stop talking about it. She reminded me it was the middle of a workday and she was trying to track down bodies to fill up her order, so we ended our conversation.

I meant to get some work done that afternoon, maybe start on a proposal, or go out and push on that Jacques Lanoir character. Instead I wound up daydreaming about Delia's legs.

Delia

I always thought if Peter had fucked more, he would've obsessed less. He was always *sublimating*. I mean it wasn't so much that I thought he was queer. I *know* he liked women. I also know, because I was close to a couple of the girls he was with that he could be pretty passive in bed. Back in school, I encouraged a couple of *my* girlfriends to sleep with him, so they could report back what he was like. I'm sure I could have done something to help him. But I needed to have at least one friend I *wasn't* fucking.

I loved him. I just couldn't see him too much. It was complicated. This dead boy hovering between us . . .

I'm pretty pissed off at both of them for checking out the way they did.

The party I invited him to was down off Wooster. I live on the Upper East Side. It's not very Bohemian, but it's where I grew up. I like feeling safe on the street. Having a cab waiting for me because that's the doorman's job. I work hard. I'm entitled to something. Anyway, I hadn't seen his new apartment, so I was going to stop by, have a drink and catch up first.

The building wasn't bad for down there. The hallway had that cheap paint smell, the kind of odor that lasts for years and covers a variety of even more noxious fumes. I briefly worked in real estate. I also used to do phone sex. Guess which felt more like prostitution? I was walking up to the fifth floor imagining how I would have described the place. Prewar charm? The authentic feel of a historic neighborhood? There was a Puerto Rican family on the first floor. Peter told me the man was the super. Not exactly a concierge, but I suppose it does keep things under control.

I must sound like a snob. I'm really not. I mean, Jade, that's my girlfriend, she has a loft in *Brooklyn*, for God's sakes.

He opened the door. We hugged. He had my drink waiting, Tanqueray and tonic. The first time I tried it, I was fourteen. Peter had mixed it for me. Just a private party, Chic and Peter and me. I remember I drank four or five and got sick. Chic joked that Peter had popped my alcohol cherry. Peter blushed the way only a fifteen year-old virgin could.

I sat down on his sofa. A little generic for my taste, but not bad. He looked thin. It worried me. The look in his eyes, the *intensity* reminded me a little of when he went through that *thing* in college. I was at Sarah Lawrence. He'd call in the middle of the night and just go on and on. He believed he'd made some great discovery about the universe, but I never got exactly what it was. His father called me. I didn't think he even knew who I was, but somehow he had my number and was asking my opinion. Did I think Peter needed treatment? Peter was almost two years older than I am. I'd thought of him as my naive but loving older brother.

There I was weighing what I should say, not knowing whether or not he might hurt himself or anyone else, but feeling that the worst thing in the world would have been if they locked him up.

And I was right then, wasn't I? He *did* come out of it.

So I was sitting on the sofa, drinking my drink, with all this *past* floating through my brain, and he started talking as though he were picking up from the phone call we'd had almost a week before. Something about a girl who'd seen something in Lenny Matthews' apartment. By the time I could get him to slow down, he was describing how the girl's mother slapped him and these goons knocked him down in New Jersey. He did his Brando imitation. I laughed. It was funny. He could be very funny, but I was frightened for him.

He offered me some coke. I didn't refuse. It was just a little coke. We weren't *shooting* it or anything. He was telling me more and more about his "work," explaining that Matthews must have had help because you couldn't just scrape the brains from a skull that easily.

The whole time in the cab downtown he was blabbing away. The driver seemed interested. "You're talking about the girl they ate," he said.

Peter told him he was writing a book about it. When we got to Wooster, the driver pulled over and turned off the meter and Peter kept talking to him.

Finally I said, "I'm going upstairs," and got out.

The loft belonged to Jim who coordinates the word processing department at Finchley. It was a birthday party for his partner, Steven. It's pathetic. Steven has Kaposi's, wasting away. There were some other proofreaders too. Mostly everyone was an actor or a dancer or something. We were all trying too hard to be happy.

So maybe the others didn't get the same feeling from Peter that I was getting. They just thought he was amusing, and what was wrong with being *passionate* about something?

I went off to mingle, but I'd catch sight of him. One time he was imitating some drag queen he'd interviewed. He put his hands on his shoulders and started to caress himself. He made his voice soft. It made me remember back at Breverton, acting scenes with him. I was disappointed when he gave it up. He had potential.

He was drinking. I don't think there was any more coke. But his energy never let up. Sometimes he'd notice me watching him and he'd smile. It's funny when you've known someone that long, the telepathy. I knew he was saying, "Look at me Delia! They like me! They're hanging on my every word."

I nodded to him. Steven of all people came over and sat down beside me. He told me I looked like something was on my mind. We took a bottle of champagne and went into his bedroom, and I just started to babble about everything, what happened in college and all, even Chic.

He thanked me. He said he was so sick of people's pity. It was therapeutic to be reminded that everyone was fucked up. We stayed there talking till about four when Peter came to find me. We shared a cab back. He was trying to entertain that cabdriver as well. Only the poor man didn't speak English, so Peter was using a lot of body language, and I was catching the driver's worried glances in the rear-view mirror.

Peter finally gave up on him and turned his attention to me. He kept poking my arm and saying, "What's wrong with little Delia? What's wrong with my doll baby?" Then he'd go back into his own stuff. He told me he'd gotten a literary agent's name from one of the other temps at the party.

When we got to his place, he grabbed my hand and kissed my cheek. I just felt so sad and scared for him – though all I said was, "Peter, it sounds like there are some bad people involved. Please take care of yourself."

He laughed. He squeezed my hand as he got out of the cab. I watched him go to his door. It was a big metal door, and as it shut behind him, it gave me this horrible feeling.

That was the last time I actually saw him. He got through the next couple of months at FLH okay. Jim let him go a little early. He told me they were cutting back but I had a hunch it was something else. Jim knew we were close. I don't think he wanted to tell me.

After the job was over, he'd start calling me in the middle of the night. He'd be talking about his book, doing the characters, the way he had at that party. It got so bad I had to unplug the phone. They need to reach me sometimes for emergencies at the firms, so I had them use the beeper. I never gave him that number.

What was I supposed to do? Call his father? I didn't know he was using heroin. Maybe, I wasn't the best friend he could have had. But if you're sitting on the ground, how are you supposed to stop a plane in the air from crashing?

❖❖❖

Peter

Most of the "seasonal" temps at FLH had been back year after year – each time imagining (hoping, praying) it would be the last – that by the next winter, some break would come. The actors, writers, artists all believed that by the following year their nights of reading briefs for formatting errors and typos would be an amusing anecdote told on a TV talk show before a delighted live audience.

It was strange returning after my "success" on the soap. More than one of my fellows greeted me with a thumbs up followed by the sharing of his or her own experiences on daytime TV – working as extras, lucky if they got a line, usually on the order of "Call the doctor, stat."

An attractive attorney about my age approached me. I remembered the previous year she'd been frosty toward all the readers. Now she was shaking her wavy blonde hair, moving her head from side to side like a cheerleading Valley girl. She asked if I'd left the series to be in a play and looked confused when I told her I'd given up acting.

"To do this?" she asked.

"I've become a serious journalist," I said before giving her an oral curriculum vitae of my brilliant career. She'd heard of the Matthews case of course, read my piece in *The Eye*, but hadn't connected it to me. As I began to tell her some of my as yet unpublished discoveries, another junior associate stopped by. He stood next to her in what I took to be a proprietary posture – perhaps in another setting he would have put an arm around her. She smiled at him and explained who I was and what I was talking about. He nodded at me. I recognized him from college. I remembered his auditioning – disastrously – for a play I directed senior year.

I went on with my account. He stood by her grimly. She was amused, self-consciously working the hair. Then her head became still and her face grew longer as I described, in vivid detail, the scene Raven had walked in on.

I had just gotten to the part where Raven went with Lenny to check out the bathtub. The home coming queen turned corporate legal lackey interrupted, placed some papers in my hand and said, "Well that's all very, uh good luck on your project and we'd really appreciate it if you could get to work on this brief right away."

As she and the one-whose-hopes-for-a-theatrical-career-I'd-dashed walked away, I heard him mutter, "What's with that guy, huh?"

I was only working on that one priority document, so every time it went back to the paralegals or the word processors, I had downtime. At some point, one of the lawyers realized that a whole bunch of legal mumbo jumbo needed to be added. Then the computer system went down.

So I spent most of the night hanging around the conference room where they'd put out the food. Delicatessen, buffet style – turkey, pastrami, kosher salami, roast beef, rye, pumpernickel, bagels, bottles of Coca-Cola, amaretto flavored coffee. All charged to some multi-national corporate client. For the temps it was a party, a chance to catch up.

I filled my plate listening to snippets of gossip and conversation.

"Did you hear that Jamey's doing rep in Atlanta?"

"Susan's given up and is going to law school."

"Michael got a soap. He's blowing the writer."

"Hey Peter, what've you been doing?"

"A book! Really? About a *murder*?"

Although I spent most of the night entertaining or being entertained by the thespians, I felt a certain restlessness and at eight a.m. – release time, I sprang out of my cage. On the subway back to the Lower East Side, I contemplated the crowds on their way to work, just starting their day, sometimes nodding off as they stood holding the poles, bodies supporting each other. The train swayed like a cradle, lulling them. Then it jarred them awake with sudden, sharp, screeching stops.

I was a different breed. Hyper-alert. Putting on dark glasses as I exited the Astor Place station, I was a vampire returning to my lair. Only my whole neighborhood was a cave, filled with other creatures of the night, who worked graveyard, or didn't work at all, haunted cafés, and stopped by bars at nine in the morning. People who shared cigarette after cigarette and story after story until their throats were raw from speaking. *Sleep* – there'd be time for that after you were dead.

I bought a *New York Times* and sat down in the smoking section of the Ukrainian, ordered a beer with my steak and eggs. Eight-thirty a.m. and the waitress didn't blink. I was facing the back of the restaurant. The next table down was empty, but there was a woman sitting facing me at the table beyond it. Every time she raised her head out of her paper, she couldn't help looking up into my face. I smiled at her.

"I am Travis, Brent's bad boy twin. I am Johnny Ramirez, " I told myself.

She acknowledged me with a smirk. She was around thirty, pretty in a slightly weary way. Light brown curly hair, olive skin, Greek maybe, or Italian.

"Nightshift?"

She nodded. "Nurse," she said.

"I used to play a doctor," I said.

"I thought you looked familiar," she said, consciously placing her eyes back on the newspaper.

I took a breath. No time for stage fright. I got up and started walking toward her table.

It wasn't my style, but I was getting off on my own audacity, transforming myself, imagining there was a weight planted inside me, slowing me down so that every movement took a little longer, was just a little heavier as though I were a man who came from a planet with a larger gravitational pull, or as though I were a man who owned time. I looked her up and down letting her know I wasn't afraid for her to see I was admiring the shape of her thighs in her tight jeans, the outline of her breasts underneath her blouse.

It was rare for me to do this kind of role-play outside of a performance. I wanted to see how far I could take it. I had the feeling I could take it pretty far.

I asked if she would mind if I joined her. She told me she wouldn't mind a bit.

Her name was Rikki – with two k's. She did per diem nursing, was also a dancer and actress. Up close, I noticed she was wearing foundation to cover some acne scars. I told her about the book and asked her questions about her work. I would have just left it at that, but she was the one who suggested we go back to my place and continue the conversation.

I took her home. We smoked some pot – a mistake. It brought down my mood. I suddenly felt self-conscious to the point where I almost couldn't talk to her anymore. So I just concentrated on the kissing.

After, she said it was "nice". She lived with someone, and hadn't done anything like that in a while. She said it was like taking a vacation.

When I was left alone again, I started thinking about how other people lived. The energy it must take to go out and pick up strangers on a regular basis. I admired guys like Johnny who could pull it off.

Dr. Leider had told me more than once "anxiety is always about the future." Those words finally made sense. I had to stay in the moment, do what was needed, *be* who I needed to be. No self-imposed rules or boundaries. No worrying about the consequences. It wasn't just applicable to picking up women, it was the journey I was on, how I would pursue my story – how I was meant to pursue it – instinct, intuition.

I slept until three. Still nine hours before I had to be at the law firm. I was ready to get to work.

First stop, the New York University Library where I looked for clippings about Robby Assad. Copied some articles off the microfiche. There was a high school graduation picture of Moira, with a caption below that read, *"Assad's girlfriend, Moira Hoffman, daughter of Newark lawyer Mark Hoffman, disappeared and is being sought by the authorities."*

Definitely the girl I'd seen the night of the riot. I looked through some New Jersey phone books and found the number and address of her father's firm as well as his residence. I tried the office first and was told by the secretary he'd just left for the day. I dialed his home and got the machine.

It was a little past five. I grabbed a sandwich, got into my bug and headed out to New Jersey.

Sitting in tunnel traffic, I read my Triple-A map and eventually found my way to the township of Eagle Heights. There I meandered awhile traversing the various "roads," and "lanes" all leading to cul-de-sacs featuring signs warning, "SLOW – CHILDREN AT PLAY."

It was getting dark and the addresses were hard to make out. After circling the same block a couple of times, I found Hoffman's home, a modest townhouse with a small patch of lawn.

I rang the bell. No answer. There was a car parked in front of a one-car garage. I decided to wait. A few minutes later, a tall, lean man in a jogging suit turned the corner. He was staring in my direction. As he came closer, I could see he was in his early fifties, not in bad shape, but with a head of receding white hair that at first glance made him look ancient.

"Can I help you with something?"

"Mr. Hoffman?"

"What do you want?" There was something pleading in his voice.

I'd come to warn him to warn *her,* but what law would *I* be breaking? Could my being here make things worse, the way my hesitation with Ingrid may have led to her death? What did I think he could tell me? Was he going to say, that no, his little girl couldn't possibly have had anything to do with Ingrid's murder? Was I even going to bring that up?

What *did* I want? I had no idea.

I told him I was a journalist looking into something I thought he could help me with and asked for a couple of minutes of his time.

"Is that your car?" He was pointing to the bug.

I nodded.

"I had one of these once," he said.

"It's kind of a private matter. Can we go inside?"

"If it's not an emergency, why don't we discuss it at my office tomorrow?"

"I think it would be better if we talked here, tonight."

He looked around, seemed to be checking the cars parked on his street. He walked me through a gate into his backyard.

"Back in a minute," he said directing me to some leaf strewn lawn furniture.

He went into the house and came back carrying a tray with a carton of orange juice, a couple of glasses though it was a cold fall evening, hardly picnic weather, and a small box of matches. He also brought a pencil and some loose sheets of paper.

I started to speak. He passed me a note, saying the house might be wired. He handed me a pencil and a notepad. As I wrote he started talking about running – how he'd topped his personal best in the New York City Marathon that year and was planning on entering the lottery again for a race slot. I scribbled something about his needing to warn Moira that the police were after the man she was with, closing in.

He wrote a note back, while giving me his opinion on carbo-loading and the consumption of beer during training. His note said that he had no way to reach his daughter.

I wrote the address I'd gotten for Blythedale.

He looked the paper over for a minute, studying it. Then he lit a match and began to burn the papers we'd written on.

I sipped my drink, then said, "Oh by the way, I was hoping you could give me a little legal advice." I asked him whether a minor's parents could kidnap her off the street and have her committed.

"Not my area, but parents' protecting their kids, pretty sympathetic."

I thanked him for his time and left.

I would have liked to have seen Kyra, but she didn't start work at the club till eleven, and I had to be in the city for my job, so I headed back to Loisaida to visit Jacques Lanoir.

I drove by the same building on Avenue C where I'd seen him before. He was standing by the stoop, warming his bony hands over a garbage can fire. I pulled over into a hydrant-space and got out of the car.

"Good evening, Jacques."

"Ah Teller," he said.

"I have a theory, Jacques. Just tell me if I'm right or wrong. Lenny knocks on your door and tells you Ingrid's dead. You go over and who do you think is there?"

He said nothing. I continued, "Joe Holiday, Moira and Kyra for starters. Was she even dead yet? Or did you help with that too? No, I think she was already dead.

"So you're helping them with the body and who else walks in? Let's see, some guy with a German Shepherd. Feed the dog, did you? Was that how you got the idea for the soup? Then there was that cute little friend of Kyra's that dropped by. Anyone else? Am I missing something?

"I bet it was your idea that head in the bucket thing. Very theatrical. When you couldn't get Lenny to shut up about it, you had to set the fire, right? C'mon, just tell me. Nod your head or something."

Even his smile was thin – the lips drawn in and the gums pulled back elongating his teeth. "And what do the police say to your theories, Mr. Teller?"

"I haven't discussed it with them yet. I thought maybe we could go talk to them together."

He laughed, then released a feeble cough from his concave chest.

I stared at him. This time determined to win the contest.

He moved away from the now embering garbage can and stepped toward me. Gaunt as he was, he was imposing. He pointed his hand, the fingers narrow as tentacles. His nails were sharp, long, claw-like. He muttered something, sounded Latin.

Then he said, "Yes, Peter Teller, it is all how you have surmised. But you will not live to tell your tale. You will be burning in the seas of hell long before I, even with my illness, reach those shores."

He turned and went into the building. I started to follow, but the door locked behind him.

As I walked back toward my car, a man was approaching me, whispering, "Red rum, red rum." Johnny had already explained to me that was one of the more popular "brands" of heroin on the street. The name was "Murder" spelled backwards, taken from the book and movie, *The Shining*.

I bought a bag without even thinking why. I wasn't planning on trying it out necessarily. I wasn't planning on anything.

I stepped into my car looking around, a little worried about police. The neighborhood cranks were right; the cops were much too busy guarding the park to worry about a drug buy.

I pulled over on Avenue B and found Johnny's clean needle guy. Went into a bodega and asked for a small bottle of Clorox. The guy behind the counter gave me a look. I felt as awkward as a teenager buying condoms.

When I got home, I took out all my little items and placed them on the coffee table. Got a glass of water and my cigarette lighter out as well. Used a tablespoon as a cooker. My hands were shaking. First I bleached the works. Then I cooked the stuff, got it into the needle and set it down. I tied the belt around my arm and tapped out a vein, but I didn't shoot. Just practiced the necessary motions over and over. Added casual conversation. Watched myself go through it in a mirror.

When I felt I'd gotten it (when my hand stopped shaking), I flushed the shit down the toilet. Johnny would have thought it was an awful waste.

It got closer to work time. I was still feeling so wired, I took a couple of Klonopin before I left. Even then, I didn't fall asleep till late the next afternoon.

❖❖❖

Raven

When she finished a two-day detox, they moved her to rehab, which was sort of like summer camp. She had two roommates. There were lame activities, only here they called them therapy – art therapy, music therapy, even sports therapy. But the worst were all the stupid "Rap Groups." It was like out of this really hysterical TV movie from the seventies she once caught on the tube in the middle of the night. They were always trying to get you to talk about your "feelings," and admit how fucked up and unhappy you were.

Of course she was fucked up and unhappy. They'd kidnapped her and thrown her inside this pretend hospital slash (as Johnny would say) pretend finishing school.

The facility didn't take anyone over nineteen so the boys were babies. Sometimes she'd daydream Johnny would come and rescue her, but she knew he wasn't the knight in armor type.

She was getting close to one of her roommates, a little blonde named Starchild by her hippie parents. Starchild had also been snatched and had had a boyfriend she missed. Only when she described the scene to Raven, it sounded like the guy had been trying to work her, and even though Raven liked the girl, she figured she couldn't have been too bright to have gotten herself into that.

Sometimes at night, Starchild would get into bed with Raven. They'd kiss each other a little and whisper. Mostly, it was just the comfort of another human being.

One day in "group," the other roommate, who'd been there before, was talking about returning to school after she'd gotten clean, and how weird she'd felt. Raven was thinking, *"Yeah, well we're teenagers. We're supposed to be alienated,"* but then it started getting to her, the girl's story about not fitting in with any of the clicks and realizing that while it was easy not to use in rehab, the real world was something else.

Raven was listening, remembering that before she'd gotten grabbed, she *had* wanted to quit, was thinking a lot about what a dead end her life was and how she might wind up.

She started to get interested in the meetings. Listening to people's stories was mildly entertaining though she thought the higher power stuff was bullshit – like Jesus freaks. Still skeptical, she talked to her recovery counselor who explained it had to do with believing in something outside of your own ego – like Buddhism, which she thought was pretty cool. It impressed her when she found out the shrink who ran the place, the medical director, had spent a year in a monastery in Thailand.

She wasn't on any kind of meds and suddenly found herself having moods. Sometimes she'd burst out laughing, and just as abruptly she'd break into tears. One day she decided that she didn't want to be Raven anymore. But she knew she couldn't go back to being Jill either.

"I want another bird. But I want it to be like a bird of light," she told her roommates.

Starchild suggested "Paloma" which was Spanish for dove. Raven liked the sound. Plus she had always had a thing for Spanish boys.

She and both of her roommates had decided to change their names and they wanted a special ceremony, which they had to get permission for because they wanted to shave their heads.

This was Raven's idea. She wanted her hair to grow back its natural color and she figured it was the most practical way to do it. The other girls just thought it would look cool and symbolize their commitment to a new life.

The therapists were worried because the Manson girls had shaved heads, but Raven and her friends convinced them.

She loved the feel of her baldhead. It was very sensitive and people were always trying to pat it. But the best was when she would take a shower. It was such an intense feeling, almost like coming, the wetness of it.

Sometimes in group or individual, she'd talk about the shit that happened to her when she used to be Raven – all the degrading things she'd done like dance around naked. Although the truth was, at the time she was usually high and it actually felt good, like she was safe and in control, but that's not how it came out when she talked about it.

But one thing she never talked about was going into Kyra's apartment and seeing Ingrid's body all chopped into pieces. It was like her life was a jigsaw puzzle and she was trying to put it together and figure things out, but whenever she thought about that day, she couldn't get how it fit in, what it had to do with who she was then or who she wanted to be now. So she just kept that piece in the back of a high shelf in a little closet in her brain.

Peter

A couple of days after my solo dress rehearsal, I wound up shooting a bag with Johnny.

I'd woken up about one in the afternoon feeling a surge of energy. Friday. One more night of work and then I wouldn't have to be back till the Monday into Tuesday graveyard. Two days to track down Kyra, maybe get an address on Raven and recover Ingrid's diary. I decided to fortify myself with some cheese blintzes and a few cups of joe at the Ukrainian Parlor. Johnny was sitting alone at a table, downing his pancakes with fried eggs and sausage – taking a lunch break from El Rey's.

I looked at his plate, "Man, you eat like that, you're not gonna make it to thirty."

"Thirty? I was shooting for twenty-six." He pointed to the empty seat across from him and I sat down. He was telling me about a delivery he'd made to a call girl in a mid-town hotel. Her client was hiding out in the bathroom when Johnny came to the door. He'd seen her around the neighborhood and they wound up making a date.

"I don't care if this one actually *killed*, Ingrid," he said, "I'm not introducing you."

I told him about the law firm gig, seeing Moira's dad, my conversation with Jacques. I told him about my "practice session" and how I really wanted to shoot for real. I needed to get into the head in order to better understand the desperation of someone like Joe Holiday. Besides as he had said, it would probably be the only way I could get Kyra to trust me.

He was smiling, but I couldn't read what his take was.

"It's like you were saying," I told him, "Why freak over needles? I've used drugs before. It's not like I'm going to get addicted the first time I try the stuff."

"What happened to your professional ethics, man?"

"Raven happened," I said watching the oil squirt out of my blintz as I cut into it with a fork. I dipped it into applesauce and sour cream and tasted all the flavors rolling in my mouth. "That girl saw Kyra in the apartment while they were cutting the body. Kyra lied to the police about that. I'd bet my life Kyra saw the whole thing."

"So you're going to get it out of her by giving her drugs?"

"I know she's the key. She's everything. If she talks to me, I've solved a crime. I'm on a mission."

"Yeah, you sure are."

"Come on Johnny," I said. "Are you holding?"

He laughed.

"I've got to be at work at midnight, that's the only thing," I said.

"You'll be fine way before then," he said.

We went to my place. I set out everything including some bleach and extra water to clean the works. I got a little jittery right before. "You sure I'm not going to OD and die from this shit?"

Johnny tasted a bit from the bag. "No, man. I know what this is. Besides, you're just going to get a little taste."

He shot first. Showed me how to "boot" the blood back in.

I didn't like seeing the blood inside the syringe, wished I'd had an extra needle, made sure to shake up the bleach and water first.

The rush didn't last long. I suppose I could tell you it felt something like the time when Chic sent the girl down to my bed. The heat, the letting go, the psychic relief. But it wasn't that. It was better.

It wasn't like cocaine either. Coke relieved my self-doubt in the sense that it made me feel I could do whatever I set out to. But this eliminated any desire, any need, to *do* anything. All I had to do was be. And I felt safe and comforted in the being. I felt at peace.

For a couple of seconds.

Then I vomited into the bowl we'd used to clean the works. Johnny had to go back to work at El Rey's. I took a couple of Valium which I thought would help with the nausea and wound up sleeping till I had to leave for work. I felt a little queasy when I woke up. Made myself some tea and toast, belched, but kept it down. At the office, I was pretty steady. though a couple of people commented that I looked tired and asked if I was getting sick.

I came home drained, but couldn't sleep which was annoying because my head kept spinning with ideas for the book and things I needed to get done during the weekend, before I had to go back to the stupid job. A brandy and a couple of Restoril finally did their magic and I woke up in the early evening.

Still a few hours to kill before I'd drop in on Kyra at the club. I started straightening up the apartment, vacuuming, dumping the ashtrays, conscious of the fact that I was doing all the stuff I'd do if I had a date who I thought might wind up spending the night. My mind was buzzing with questions about my own intentions. *Was I planning to seduce Kyra? Would she be more interested in drugs and a place to crash? If she did spend the night, would she even tell me anything, and would I ever get her to leave?*

Then I remembered my own resolution: instinct, intuition. This wasn't a story about a murder in the Hamptons, or Yale, or even the Upper West Side. This was a story about Loisaida, and I was determined to play it by Loisaida's rules.

Chapter 13

Winter

Kyra

The light's in my eyes. It's hard to make out faces. I see Peter, and then I don't, so I could have imagined it, but there he is waiting in the dressing room when I go on break. It's like Lenny being in love with Ingrid, or Joe hating her so much. He can't let this thing go.

He says, "I couldn't stay away from you."

I laugh. Look down at his crotch. "The only hard on you got is about your stupid story."

Shit, he's *jonsing* over it! The police, the DA, everyone but this joker's dropped it.

He's staring at me with those movie star eyes, and this *momma's been mean to me but I still love her* smile. Boyish, you know? But tall with a big Adam's apple and big hands. His hands are smooth too, like he must take care of them.

He's sitting in this ratty chair, one hand resting on the arm. I grab it. "I used to read palms," I tell him.

It freaks me when I look at his cause the lifeline is short with a big skid in the beginning and a lot of little fuck ups at the end.

"Let me read yours," he goes grabbing my hand. "Yeah, I see it. You've seen some terrible things. People treat you badly, so you're not very trusting. I see you getting into a yellow Volkswagen with a great looking guy giving you a ride into the city after you finish work tonight. What's this? He's buying you breakfast."

"Yeah, you can do that." I need a lift. I'm staying in a sublet on 3rd off of 1st, very short term. Cab fare's eating me and the PATH hardly runs at night.

We're in his car, and he's just telling me about some bullshit job he's doing to pay the bills and asking my opinion about night work. Do I think it's fucking with my bio-rhythms?

I ask him to stop over on Rivington cause I need to see my man, Morris. He tells me, "no." We're going to *his* guy. It's his "treat."

"What do you get out of it?"

"I want to get some pancakes. I want your company."

So we make the buy on Avenue A. Then he makes a second stop, runs into some bar to buy coke. Gets back in and starts looking for parking, asks me where I want to have breakfast.

"Breakfast? Shit. I gotta fix first, if you wouldn't mind?"

He tries to convince me to wait. Like it's gonna be better if we do the shit later. I go to get out of the car. So he says, "Okay, but lets save the coke then, for after we eat? Dessert?"

I'm thinking the scene is getting weird. It's not a shock, his using. I've seen Wall Street types with habits. But I'm getting a bad feeling about the whole way he picked me up at the club. All I want to do is go to work and use enough so I don't get sick. I don't even want sex anymore. It just messes things up. I want money to maintain my own space and I want peace of fuckin mind. But he's out for what? Information for his precious story?

We wind up at his apartment, which I don't get why we had to bother with the stairs and all, but he doesn't wanna shoot in the car, and it's his dime. We do the shit, and right away, he was like, "let's go eat."

I'm like, "Peter what is your fuckin hurry, man?"

So we drag our nodding butts down to the Ukrainian Parlor. Where I might add, the snotty Polack waitress gives us some major attitude.

We're making polite chitchat. Then he goes, real casual, "You happen to know where I can find Raven?"

I just kinda stare at him hoping he isn't gonna notice the way my stomach jumped up into my throat. "Excuse me?"

"You know her, right? Worked at your club. She was going out with a friend of mine."

I figure I gotta be cool with this. "Puerto Rican? Good looking guy? That's your friend?"

"Yeah," he says.

"One day she didn't show up. You mean she didn't come home?"

"Her boyfriend doesn't know where she is." He shoves a forkful of blueberry pancakes into his mouth. "You worried about her?"

The truth – damn straight I was worried. My first thought when she didn't show, Joe's back in town and he's cleaning house.

"Worried? Nah. I figure she got another job. Happens a lot. Probably had a fight with your friend and took a geographic."

"That must be it," he goes.

He doesn't say anymore about it. We're mostly sitting back. Bullshitting. I tell him how they dropped me from my program for dirty urine. Time for Plan B. Just try to keep things under control.

He starts talking about how things are different in Europe. It's legal there, and free – medication. Then he's talking about some plant that may end dope craving and people he knew were investing in it.

"You can sign me up," I tell him.

I'm ready to go back to my place, but he reminds me about the coke.

"One time, in my life, I want to say no, man. I told you, I'm trying for *control*."

"It's not like you're buying."

"I don't think so."

But he goes, "Please, please come back with me," like a little boy – he's holding my hand and swinging my arm, like some kid's game. What woman can resist that crap? So we head to his apartment again, back up the damn stairs.

I get myself comfortable on the couch. Shoes off, feet up, music on. He hands me a drink, a screwdriver, which I don't particularly need, but I don't say no. We do the coke. I'm starting to feel pretty fine, thinking, maybe he brought me here to show me what a man he is after last time. That wouldn't be bad. I'm thinking I want it. I want him to be gentle. I'm betting a guy like that would know how to be *easy*. Shit, I just put my hand on my thigh and I could feel like he was already inside me.

He's sitting next to me on the couch. I'm waiting for him to make his move. He looks at me and says real soft, "Kyra, tell me what happened that day in the apartment with Joe and Moira and Lenny and Ingrid and you. Tell me how Ingrid died."

It's like a car crash. Time stands still and then, boom, *impact*. I feel something coming up and run over to the john. Almost make it, just a little on the floor. And no way I'm gonna clean it after what he's pulled!

I rinse my mouth, come back into the living room, and start putting on my shoes.

He's still sitting there. "I'm sorry, I'm sorry I upset you, Kyra." He's going on about how worried he is. He doesn't want me to get hurt. He tells me how he's heard stuff. He knows I was in the apartment.

"Who the fuck told you that? *Raven?* She wasn't there, man!"

"Not when it happened, but she told me what she walked into.

I'm somewhere between stone numb and Bellevue crazy. That whole ugly trip was coming back to me.

"You taking this to the cops?"

"They're asking me about it. But it's like I said. I protect my sources. I'm protecting Raven. I don't want to hurt you either. I just want you to tell me what happened. I know it's hard."

"Jesus, Peter. I feel sick. Could we shoot another bag?"

He pats my hand. He goes over to the bathroom. Cleans the puke up and comes out with a couple of tiny pills which I recognize. Valiums. He puts my drink in front of me, and tells me it'll make me feel better.

I swallowed the meds and sat there a minute, then just started sobbing and it felt like I was somewhere else far away just watching this crazy bitch crying on a couch.

❖ ❖ ❖

Peter

I went too far with Kyra, too fast. When I told her I knew she was there when Ingrid was killed, it was a bluff. All I had was Raven placing her there *after* the murder, but judging by her reaction, it was a good guess. I think she wanted to tell me, but she wasn't ready.

She was volcanic. Tears pouring from her eyes, her nose running, and I felt her wet mouth as she leaned into my neck.

At first, I thought it was an act. Sure she was upset, but she was probably putting it on a bit to get me to lay off. But she kept it up too long for that. I put my arms around her, trying to calm her. I felt a kind of envy for the way she could release everything. Even though her face was red and swollen, it was strangely attractive. I wanted to lick those salt tears, taste their power.

I was wondering at what point I'd have to drive her to a hospital, and how I would explain what had happened. I was thinking about calling Dr. Leider for advice.

Her body began to relax in my arms. Her breathing became slower, fewer gulps. The coke was wearing off. I guess we were both dead tired. I walked her to my bed. We lay down together fully clothed. I was frightened, not sure whether or not she'd really be okay. I kept listening to her breaths, which by then were quiet and steady. She must have fallen asleep. Then I did as well. The next thing I remember hearing was some rustling. I was still out of it, figured she was probably getting ready to leave. Part of me wanted to wake up and stop her, apologize even, but I didn't have the energy. I heard my apartment door close.

When I woke up again it was going on nine o'clock, Sunday night. I'd slept over twelve hours, and in twenty-four I'd be getting ready to go back to the law firm. My body ached as I left the bed. My head felt like it was undergoing construction. I wished Johnny had had a phone, because I wanted to call him just for reassurance that it had to be a hangover from the coke, that I couldn't possibly have already developed a physical addiction to the smack.

I still had two bags from the buy and wanted to do one for my head. But when I checked my jacket pocket they were gone. I guess she deserved something. I was glad she'd taken the dope because it kept our connection. I could confront her the next time I saw her.

I searched and found a couple of Fiorinal in the back of my medicine cabinet. They were Delia's – for her migraines. I couldn't remember exactly how, when, or why I had them. I downed one with a stale piece of bread and then made it out to the street.

I thought of stopping in to see Johnny and passed by his place. I could see his lights, but I rang the buzzer and didn't get an answer, so I walked on. Found an unsold copy of *The Sunday New York Times* and went over to Diner-Diner which is overpriced and not as good as the Ukrainian Parlor but I try not to walk into the same restaurant twice in a twenty-four hour period.

As I waited for my order, I started skimming the paper. Buried deep in the *Metro* section, I came across a filler: *"Activist" Seized at Airport – Claims hallucinogen will cure opiate addiction.* Sean had arrived home.

The article was classic Sean. They quoted him saying, *"The government's persecution of myself and others in this matter is yet more evidence of their enmeshment in the sale and distribution of narcotics. The medication which I had in my possession could end the so called 'drug-problem,' overnight."*

I was thinking I could put together a piece for *The Eye*. I must have been operating on the same channel as Sean because when I got home and checked my messages, the man himself had invited me to dinner, date and time to be arranged.

Johnny

The way Johnny figured it, you couldn't really blame him for how it finally went down with El Rey.

It was the fault of market forces. Federico himself was always pointing out how the CIA, in order to finance their cocaine sponsored Contra War, was flooding the streets with cheap white powder leading to a reduction in demand and subsequent profit for pot.

His supply came mostly from a cooperative of organic growers in California. The quality was high, but lately there'd been problems with arrests and seizures. A shipment was supposed to have come in a week ago, but the carrier had gotten busted. The two and a half pounds they'd been keeping in the refrigerator at Johnny's was the last they'd have for at least another week.

Johnny was setting out for the office with the dope tucked securely in the inside pocket of his overcoat. He was going to meet El Rey who wanted to "supervise" – "watch the scales – as they'd weigh it out into eighth and sixteenth of an ounce bags. The plan was to sell small quantities and then go on "vacation" until they could work out the supply problem. The silent partners had offered them some Mexican, but El Rey thought it was inferior product and probably full of pesticides. He wouldn't even consider mixing it in.

"Better to close down then screw with the integrity of our brand," he insisted.

Johnny left his building for the eight-block walk to the office. It was windy, maybe lower forties, but he didn't feel the chill. His new girl, Victoria had bought him a camel hair coat at Barney's. He'd never even been inside Barney's before. He really dug Victoria, too. She worked for Sophisticated Escorts. He could already see how her age obsession might get to be a problem. She was thirty and kept saying it was a drag because the men were always requesting under twenty-five, and at $300 an hour they got what they wanted. But she was *fine*. Smart and funny too. Johnny didn't expect it to last forever, but it was a beautiful morning full of possibilities.

He was passing by the headquarters of the Revolutionary Anarchist Action Network, a small sub-street level storefront of a three-story apartment house. A guy he vaguely knew from some community meetings was taking boxes out of an old station wagon parked in front of a pump. The guy, Earl, said "hello" and asked him if he wanted to help.

At that moment, two cute girls came out of the basement. They both had long reddish hair and there was something about the way they were looking at each other that made Johnny immediately suspect they were lovers.

He had plenty of time to get to the office, was going to stop for coffee anyway, so he started to pitch in with the boxes.

He began chatting with one of the girls who explained that she and her friend had been attending a women's Wicca workshop, and they decided to stay around and assist Earl with the boxes because the Network was such an important community resource.

The girl started to complain about how some man wanted to come in and use the Anarchist Library during their class, and accused them of being fascist because they weren't allowing men. Johnny said something about supporting women's spirituality, and this seemed to please both of the girls.

Then after they'd finished the task, Earl, who knew that Johnny worked for El Rey, asked him if he had any pot. Johnny figured they could roll a joint from the stash. He'd tell El Rey and let him take it out of his pay. He was getting worried about being late. So just to be extra responsible, Johnny went to the corner and called the office leaving a message on the machine (which answered with his own resonant voice) informing his boss (who probably hadn't arrived yet himself) that he was delayed and would be in shortly.

Earl took out his pipe and they were burning a few bowls with the girls when this Brit named Greg stopped in with his girl. They were passing by and smelled the party. Greg was tall, thin and pale with that classic tubercular look that artistic women always go for. Johnny thought that if he were a girl he'd go for Greg. It made him wish he could get it up for a man because he was willing to bet Greg would be a grade-A lay.

Johnny was thinking he should get a move on soon, but Greg's girl was doing some heavy flirting and he didn't really want to leave. Then Greg said, "We're all such fuckin beautiful people. We should have an orgy."

The Wicca girls giggled and one asked him to explain exactly what he meant.

He said they should start by just taking off their clothes partnering up and seeing what happened.

"Boy girl, boy girl?" someone asked.

Greg laughed, "We're fucking anarchists. It doesn't matter."

There was no way at this point that Johnny was going to say, "Oh excuse me, I have to get to the office."

There were some old futons on the floor. Red and black paint covered the storefront window. Earl locked the door and they all undressed.

The Wicca girls took a futon and started touching each other. Greg and Earl both watched stroking themselves. Johnny was feeling a little self-conscious when Greg's girl tapped him on the shoulder and pointed to a futon. As the other's joined in, it wound up being his first five way, six if you counted Earl who was standing, hovering, pipe in mouth, hands on prick taking in the scene.

The party dissipated slowly. Earl wandered away at some point. Then Greg and his girl said they were going to get some food. The Wicca girls invited Johnny to go with them to the witchcraft store. He declined. He went to use the toilet and when he came out discovered he was the last one remaining. He put on his clothes and looked for his coat, but it was gone along with his beeper and whatever had been left of El Rey's stash.

The last place he wanted to head for was the office. He knew he'd have to talk to El Rey eventually. Tell him he got mugged or something. His boss wouldn't buy it and his ass was fried. At least, if he were apologetic and promised to pay back the value of the dope – which of course he'd never be able to do – El Rey could provide some cushion between him and the silent partners whom he did not want coming after him with baseball bats. But he was not looking forward to the inevitable look of hurt and disappointment on El Rey's face. He could already see him shaking his head, saying, "Johnny, Johnny, you're such a smart boy. How could you do this?" Same as his grandma.

He figured before facing that, he might as well go back to the apartment and gather his stuff. It would have been looking like another bleak Christmas if Victoria hadn't already offered to move him in. She was staying at the Floradora, a renovated Yuppie condo across from the park. This john with whom she was kind of friends, had bought it as an investment, and was renting it to her in return for trade. He was in his seventies and still had an active libido, loved his wife but didn't want to fuck her anymore and came by maybe once or twice a week. Probably wouldn't be crazy about her moving her boyfriend in, but he always called first. They'd just have to be discreet.

Johnny hoped she wouldn't get on him too much about getting another job. He'd need to keep a low profile for a while and after the shit he knew El Rey would throw at him, he was going to need a long vacation.

Peter

I was standing in front of Sean's house, imagining that as soon as my finger pressed the front door bell, time would be displaced. Judith was going to answer the door, so tiny in some oversize tee shirt. She'd yell for Chic. I would be welcomed and fed and who knew who might drop by? Kunstler, Abbie Hoffman if he wasn't on the run. Or maybe one of Judith's artist friends.

I'd run in to Sean in the late spring shortly after I moved down. Still, when he opened the door and greeted me with his traditional bear hug, I was, as always, startled by his appearance.

The first time I saw him, he was a burly Celt. Well over six-feet tall, broad shouldered, with long red hair and eyes so light blue that in photos his irises were invisible. In those days, the little color in them sparkled. He'd wink at his own jokes. Now those eyes were devoid of any emotion. They functioned – recognized faces and forms. Sometimes he'd look from side to side, searching for the hidden recording device he was certain the government had left, or he might stare straight through you as he'd talk, without stopping even for breath, going on and on about the latest outrage inflicted on the people. His thunderous voice the only feature unchanged by time.

The most dramatic difference had to be the hair loss. Even his eyebrows were gone. At first, he'd worn wigs, but soon gave up on that. I never asked him about the condition. The one time he'd mentioned it in my presence, was during one of his tirades involving both the incompetence and ignorance of Western medicine and the deviousness of the COINTELPRO conspiracy.

As he'd gained weight around his middle, he'd taken to cultivating his Buddha like appearance by wearing robes ordered from a meditation center.

Despite the extra girth, he always seemed smaller than I remembered, probably because that first time I'd been shorter than he was and had spurted up later.

"Good to see you, Teller," he said. "Welcome home."

His living room smelled of residue pot and mildew. He invited me to sit on the couch, the same couch I'd sat in ten years before, which was hardly new then, and now featured a spring visibly popping up and innumerable scratch marks left by innumerable cats.

He went into the kitchen, and I heard the whirring of his juicer. He emerged a couple minutes later, a proud smile crinkling his features, as he handed me a celery, beet and carrot with wheat grass juice.

We toasted, naturally enough to good health. He lit up a joint and immediately launched into a monologue on Africa, the iboga plant, and US customs.

As he didn't allow the use of recording devices for interviews, I struggled with my notepad to catch the gist.

"Fix your mind on it Teller. Imagine! I don't know that it'll make a difference with this crack thing. But all the heroin addicts, overnight. Cured! *Cured.* And that's what our government wants to stop. They're bringing the shit in. You know what the opium of the masses is in this country? It's fuckin opium, man."

He went on in this mode for close to an hour telling me more than anyone needs to know about body cavity searches. Then he stopped abruptly and said, "Guess it's time for dinner."

He went back into the kitchen and returned carrying a tray with two steaming bowls of soup. It was a variation of the soup that Judith had made the first night I'd been in that house. Broth seasoned with cilantro, garlic, lemon grass and pepper. Filled with shrimp, mussels, clams and squid.

"So what's up with you, Teller?"

"I guess I'm okay for a man cursed to eternal damnation," I said while stirring the pungent liquid, taking in the mingling aromas.

He asked me what I meant, so I laid out the whole saga for him, beginning at the beginning, the first night I'd laid eyes on Ingrid at Wigstock and ending with Jacques Lanoir's hex – minus a few details such as sex with a minor and my own excursions to Needlelandia.

It was good to watch Sean as he listened. He laughed in the right places. His eyes had the old gleam. But by the time I'd finished, his forehead was so furrowed that if he'd had eyebrows they would have met in the center of his face.

"I'd be careful around Jacques," he said.

"You know him?"

Sean laughed. "Teller, haven't you figured it out yet? I'm God. I know everyone."

"He's been on the scene awhile?"

"Yeah," Sean said. "You could say that."

"I know you've got some story to tell me, McFarland."

He rubbed his hand across his baby smooth chin. "Put down the notebook Jimmy Olsen. What I got stays between friends."

Sean began to tell me how sometime back in the late sixties maybe early seventies, a couple of guys came to him with an idea. The guys were his friend Federico Fernandez, these days better known as El Rey, and a friend of his, French-Canadian, named Jacques.

Federico had just been down in Mexico where he'd done some peyote. A fellow traveler had informed him that the stuff was legal in the US for ritual use by certain Native Americans. Federico found this to be a revelation. He started thinking about the Rastas and how come they couldn't use pot legally. Had to be a racial thing. Then his mind kept going. Okay, what if there were white Rastas? Or Latinos who believed in Native American practices? The first

Puerto Ricans, after all, were Boricua. Federico didn't know a lot about that history, but maybe they could get an anthropologist to look into it and uncover legitimate ancient practices involving marijuana. As Federico went on, Sean was starting to wonder what the angle was. What did they want from *him*?

Federico slowed down enough to explain. He wanted them to start their own religion. They should make it as legitimate as they could, write a bible or something. Federico was thinking that Sean was an educated man and could help, not only with ideas, but contacts too. They could rent a church. Charge for membership and ask for donations. They'd conduct daily services using marijuana as a sacrament. Maybe add on the occasional peyote ritual. Federico was already planning to wear a flowing robe – something Pope-like but with a little extra glitz. He even had a boyfriend who owned a religious supply store so they could get the decorations wholesale.

"There will inevitably be certain legal complications," Sean pointed out.

Federico was undaunted. "So we're gonna be discreet. We invite people like any religion. We talk about the experiences, the prophecies. We *promote*. Maybe we make the ceremonies like members only. If we get busted, we take it to court. We get lawyers like those Indians. And then after we win, shit everyone's gonna wanna join the church. That's how we legalize it, man."

"Lawyers?" Sean asked. "Lawyers cost."

Federico admitted they were hoping for some support from him on that. "Look man, if this thing works, it's gonna put your business through the sky."

Sean, who hadn't met Jacques before, asked him what his connection to this was.

Federico talked for his friend. "Oh man, this guy is like an expert in ceremonial shit. He's my consultant."

Sean felt this was not for him. First off, despite his anarchist leanings, and distrust of all forms of organized power, he still had never quite lost his college freshman enthusiasm for Marx. Religion, even a *sham* religion set up as a business venture did not sit well. He was sure there would be followers, vulnerable idiots lacking any sense of irony who'd actually believe in it.

Second, he knew there was no way they'd win legally, and while he was not averse to supporting lawyers fighting the good fight, he preferred to choose battles with at least slightly better odds.

Yet, he found his friend's energy appealing. He didn't wind up giving his official sanction, but he did agree to lend Federico some startup funds, and talk to legal contacts about doing *pro bono* when there was a bust.

Federico, for his part, listened to Sean's advice about never keeping too much product on the premises. The two of them, with very little input from Jacques who spoke and moved so little, that Sean assumed he was on some kind of trip, spent an hour or so coming up with different names for the new sect.

They discussed and rejected, Church of the Boricuan Warrior, Aboriginal Church of America, Church of Maria y Juan, and Church of the Peaceful Pipe. They finally settled on The Church of Joy and Abundance.

I was enjoying the story which Sean continued uninterrupted as he journeyed to and from the kitchen refilling our soup bowls. But he had been going on for a while, so I waited till he was chewing a piece of delicious but slightly tough homemade multi-grain sour-dough, and I asked, "And how again does this relate to my being careful around Jacques?"

He gulped the last remaining soup from his bowl, swirled it around his mouth and swallowed. "Oh yee of little faith, have patience."

Sean never expected to see a return on his investment in the Church. He was in it purely for the entertainment value. He rented El Rey a storefront on East 10th, in a building he owned through a dummy corporation, charging a dollar a month. He'd stop by sometimes and watch as his friend ardently oversaw the renovations. It was theater. Even Federico's vestments were made of cardboard, foil and tissue paper, liberally sprinkled with glitter. They had a large opening "ceremony" in which Federico gave communion, using as wafers, oatmeal cookies garnished with

Acapulco gold. After that, they'd have services a couple of times a week. Federico would greet the crowd, and everyone donated five dollars upon entering. They'd do some chants and have a party. The place began to get a rep.

Federico mentioned something about mice, so one afternoon Sean decided to stop by in his landlord capacity and see how bad it was. Maybe lay out a couple of traps – the no kill kind of course. He heard some sounds inside which seemed a little strange, but figured Federico was probably letting some kids crash. He turned the key and opened the door.

"Jacques was there in black robes. The crosses were, I shit you not, upside down. There were four or five kids with him . . ."

"Children?"

"Teenagers. Boys and girls. Naked. One little girl, she had this really strange look on her face and she was holding a chalice. She sees me and spills it. There was blood in it, Teller. This was like right when the Manson thing was happening in California. *Not* something I wanted to be associated with."

"So what did you do?"

"I said 'What the fuck is going on?' Jacques tells me, he's conducting a sacred ritual which I've disturbed. He kind of nods towards the kids and they start getting dressed. Then they leave. I told Federico about it. He said he thought Jacques was okay, but he'd tell him to cool it.

"I mean it's not like I found him strangling a goat or anything. Though, maybe that would've been better cause at least then I would've known where the blood came from. But you can see why I have a weird feeling about the guy."

Sean went on to tell me about the final days of the church. A Saturday night mass got busted. Just a passing patrol car hearing music and smelling the smoke. Federico wanted to push the religious aspect. Sean got a lawyer friend to advise him, but Federico represented himself. The lawyer talked Federico into claiming the whole thing was meant as a statement, a satire of organized religion. Federico was giving a performance and it wasn't his responsibility if some of the patrons decided to light up. There was no evidence of sale and Federico got off.

"What about Jacques? I mean, all you have is this one wacky ritual that may or may not have involved the use of blood, which may or may not have been human. Don't tell me you believe in the guy's curse."

"Of course I don't, Teller. Look, all I'm saying is, there were a lot of young kids drifting through in those days. Runaways. More than now. And that guy, he could *influence* people. I mean, look at Lenny.

"It just got me thinking. Let's say a young person disappeared suddenly. No one would have thought anything about it."

He sat back for a minute leaving me to ponder his statement.

"Are you telling me there was human sacrifice taking place in the East Village? Because if that is what you're saying, I wish you'd fill me in on some details so I could collect my Pulitzer."

"It's not what I'm saying. All I'm saying is that this Jacques guy, might be dangerous. Maybe even if he wasn't involved in the Ingrid Hess thing the way you think, he's got something else to hide. This could be like throwing shit in a sandstorm. Piss some folks off."

"Like you?"

"I don't know what good it's gonna do me if you start writing about Lenny's working for Federico. I don't know what good it does anyone for you to say it was some kind of anti-yuppie backlash motivation for killing that girl. That's just how I feel. I'm not gonna do anything about it. But maybe there's people out there with stronger feelings."

I wasn't sure if it was that number we'd smoked making me paranoid. Was Sean threatening me? Giving me some kind of veiled warning about someone else who might want to stop me? Maybe he was just projecting his own conspiracy obsessions. I changed the subject. Asked him some more about Ibogaine. He lit another joint and we had tea and dessert.

Before I left he touched my shoulder and said, "Peter, I wasn't trying to discourage you. You do what you have to. I just don't want to lose you man. Be careful, all right?"

❖ ❖ ❖

Dr. Sharon

Dr. Sharon Horowitz had not yet met the young reporter who was pestering her with phone calls, though she had finally agreed to meet him for lunch.

He'd "check-in" about once a week, always wanting to see Lenny who still refused to talk with the press. She made it clear she could not be persuaded to influence her patient in that regard. Nor could she break his confidentiality by discussing his case. Peter Teller, for his part, was always dropping hints about what he knew.

"Look I'm not the police," she told him. "Talk to them."

He told her he had, but they needed Lenny to tell them the truth.

"My job is to treat the patient, not solve a crime."

He pushed the angle that they should meet anyway, so he could get more background. She put him off, but was beginning to enjoy the way he was trying to charm her, telling her what an important underappreciated job she had, mentioning how much he looked forward to their conversations. She wasn't planning on straddling an ethical divide by meeting with him, but it was nice to be quasi-flirted with by someone with employment, someone who wasn't strapped down in five-points trying to beat a rap.

When she found out that Peter had played the original Travis Harrison on *The Wild and the Innocent*, it was too much to resist. It turned out a friend of hers had enjoyed a short "fling" with him the previous summer.

Her friend, a lawyer, filled Sharon in on her brief "romance" with Peter.

"You know actors. Self-absorbed, non-committal. It went great as long as we were talking about *him*."

Suddenly Sharon was entertaining some serious fantasies about their potential lunch. It wasn't that she was out to seduce him or let herself be seduced by him. It was just the idea of sharing a meal with a handsome single man. She'd watched the soap on and off since high school, sometimes still catching a minute or two as she passed the "recreation room" on the unit. She remembered his brief portrayal of Brent Harrison and his twin. Travis was still a character on the show, though they'd killed off Brent who was accidentally murdered by someone who mistook him for his brother. Then Travis had to pretend to be Brent, a neurosurgeon, for several months.

"Don't talk to him about the soap," her friend warned. "He's a snob about it. He went all moody and passive aggressive on me when I mentioned it."

Sharon decided to play it "cool." She waited for his call, then firmly told him, "Well, as long as we're clear about my limits with patient confidentiality, I suppose I could just talk to you about the general concepts of my work . . ."

She agreed to meet him at some blintz joint in the East Village. She was a little leery of going down there, but the East Village was supposed to be the coming thing, so when he suggested it, she didn't want to say no and seem unhip.

She'd never been much of a clotheshorse and usually wore scrubs at work. She put on jeans and a simple silk blouse, along with a black blazer she'd found in a consignment shop on the Cape. Looking herself over in the mirror, she didn't think anyone would take her for an actual neighborhood denizen.

Her four-year-old daughter, Nicola, noticed something different that morning, and murmured approvingly but with just a hint of anxiety, "Mommy you look pretty today."

Pretty. That was it. She wanted to concentrate on that. Put on some lipstick. Transform her even more. She examined her face in the mirror, observing each freckle and wrinkle as carefully as a dermatologist. It wasn't that she was bad looking. She had what her ex had called a "simple peasant look" although she was never sure how he meant that. Wide Semitic nose, hourglass shape that tended to get a little *zoftig* if she wasn't careful. Her best feature was her hair, long and thick, the color of dark honey with just a hint of red. Usually she preferred to tie it back and not wear any make up – fewer hassles with patients, and she thought her male colleagues took her more seriously as well.

She dropped her daughter off at the hospital staff day care center and at lunch time took a cab down to the Ukrainian Parlor, arriving a few minutes late on purpose. She removed her bulky but functional down coat as soon as she stepped through the door. Peter Teller was already there. She didn't want him to know she knew what he looked like from the soap, so she glanced around the restaurant as though she were wondering whether the tall blond man with the gray sports jacket was the same tall blond man with a gray sports jacket that she'd been told to look for.

"Dr. Horowitz, Sharon?" he asked.

"Peter Teller, I presume," she said shaking his hand and hating herself for the preciousness she heard in her own voice.

She looked over the menu while he made small talk. He appeared younger in person than she remembered his being on TV. *"Twenty five,"* she thought, *"Maybe he's twenty-six. Definitely too young for someone over thirty. What was I thinking?"*

He was telling her how happy he was that she'd agreed to come. He was saying that for the past few months "the Matthews thing" had been his life. Despite his height and the jacket and tie, she felt there was something unformed about him, boyish. She observed the way he was drumming his fingers on the table as he spoke. At first she simply noticed the fingers, long and smooth, but then she realized how quickly they were moving, out of rhythm with his speech. She was conscious that she was observing this *clinically* and wondered whether his "nervousness," if that's what it was, had anything to do with her.

It was strange. He was a reporter. She'd expected him to "pump" her. But instead he just went on and on, telling her about his theories. He thought other people had been involved. He didn't think Lenny had even been the one to kill Ingrid. She wondered if he was trying to trick her into giving him some information.

"It's like I explained to you on the phone," she said, "I can't discuss *anything* Lenny has said to me. I can't confirm or deny if he's even brought up any of those people you've mentioned. All I'm willing to do is in a very nonspecific way . . ."

"Okay, okay," he said quickly, "Let's say in a very general way, yeah, there was this guy, he's kind of crazy, I'm sorry I mean let's say he's a schizophrenic, he has a *chronic mental illness*, okay? And he's talking about killing someone, only then he has this friend who's even more crazy, violent, and this friend kills her, and then maybe they try to convince him that he did it. Like could they do that, a schizophrenic say, convince him that he did it?"

"Theoretically?"

"Yeah, or like could someone be a schizophrenic but also be sane enough to be scared shitless to the point where he's willing to take the rap?" He was speaking loudly enough now that other patrons were looking.

"Hypothetically?" She asked. Noting to herself: *rapid speech, voluminous, interruptive.*

"Hypothetically," he agreed. The food had arrived. He'd ordered potato blintzes with applesauce and sour cream. She'd gone for the water packed tuna with a salad consisting mostly of iceberg lettuce. She stared with envy at his plate, which he hardly touched.

"We know that schizophrenia is a disease," Sharon said, hoping she wasn't sounding too pedantic, conscious that the man across from her used to play a doctor on TV. She was wondering why he couldn't stop moving his hands. She was looking into his big blue eyes and thinking that he couldn't possibly be Jewish. "Just like cancer is a *disease*. We don't know exactly what causes it. But, yes, a person with schizophrenia would still react to fear, to threats. They might *perceive* situations differently because . . ."

"Because of the illness," he finished for her. "Yeah, that's it. Thanks. It just what I was thinking. Lenny's petrified, right? Joe could come after him and . . ."

"Peter, look, I really can't discuss it with you. Let's stick to the general or change the subject. What got you so interested in this anyway?"

He shook his head and smiled. She imagined he was one of those slightly dangerous men, always a little out of control, the kind she had dated in college, before settling for the supposedly reliable ex, whose M-CAT scores were lower than hers, so he'd wound up being an embittered dentist who'd left her for his hygienist.

He laughed and said, "Oh I get it. Right? You're analyzing me! Brilliant. Sharon, do you believe in fate? Man, if I started to tell you, really tell you about some of the things I've uncovered, some of the things I've *experienced* since I've been working on this, you would think, oh Jesus! I'm sorry the way I'm going on. I didn't get any sleep last night. I've been working nights, proofreading?"

"Tangential," Sharon thought as she listened, *"That's rapid voluminous speech, interruptive, lack of appetite and now we've got tangential."*

"I mean there I was sitting on a bench when I saw Ingrid Hess. Then she's in the papers dead two months later. That's what I mean. It's like destiny. And it doesn't stop there. I have this source I found, he knows these people and . . ."

Grandiose. He ran off in so many different directions, talking one moment about a warlock's hex and how there might be human sacrifice going on around the block, then some story about a lawyer making him write things on paper because of government surveillance, and now he was jumping to a description of a strip joint in New Jersey. Sharon tried to slow him down, make sense of everything he was telling her. It was something she was good at, making sense of other people's stories. By the time he took the check, she had come to several conclusions.

The first was that Peter Teller was in all probability suffering from bipolar disorder in its hypo-manic, or milder, phase. The implications were that he could become fully manic – even psychotic, or he could crash into a deep, possibly suicidal depression. He might be prone to alcoholism or drug abuse if he wasn't being properly medicated and monitored.

The second conclusion was that though he was somewhat higher functioning, he was not very different from the patients she saw every day at the hospital.

Despite these beliefs, she hoped he would not, in the disorganization of his mania, lose the home phone number she'd given him, because if he ever called her, she would eagerly run to his rescue.

❖❖❖

Peter

The night work was screwing with my bio-rhythms. I was using all kinds of chemicals to keep my sleeping and waking hours straight and get my real work done.

Weeknights I'd wake up around ten thirty, make myself some coffee, mix in a little brandy, maybe some rum. Sometimes I'd snort a few lines of coke if I had any around, just an eye opener – too much and I'd be crashing at work. It wasn't as if the yuppie lawyers weren't doing it themselves all night long. Then the car service would come to pick me up and I'd try to get through the next eight hours at the office, a model of efficiency. Come home a little hyper, work on my notes for a while. Go out and have some breakfast, sometimes shoot a bag to mellow out, listen to music, do some notes on the book or on a freelance piece. I'd need a Restoril and or Klonopin to actually fall asleep. Even with the pills I'd usually wake up four or five hours later, run necessary errands, write more until I crashed again, then wake up around ten-thirty and start the cycle once more.

One Sunday night, I figured it was time to follow up with Kyra so I went back to the club and found she was gone. The owner didn't have a current address for her. I brought up Raven and started to bluff about knowing he hired underage girls. He showed me her employee card, which had a Xerox of a driver's license saying she was eighteen. I wrote down the name – her real one, maybe.

Johnny said she was from Long Island. The name on the card was Jennifer Goldberg and there were about a hundred Goldberg's listed in the Nassau county phone book.

Sometime Monday afternoon I heard my buzzer and made my way toward the intercom. It was Ouspenski. I'd been meaning to call him, trade some info, but I was holding and didn't particularly want him in my home. I buzzed him up anyway and spent the time it took him to climb the stairs hiding whatever incriminating evidence happened to be laying around.

I offered him a cup of coffee.

He told me he was just passing by. Hoped I'd had a merry Christmas or whatever I celebrated. Asked me again if I was still looking into the Matthews thing.

I told him I was going to write a book about it.

"A book," he repeated smirking like it was a punch line. "Yeah, I heard you was telling that to his shrink."

"I guess that means *you* still consider it an open case?"

He smiled. Said he still talked to Lenny occasionally. It looked like they were going to declare him competent for trial. The district attorney and his public defender would both agree he'd done it and was crazy. He reminded me there was no statute of limitations on murder. If they had the evidence it might be possible to indict others as accessories later on.

I was thinking by now Moira's father had had enough time to get word to her, so I told him I'd heard Joe might have gone to a commune in Oregon called Blythedale, that his real name might have been Jerome Comb or Combs, and he'd spent time or done some, in Ohio.

He asked me where I'd gotten my information. I reminded him that I couldn't tell him my sources, but I would encourage them to come forward.

"And I suppose you're telling me this because you're a concerned citizen."

"I told you I'd let you know when I found anything. Besides, I'd like to find out more about this guy myself. If you can tell me where he lived in Ohio, his record, any background. . ."

"Sounds like you think he was involved. What would make you think that, Teller?"

I figured once Joe was in custody, maybe I'd be able to convince Mirabella to go to the police. As for Raven, I'd try to get Ingrid's diary if I could, but I wanted to keep the girl out of it.

"Nothing very specific. Word on the street is he's not a very nice person."

"Word on the street?" he repeated like I'd just told him another great joke.

We ran out of conversation. He finished his coffee. Thanked me and announced he had to go. He told me he'd let me know about Joe.

"Don't work too hard, Teller. You look like you're losing weight," he said.

I looked at his stomach and patted my own. "Jealous, detective?" I asked, trying for a tone of lighthearted banter which under the circumstances felt about as natural as a McDonald's milkshake.

Chapter 14

Dinner at Eight

Johnny

It was a month since that horrible day when El Rey shook his head exactly the way Johnny had imagined, and told him to stay away from Little Italy and the safehouse because though he would do his best to convince the silent partners that it had been a freak occurrence which went down exactly the way Johnny told him – some kids, (*mooleys*, the Italian's would assume, and he'd let them) a wolf-pack running wild, mowing down Johnny while he just happened to be transporting product – El Rey was not certain the partners would be convinced.

Federico's parting words of wisdom were, "If I was you man, I'd go Greyhound tonight, and don't even think of asking me to lend you dinero for that."

Johnny could almost laugh about it now as he sat in the rooftop atrium café of the Floradora, savoring his second cappuccino, overlooking the swimming pool and thinking that things had not gone too badly after all. He was tempted to go back and tell his old boss, "See, I'm doing all right. I'm not such a fuck-up."

On the other hand, Federico might then ask him to pay him back for the stolen product.

Victoria was in the apartment with her old man. She'd told Johnny to wait for her to fetch him, which he was obediently doing.

In addition to letting her stay rent-free in the space, the geezer usually tipped her a couple of hundred which she and Johnny would likely spend on a fine dinner with some wine and maybe a little blow.

He was pretty satisfied with the relationship. Victoria had black hair like she must have been part Native American, green eyes with dark flecks. Her breasts were small but he liked that she'd never had them "done." They stood up on their own and her nipples were the color of cocoa. There was enough of a butt to grab onto, and long thin legs which she could wrap around him in innumerable combinations, though she didn't seem crazy about penetration – got more of it than she needed from her clients, she'd say.

Like all women, she had her moods. Sometimes she'd go off about how she'd wasted her whole life and now it was too late. She'd come to New York when she was seventeen. Some photographer passing through her town had told her she was pretty enough to model. It hadn't been the first time she'd heard that. They boffed a couple of times and he did some portfolio shots for free. Told her he could get her some work in New York, so she'd gone with him.

The "work" of course was all nude. Plus the guy tried to pimp her out to his "friends." She was smart enough to get away from that scene. Took her pictures and went to some legit modeling agencies where she was told to come back after she lost weight, got a nose job and better teeth. She eventually shed the pounds, had her nose fixed and capped the broken front tooth, all thanks to the money she was by then earning as an escort. She went back to the modeling agencies, but gave that up after finding out that even if they'd sign a girl "a shade under" five foot six, there wasn't going to be much work, and besides it was just as easy to fake an orgasm for some guy in a hotel room as for a photographer in a studio.

Thirteen years later, no money saved, most of her daily earnings spent on smack and blow, she was beginning to worry.

Johnny for his part would listen sympathetically when she went on about her troubles. He resented having to vacate when the old man came, but knew he wasn't exactly in a position to vent his feelings on the subject.

He *was* grateful to Victoria for letting him stay. That first night he'd showed up – his best clothes and assorted paltry possessions stuffed in a duffel bag, the rest abandoned, without even cab fare for the five block trip – she'd looked at him like he'd been expected.

She didn't press him about what happened, but managed to ask a question or two, and let him know when some part of his answer didn't make sense, so finally by the next afternoon, she'd heard everything.

"I think it's very sweet, you letting me stay," he told her.

"You know, Johnny," she said biting her lip the way she sometimes did, "Most guys, they see a woman in the profession I'm in, they want to rescue *her*."

Johnny looked around the living room, taking in the white carpet, the leather sofa with matching chairs, the blond hardwood table and bookcases, the paintings – landscapes mostly which the old man himself had done. He looked at the stereo and the shelf of CDs, the TV and the VCR.

"I don't know," he said. "You don't look like you're doing too bad."

They'd had their worst argument earlier that morning. She'd wanted him to vacuum and straighten the place up while she got herself ready for her patron's visit.

Johnny didn't mind helping out. But she started bitching at him, reminding him to hide the shaving cream and other things he'd put in the medicine cabinet.

"I'm beginning to feel like there's not much difference between what you got going with me, and what that old man's got going with you."

She slapped his face. They were both quiet for a couple of very long seconds. Then she said softly, "Maybe you wouldn't feel that way if you got yourself a job."

That was when he started to grab his stuff.

"What are you doing? Where are you going?" she asked.

"Yeah, right," he said, "What kind of a job is a guy like me going to get? Security? Five dollars an hour, maybe? While you're making two hundred on your back. C'mon. You wanna stake me, maybe I can get something going, but you already made it clear you don't want me dealing out of the house, so don't start telling me to go find a job."

She started to cry, told him she was in love with him, that the last month had been the happiest of her life. He comforted her, whispering in her ear that he loved her as well. She told him she was sorry for acting like a bitch and asked him to please take back what he'd said about their relationship being like the one she had with the old man.

Johnny apologized, said of course it wasn't the same thing at all. They would've screwed except they had to hurry because of her client.

As they both worked on getting the place in order, she was talking about how she just wished they could be more "normal." Sometimes she thought of going away, maybe to the country. They could kick drugs and get jobs – waiting tables in a diner, or working on a farm.

Johnny nodded like he thought it would all be wonderful. She went on about what losers all her friends were, how she wished she could meet some people – other than johns – who were *doing* something with their lives.

He told her that maybe if she could just lend him the money for a health club membership, he could work on his body and who knows, get a job in construction or as a Chippendale or something.

She told him she'd start by giving him a couple of guest passes to her gym and see how that went. She kissed him good-bye and sent him on his way. He went to the roof with his newspaper. He was thinking about what she'd said about wanting to meet people and he thought of Peter. He was educated, good-looking, writing a book. Yeah, maybe they could invite Peter over, with a date even. Besides he wouldn't mind showing her off to him.

Peter

I hadn't heard from Johnny in a while. At first, I figured if he had anything new for me, he'd get in touch. Then I wanted to sound out some ideas, so I called Royal Messengers and was told by El Rey, "He don't work here no more." No details, followed by a click. I walked past his building where his name was no longer on the buzzer, and a moving van was delivering someone else's furniture. I thought I recognized a chair left on the street being used as a dog urinal.

From the stories Johnny had told me about his life, I half expected I'd find him waiting on my stoop, asking if he could crash on my couch for a few nights that would turn into months. But it was a about three weeks later he left me a phone message with a number. He sounded good.

I called, heard a woman's voice on the machine, started to speak and Johnny picked up.

I asked him about the job. He said things had been slow, supply problems. He was going to start working out, get his upper body into shape, and look into a minority apprentice program in the construction trades.

"My grandma used to say if you don't get an education, you better have a strong back."

"What about school?" I asked.

"People in construction make good money, man," he said. "I could start paying off the loans. Go back part time."

He asked how I was doing, so I mentioned meeting Lenny's shrink who could maybe be persuaded to help me get in to see him.

"She sounds substantial. Smart, a doctor. Good luck."

"It sounds like your having some luck yourself."

He told me about his new girl and the apartment. "Look, you want to come over sometime, dinner? She'd love to meet you. You could even bring your doctor friend."

I was touched that Johnny was asking me to his home. It wasn't about the story or what I could do for him. I told him I'd come. Couldn't vouch for Sharon. I wanted to go on a night when I wouldn't have to work, and he told me that Victoria was usually "booked" Saturdays, so we arranged it for Sunday.

After we hung up I knew I wasn't going to ask the good doctor.

I could try giving Delia a call, though she was usually pretty "booked" herself. But Dr. Sharon Horowitz? What could I say? *"Sharon, this is my friend Johnny Ramirez, former pot dealer and wanna be pimp. He used to live with cannibals. And this is his lovely companion, a prostitute..."*

Johnny

Johnny and Victoria have planned a quiet day, *Sunday New York Times*, leisurely breakfast, clean the house before Peter arrives for dinner. Then her agency calls to tell her that one of her regulars is in town.

"You were going to take the day off," Johnny reminds her.

He does not feel like spending the day scrubbing the toilet while Victoria is out getting laid in some fancy hotel by a guy probably feeding her champagne and blow the whole time.

"Look, he's got a train to catch. I'll be back before five," she tells him.

"Let's get a cleaning service," he suggests.

"On a Sunday? You're nuts. They'll charge more than I get. All you have to do is clean the bathroom and vacuum."

"I was going to start my work out program today."

"Maybe you could start by working around here a little."

"I thought I did enough around here." He is referring to the forty minutes he spent that morning going down on an unresponsive Victoria. She'd asked him for it, then just lay there still as stone, occasionally moaning, "Softer, honey. Just be soft." Finally she kissed him and thanked him for understanding that she was too "worn out" to do anything.

It is obvious by the way she is chewing her lower lip that she has caught his reference. She grabs her briefcase and coat with overdramatic exasperation and leaves.

Johnny shoots a bag, spends a few hours on the couch watching the public access porn shows in a pleasant nod, and eventually gets up and starts moving the vacuum slowly back and forth across the carpet. The late afternoon light is golden orange and from the living room window facing northwest, he can watch the sun setting over the Chrysler Building. He is thinking about Raven and how *she* never would've tried to push him around that way.

He does another bag and lies down. Gets up, lights a joint and continues to vacuum. A book on the shelf catches his eye and he pulls it down, *The Portable Nietzsche*. The word *ubermensch* pops into his brain and he sits on the floor, vacuum still running and starts to read. At some point he turns the vacuum off and falls asleep on the carpet, the book by his side. A long ringing sound wakes him. It takes Johnny a moment to recognize that this is the lobby intercom. He answers and tells them "yes" to let up Peter. It's ten to eight and Victoria still isn't back. Fuck it. They'll start without her.

Peter enters carrying a bottle of champagne. He looks around approvingly and tells Johnny he's "moving up in the world."

They decide to wait on the bubbly till Victoria arrives, and take a couple of beers from the fridge instead. They look over the take out menu from Empire Palace, which they both agree is the best Szechuan in the neighborhood. Johnny calls in the order.

They hear the key in the lock and Victoria enters. Before she even has her coat off, she's unpinning her hair. She wears it up sometimes like the blondes in a Hitchcock film. Johnny checks out the way Peter is watching her. Johnny goes over and kisses her hello. He introduces her to Peter while keeping an arm around her waist.

"Victoria Johnson, Peter Teller," he says.

Victoria reaches out her hand. Johnny wonders for a second whether his friend is going to shake it or kiss it. He shakes it.

"Johnny tells me you used to be an actor," she says. "I think I saw you in some movie. A coming of age thing."

"I was in a couple of those."

Johnny notices that his friend is beaming, which is a relief because he knows Peter is a little embarrassed about the whole acting thing, and he'd meant to warn her not to bring it up.

Victoria takes off her coat – a gray fox she wears in spite of the animal rights fanatics. She has on a short black dress, low cut but not vulgar on her slim body. Johnny is feeling like a very fortunate man surrounded by his friend Peter and this beautiful woman in their luxury co-op. Johnny is wondering what further miracles will occur when Victoria takes out a plastic bag with the remains of an eight-ball of cocaine and announces, "Leftovers!"

She goes into the bedroom to change. She likes to wear sweatpants and a tee shirt when she's just hanging in the apartment, but this time she comes out in a long dress. It's some kind of seventies "peasant" style thing. Paisley print, cinched in at the waist. With her long hair – wet from the shower, she looks like a hippie girl.

Peter opens the champagne as Johnny answers the door for the deliveryman. Johnny pays with the cash Victoria had earlier slipped him and tells the guy to keep the keep the substantial change.

They put the blow in a bowl and snort a little here and there throughout dinner and after.

Peter is telling Victoria about the Ibogaine piece he's just sold to *The Eye*. Johnny interrupts, reminding him that he was the one who first put him on to that, but Peter is rolling ahead describing his dinner with Sean, and Victoria is lapping it up.

Johnny drifts off in his head. He's alternating between feeling like this is the best time he's had, and wanting to bash in Peter's skull. He's vaguely recalling some Shakespeare play he saw a production of at the university. In the first scene, some cranky King becomes convinced his pregnant wife has been screwing his best friend (with whom she had been flirting). Much chaos and nonsense ensue including bears.

When Peter brings up Lenny, Johnny jumps in with his own story, but Victoria ignores him and interrupts to ask Peter if he wants some dessert. There's mocha chip, Frusen Gladje. Peter is talking about how he's got himself an agent. The agent set up a lunch for him and a couple of guys from Random House.

Johnny tells his friend what great news that is.

"Hey man, your help was critical," Peter says.

Johnny wonders if he should be writing his own book. But without those "old school ties" and all the other connections Peter has, what chance would there be?

Peter is talking so much his throat is hoarse. Johnny notices the way Victoria is looking at him, the way she moves her body around, displaying herself – posing, as she listens. It hits him she'd rather be with Peter. But she probably figures a guy like that wouldn't put up with a girlfriend making a living on her back.

The evening ends late. All the coke and champagne is gone. Even the beers. Peter gives Victoria a little hug and a peck on the cheek. Then he gives Johnny an even bigger hug.

"Thanks for the dinner. Thanks for everything. Really, man. You've been such a help. I'll call you next week."

Johnny closes the door behind his friend. He goes into the bedroom. Victoria is already running the shower. Johnny is thinking how she took a shower with him that morning, another probably in the hotel, a third when she got home and changed, now this. Johnny has to take a piss, but the door is locked. He makes a fist and punches the wall between the bathroom and the bedroom, cracking the plaster. Then he walks to the half bath off the living room.

Victoria wrapped in a towel comes into the living room bathroom while his stream is still flowing.

"What the fuck was *that* about?"

"Sorry," he says sheepishly. "I had to take a piss. Guess I should lay off the blow."

She turns around and walks back toward the bedroom where Johnny joins her after he's done.

Chapter 15

A Fine Madness

Peter

It was a few blocks from Johnny's back to my apartment. I hadn't taken my car as it was parked in a spot "good" for two more days. Even on a cold winter's night it wasn't worth giving up a space. So when I emerged from the "East Village's Premier Luxury Co-Operative," my options were cab or walk.

I was still feeling energetic, so I strolled past the park on Avenue A. The patrolmen guarding it had their arms crossed. They spent the night with their butts pressed against the wrought iron fence, occasionally ducking into smoke filled patrol cars for warmth. Going by the number of cops per square foot, Loisaida should have been the safest neighborhood in the city. Across the street, the newspaper stands and diners were still open and doing business at past two in the morning. I turned onto 7th and started west toward my apartment.

7th is quieter than the avenue blocks, and not as well lit. As I walked down the street, I became aware of a red glow moving back and forth in front of my building. Coming closer, I realized it was a lit cigarette being smoked by someone sitting on the stoop. I approached with caution, anticipating another encounter with a homeless drunk I'd have to step over before I could gain access to my home. Then I recognized the woman huddled in the ratty raccoon coat, rocking herself back and forth.

"Kyra?"

She dropped her cigarette and stood up. She put her hands up and came towards me. I thought she was reaching out to hug me, but instead she started pounding my chest with her fists.

"You son of a bitch! You screwed it all up!" She was whispering but loud enough for someone on the first floor to turn on a light. She was crying, managing to both pull me toward her and push me away at the same time.

"Why don't we go up to my apartment and talk?" I suggested taking her hand.

"I'm fucked Peter. I'm fucked," she announced inside the hallway.

I put my finger to my lips gesturing for her to stay quiet. But there was nothing quiet about her. She was wearing boots that looked like leftovers from a transvestite's glam rock phase. The clunky heels came down on the tiles as loud as glass breaking on metal. She was dragging a large canvas bag that thudded on every step.

We got into my apartment. "I'll make you some tea," I said. I went to the kitchen and nuked some water.

She sat down and lit another cigarette.

I tried to keep my voice as calm as I could. "You're safe now. Can you tell me what happened?"

"You told me you weren't going to the police, you shit!"

"I didn't go to the police. What are you talking about?"

"Okay, okay, okay," she said making a gesture that looked like she was pushing the air away with her palms. She was breathing heavily and I couldn't help but watch the vertical motion of her breasts, her nipples so hard and sharp they cut a crease in her blouse.

"Then how come Ouspenski's back on me? Tells me he knows I was talking to you about Joe and they're going to find Joe eventually, so why don't I tell them everything and save myself."

I flashed back to my last conversation with the detective. "He's just guessing," I said. "He's no idiot. I'm sure he figured you were holding back. It's nothing he got from me."

"Yeah, well I wish it was just that. You got me in a mess of shit. What the fuck did you tell Jacques?"

"Jacques?"

"Don't act like you don't know what I'm talking about."

"Look, the last time I talked to Jacques, maybe I mentioned I thought you were at the apartment, but . . ."

She started punching me again. Screaming obscenities loud enough to wake neighbors on the other side of the river in Brooklyn. I slapped her. Not hard. Like they do in the old movies when someone's hysterical. Thought it would calm her down, instead she stood up and kicked my shin with those damn boots.

I screamed in agony and *that* finally satisfied her.

She'd run into Jacques who told her he knew she'd been talking to me, and warned her she'd experience the same fate as I would. What really shook her up was when he said her son would also be cursed.

"I haven't seen the kid in years. I never told him I had a son. How the fuck did he *know?*"

"You must have mentioned it to Lenny or someone who told him," I said patting her hand. "There's nothing mystic about it. Look at the guy. If he had any power, he wouldn't be dying of AIDS in a squat."

She looked around the room like she was thinking of something else. "You holding?" she asked.

"I got some Valium."

"Christ. Can you lend me some money? I gotta get out of here. I don't want Jacques . . ."

"Or Joe," I said.

"Oh fuck no! He's back?" She yelled.

"I don't know. Why would he come back with the police looking for him? Listen, I'll help you get out of town if that's what you want, but Kyra, you're going to have to talk to me first."

She wanted to fix. We drove to her guy on Rivington. He was standing outside, came down to the car and we did it right there. She started telling me about going to Boston, looking for her kid.

"He'd be almost fifteen. My baby." She shook her head and stared out the window as I made it back to my place.

She told me she wanted a thousand, "startup" money for her story. I pointed out she wasn't exactly going into hiding. We bargained it down to five hundred, cash. I'd go to the bank with her in the morning.

She agreed.

Back upstairs, I brought out my tape recorder and said, "Tell me what happened that day in the apartment."

"Jesus, Peter do you really need that thing?"

"Yeah."

"The police could get it."

"I won't let them."

"This might be the last time we see each other. Maybe there are better ways we could kill time."

"C'mon Kyra. You need to tell someone."

She was quiet a moment. She closed her eyes and said in a monotone, "We were just sitting around."

"Who?"

"Lenny. PD. He'd come with Joe and Moira."

"And Ingrid, of course," I added. "The guest of honor."

"No, not yet. It wasn't like it was planned, I don't think. They were just hanging out. Ran into each other."

"Were they talking about killing her?"

"No. Lenny was always saying shit about that, but I don't think, no. They were talking about the riot. PD had filed a report with the commission about the brutality. Joe was saying that was all bullshit, waste of time. Wasn't going to change nothing."

"And then?"

"Then *she* comes in."

"Ingrid?"

Kyra nodded. "Oh she was pissed. Slammed the door. Yelling. Screaming at Lenny because this guy she had lined up for the apartment backed out. She was blaming him and me because we wouldn't leave, so now the landlord was going to throw us all out and keep her money."

"What did Lenny do?"

"He was cool. I'd told him before just ignore her if she got that way."

"So what happened?"

"Joe. It set him off. He's on Lenny about letting her whip him like that. He starts saying that it's yuppie trash like her that caused the riot. She's what they were protecting the park for. He's saying to Lenny, 'Just do it, man! Do it like you said!'"

"Was she afraid?"

"She had no idea. She's just giving it to Lenny and he's taking it from her and from Joe too. Finally Joe yells, 'Just kill her man.' And Lenny says, 'I'm gonna kill her.' And then he was charging at her and all of a sudden she sees it. But it's too late."

"Joe?"

"No, Lenny. It was Lenny. He was pounding her."

"Show me, Kyra. What was he doing, exactly?"

She placed her arms on my shoulders and started pushing back and forth. "She was fighting back. She was a big girl, you know? But he got her down to the floor and he kept pushing."

"Did any of you try to stop it?"

"It was happening so fast. Joe was there like the coach. Telling him to get his hands around her throat. I shot a look at Moira but she was blank, and PD was like having some kind of riot flashback."

"He strangled her?" I asked.

"No. I don't know. I mean I don't think he got his hands around her neck. He was pushing her shoulders, knocking her head against the floor. You could hear it, the sound of it hitting. She was kicking and that just made him madder and he pounded harder and then she was out. Then his beeper went off."

"His beeper?"

"Yeah. It goes off and he's on top of her and I think there was some blood by her head. He looks at Joe and asks what he should do about the beeper. And Joe looks at Moira like he's reading her mind for the words. He tells Lenny to do whatever he'd normally do, so Lenny carries Ingrid to her bed and leaves."

"Why does he carry her to the bed?"

"I don't know. I guess he didn't wanna leave her there like that."

"Okay, so then what?"

"I wanted *out*. PD and me, we exchanged looks. Joe was smoking a cigarette. I started to get up. He goes, 'Where the fuck you going?' I said to use the can. I knew I wasn't getting out of there till it was cool with him."

She stopped talking and lit up another Camel. I waited for her to go on.

"Jesus, Peter. Can I have a couple of those Valiums? I'd really like to get to sleep."

I was thinking about what Mirabella had told me. I was thinking about what I knew in my gut. "She wasn't dead yet. Was she?"

"Oh Christ. What about we slam another bag and forget about it, okay?"

"Did she get up, walk into the living room, her head dripping blood, begging for help?"

"Stop it! Just fuckin stop!"

"Tell me," I said. I was holding her wrist now. Squeezing it.

"We were all just sitting there. I don't know how long. Could've been ten minutes or longer. Nobody's saying nothing or even moving and then there's this moaning from the room."

"Could you see her?"

"The door was open. From where I was sitting I could see her feet."

She looked off into space watching the cloud of her cigarette smoke.

"Joe went in there. Didn't he?"

She nodded. "Joe went in there," she repeated.

"Go on."

"I don't know. He closed the door."

"What did you hear?"

"Christ." She stared at me a moment before she continued. "Groaning? Then it stopped." She was crying now, her voice was cracking, and she was taking little breaths. "I heard the sounds. The springs squeaking. And when he came out, oh God, he was zipping up . . ."

I hugged her. "It's okay, Kyra," I said. "It'll be better now, you'll see. It's better that you told somebody."

We shot the last bags we'd bought. Then she told me what happened next. Joe sat down. No one asked him anything and Kyra finally got up, said she was supposed to go to her program. Joe gave her permission to leave.

"Don't forget," he'd told her, "You're a part of this too." He ordered her to knock on Jacques's door on her way out and ask him to stop by.

"I thought about not going back, but my stuff was there and I was trying to act normal, you know? I guess I didn't think she'd still be there."

She gave me a few details about what she'd seen when she returned, and who had "dropped by." Her story confirmed what Raven had told me and included Johnny's friend Lobo taking down body parts in a trash bag. Raven hadn't been the first to raid the room, although the others had looked for cash, not keepsakes. From what she'd seen, Moira had been pretty active in helping with the body, but it didn't sound like she'd been in much of a position to argue with Joe and Jacques.

We were both beat. I was set to give Kyra the bed and take the pullout myself. She asked if we could share, said she needed someone to hold. We lay there together both stripped down to just underwear. A little street light piercing through the shade.

We were speaking softly. I tried to convince her to stick around, go to the police. She didn't want to hear it. Her breasts were resting against my chest. I asked her if it would be okay for me to touch them. She smiled and said of course. They felt colder than the rest of her, surprisingly dense.

"Kyra," I asked, "Did you ever tell Lenny? I mean, does he think that he . . ."

"Right before the police got him. First, I didn't see the point in it. I mean it could've been him. But then he was starting to feel so bad, talking about turning himself in, or offing himself. So yeah. But

I also told him that Joe would kill me if he knew I told him. Then the police got him, and I guess he was scared for me or him or he just wanted to be a man."

Nothing else happened between us. We both fell asleep.

I woke up at two in the afternoon. She was gone. In lieu of the five hundred, she'd taken my Rolex and some cash I'd buried in my sock draw. The tape recorder was there, the cassette gone.

I looked out the window and discovered that the Beetle, which had wound up parked on the wrong side of the street after our run, had been towed.

I hadn't even bothered taking notes while I was listening to Kyra – depending on the now and forever missing tape. I sat down at the computer, transcribing from memory. Was I remembering what she had actually said? Or was it what I had wanted her to say? Maybe we'd both nodded into sleep and it had all been a dream. Or maybe even finding her so conveniently waiting on my doorstep had been a hallucination.

Monday. In a few hours a car would be coming to take me down to Wall Street and the world of work. I felt like crap. I called Johnny, worried that I could already be developing a habit. He laughed it off, said it was probably a cold. I went to see my man, who now greeted me as cordially as any of his regulars.

I called in sick. Went back to sleep till Tuesday morning when I woke up feeling slightly better, if not renewed. A craving, but no real need to do anything about it. I called in again and treated myself to a serious Ukrainian style breakfast before taxi-ing up to the impound lot, major credit card in hand to bail out the Beetle.

Hands on the steering wheel, I was fantasizing about driving straight to Boston and searching for Kyra in every dive of the Combat Zone. If only the trunk had been bigger, I could pop her in and deliver her to Ouspenski.

"Good work, Teller. Where would NYPD be without you?"

"It was nothing, sir. Glad to help."

But I knew even if Kyra cooperated, it wouldn't be enough – one witness, arguably a co-conspirator, and with her own previous conviction.

They needed more. I called Lenny's father in Texas – something I'd been doing on occasion for awhile. He was always friendly, if a bit distant. Wound up telling him more than I should have – that I'd spoken to an eyewitness, a friend of his son's, who now admitted that Lenny hadn't actually killed Ingrid.

"So are you going to the police with that?"

I explained why I couldn't. My witness was gone, and in any case, I couldn't reveal the source. But he had to get Lenny to talk about what really happened.

"What makes you think my son even *knows* what *really* happened? His brain is so fried, he's got grease dripping from his ears."

The old man had a point. Maybe in spite of what Kyra had told Lenny, he believed he had killed Ingrid. There hadn't been much of a body left to autopsy. Who was to say whether or not the blows to her head were fatal? She could have already been dying when Joe got to her.

I spent the rest of Tuesday afternoon and evening on the phone.

I tried calling Sharon several times at her office. Finally got through at home. She wasn't interested in my revelations, particularly when I suggested she confront Lenny with them.

"Don't you think it would serve some *therapeutic* purpose for him to know he isn't a killer? That someone else shares the blame?"

"This isn't a movie where the hero recovers his sanity when he remembers some childhood trauma. Lenny is going to be just as psychotic whether he killed her or not."

She went on to remind me that it wouldn't do much good for the doctor-patient relationship if he knew that she was talking to a reporter behind his back – much less a reporter with whom he still refused to speak.

Then she started asking me questions about my sleeping habits and set out the possibility that I was thinking about this too much.

"Thanks for the analysis, Doc. Will you be billing me for that?"

"I'm just concerned."

My own shrink, Dr. Leider, had left several messages. I'd canceled a few times, but didn't want him cutting my meds, so I finally reached him at his office where he agreed to a fifteen minute "phone check-in" and called in my scripts for the month.

I continued my efforts to contact my alleged literary agent and the two guys from Random House she'd gotten me the lunch with. According to the secretaries everyone was "traveling."

Next on my list, Ouspenski. I was tempted to tell him everything "my source," had told me Sunday night. Tempted, but knew that without Joe Holiday or Lenny to at least back it up, it would be meaningless.

"Teller, I'd been meaning to give you a call. You happen to know where Miss Kyra Vanovowich might be?"

"Kyra? Last I heard she was living on 3rd."

"Not there anymore. Thought you might know since you're such good friends. Always dropping by the club and all."

"Well, I hear she has people in Boston," I said, unable to believe I'd let it out that easily, while at the same time realizing it was a conscious choice to let him know I was with the program. "I don't have an address."

"Thanks, Teller. And what is it I can do for you?"

"You didn't happen to find anything on Joe Holiday. I mean, after I gave you the name."

"Jerome Comb, DOB 8/5/53, Detroit. Dropped out of sight after completing parole in a town called Sulvan, Ohio outside of Cleveland.

"What'd he do?"

"Mostly juvenile beefs. As an adult assault. A little burglary. Nothing we know about for the last twelve years." I pressed him for more details, the name of his parole officer, dates.

"So will you be going out to that commune I mentioned. Looking for him?"

"For what, Teller? As far as I know, as far as anybody knows, he's just, maybe, a witness to something. Lenny Matthews acted alone. That's the story he's telling me and nobody's come to me with a different story. You hear something else, let me know. Meantime, the City of New York is not going to finance an out of state excursion. I did speak with the sheriff of Bumfuck Oregon, who assured me that if he did take a trip out to the hippie farm, they'd lie to him on principle. Of course, *you're* a free agent. You happen to be going out west and hear anything, you might think to give me a call."

I explained that I didn't think I'd make it "out west" too soon. I still had to hold on to my day, or in this case night job.

After we hung up, I thought about the implications of what he'd said. There wasn't much he could do. People who wouldn't talk to the cops, would talk to me. I'd already gotten further than they had. He knew it. He *wanted* me to go out west and bring him back something solid. I was part of it, not just reporting.

I wanted to be part of it.

I checked my mailbox and found a holiday greeting card from my father, stuffed inside was a check for two thousand dollars. It was his custom to send me his gift after New Year's, for tax purposes.

I called his office to thank him and found out he was in Florida with Peggy. Peggy, being a name his secretary assumed I – the only son, would have heard before.

The money could finance a trip out to the commune. Maybe Joe Holiday was still there, or PD. Confirmation of Kyra's story from him might be all they'd need. I wondered if Moira would be there as well, or if she'd gotten the warning and left. Moira could be the key. She would have seen everything. She would have known what Joe was thinking. Of course she couldn't go to the police, but maybe if I could find her, I could get her to tell me. Maybe it could even lead to something for her, testimony against Joe in exchange for the old charges being dropped.

I could still see Moira in my mind the way I saw her the night of the riot. Just for a moment I thought it was Ingrid – but Ingrid was about artifice. Moira tried to be anonymous, play down those looks, but there was something luminous about her.

But I couldn't just take off. I'd promised Delia I'd finish the temp assignment.

I finally made it to FLH again on Wednesday night. Some of the other temps were concerned, asked me how I was. I don't know that the lawyers had even noticed my absence. The agency had no doubt sent another articulate cog as a replacement.

They pulled me to work on a brief they needed to file in the morning. The lawyers working on it were my old buddies – the Valley Girl Attorney and Lawyer Lipshitz – the one who hadn't made the callbacks.

If there had been anything "unusual" going on, I hadn't sensed it before. We were always telling each other stories about our auditions or rehearsals or classes. Our real lives. It was never an issue. So of course, I'd talk about my work. There had been that one time a couple of weeks before when Jim Lawson, the Word Processing Coordinator, who was also the liaison for the temps, and therefore nominally my supervisor, had said something to me about "decorum."

I'm sure what happened next had more to do with Lawyer Lipshitz settling what he thought of as an old college score, or maybe he didn't like the way his golden haired friend was eyeing me. That night, Lipshitz, who I might add had a reputation for frequent trips to the executive washroom where he often left wiping his nose, was in a huff because some poor word processor, a temp they'd gotten in especially for the job, had screwed up some edits, probably due to the fact she couldn't make out his hand writing.

He started laying into her, more than necessary or appropriate. Understanding my place in the corporate food chain, I hadn't intervened, but once he seemed to be safely down the corridor I'd gone over and told her that he was an asshole, and she shouldn't let it get to her.

Right before quitting time, Jim asked to see me, mentioned that things were tighter in the post-crash world, and they'd decided to let some of the temps go early. My services etcetera and so on. I would still be getting the ten percent bonus.

I asked him if there was any problem with my work.

"No, nothing like that."

"Then why me in particular?"

"The truth is Peter, you seem a little too 'high energy' these days. A couple of people have told me that they feel uneasy around you. It's nothing I'd mention to Delia."

I caught Lipshitz on his way into the men's room and called him a piss-ant fascist bully. He gave me a look, mingling incomprehension with pity. Being of sound mind and reasonable temperament, I resisted the impulse to chase after him and pound him into the ground.

It wasn't till I'd come home and chilled out that I realized it was the best thing that could have happened. Nothing holding me back from a trip out west.

❖❖❖

Dr. Sharon

Dr. Sharon Horowitz had lately taken to using her beeper for night emergencies and keeping the phone unplugged. It was hospital policy not to give the beeper numbers to anyone, but Peter Teller had somehow gotten hers.

After returning one of his middle of the night calls, and spending the next hour and a half listening to his ramblings, Sharon had come to regret her earlier interest in him, and decided only to answer the pages she recognized as hospital extensions. Her plan worked until the night he managed to get passed the doorman and started knocking on her apartment door at three a.m.

She told herself that whatever mild infatuation she'd felt had to be over. Yet she invited him in and gave him what she hoped would be a pacifying drink of homebrewed tea made from valerian root, hops and yarrow – a recipe her homeopathic mother had clipped from *Prevention Magazine* and insisted was better than the drugs she prescribed.

He *did* apologize for the hour. Reminded her she had told him she kept odd hours herself. Explained that he was out with friends who lived nearby and had tried to call her before dropping in.

He started telling her about the drag queen in the hospital with hep B who was still refusing to talk to the police. He told her of his "progress" with Lenny's father.

"Peter," she said quietly, unable to keep herself from staring into those Caribbean-sea blue eyes, "It's not uncommon for creative people like yourself to get so caught up in their projects. They start to lose sleep, not eat very much. The body is thrown off balance and . . ."

His voice got louder. She worried he might wake Nicola. "I'm not *delusional*. This is what's happening! It's exciting that's all. Life is supposed to be exciting!"

He took her hand. She caught him staring at her cleavage – just visible through the opening of her bathrobe. She felt her thighs turning to warm Jell-O, while at the same time she noted to herself that his ardor was nothing more than the hypersexuality associated with the manic state.

Interlacing his fingers with her own, he was talking about the trip he would be taking to Oregon and maybe from there to wherever his "research" would lead him. It took her a moment to grasp he was asking her to come along.

"You could be my expert. Tell me the *clinical* interpretation. Think about it Shar, a hippie commune! Like some time trip back to the sixties. Then we get the bad guy and you save Lenny."

She pointed out the dangers of what he proposed, that it was police work not journalism and certainly not medicine. She wondered whether he was aware of how close to the edge he was walking, if that was the unconscious reason he wanted her to go or maybe to talk him out of it.

He told her about a conversation he'd had with Ouspenski, and his interpretation that "between the lines" the detective wanted him to make the journey.

She tried to pin him down on what *exactly* the cop had told him. She let him know that she didn't share his perception.

The herb tea didn't slow him down. She finally walked him to the door, insisting on her own need for more sleep. He took her hand and kissed it, assuring her that he'd "stay in touch" while on the road.

Sharon went to check on her daughter, still sleeping soundly.

Of course he was ill. Still she wondered what life would be like if she didn't have her little girl and the obligations of her job. What *if* she could just take off with him in search of whatever? She smiled and shook her head at the very idea, while acknowledging that when she returned to bed and turned off all the lights, it would be his face she'd imagine beside hers.

Chapter 16

On the Road

Peter

It took me a couple of weeks to escape from New York.

My so-called agent finally returned my calls with the news that while Random House would be interested in seeing the finished product, they were making no commitment. She made suggestions for a proposal rewrite, and then she said some things and I said some things, and I'm not sure, but she may or may not have dropped me, ending my fantasies of an imminent advance.

If I wanted to hit the road in search of Joe Holiday and whatever truth I might find, it would be a self-financed trip.

I visited Mirabella in the hospital. She (and in that vulnerable state, she seemed female) told me it was her hepatitis and insisted she was dying.

"I doubt that, Mirabella. You're a survivor," I said trying to put sincerity into words I knew were lame and trite.

I suggested maybe now would be a good time for her to make a statement to the police about Joe.

"I don't want to spend my last days worrying about *him*."

"I doubt Joe'll be back, unless it's in handcuffs."

She took Ouspenski's number and said she'd "think about it."

I still didn't have a full name for PD, so I contacted the police press liaison I'd used on my riot article. After several pleading phone calls, she succumbed to my charm and agreed to get me a copy of the list of people who'd filed brutality complaints. I found one Patrick Donald Brewar listed at the address of PD's squat.

In the midst of getting all that done, I'd purchased a plane ticket to Portland, thinking about, then rejecting, a stopover in Seattle to visit some friends.

I took an early flight, arriving late-morning, West Coast time, groggy from the Klonopin – a medical necessity to keep my brain from realizing my body has left the earth. I wanted to get out to Blythedale but decided, after nearly falling asleep behind the wheel of my rental car, I should stop off first at a hotel.

I woke up in the late afternoon, the setting sun shining through my western facing window. I hadn't visited Portland before, so I decided to take a walk before dark, see the town. I passed a park where just like home someone came up and asked me if I wanted to make a buy.

I did a double take past a teenaged girl sitting on a bench. Dyed black hair and dark make-up just like Raven. The girl, who was not Raven, turned out to be from Castle Rock, Washington, a tiny town near Mount Saint Helens which she described as the dullest place on the planet. I wound up talking to her and her friends, all runaways more or less, from surrounding towns or states. They took me to the house where they were staying. We wound up shooting some bags together, and I fell asleep on the couch, waking early the next morning and somehow making it back to my hotel and car. I figured I might catch them again before I left – maybe do a piece on the Portland youth scene for *The Eye*.

After a decent diner breakfast, I followed my maps out to Blythedale. It was a couple of hours south, actually closer to Eugene where I probably should have come in.

It was cold, not New York cold, but in the forties with a steady drizzle, and the clouds looming so low I could feel their weight. I was on a muddy, dirt road wishing I'd rented a Jeep, or at least something with four-wheel drive. I felt grateful to whatever gods had seen me through when at last I passed the sign welcoming me to Blythedale – painted in what must have once been psychedelic, bright colors, now gone to mushy rain-washed pastels. There was an old house on a hill, rambling Victorian that seemed to lean. Surrounding it, various types of shacks, the sturdier ones on cinderblocks, a few log cabins. Several old vehicles – VW mini-vans and decrepit school buses had been converted into makeshift housing. No people were out. Smoke was coming from the chimney of the big house and those shacks that had chimneys. There were various pick-ups and older cars rusting on the property.

A group of children came toward the car as I was parking. They were all white, except for one or two who looked biracial, but there was something about the way they were gathering in fascination around my late model rental that made me feel like I'd landed in a third world backwater.

A tall, man with graying hair down past his shoulders, smoking a home rolled cigarette, tobacco by the smell, approached.

"Can I help you with something?"

Emerging from the car, I reached out my hand. Told him I'd read about the place and showed him the alternative community guide. Mentioned I was a writer, wanted to check it out.

"Cool man. I'll give you the tour."

His name was Gary. He looked to be around forty, was wearing round wire-rimmed glasses, the lenses so scratched I wasn't sure how he could see.

We started with the big house, which he referred to as – "the main." There was a fire going and the children, about a dozen of them, from around four to maybe ten or eleven years old, were drawing pictures and running around under the somewhat lackadaisical watch of a couple of women. One of whom, large with child, was saying to the other, "Well, if you believe in science, Gypsy's probably the father, but if you believe in magic, it had to be Zephyr."

Gary gave me a quick history. The house and land had been left to Jerry who had drifted in one day and made himself useful to the old woman who'd owned the property. There was a tax lien and Jerry got a few of his friends – "the founders" – to chip in and help. Other people discovered the scene and Jerry would find things for them to do to earn their keep. There was a group back in the seventies that had tried to organize things, sounded like a cult. Most of them were long gone, but a little of the structure remained.

Gary explained that a few of the old timers lived in the upstairs rooms of the house, but the downstairs, where we were standing was used as a school for the kids.

"We're not certified, so when they're six they got to go to the regular county schools. That is, if the state knows about them."

He showed me an old barn, one of the more substantial structures besides the big house. "This is the factory," he said. There were only four people working including a couple of children. It looked more like an arts and crafts class. A woman was doing beadwork in the glow of a small black and white TV with fuzzy talk show images. The kids were dipping candles.

The products would be sold from carts in towns and at concerts and fairs, I was told. The profit went back to the commune.

Gary admitted they still ran in the red. Jerry usually wound up paying the taxes or major repairs out of his own funds. He had a successful farm a couple of hours away. I didn't bother asking what he grew.

"A lot of the women here with kids get the AFDC. Some folks got SSD and help out with that. We encourage people to pool the money. Also barter."

I acted impressed, jotting notes.

"I think I might know one of your founders from New York. Might even be staying here now. Patrick, goes by Pirate Don sometimes, maybe PD?"

"You knew PD?" he asked.

Knew. "Uh, yeah."

"Oh man, I'm sorry. I guess you don't know what happened."

Gary told me. A week before, a couple of cops from a town called Afila, down by the California border, had visited with the news of PD's death. His body had been found in the woods, decomposed, partially eaten by animals. No ID but someone remembered the disabled van that had been found by the side of the road around the time the death would have occurred. The plates had been removed but there was a sticker left and they'd been able to trace it to PD at his Blythedale address.

The police had come to the farm asking a lot of questions. Gary told them how PD had shown up a few weeks before with his friends Joe and Maureen. They worked on an old vehicle of his that he'd left on the farm years before, and once they got it roadworthy, they'd taken off, vague about the destination, but Gary remembered hearing something about San Francisco.

"So the police are thinking this uh Joe and Maureen may have been involved in the death?" I asked.

"I dunno. She was okay. I don't know what her boyfriend's problem was."

"You remember that cop's name?"

Gary didn't and somehow the subject changed itself. He invited me to stay for lunch, told me there was a lot more for me to see. I declined. Once I'd cleared the property, I had to pull over. I popped a couple of Valium, not great for driving but I needed something. It was hard for me to catch my breath. I could feel the sweat along with the increasing tightness in my chest. I closed my eyes and tried to concentrate on keeping my breathing slow and steady, but it was getting faster along with my thoughts.

Joe had killed him. No other explanation. But what role had I played with my warning to Moira? Could she be dead as well? Another body they hadn't yet discovered? Why hadn't I just told Ouspenski the day I heard the word Blythedale?

I was tempted to head back to Portland, see my new young friends, get some dope and try to forget – even for just the rest of the day. But when I felt stable enough to drive I headed south, three hours to Afila – *"a University town of pleasant tree-lined streets and cafés, where the ratio of massage therapists and new age healers per capita is perhaps higher than in any other U.S. city outside the Bay Area,"* or so said my Pacific Northwest guide book. I hit the main drag and asked where I could find the police station.

I parked in front of a building that bore an eerie resemblance to the sheriff's station in the mythical town of Mayberry. Something stopped me from getting out of my car and going inside. A little voice of reason whispered that maybe I needed to first get my story straight in my brain if I didn't want to wind up answering questions under bright lights in a back room, or maybe like that guy in Texas passing through who wound up on death row. I got back in the car.

Chapter 17

Father and Son

The Major

The Major had never been to New York City before, nor had he ever experienced the desire to visit. When he was active in the service, he'd lived in or near many cities. It wasn't that he was some small town boy afraid of having his pockets picked; he just preferred a quiet life.

There was plenty at home keeping him busy too. Had a little dog breeding business going – wirehaired pointing griffons, the best bird-dogs in the world. This had come about through his lady friend, a divorcé, quite a bit younger than himself. She groomed dogs for a living and talked him into using his land for a kennel.

Life was going along about as well as he could imagine until the thing came up with Lenny. He'd thought of flying east right away, but Estelle convinced him to wait.

He should've gone though. Felt bad when the lady doctor had called him. He made a reservation. But then his angina had started acting up, and Estelle drove him in to see his cardiologist who'd put him in the hospital and ordered an angiogram.

Turned out he needed a quadruple bypass and a couple of valves replaced.

Three months later he still felt like crap even though the doctors assured him he'd be good to go for years. Before he still felt young, now every day seemed like borrowed time.

Reporters had called him after the murder, but he hadn't spoken to them. The Major was at least relieved it had happened far away enough that no one knocked on his door. But that one reporter, Teller, was different. He seemed genuinely concerned about Lenny, told the Major he thought there had been some kind of "miscarriage of justice." Maybe Lenny wasn't such a monster. Maybe he wasn't even the one who did it. It made sense to the Major. His son had always been easily influenced – a "go alonger." The Major wrote Lenny asking if he was covering for a friend or if someone was threatening him, but he didn't get any letters back, and his son refused to talk to him over the phone.

When he was finally feeling up to it, he made a reservation. Estelle decided she might as well go too.

"We could stay someplace nice," she said. "See *Cats* or that other one."

"This isn't going to be a pleasure trip," he said.

"I know that shug," she replied, running her fingers through his full head of white hair. "But that doesn't mean the two of us can't find the time to have a little fun."

So there he was walking through endless corridors at the Municipal Hospital. Slow going, his leg bothering him where they'd taken the veins. He found the sign for the State of New York, Division of Mental Health, Unit 5. It was a locked ward with bars and a thick metal door with a buzzer outside. He pressed the buzzer and emptied his pockets. A female guard sifted through his belongings while her male partner frisked him. Then they buzzed him through another door. Once he was inside, it was the same as all the other units on which he'd visited his son. The nurse, little Mexican girl or more likely Puerto Rican in New York, led him to the day room. She didn't seem to have any fear of her charges, and neither did he. They found Lenny absorbed in a soap opera. They'd cut his hair and shaved off his beard. It was the first time the Major had seen him clean shaven as an adult. The old man was startled to see the mix of his own features with his wife's coloring on his son's face. The nurse called his name and Lenny turned around.

"Hi Daddy," he said.

Lenny

They'd told him that his father was coming, but it was hard to keep track of everything they told him, and what day it was and whether it was something that had happened already.

Time was an illusion. Most people didn't understand that, but there was an orderly, Hispanic guy who seemed to get it. Mike, his name was. Used to say how he and Lenny should collaborate on a book, bestseller, but he got fired. Lenny heard he was caught boosting meds.

"Shrooms," Lenny thought. *"Shrooms would seriously help the people here."* He daydreamed about getting out and coming back to visit and smuggling in shrooms for everyone, the doctors included. But he knew he probably wasn't going to get out for a long time.

Kyra had come to see him a few weeks before. She'd told him that Joe was gone. Lenny didn't believe it. The last time Stan had come, Lenny was sure that Joe had taken over the cop's body, and was trying to see what he'd say.

He was happy to see his father but a little suspicious too. In the past, his father had been taken over by evil spirits.

He felt safe on the Unit though, and Doctor Sharon had assured him that his father's visit would be a good thing.

They went into the "snack room" to talk. It was the middle of the morning and not too many people hung out there. His father got himself a coke from the machine and brought Lenny an orange soda, his old favorite.

"How are they treating you, son?"

Lenny told him what he liked and what he didn't.

His Daddy told him a little about his life too, that he had a girlfriend now, and some dogs.

"I used to have a rooster," Lenny said.

After a while the conversation slowed. Finally, the Major said, "Son, there's something I want to talk to you about . . ."

Because he could see the future, Lenny knew his Daddy was

going to ask him something about the murder.

"It's just that, you've always been such a gentle boy. I know you get angry sometimes, but what happened with that girl . . ."

"She was sent to torment me. She was going to send me out to wander in hell."

"Yeah, I understand that boy. But what you did to her, it's so unlike you. Did somebody tell you to do that?"

Lenny looked around the room. There were a couple of nurses gossiping at a table far away. He looked at the corners where the walls met. There was a cockroach crawling up the side of the candy machine. He wondered if it could have been Jacques transformed, or if Jacques could have sent the insect to watch him. He didn't sense Joe's presence.

Lenny gave his stock reply. "I prayed to Satan for guidance, and he sent his emissaries to help me."

"Yeah, son. I heard that."

His dad looked like he was thinking about what to say next. Lenny felt scared because he was sure that if anyone would ever ask him the right question, it would be his father.

"Leonard James, these emissaries, in what form did they come to you?"

Lenny's heart was pounding so hard he thought maybe Jacques had put a spell on him and it was going to explode. He took a couple of breaths and was relieved to discover that he had not been transported to the gates of hell. The Major was waiting for an answer.

"One came as a female, beautiful in form and the others came as men," Lenny told him.

"They have names, these entities?"

"There was demons named Jacobo and Josephus."

"Okay, Leonard. What were their *earthly* names?"

Lenny was now compelled to reveal them because his father had finally asked the right question.

❖❖❖

Chapter 18

On the Road Again

Peter

I checked into the Stay-a-While Motor Inn on Main Street, Afila, southern Oregon, and drank my dinner at the adjacent bar. The next morning, I called the hotel in Portland where I'd left my luggage. They agreed to store my bag. I groomed myself as best I could without a change of clothes, ate a good breakfast, washing down a Klonopin with my coffee, and in the guise of intrepid young reporter entered the police station.

The receptionist called for a Detective Voight in response to my request to speak with whomever was in charge of the investigation into Brewer's death.

Voight wasn't the beefy small town cop I'd expected. He was around my age with an earnest baby face and slight build. He shook my hand and carefully looked over my press credential, as I began to explain that I'd come to do a story on alternative communities in the Pacific Northwest, was given Brewar's name as a contact and now discovered he'd been murdered. Thought it would be worth looking into.

"So you didn't know him?"

"I don't think so. I know people who know him. It's possible I've seen him at a community meeting or someplace."

"And these two?" He showed me a sketch. Composite

drawings of Joe and Moira. Decent likenesses.

"Never saw them before," I said maybe a little too quickly. I don't know if I should have told him everything then, but I was still thinking about Moira facing jail and once I said it, it was said.

He asked me what I knew. I told him what Gary had told me and asked him what he had.

"The body was found in a ravine. There are *indications* of a blow to the head. But coyotes and raccoons found the body before we did. Might have even dragged it some. It's possible the guy could have fallen, hit his head, rolled, been moved by the animals. We don't know what we got, except those friends are gone and somebody took the plates."

He pulled out some photos of the body. I concentrated on holding down my breakfast.

He added that the sketch of the couple was being circulated up and down the coast. A hotel clerk thought he might have recognized them. If it was them, the man had checked in as Jim Roberts and given a non-existent Seattle address.

As for the van, a service station had a county towing contract. They'd seen a vehicle illegally parked by the side of the road and had brought it in, waiting for the owner to come looking. That was before the body was found. Later, when the vehicle was connected to the body, the only fingerprints found belonged to some local juveniles who'd admitted breaking into the *already* impounded vehicle and stealing tapes and camping gear.

"Those friends of his, your contacts in New York, it would be helpful if you could give me their names, addresses, phone numbers," Voight said.

I fumbled a minute. Told him I didn't have the information off-hand, but would be glad to check my records when I got back to the city. He asked how he could reach me there. I handed him my card. He looked it over and said. "Mind if I see your driver's license? I can make a copy. Harder to lose."

I gave it to him, asked for his card and a copy of the sketch as well. We shook hands as I left.

I went back to my hotel and called Ouspenski in New York. He wasn't in. I don't know what I would've said to him if he had been. I wrote him a note. Kept it short and to the point:

"*. . . Joe Holiday showed up at Blythedale with a man named Patrick Donald Brewar a.k.a. PD or Pirate Don – also from New York. They left the farm. Brewer's body was found a few weeks later. The investigating officer is detective Voight, Afila Police. According to one of my sources, Brewar was present at Ingrid's death and Joe was the actual killer . . .*"

I don't think I really had my next move planned when I checked out of the motel and got into the car. I was driving south on the highway, taking those mountain curves faster than I should have. I was beyond the normal clarity we associate with thought. Some inner voice was telling me to head for San Francisco, to find Joe myself before he could do further damage, telling me that I *could* find him, *would* find him. I knew how he thought, what he liked. I could hit every shooting gallery, every low-life drag bar, soup kitchen, SRO and squat.

Five or so hours later, the voice had guided me into a strip mall in the suburbs of the Bay Area where I found a huge Goodwill. There I bought myself another pair of jeans, a couple of shirts, a very worn leather bomber jacket with torn lining, and a duffel bag. As I was about to leave, I passed the store's shoe section and found myself reaching for a pair of motorcycle boots. Perfect fit. The second I touched them it came to me that the wearer of those boots had perished in a bike accident. His old lady had given them away.

Just outside of the city, I stopped by a K-Mart for a few other essentials and called the Portland hotel once more, this time discussing their shipping my stuff back to New York. Also told the rental car agency about my change of plans. I took a final look at my maps and drove to the Tenderloin, stopped at a dark little bar where the floor kissed my boots with each sticky step, ordered a scotch and tried to get into character. Concentrating on how the muscles of my face should set, how to move my hands and pitch my voice.

I wondered if Joe had been by this place, thought of asking the bartender. Describing my friend from New York who "might a been lookin' for me." But I wasn't ready yet.

I left, got the duffle from the trunk and walked a couple of blocks finally passing a hotel that somehow felt right. I wasn't so far gone I expected to find Joe Holiday in the lobby. I just needed a place.

The Hotel Grand Paradiso probably wasn't the seedy, center of iniquity that I imagined as I walked over a threadbare puke green gone to gray carpet toward the reception desk. They didn't rent rooms by the hour. Later, I even discovered it was mentioned in my guidebook, *San Francisco on a Shoestring* which stated, *"You will probably not be killed in your stark little cubby-hole, but ladies might think of moving their dressers in front of their doors at night, and if you choose one of the less expensive rooms lacking a private bath, remember to always lock your door. The staff is relatively honest and will keep your valuables in the office safe."*

The clerk was an attractive, if somewhat butch, Latina or I guess in that part of the country Chicana woman, maybe a few years older than myself. She was wearing a leather cap over her short curly hair and had a seen-it-all smirk.

"Yeah? You need something?"

"A room."

She looked me over. "You sure you wanna stay here?"

"Any reason I shouldn't?"

She scanned my duffel, checked out the boots. "Nah. I dunno."

I took a single. No bath. She tried to talk me into a double. "They got private showers and everything. Even a phone."

"Sorry," I said. "Tight budget."

She handed me a towel the texture of sandpaper, a bar of soap and my own private roll of toilet paper.

"Guard this with your life," she told me. "Do *not* leave it in the toilet."

There was no porter, but at least the elevator worked. The room was no wider than the width of my arms. I pulled opened the window, which was curtained by gray paint, and saw that the view was of another identically painted window across the airshaft. I heard the murmur of voices from that direction. As I shut the window, I had the fleeting thought that Moira and Joe could have been staying in that opposite room. Moira waiting for the opportunity to escape, sure that Joe will turn her in to make a deal, or kill her if he gets the chance. Joe thinking the same about her.

I had several ideas about how I might spend the approaching evening. I could walk around, maybe flash some cash at other "budget" hotels and outside the shelters, show the sketch of Joe and hope for luck. But what if I showed it to the wrong person, and Joe found out? What if my meddling caused him to run? I considered a trip to the Castro. I could check out the dicier drag bars, look for Joe's kind of place.

In the end, I decided to head out and see where I'd wind up. I hadn't been to San Francisco in years. I knew a couple of people from college, but I wasn't planning on visiting.

I was trying not to think of copping some smack. I hadn't indulged since that day with those kids in Portland, hadn't even thought about it, which at least made me less anxious about having developed a habit. But now the desire to blot out everything was strong.

I felt a hyper-awareness of my body, my skin, my thoughts. I needed to turn down the volume. It wasn't quite a physical need, at least not yet. But it was a longing for an illusion of wholeness. Something I hadn't felt in any woman's arms, but imagined was what they meant by being "in love."

Delia once told me about a man with whom she'd had an affair. Older guy, friend of her father's. She despised him, his face, his clothes, the sickening sweet smell of his pipe. But one summer, when she was seventeen, she was doing an internship at his magazine, and they started sneaking around. For the next six months she couldn't think of anything except when she would have a chance to fuck him again. They did it everywhere they could, offices, cars, supply closets, restrooms.

He was the one who wound up ending it. She even tried to blackmail him into continuing, threatening to tell his wife.

That was as close as I can come to describing my feeling for heroin. I found the idea of it repulsive, but it gave it me a vacation from the noise in my head.

Following the guidebook's advice, I left my credit and bank cards in an envelope at the front desk, taking some cash with me.

I stopped at a nearly empty diner and bought a chicken salad sandwich. The bread was toasted black and tasted of old bacon grease and whatever else had been left on the grill. I had a vision I would wind up in an emergency room with food poisoning.

I walked on and came to a little triangle of a park. It wasn't quite dark. A few people were gathered, talking by one of the benches – a couple of older black men, a younger man, maybe my age, a fat white woman with stringy hair passing a brown paper bottle, another woman, wiry Latina, reminded me of the hotel clerk. None of them were wearing rags or seemed deranged, but they all had the unmistakable look of those with nowhere else to go.

I would've walked right past them, except the young guy asked me for a cigarette and the fat white woman wanted one too. Then we started talking and I wound up sitting down. Soon the old guys and the wiry woman were taking off. Something about getting to "the church" for supper. They invited me. I thanked them, told them I'd eaten.

After the others left, the fat white woman offered me a swig from her bottle. I drank to be polite. The young guy was friendly, talked a little too fast, like he might have been nervous. We were talking about New York mostly. She'd never been east of Chicago. He had.

Then he asked, "So young brother, what is it you're looking for?"

I said I wasn't looking for anything. I was about to add, except maybe this guy, named Joe, from New York, owed me some money. But he cut me off.

"Everybody's looking for something. Come on. Whatever it is, I'm the man to see," he turned to the woman. "Ain't that right, baby?"

She made a sound between a cackle and a groan. "That's right. Clarence is the man to see."

I shook my head.

"Now a fine young specimen like yourself. Maybe you be

wanting some pussy," he laughed. "Maybe you be wanting the kind of pussy you smoke."

"No Clarence, I'm not looking for anything to smoke."

I finally did ask him, for the hell of it I guess, where a man might be able to find some smack and a clean set of works.

He laughed again, told me I'd definitely come to the right place, "oh yeah." Told me I should go see his friend, Earl. Over on Lombard. Gave me an address and directions.

"What do you get out of it?" I asked.

He smiled. "Hey, this ain't New York. Just being friendly man. Ain't my scene. But Earl'll take care of you."

I had a bad feeling and figured there was no law I had to follow through. I left the park. Looked at my tourist map. If I walked to the Castro, I'd still pass right by the street Clarence was sending me to. I didn't see any harm in going past the building. I didn't have any intention of stopping.

When I got to Earl's street, I was barely noticing the addresses. Someone called out, "Hey, you. You Clarence's friend? It's cool. He told me you was coming."

I went over, maybe just to check out the scene, take it a little further. We weren't even in the building when suddenly I felt something hit the back of my head.

I don't know how much later it was when I came to. Someone must have dragged me to the side of the building. A couple of uniformed police were pushing at me.

"Jesus, there's blood," one said.

"Ah shit. You touch it?"

"Fuck no. Let's call."

They radioed for a medic. "I'm okay. I'll be okay," I struggled to my feet, realizing my boots were gone.

They were asking me questions. *How'd you get cut? What's your name? Who's the president? Did you see the guys?*

I felt the back of my head. There was a large bump and blood. I vaguely remembered hitting something, a step or a wall on my way down. I told the officer I had no idea. Must have been hit from behind. I checked my pockets. Cleaned out.

The medics arrived. They repeated many of the same questions the cops had asked. They assured me it was only a tiny gash, looked worse than it was. But they thought I should go to the hospital, stitches. One of the cops handed me a card with the precinct number on it and told me to call after I got treated. They'd send a detective to take a report. I thanked him and walked on board the ambulance.

It was a couple of hours before they finally treated the wound and took some x-rays. While I was waiting the clerk popped in to take my insurance info. Then after, the doctor told me to wait in the room a while and ring for a nurse if I felt dizzy or nauseous. Another hour and a half till he came back to tell me my skull was not cracked. The doctor thought a concussion unlikely but advised me to come back if I had any symptoms. Then I waited some more till the nurse came in to repeat his instructions and sign me out.

She was good about getting some cardboard slippers for my shoeless feet, but stubbornly refused to part with a cab voucher, insisting that if I called the police from the pay phone, the officer who came for my statement would give me a ride.

I left the hospital thinking I'd find my own cab and pay it back at the hotel. Instead I wound up walking the five blocks. The hotel clerk noticed my slippers as I approached her desk for my key.

"You was robbed," she stated flatly.

"I was robbed."

"They took the boots," she said with a touch of concern, more for the boots than for me from her tone.

"They took the boots," I confirmed.

"You look like shit."

"Thank you."

I asked for my wallet and as I inspected the contents she said, "You're not here to do the big check out, huh?"

I looked at her blankly.

"I mean, we get like at least two people a month that, you know," she said. She cocked her head to the side rolling her eyes back and sticking her tongue out loosely as she raised a fist vertically above her for forehead.

"No, I hadn't planned on killing myself. Although you certainly create an inviting atmosphere for the act."

"It's just tha' people, they think it's something they do to themselves, but you know somebody's always gotta clean it up."

"I'll keep that in mind," I said heading toward the elevator, wondering whether that conversation had really taken place or if I was out cold dreaming it.

I stopped by the ice machine in the hallway and got a bag for my head. The doctor or the nurse had said something about not taking anything at least till the morning.

The clerk was wrong. I wasn't feeling suicidal. Depressed, humiliated, defeated – but not like killing myself. The voice in my head had stopped talking to me. Stopped telling me to go find Joe. I wanted to go home. I wanted to sleep in my own bed instead of on a lumpy mattress that smelled of Kwell. I wanted to find my dealer on Avenue A, who after such a short acquaintance greeted me by name and would never try to beat me.

I looked at the clock. One in the morning, which would make it four in New York. I went back down to the lobby and into the phone booth. Called Johnny. Apologized for the lateness of the hour though he sounded awake.

"I was catching some tube. Cable," he told me. Victoria was out.

I told him about PD and my conversation with the police in Afila. I told him how I wished I'd told Ouspenski everything. Maybe PD would be alive if I had.

"It's not your fault Joe Holiday kills somebody."

He gave me a brief update on the hometown news. The police had been closing down squats since the park closing. PD's building had been fighting in court. Had some good lawyers and tenants' rights groups backing them. But as soon as the decision came down against them, the police and city sheriff had shown up to clear the place.

It made me realize that I should be back there, covering the city I knew, not searching for phantoms on the west coast.

I told him I missed home. Then added that one of things I was missing was my easy access to smack.

"You can find dope anywhere," he said. He'd been to the Bay Area himself once. Mentioned a couple of streets, including the one I'd got beat on.

I didn't tell him what happened, only started to say I was a little worried. Maybe I liked it too much.

"You can kick," he said. "I've done it lots of times."

"Yeah," I said. "But if I quit, I want it to be forever."

"What are you worried about? With your bucks, you can stop and visit Betty Ford on your way back. Do the Ibogaine thing."

I returned to my cell. Decided the idea of finding Joe was absurd. If he had killed PD, and I was sure he had, would he then be stupid enough to go to the city where he told people he was heading? I packed my bag with the idea of getting to the airport in the morning and getting a flight home. Despite the ER doc's advice, I popped a couple of Restoril to take my mind off the smell of the sheets. I was out till eight a.m. – a solid five hours.

When I woke up the voice was back in my head, just a whisper at first, then getting louder and gaining confidence throughout breakfast. Sure going back home and doing a freelance piece on the evictions would be a fine idea. Plus I could keep the pressure on Sharon for me to see Lenny. But wasn't there something else? Something nagging at me, ever since Ouspenski had told me there was no record for Joe Holiday or Jerome Comb since he left Ohio.

It was what Johnny said about Joe's thinking the police were looking for him. It had to have been a pretty big deal for him to leave, change his name, and avoid the cops for ten years. Maybe I could find out what. Not just for the sake of my book, but because the guy was a menace and no one was even looking for him. He'd nearly killed Mirabella, had killed Ingrid and probably PD.

So when I got to the airport, I changed my ticket for a flight to Cleveland, from there, I rented a car and found my way to Sulvan.

❖ ❖ ❖

Chapter 19

Hindsight

Johnny

I had this girl. Back when I was at NYU. Pre-med, lots of interests. Always trying to get me to go dancing. Said she couldn't believe I was Latino cause I didn't dance *or* speak Spanish. She was fluent. Spent a couple of summers building latrines in Guatemala or something.

Big boned, but not fat. She could carry it.

She was pretty into me at first, but I knew it wouldn't take her long to figure out that Johnny Ramirez might be a great guy to sleep with on occasion and a good dinner companion, but he really doesn't *do* very much, does he?

It was winter. Her parents had a country place, upstate. They were in Florida. So she invited me up for a romantic get away. Made me a little nervous. What's there to do there?

She started working the fireplace while I started working on her daddy's scotch. We made love on a quilt by the fire, and the next morning she made pancakes. So far, not bad.

Then she announced we're going skiing.

I told her I didn't have the money. She laughed, said she meant cross-country, right outside the door. She was sure her brother's boots would fit.

"It's easy," she said, "Like walking."

I put on the skis. I could hardly move. Looked like a throwback wingless duck. I'd fall at the smallest decline, and uphill I fell backwards. She kept trying to show me, but I couldn't get it. Eventually, she left me there to figure it out for myself.

I watched her taking off into the woods. Her skis made this sound as they touched down in perfect rhythm, *pit-pat-pit-pat*, fading away.

I went back in the house, polished off what was left in the liquor cabinet.

Most things are like skiing. They take time to learn. More than time, you gotta have patience and faith, belief that if you keep at it, you'll get somewhere.

Not heroin.

After you throw up a couple of times and figure out how to tap a vein, you're just as expert as the guy shooting next to you with the twenty-year habit, no matter what his bullshit.

I *never* told Peter Teller to stick a spike in his arm.

I mean, not like a serious suggestion. Besides, why would a guy like that, a Yale man for Christ sakes, take advice from someone like me?

That first day we'd met for lunch, it might have gone down something like this. He's telling me his problem getting people like Kyra to talk to him. I'm laughing because he's this slumming movie star, and why should she trust him when she could wind up in jail? So maybe I said something as kind of a joke. But that doesn't mean I'm therefore responsible for whatever happened to the guy.

It's not like he wasn't around drugs before. I mean, c'mon, he was *best friends* with Sean McFarland's kid, and he didn't need me to fill up his medicine cabinet.

He had that IV block going, like in the fifties when women wouldn't give it up till they got married, but might do anything but. Like sure he'd dropped acid, do coke at parties, but only a lowlife is gonna jab in a needle.

Shit. The boy sure took to it once he started.

I told him to be careful.

What I think it was really, that got him in the end? I think it was a curse.

Back when I was a kid, even my Grandma, good Catholic woman, every once in a while, like when I'd get into trouble, she'd go see these ladies with the chickens, *Santeria*.

And I used to know this biker chick. Witch. Guy crossed her old man in a deal. Guy wound up dead in a car crash. Okay, maybe he was shitfaced at the time. But that's how it's supposed to work. Like Joe put it, "Natural order of things."

Peter kept confronting Jacques, trying to get him pissed off enough to say something. Finally, Jacques *did* say something. He said Peter would be dead before he was.

It was after that he started using smack and things got out of control.

You think it's a coincidence?

Maybe that's what you're supposed to think.

Chapter 20

Enlightenment

Peter

Sulvan, a small college town with a veneer of hip combined with a laid back anachronistic crunchiness, features a wide main street off the interstate. I pulled into the College Motor Inn, AAA recommended, and got a room. With the flying, the driving, the time change, I was beat and settled down for a nap. I awoke a short time later in a panic, thinking the room was on fire, but it was only the industrial orange glow of the setting sun piercing through the thin hotel curtains.

It was dark by the time I left to forage for food. I passed first an old man's bar, next a collegiate sports bar with giant TV, third a small veggie sandwich place filled with the anemic, and finally a diner where I ordered a sandwich. A copy of the local paper, *The Sulvan Register,* my dinner companion.

After Ouspenski had mentioned the town, I'd done a little research. Enough to find out that the downtown had been renovated four years ago and now boasted a three block cobblestoned pedestrian mall designed to rival similar ones in Boston and Burlington, Vermont. Victorian houses were being renovated by ambitious academics, and gentrification had become a part of the lexicon. But ten years ago, when Jerome Comb was living there, it had been different.

Back then the new state university center wasn't fully operational. The construction jobs it had provided were ending, and the low paying service positions it would provide weren't going to make up for the factory production work being lost due to plant relocations and recession. Meantime, the citizens hadn't yet organized against the dumping in their community of many of the rootless souls released from the state prison in Grenville, next exit on the turnpike.

I left the diner and stopped by a liquor store on the way back to my motel. No more adventures purchasing illegal substances in strange places for me. I bought a bottle of scotch and when I reached my room, happily poured myself a glass, downed a Klonopin and turned on the TV which happened to be tuned to some cable soft-core.

I had a plan for the next day. Try to find Joe/Jerome's parole officer, and go to the library to research old copies of *The Register*. I wasn't sure what I was looking for. Some unsolved crime around ten years ago. Something that would smell like Joe Holiday.

I was feeling restless, so I made a couple of calls to New York, but no one was picking up. Meantime on the screen, a blonde with enormous breasts was rubbing herself and moaning in a giant circular bathtub. An Asian woman, of equally unlikely proportions was about to join her.

I was thinking of Victoria – remembering that glimpse of cleavage I'd caught when she took off her coat. I would have rather have had those small breasts in my hands, in my mouth, than both the women I was watching on the screen. I was thinking of Raven's body as well, the smoothness of it. I was absently stroking myself, wondering what Dr. Leider would say about the two women on my mind both being Johnny's.

I glanced at the phone book, curious about what services might be available to a lonely young man in a town like this. Nothing in Sulvan, but naughty Grenville had a few listings. I looked to see if there were any drag queen services – maybe a link with Joe. There weren't, but one of the other ads caught my attention. *"Elite Escorts Ltd. The most sophisticated gals in the Buckeye State! Coeds! Models!*

Hotel outcalls. 24 hours. All major credit cards honored!"

I'd never paid for sex before. The idea was somewhat revolting. But Johnny had explained something to me about Victoria's line. The men weren't just paying to get laid. It was companionship – a drinking buddy who'd also suck your cock, tell you how great you were, stay up all night snorting coke with you, listen to the stories you can no longer bore your friends with, or leave, no hard feelings, the second you said, "Go."

I dialed the number. The receptionist or dispatcher asked a number of questions including whether or not I had any affiliation with law enforcement and what if any were my "special needs." My mind still picturing Victoria, I asked for a leggy brunette with long hair.

The girl showed up about forty-five minutes later. Her name was Gina. She did have long brown hair, but it was teased and sprayed as though she were ready to put on a swimsuit and walk down a runway. Young, though definitely legal. Her teeth had never been straightened, which I noticed though I didn't think it detracted from her "looks." She wore a clingy wool dress that showed off her shape. It was a nice shape. But she lacked Victoria's elegance and whatever mysterious force it was that formed beauty.

I handed her a drink as she entered the room. She seemed relieved when she saw me, but looked around cautiously as though someone more sinister might be lurking in a corner.

"I've never done this before," I said.

She eyed me from head to foot and said, "You don't look like you'd need to." The flatness in her voice made me wonder whether she meant it, or if it had been a rote response.

We talked business first. I explained I didn't know exactly what I wanted, mostly just to be with someone. What would it cost, "all inclusive" for the night?

She scrunched her face. Her nose wrinkled. She said she wasn't sure. She called in to check, asked for Jake, told me $500 while he was still on the line. I grabbed the phone from her. Talked him down to $350. When I hung up, I told her I was a good tipper.

She didn't say anything. I'd also run out of conversation and realized that the erection I'd had while I was waiting had headed south. I felt seized with self-consciousness, almost dizzy. I sat down.

"You all right?" she asked.

I nodded told her I'd be okay.

She told me she had a joint in her bag. Maybe it would help me loosen up. I told her it wouldn't, but it was fine with me if she smoked. She took her clothes off, got on the bed and lit up. I thought about telling her what would help me, but this was Ohio, not New York or even San Francisco where heroin was becoming fashionable. I thought of Johnny's tirades about the prejudice against needle users. I didn't want the hooker to think I was a low-life.

"What about some coke?" I asked.

"You got any?"

"No, can you get some?"

She made a call. My bet it was Jake again. Twenty minutes later there was a knock on the door and I was out another hundred dollars, but the evening improved considerably.

I told her more or less why I'd come to Sulvan. She wasn't from the town and couldn't think of any crimes that far back. I asked her where she was from, but she seemed shy about telling me. I was starting to imagine the whole scene was research for some as yet unwritten piece. She said she hadn't been hooking long. Wanted to save some money, go to Chicago or New York. Dreams of being a department store buyer. I took another drink, and tried not to think about the fact that there were several women I would rather have been with. Their names, faces, bodies kept running through my mind, *Delia, Sharon, Raven, Raven, Raven, Victoria, Moira, Ingrid, Ingrid . . .*

Incredibly there was a movie I'd been in playing on cable. I caught it channel surfing and left it on. We were naked in bed talking, snorting, half-heartedly groping each other with the TV in the background. She finally noticed a resemblance between the snotty brother of the hero's best friend and myself. She shouted, "It's you! Oh my God, it's you!"

The only sex we had that night was a blowjob, shortly before we both fell asleep. My hand was on her hair, I tried to imagine it was Raven's hair, but sex shouldn't feel like an acting exercise.

We slept in. When we woke, I started kissing her. She kissed me back and we screwed. I don't think it was on the clock, though I did give her a hundred above what she took off my VISA.

After she left, I popped some aspirin for my head and went back to sleep, but made myself get up before one. I didn't want to lose the day.

I had a quick diner breakfast and headed for the town library where I scanned many copies of *The Register* from the time period of Joe's parole and a bit beyond.

There'd been a series of break-ins. A bank robbery, but only two guys had been involved and neither of them fit Joe's description. A warehouse break-in, one masked robber. I skimmed for a follow-up. It looked like there hadn't been any arrests. At one point suspicion focused on the security guards – one of whom had taken off on a scheduled vacation the day after and never come back. The guard's family insisted they had no idea where he was. A police detective had gone to Puerto Rico looking for him, but returned alone.

The same night as the break-in, though it didn't make the papers till the following day, there had been a murder. No connection. Just an unusual crime spree for Sulvan. Plus a suspicious house fire as well.

The murder victim had died in the early morning. Susannah Martin, age twenty-three. Waitress. Studying for a degree in "veterinary assistant" at the local community college. Someone had broken into her apartment, raped and strangled her. As I read the article, I was thinking about what Kyra and Mirabella had told me about Joe's quirks. I was wondering if the victim had been strangled, *then* raped.

I went through more papers. They were all there, on microfiche, but not indexed, so it was slow going. There had been an arrest a week after the murder. Ex-boyfriend of the victim's. The police had been called a couple of times by neighbors when they'd fought. She'd complained about his violence to friends.

It had gone to trial, though there wasn't a lot of physical evidence. There was a neighbor, an eyewitness who had seen the back of someone leaving Susannah's apartment, but she wasn't sure it was the defendant. Thought it would have been a smaller man. The accused, Raymond (Ray the Man) Carter, had been a high school football hero. Got a scholarship to a college in Texas, got injured, left school. Returned to Sulvan where he held a series of jobs.

Though both the victim and the alleged assailant were black, there were charges of racism. Many of these accusations were made by Raymond's mother, Destiny Carter. She was a widow who supported three kids, and Raymond was her baby. She was ready to shout his innocence on every street corner and nearly did, organizing daily rallies in front of the courthouse to protest "the outrage" of his arrest.

The defense contended that the victim – who according to her friends was studious, hard-working and "going places," – also liked to use cocaine on occasion and was known to have taken up with several men before, during and after her romance with Ray the Man. These charges were met by pickets and protests from local feminists, who accused the public defender of "smearing the victim."

The judge wound up dismissing the case – lack of evidence. The prosecution never reopened it.

By the time I finished my reading, I was anxious to talk to that district attorney and maybe the arresting officer, find out if the name Jerome Combs had ever come up in the investigation. But it was nearly four o'clock, so I just gathered my copies and returned to the hotel with the idea of actually getting some rest and an early start the next day.

No company that night and no substance beyond my medications. I even got a decent amount of sleep, but it wasn't restful. Ingrid was in my dreams. She was wearing those thigh-high boots from that day I'd seen her. They made a rhythmic tapping sound. She wanted me to follow her somewhere. We seemed to go from the park to PD's squat to some other place I couldn't quite recognize with stark white corridors and an anti-septic smell. Then I knew. She was going to show me a body. I was thinking it might be hers, or Susannah's, or Moira's. We were approaching a slab. The body was under a sheet. She looked at me, smiled, winked. I understood before she lifted the sheet it would be my body on the table. I screamed myself awake.

It was already morning. I showered, shaved and dressed, put on the new shirt and tie I'd picked up in town the previous day.

It was gray, cold and drizzling. I ate in the motel restaurant and ducked into my rental car even though it was only about four blocks to the courthouse and as a New Yorker it was against my religion to drive where I can walk.

It didn't take long to find the parole office, but I hadn't called in advance and had no idea whether, David Feinmann, the name I'd gotten from Ouspenski, would still be working. Luck was with me. I passed a door with his nameplate.

I showed him my press ID and explained as much as I thought he needed to know. He told me he didn't like the idea of discussing his clients with reporters.

"You're an officer of the court," I said. "Not his therapist."

It was the wrong thing to say. He pointed to his diploma on the wall. David Feinmann, M.S.W. He went on stroking his beard and talking about the ethics of his profession.

I told him my work was important too. I told him about Ingrid's murder and that Joe/Jerome may have had a role.

"Why aren't the police here?" he asked.

"They will be if I keep digging."

There wasn't much in the parole report. Jerome had been a good client. Got himself a job and kept his appointments. His last meeting with Feinmann had been a couple of months prior to Suzie's murder.

Feinmann remembered him, or said he did. "He was an angry kid, and an angry young man. I'm sure he's still angry."

"Do you think he could have been a killer?"

"Listen, my easiest ones are the murderers. Most people kill someone, it's a bar fight that gets out of hand. Or a crime of passion kind of thing. They have jobs. They have families. They're not usually career criminals."

I jotted down the address of the convenience store where Joe had found a job. Feinmann said he thought it was still open. As for the rooming house Joe/Jerome had moved into, he was certain the whole block had been raised years ago for student housing.

"Why do you think Jerome left town?"

"Find work, travel, start over. He completed. Never missed an appointment. As far as I'm concerned Jerome Comb was one of my successes."

"Why would he change his name?"

Feinmann leaned back in his chair. He took out a handkerchief and started to polish his eyeglasses. "Jerome Comb grew up being shoved from one foster home and institution to the next. Had a mother who was abusive. Didn't have a daddy. Why the heck wouldn't he change his name? *Especially* if he was going to leave and start fresh?"

I stopped by the D.A.'s offices down the hall. The secretary told me everyone was in court, no one working there now had worked there ten years ago, and the earliest I could see anyone would be next week.

I went downstairs to the court archives and spent some time going through the transcripts of Ray Carter's abbreviated trial. No mention of Jerome.

After a lunch break, I headed for the police station with the idea of speaking to Detective Novak, who of course had retired. His partner told me what he remembered – the detective had never doubted it was "the boyfriend." The name Jerome Comb wasn't familiar to him. He gave me a number for Novak in Florida and told me to give him his regards. I tried the number, but it had been disconnected and there was no new listing.

I wanted to speak to Raymond himself. Find out if he knew Jerome. There was no listing for him in the book, but there was one for Destiny. I glanced at the tourist map I'd picked up at the motel. Her street was nearby. The rain had stopped so I walked over. The building was larger, more institutional looking than those around it.

I realized from the tenants I saw going to and from, it was some kind of seniors housing project.

The main door was open. I found my way to Mrs. Carter's apartment and rang the bell. She answered on the chain. Looked at me like I was crazy and said that Raymond was "five years dead."

When I told her I was doing a story on the Martin case, and thought her son was innocent, she let me inside and we talked. She told me he'd died of a drug overdose – pain pills and alcohol according to the doctors. Shame was Destiny's assessment.

"Not cause he killed that girl," she said. Ray, she told me, had gone off to college with big plans, and never gotten over it when they hadn't worked out. The trial had been the breaking point. He'd been hoping to be vindicated, not "dismissed." He was "too sensitive" to live under suspicion.

Before I knew what was happening, Destiny had me sitting on the couch, drinking instant coffee and looking through the photo albums and scrapbooks she kept of her son. She was crying by the time we'd gone through them.

Before I left, I asked her if she'd ever heard of Jerome Comb. She told me that she hadn't known many of Raymond's friends and she certainly wouldn't have known any of "that woman's."

Suzie didn't have any family for me to harass, which was just as well because I was beginning to feel like a creep for bothering Mrs. Carter. I wanted to quit for the day. Quit for good, thank you very much. So far I had no evidence that Jerome Comb had even known Susannah Martin, much less had had any reason to kill her. The whole trip had been a waste of time. I wanted to go back to my motel and get fetal for a few hours.

But first, just so I could say I tried, I walked over to the convenience store where Joe had worked. I didn't think it likely anyone would remember him, but I thought I might be able to get a next of kin's name, a new address, something.

The store was part of a local chain. There were two people working and no other customers. The woman behind the counter smelled of soap or perfume and might have been a disfigured burn victim behind the thick layer of foundation on her face. Her nametag said, "Lillian." The guy was younger, oily hair and pimples. The fluorescent lighting didn't help either of them.

I flashed my ID while explaining I was looking for some information about a man who'd worked there ten years ago. Lillian said she didn't know anyone who'd worked there that long ago. I told her I needed to see their employee records for ten years back. Were they on the premises, or would I have to go to a central office?

"The records are back there," she pointed to a door in the back of the store. "But we're not allowed to just . . ."

I casually slipped her a twenty while keeping my eyes on her face and telling her I was only in town a short time, and it would be so helpful.

The kid saw the money and said, "I can take him in."

"No, I'll go," she said taking me to a storage room lined with stacks of boxes. In one corner, there was a desk and a couple of four-draw file cabinets. She went over to the bottom drawer, pulled out some folders and placed them on the desk.

"I don't know how far back, we got em, for." she said.

As I deciphered the filing system, she rambled. Said it must get lonely, traveling for my work. I tried to sound friendly and non-committal.

There were more forms than I would have thought, but I found Jerome's application and an employee information card.

There were no payment records or anything to indicate when he'd quit. Lillian wasn't sure where that would be. "You could ask the boss. He's on vacation now. These are the only records I know."

The card had originally been filled out in blue ink. The rooming house address was crossed out. Another address was written above it, in black ink with a phone number. Also in black, the name "Emily Wojinski" had been filled in next to the emergency contact slot. The phone number was the same as the one in the new residence. I copied the information.

Lillian was standing over me as I wrote. "That's a couple streets down, near the community college."

I thanked her for her help.

"Where you staying at?" she asked. "In case I talk to anyone who'd know something."

I told her I'd probably be leaving the next day and thanked her again. The address was in the opposite direction from the courthouse in front of which my rental was still parked. But I walked, almost jogged to the street. I felt like I finally had something. A name. Someone who had known Joe. A lover, probably. Though for all I knew she could have been a sweet old lady who'd rented him a room. Maybe she was someone with whom he still kept in touch. Someone he could turn to when he wouldn't be able to trust anyone else.

The block was well kept. Neat row houses, some with bay windows overlooking small front gardens.

I reached the address and walked up the front steps. The buzzers were in the vestibule under the mailboxes. There was no Wojinski listed for 2A or any other apartment. I thought of going back to the motel and checking the phone directory but decided while I was there, I might as well see if anyone remembered them.

I rang 2A. There was no intercom, but someone buzzed me in.

A young woman wearing (as far as I could tell) only a long tee shirt, her wet hair turbaned by a towel answered the door. It was obvious from her expression that she'd been expecting someone else.

I told her I was a reporter doing some research, looking for a couple that used to live in the building, in that very apartment, ten years ago.

"Ten years ago," she repeated.

She told me to wait for a minute. Closed the door and came back in a bathrobe. She invited me in and introduced herself as Janet. She didn't think anyone living there now had lived there that long.

"I think it's all students now. State or the Community. I'm State."

"Did you know the previous tenants?"

"Grad student. She was moving to Cincinnati. I'm sure she wasn't here back then."

"I guess I'm wasting my time and yours."

"Sorry."

"I don't suppose you'd happen to know anyone named Jerome Comb . . ."

She shook her head.

". . . or Emily Wojinski."

"*Professor* Wojinski?" She asked. She sounded stunned, though not as stunned as I was. "She used to live here?"

I sat down.

Janet told me the little she knew about the professor. Wojinski taught literature. Janet hadn't taken her class, but knew her rep as a tough grader though she was "very popular with the artsy types." No idea where she lived now or with whom.

I asked to use her phone and called the number I'd copied from the form. It was answered by a child who told me it was a wrong number and hung up. I tried again, spoke with his dad who said they'd had the number for years and he didn't know who'd had it before. I borrowed Janet's phone book, but there was no listing for Wojinski. Janet found a University map and pointed out the Humanities Center where I could find Wojinski's office. I thanked her profusely and might have asked her to join me for dinner if the buzzer hadn't rung. We were soon joined by her large baffled boyfriend for whose benefit she quickly explained my presence.

I walked back to the courthouse to get my car. I figured it was too late to try Wojinski's office, so I returned to my room. Desperate for company, I even thought of calling Gina again. Rejected that idea, phoned Delia at three different numbers, phoned Johnny, phoned Sharon. Nobody answering. Called my home number to check my answering machine. Ouspenski must have gotten my letter as he'd left several messages. There was also something from Lenny's father who seemed to be in the city.

I decided with the Major in New York, and Ouspenski's being so anxious to get in touch with me, I should get home. Wherever this Wojinski thing was leading, I couldn't give it that much time. I called the airport and booked a flight back from Cleveland for the following evening.

I was too restless to stay in my room, so I went for a walk

through town. Stopped in at a couple of bars. Wound up drinking and dancing someplace where the music was too loud for much else. Came back alone and collapsed on my bed.

I woke up late morning when the hotel maid came knocking on my door. My clothes smelled of perfume, tobacco and sweat. There was no way I could wear my jacket. I didn't even have an overcoat, just the bomber I'd picked up in the thrift store outside of San Francisco. So I stopped by the men's store in town before going to meet Miss Emily.

There happened to be a sale and an Armani that fit. The temperature was in the forties, and it was drizzling. I couldn't see wearing a ripped leather jacket with the suit, so I got myself a new faux-Burberry as well. My credit card would cover everything. I'd just have to pick up some freelance work when I got back.

I drove onto the campus and followed my map to the Humanities Center, found the English Department offices and finally a plaque for Dr. Emily Wojinski. The door was closed. I heard a muffled one-sided conversation inside. A girl with a near crew-cut wearing jeans and a flannel shirt came by to wait as well. I caught her staring at the suit.

"Job interview," I whispered.

After a few minutes, I heard the sound of a chair scraping the floor as someone rose. I'd been standing on the hinged side of the door, so I moved around it as it opened. The crew cut was already standing in front of it.

"Come in Diane," a voice from inside called.

"He was here first," she said looking at me.

I was now standing in front of the open door looking at the woman. She was crouched down by a bookshelf. She grabbed a volume, and returned to her desk. The office was cluttered with figures of deities and animals, which I later learned were of Polynesian, Hindu, Mayan, and Inca origin. The woman was wearing a loose cotton blouse, and a multi-colored skirt with a complicated pattern. The ensemble looked hand made, something likely purchased in a third world market in a country featured in the travel posters decorating the walls.

The woman herself looked like she might have been a native of one of those countries, though I couldn't figure out which. She was short. Her body not unlike that of one of her fertility goddess miniatures. Large breasts, waist small, round, childbearing hips. Definitely too heavy, too womanly for the pages of *Vogue*, but not fat. Her large brown eyes looked vaguely Asian, as did her wide flat nose. Her hair, black and curly reached her waist. Her lips were full and like those eyes, expressive. The eyes were expressing amusement.

"Groovy threads," she said.

"Thanks. Dr. Wojinski my name is Peter Teller and I'd like to speak with you a few minutes. I . . ."

"Books?"

"What?"

"You're the textbook guy, right? Look, I put together my own materials for my classes. I have a seminar in twenty minutes and I've got to see this young lady about . . ."

"Woman," the crew cut interrupted.

"*Really*? Lady is offensive?"

"Yeah, Emily. It's a class thing. And 'young' is ageist anyway. It's a diminution."

Emily was shaking her head.

"Dr. Wojinski, I don't sell books. I'm a reporter from New York. I'm working on a story and I need some information about a friend of yours. Jerome Comb."

There was the briefest flash of panic in her eyes. I don't think the crew cut caught it.

"Diane, I'm running so late today. Can we meet after the seminar?"

Diane shrugged her shoulders and nodded. I walked into the office and shut the door.

"What's he done?" Emily asked.

I told her he was friends with a man in New York who had allegedly sliced and diced his girlfriend. The police wanted to question him about what he knew and he'd taken off.

"No, no, no, no." Her arms were folded sternly below those

large breasts, but she was smiling. "That doesn't make any sense. You would have had to do some work to find me. I haven't seen him in over ten years. What could you possibly want from me?"

"You're right Dr. Wojinski. There's more to it. I think he may have been directly involved in the murder. I think he might have been involved in a lot of things. I'd like to know more about him. Who he was when you knew him. What he was like.

"Look, Mr. . . ."

"Teller. Peter," I said putting out my hand for her to shake.

She looked at it a moment, but didn't take it. "Peter. I don't have time for this. I really do have to teach a seminar in ten minutes."

I sat down in the chair in front of her desk. I leaned forward. "Please. I'm trying to find out what happened. Why it happened. I may have already messed things up. I think he may have killed a man in Oregon because of something I did, or failed to do . . ."

"What does . . ."

"I don't know. Maybe there's something you can tell me that'll make it make sense."

"This isn't the place."

"Later, after you finish?"

"I have to think about this."

"Please Emily. I'm leaving tonight. Can I buy you dinner?"

She started writing something down. "This is my address. Come over at six and we can talk."

I asked if we could we meet earlier. She told me she'd be home by four.

Her address was on the way out to the airport, and I had to check out of my room, so everything went into the trunk of the car. I was feeling self-conscious about my suit, but didn't want her to think I'd dressed down for her benefit so I wound up wearing my jeans with the new jacket. I got to her place around three-thirty. It was still raining so I stayed in the car with the heat and the radio on until she pulled up a few minutes later.

She also had a Beetle. Hers was cherry red and decorated with numerous bumper stickers including such favorites as,

Silence=Death, Protected by the Goddess, and of course *Dukakis/Bentsen*. When she saw me, she noticed my jeans.

"You changed."

She walked in the door throwing her keys and coat on a small table.

"I'm hungry," she said. She led me into the kitchen where she took out spinach, tofu, carrots, several variety of mushrooms, and many other vegetables. She handed me a knife and told me to start chopping.

She lived in an older part of town. The first floor of a Victorian renovated to a two unit. Her apartment looked like an extension of her office. Large color photos of exotic locations. Books. Deities.

I commented on what a nice place it was. "Do you live here alone?"

"I do now," she said chewing a carrot as she chopped one into the bowl.

As we peeled, grated and sliced, I learned a few things about Doctor Emily Wojinski. She was from Hawaii, her mother some combination of native, Tahitian, Japanese and missionary, her father a merchant marine from Ohio. She and her mother had moved to Cleveland when she was seven to search for him after he'd disappeared from their lives. Emily had gotten her Ph.D. in American literature from the same institution in which she taught.

She heated blue corn tortillas in the oven and brought them to the table.

"Emily," I said. "Tell me about Jerome."

She wrapped some salad into a tortilla. "You tell me first. This isn't just some article you're writing. What you were saying in the office, it's personal. You tell *me* about it."

I spent the next hour telling her. I started from the day I saw Ingrid in the park. She stopped me. What was Wigstock? How could people live in the park? She had a talent for listening, drawing me out. I didn't tell her about sex with Raven or getting beat in San Francisco. But I told her most of it. When I mentioned Joe, sometimes she'd ask a question or make a comment. She didn't flinch when I told her about Moira or Mirabella or what Mirabella had told me.

"He only hit me once," she said, "and that was the day he left."

There was something about her presence that calmed me. Slowed me down. I could see her being the quiet woman, the muse, behind some great man, a composer or even a writer. I couldn't imagine her with Joe Holiday.

She didn't want me smoking in her house, so I took a cigarette break in her back yard. It had gotten colder; a light snow was falling. I inhaled as deeply as I could, trying to get the most out of every drag. When I went back inside, she was in the living room and had put out a platter of fresh fruit. There was also some kind of steaming glop in ceramic bowls. She told me it was rice pudding. "Brown rice," she said, "with rice milk. I'm working up to vegan."

She didn't have coffee, but offered some herbal chicory concoction with twice the caffeine.

"Now it's your turn." I said.

"Joe Holiday," she said repeating the name I had told her.

I took a spoonful of the rice glop, tasted cinnamon, nutmeg, honey and ten things I couldn't name. It was surprisingly wonderful.

"You told me you don't know why he changed it. But do you know why he chose that name?"

"No idea," she said. She looked away. It was the only time that night I thought she might have been holding something back.

She told me they'd met when she was teaching at the community college. She taught mostly remedial courses, though Joe – Rome – she called him, had been placed in what was considered a freshman college level class. He hadn't been a stand out student. Wasn't very different from the others, except for the attention he paid her.

"I only had my master's. English Arts. It's basically a teaching degree. I went to the state college in Athens. Everyone was always encouraging me to teach. I don't think I really thought about it. I certainly had no plans to go on for a doctorate. I came to Sulvan to teach high school. But I couldn't do it. The students were horrible to me. That's why I wound up at the community college. I wouldn't have been able to get tenure even at the community without a doctorate. But at least I could work with adults. Mostly working people."

"I can't imagine your being intimidated by a bunch of kids," I said.

"You can't imagine, Peter. I was different then. I guess that's why I fell in with Rome."

"Different?"

She kept one hand on her teacup and briefly put the other one over mine. "I weighed about eighty pounds more than I do now. I'd always been heavy. Later, I learned that, well, the weight, it can be a way of being invisible. And I was invisible for a long time. It was like I was living under a kind of spell and nobody saw me until Rome.

"It wasn't an issue for him. It confused me at first, his attention. His acceptance of me the way I was.

"For the first time, I felt normal. I felt loved. Later, I would look back and think there were all these signs, even from the beginning. But I suppose that that kind of love, romantic, obsessive, whatever name you give it, it's like . . .

"Have you ever been on stage?"

"Yes," I said imagining she had suddenly recognized me from some straight to cable fiasco.

"It's like being on stage and you can't see past the spotlights. Only the light itself."

It had really only been a few months, their life together. After the first weeks, he'd come home late, if at all. Then one morning he told her there was someone else, packed up his stuff and left.

"The suddenness of his leaving, wasn't it strange?"

"Not really. I knew things weren't right, and I'd grown up on stories of my father's disappearing. There was one odd thing. That old car I'd given him. He just left it. At first I thought he was around, parking it, but then it hit me, he never moved it. One day I realized it was unlocked. He'd left the key and the title in the glove box. I checked at the store, but he hadn't shown up for work in weeks. I figured he must have just left town. I had the feeling he left the car for me to find, his way of saying he wasn't trying to rip me off."

"What did you do with the car?"

"I sold it."

"When did he leave, Emily?"

"Told you. Must have been '79."

"What was the date?"

She went into the kitchen to put up some more water. "What makes that important?"

"I know he completed parole at the end of February 1979, so he was in town at least till then. Sometime after that he walks away from a job, a car and you. He starts using a fake name. Ten years later he even tells a guy he *had to* leave town. There were a lot of things going on back then. If I had the date maybe I could figure out which thing hooks up with Joe's leaving."

"What date did you break up with somebody ten years ago? I don't know the date. Which *thing* did you have in mind any way?"

"Susannah Martin's murder."

Emily put down her mug. She stared at the steam coming out of it. "I knew Suzie. She was one of my students," she said quietly.

"I'm sorry."

"She was killed on a Saturday morning but it wasn't in the paper till Sunday. I remember it clearly because Rome left Saturday morning and I hadn't been out of the house all weekend. I was home reading the Sunday paper and thinking that I shouldn't be feeling sorry for myself because at the same time that Rome was breaking up with me, this girl was being killed."

"Did he know her? From the school?"

"I don't know. But I don't think he would have left me and raced out to kill someone."

"What if she was the one he was leaving you for? What if he went to get her and she said no. He's just left you and now she's rejected him. He kills her in a rage."

"Peter, he left me for a man. I didn't mention that detail before because it didn't seem relevant."

"What about the warehouse robbery? Did you read about it?

That would have happened earlier, the same night."

"Look, she said her voice getting louder and faster as she spoke, "He had some whole other life I didn't know anything about. I have thought about it before. I can't imagine the circumstances where he would've killed her. It doesn't mean it's outside the realm of possibility. When I read about the murder something flashed through my mind. The warehouse too. But the Jerome I knew, he wouldn't have had the, the initiative to pull off something like that. I mean the first week a guy gets his driver's license, he commits an armed robbery?

"I'm sorry, Emily. I'm sorry I came here and asked you. I didn't mean . . .'"

"I think I half expected the police to come to me years ago asking questions about him. But they never did."

We were silent for a minute. Sitting together on her living room couch. I was cradling a warm mug in my hands. She'd put on a record, authentic vinyl, Diana Washington. It was still early enough that I didn't have to leave for the airport yet, and I didn't want to.

I wanted her. It felt strange. Did I want her because she had been deflowered by Joe Holiday? It wasn't so much that I wanted to fuck her. I just wanted to be with her. To lean my head against those breasts – which I was certain would be soft and warm, the opposite of Kyra's. I wanted to wake up entangled in her hair.

But it wasn't the vibe I was getting from her. She seemed interested in me, wanted to talk. But I had the feeling I was reminding her too much of her pain. Maybe there had been something recent too. The way she had said, "I do now," when I asked her whether she lived alone.

I got up and started looking at some of the statues and carvings.

"Tell me about, after."

She smiled. "It's not for your book, is it?"

"No."

"After I was a mess. It wasn't like my life was going to be any different than it had been before. But I couldn't go back to what it was."

"To being invisible."

"More than that. I couldn't go back to sleepwalking through my life. I was going to be aware of my pain, my loneliness. That was too much. I wanted to kill myself."

"Oh Emily."

"I didn't know how. I had an electric stove, I was afraid to cut, and my God I sound like that Dorothy Parker poem. But I couldn't stand it anymore, so one day I walked into an emergency room and signed myself into the hospital. It was a mistake. There were these teenagers there. Two of them. They'd tried to kill themselves, or maybe their parents needed a break. It was like teaching high school again. They were awful. I got worse. I wanted to leave. But the doctors wouldn't let me because they were afraid I would harm myself. Finally I tried to walk out and wound up on the locked unit, surrounded with really ill people. I knew I'd have to figure out something else, some other way to be, because this was not the path I wanted to be on."

I nodded.

"So when I got out I found this therapist. My insurance didn't pay for it and even with the sliding scale I used all my savings. But I learned a lot and it helped. I'd stopped eating because of the depression. Lost about thirty pounds. Then I became obsessed with that too."

It struck me that her voice, her speech, was as good as any I'd heard on a stage. She spoke with a compassion toward herself, a sense of irony and no self-pity.

"Learning to accept this body wasn't easy. One time in Nepal, I was hiking. I got lost. It started to snow, and the trail was gone. I remember realizing how strong my body was and what a good job it was doing keeping me alive, and I thought I can't afford this obsession with weight. We get so little time as it is."

"How did you wind up in Nepal?"

"I wanted to get away from the apartment, the town. I needed money. I found out about a position in Japan teaching English to businessmen. I got it."

"How'd you like it?"

"I didn't. At least not the first few months. I kept thinking they'd made a mistake. I wasn't their idea of what an American English teacher should be. You know tall with blue eyes and blond hair and oh God, Peter, I didn't mean . . ."

"It's okay."

"But something started to happen. I realized teaching could be like my art? I never felt like a *seductress* before, but suddenly I was getting these tight-ass Japanese businessmen to loosen up and laugh in the classes. Then I did the backpack thing. Over a year before the money ran out."

"You came back here?"

"The U was open. I got a job in recruitment. Can you believe it? Talking to high school kids. Went back for my Ph.D. and voila. Oh Peter! Your flight!"

I wanted to tell her that it didn't matter. I'd get another. I called the airport. The plane was delayed due to weather.

"I guess I could drive out now."

"You've got a little time. You're welcome to hang out," she said.

"I'd like that. Can I ask you something? The blinding light? Have you seen it since?"

"I've had lovers. I've had relationships. I don't know that feeling like you've returned to Paradise? Getting that from another person, it's like getting it from a bottle or a drug. It's an illusion."

"That's not very romantic."

"Have you seen the light?" she asked.

I thought of that time with Raven, but I knew it wasn't what she meant. There was the feeling I had on smack, but that was her point.

"Maybe I've come close."

I went outside for another smoke on her porch. The snow was just beginning to stick. When I came back in she was using the bathroom, so I looked at her books. I saw a small section on astrology, witchcraft, and tarot. There was something wrapped in a lavender silk cloth. Johnny kept his tarot cards wrapped in a cloth like that.

She returned to the room.

"You read cards?" I asked.

"Not in a while, but yeah."

"You believe in it?"

"I believe it's a good instrument for getting in touch with the unconscious."

"You can't tell the future?"

She smiled. I knew she had to be in her thirties, but when she smiled she looked like a kid. "I like to believe we create our own futures. But sometimes when I've done readings, I've gotten feelings, hunches that came true."

"What happens if you get a bad feeling? Do you tell people?"

"It's better to know. Face it."

"Would you read my cards?"

"If you like."

We sat down on the floor. She unwrapped the deck and handed them to me. Told me to think of a question that couldn't be answered with a yes or no.

"It's best to choose one area – work, love. The cards are good at advising, telling you the pitfalls, what you need to know."

I shuffled and cut them as instructed while concentrating on my question – *What would be the result of my work?* I selected ten cards. Handed them back to her and she threw them. I didn't believe in it, but still it shook me when I noticed the Tower, the Devil and Death.

She was concentrating on the spread, engaged in an animated internal discussion which included pointing at cards, mouthing words, nodding her head.

"You can tell me your question or let me give my impressions first."

"Tell me what you see."

"You haven't had your cards read before?"

I shook my head.

"There are two types of cards. The Major Arcana – the picture cards, and the Pips – the ones with numbers and suits, precursors of our playing cards. The Major Arcana are more about fate if that makes sense. But they only comprise a third of the deck. Seven out of the ten cards you picked are Major Arcana. That would indicate you're at some critical juncture."

"Go on."

"The Knight of Wands here in the center represents you. He's a knight. He's on a quest. Court cards often stand in for people. Wands represent fire, passion. More negatively, ambition, but not greed. He's crossed over by the Devil."

"Which means?"

"This card comes up a lot around alcohol issues or drugs. Often there's a need to confront what you find shameful. It may have to do with self-deception, especially as it would affect the mission of the Knight. Here I'd interpret it as the need for you not to get sidetracked by delusion in the pursuit of a goal.

"Above that in the position of the conscious world is the Ace of Swords. Aces often herald adventures, journeys – though not necessarily physical ones. Swords are contentious. It's difficult the journey you're on. Dangerous. The swords are analogous to spades. When regular playing cards are used for divination, the Ace of Spades signifies death.

"Below in the position of unconscious forces stands the High Priestess. She represents spirituality but also dark forces. The occult. Mysteries. She's reversed which makes her even more ominous. Her position indicates that you may not be as aware of her, of her power, dark forces, as you need to be."

"Emily, you're not exactly describing a day at the . . ."

"Would you like me to continue?"

"Oh yeah."

"In the recent past we have the Queen of Cups. Also reversed. She might represent a woman. A beautiful woman, but unknowable and dishonest. You shouldn't trust her. It could also indicate some other kind of seductive force."

"What other kind?"

"I'm not sure. In the near future, but not the final outcome, we have the Death card, which does not necessarily mean anyone is going to die. It may be some finality you have to accept to move on."

My mind was sticking on the words, "not necessarily."

"The Tower is in the seventh position, which is similar to the first. It represents you, your energies, where you find yourself. It indicates . . ."

"The destruction of all existing forms. A friend told me."

The card above the Tower featured a man carrying a stick with a sack tied to the end of it. He was obliviously looking at the sky while dogs nipped at his heals, and children laughed as he was about to unknowingly step off a cliff.

"That's the Fool," Emily explained. "Sometimes he can be lucky. We have to take risks on life's journey while retaining our innocence. He's reversed here which could indicate danger. He's in the position of how others view your journey.

"Above him is the world, which is the ying-yang, coming together of all the elements, complete spiritual integration."

"That's what I get?"

"No, that's what you hope for. The final outcome is the next card, The Sun. It indicates rational enlightenment. You get the truth, knowledge, an understanding of the big picture. Was your question about your work?

"Yes."

"The cards indicate you'll find the answers eventually. But the danger is if you can't distinguish the truth from your desires, your 'lusts' – that's the Devil."

I felt as Raven might have put it "creeped out."

"Peter, it's only a deck of cards. Just stay pure in your purpose. The Knight on his quest. You'll find what you're looking for. I promise."

"That's within your power?"

She laughed. "'If a fool pursues his foolish path to its end, he will gain wisdom.' William Blake."

We drank more tea. She put on a Bucky Pizzarelli album and smiled when I recognized it. We sat for a while watching the snow.

She was asking questions about New York. She'd only been there in transit. I wrote my number for her, "in case" she was ever in town. I wanted to put my arm around her, but didn't. I called the airport again. No further delays. Time to head out.

I put on my jacket and coat. I was by the door when she said, "Peter maybe it would be better if you didn't go tonight."

I felt the air leaving my body.

"I mean," she continued, "the roads must be slippery. You can stay on the couch."

Emily's couch. Emily's house. Emily. I wanted to stay. I should have stayed. But I'd started feeling that restlessness again, that voice in my head. Now it was telling me I had to get back to New York. Tell all to Ouspenski.

I thanked her for everything.

She stood on her tiptoes. I bent down and kissed her warm cheek as we hugged good-bye. "Take care of yourself," she said.

More than once I almost turned around on the drive. I was giddy thinking of her. She wasn't even my type. Short, heavy, older. But suddenly short, heavy, older *was* my type. I was thinking about how I'd been living those past few weeks, the booze, the drugs. My "desires" she called them. "Lusts." But I had hardly even felt the need for a cigarette when I was with her. I wondered if that's how Joe had felt as well – that she could save him in the warmth of those breasts, of that heart.

It was sometime past two in the morning when I got back to my apartment. I was feeling a thousand different ways. Exhausted, but still hyper.

I decided I'd call Emily in a few hours. Let her know I'd arrived safely. I wondered if I could find some excuse to see her again, and thought about what might have happened if I'd stayed.

I checked my new messages. One from Johnny, wanting to know if I was back. Said he knew about a squat organizer I might want to meet. Also left me a pager number where I could reach him. I tried Victoria's first, but there wasn't an answer, so I dialed the beeper.

He called a few minutes later, sounding as awake as I was, though his voice was a little slurred. I heard music, other people behind him. He started updating me on some demos and giving details about the latest round of evictions. I was thinking it was more Laura's beat than mine.

"So maybe I could help you out on this. You know, research?"

"That's cool man. I'd appreciate it."

"Yeah, like the thing is, I could use the bread."

"You'd get a research byline, if it was significant," I said, "But I don't get much for the articles."

"Yeah, maybe it could lead somewhere."

I felt awkward having this business discussion with him in the middle of the night. I'd just wanted to talk – tell him about the Suzie Martin murder and my suspicions. Tell him about Emily.

"You want to come over?" I asked.

"Now?"

"Yeah," I said. "Why not?"

"I'm with some people. It's raining. We can sit for coffee tomorrow."

"It's just, I'm feeling kind of fidgety here."

"Fidgety?"

"Yeah. You could find us a couple of bags. I'll reimburse you. Cab too. We can talk about your ideas, on the squat thing."

He told me to hold on a minute. There was some muffled talking. It sounded like he'd put his hand over the receiver. Then he came back on line.

"Yeah. Okay. How much do you want?"

He could get the dope from the people he was with. But he didn't have any money, so someone would be coming with him. I buzzed him in twenty minutes later. Gave him the cash. He went down to his friend waiting in the taxi, then came back up.

I was describing the parole officer as he took out a set.

"Clean?" I asked.

"That's what the man told me."

I was bleaching it while he cooked. I handed it over to him. He filled it and handed it back to me. I cleaned it again and kept talking as I shot, then gave the needle to him.

"But I still can't figure out what motivates the guy? Why did Joe kill Ingrid? She wasn't a threat to him. Why take the risk?"

"I don't think he saw it as a risk," Johnny said. He was about to refill. "I don't think he thought he had that much to lose."

"Aren't you going to clean that?"

"I trust you," he said plunging the spike into his arm.

"Why take a chance? You could . . ."

Johnny leaned back, closed his eyes and laughed. "Look at yourself, man. Look at what you're doing. You don't get it. What's the incubation? Ten years? You're worried about getting sick in *ten* years. We'll be dead way before then. This trip is about death."

I stared at him, not sure what was going through his mind or what to say. I finally asked, "Is something wrong? What's with you and Victoria?"

"Look, I'm not one of your old school chums. I don't have a girlfriend named Miffy and a job at her daddy's firm. I'm here at fuckin three in the morning because you called and offered to stake me for some dope if I showed. I *do* like you, Peter. But don't kid yourself, the only difference between Joe and me is I got a better vocabulary."

"You're not a cold blooded killer."

"You're right man. That's another difference. If I'd a been in that apartment, I woulda shit my pants. Joe's got more balls than me."

Even with the heroin to numb every bad thought, there was something ugly hanging in the air between us. Maybe it had always been there, but now it was going to be harder to ignore. I thought about apologizing for the way I'd pressured him into coming. But I didn't. I kept talking about the case.

"Ingrid looked kind of like Moira. You think he might have been acting out some kind of resentment toward her?"

"Toward everything." Johnny said.

"The parole officer said even back then he was angry. Abusive mother. Maybe he just hates women."

Johnny took a deep drag of his cigarette. "Maybe he was just born mean. Maybe it was her time to die."

The silences between us were getting longer. Johnny said he was heading out, wanted to get to sleep. He staggered up.

"Could you spot me taxi fare?" He asked.

I didn't have anything smaller, so I gave him a twenty. As I handed him the money, I felt a flash of awkwardness, remembering the money I'd given to Gina. He must have sensed something, because when I looked at him, his eyes met mine with concern. He patted my arm with his hand. "See you, man."

I sat for a while, listening to music. The thoughts were floating on clouds drifting through my brain. I could catch them if I tried or let them pass.

What were Johnny and I to each other? Friends? I could have gone out to cop. Why had I dangled the possibility of work in front of him?

I tried to put myself in his mind. It was strange, the way I'd thought of us as evenly matched – looks, intelligence, humor. But we weren't even. We never could be. He'd said things before to try to get me to see it. I hadn't wanted to.

There were differences between us – who we were, how the world treated us. Johnny wasn't lying when he said he liked me. But on some level, he hated me for those differences.

I imagined that that's what Joe had seen in Ingrid. She wasn't one of them. There'd always be a way out for her if she wanted it.

Ingrid had come into his world and she'd broken the rules. He was going to make sure she was punished.

I fell asleep in my chair. The hiss of the steam heat coming on woke me a while later. I didn't want to go back to bed. I wanted to do some work. I lit a cigarette. Made myself a cup of coffee and drank it black because the milk had spoiled. I sat down at my machine and noticed the last packet left by Johnny on the coffee table.

I had this vision of flushing it down the toilet and calling Emily. I didn't think Emily would have wanted a druggee in her life.

But Emily was in Ohio and I didn't know if I'd ever see her again, and lately my mind had been racing too fast for me to even sit down and work. I looked at the bag. It wasn't the same as the one we'd shared earlier. It had a stamp I hadn't seen before, *Oblivion*.

Like Johnny said when I called him from Frisco, I could always take the Ibogaine cure if it came to that. By that time, the book would be on its way to print, and the addiction developed in the process of writing it would only add to the public's interest. Who knew? A second book, maybe, *Loisaida, the sequel.*

The apartment was boiling. I cracked open a window though the temperature outside was below freezing. I took off my shirt. Threw it on the couch where my jacket was draped. Missed. It wound up on the floor. I'd get it later.

I checked out the needle. Dull but serviceable. Bleached it over by the sink. No matter what Johnny said, death wasn't my intention. Went to my desk. Put the diskettes into my computer and turned it on. Cooked up some dope. Filled the syringe. Tied my belt till my vein was popping, and jabbed in the spike.

It felt different. Everything went quiet suddenly, except for the pounding from my chest and some high-pitched noise I couldn't identify that felt vaguely familiar. I could feel the weight of my body forcing the chair off balance. I could hear the thump of my head hitting the floor, but there was no pain. No pain even as I tried to grasp the air, my lungs shutting down as if some plug had been pulled. But I wasn't afraid. I even saw that cliché tunnel and the light, brighter, a thousand times brighter than the one Emily had described. There was a blonde in the tunnel too. I couldn't make out her features, but she was beckoning me with her finger, the way Ingrid had in the dream. She wanted me to fly or float down towards her, and I wanted to, Jesus Christ, I did, but something held me back, and the light went out and I found myself floating like the dead guy in the pool, telling my story over and over.

Chapter 21

Another Summer in the City

Terri

Terri was watching Stan Ouspenski slurp down borscht at the *Ukrainian Parlor*. She couldn't imagine anything more unappetizing than cold beet soup. She wasn't too sure about Stan either. She was vaguely attracted to him, but aware she might not have been if he weren't in a position to help her career. Maybe, it was his stories she liked. For a Polish guy, he was a pretty good storyteller.

If only he weren't so damned fat.

Their "association," Terri couldn't think of how else to describe it, had started that day in the dead guy's apartment. Ouspenski had read each page as it emerged from the printer. It was mostly notes and impressions – nothing that made much sense to her. But it did to him. He told her he'd fill her in sometime and took her out for coffee a week or so later.

He'd call her from time to time after that. Tell her about his progress or lack thereof. Teller's "masterpiece" (as Stan referred to it) was full of disjointed speculation and theories. He'd used aliases for all his sources, worried that the police might subpoena his notes. Some were pretty easy to figure. Others, Stan thought might be composites or products of an overwrought imagination.

The department considered the matter closed, so he wasn't getting much support. There were plenty of ongoing investigations that needed to be worked. He talked the case up to one of the assistant DA's who looked at the printout and returned a verdict of "Hearsay." Told him to come back when he had something she could move on.

Terri looked forward to Stan's calls and updates. She was taking a couple of courses at John Jay, getting her bachelor's degree, so she didn't have a lot of time, but she agreed to do some leg work for him.

She accompanied him, both of them on their own time, to talk to Federico Fernandez aka El Rey. See if he could give them a name for the guy Peter referred to as Nexus due to his association with so many of those involved.

El Rey was now residing in the Downtown Correctional Facility, awaiting trial in federal court on drug trafficking charges. He had not been unwilling to help them – especially when Terri gently explained that the boy was not going to be subject to any charges. He gave them a name, Johnny Ramirez, but added, "I fired the bum months ago, I couldn't tell you where he is."

The biggest break had come four weeks before. Joe Holiday had been picked up passing a bad check in San Francisco. Stan and his partner had gone out to accompany him back. He told them the same story he'd told Johnny about Lenny's threatening him at the apartment. He denied having had anything to do with the murder or getting rid of the body. Said he was too high at the time to remember who else was there.

Stan had been pushing the police in Oregon on the Brewar murder, but that wasn't going anywhere.

Kyra had been given immunity and was supposed to testify against Joe in front of the grand jury. In addition, the jury would be hearing the evidence against Jacques Lanoir who was now a resident of the Bellevue intensive care unit, dying of AIDS related pneumonia.

The DA was not looking for an indictment against Moira, as she was still a federal fugitive wanted on many other charges, and besides it was unclear what if anything she had actually done.

"You must be excited," Terri said enjoying the sweet cheese

inside the blintz she was chewing. "With it all finally going to the grand jury."

"Connor, it's over. The train has arrived at its final destination."

"What do you mean?"

"No one's getting indicted. No one's going to jail over this. It was a waste of my time and yours."

"But you're a hero, Stan. What about the stuff in the newspapers?"

"Have you *read* the papers? *The Post* is playing this like I uncovered a coven or something, which the lawyers are going to turn into a joke. *The* fucking *Eye* makes it sound like the police are spreading dirt over the good citizens of the East Village, maybe as retaliation for all those brutality charges from the riot."

"So Peter Teller's notes, they aren't worth . . ."

"Shit, Connor. They aren't worth mouse turds. It's not even hearsay. It's gossip. What a piece of crap he was. We would've had Joe Holiday months ago if he hadn't leaked it to Joe's girlfriend we knew where they were. If he was alive I'd haul his ass in for obstruction. He was a fool, Teresa. It's like Faulkner said, a tale told by an idiot, full of sound and fury, signifying nothing."

"That's Shakespeare," she said.

He dunked a potato pierogi into sour cream and swallowed it whole. "I thought it was Faulkner."

"Well, Shakespeare said it first."

"Smart girl." He winked, shot her a smile that made her think that maybe he would be kind of fun in bed. "What do we got? *Kyra*? Who knows what that burn out's going to say when she gets on the stand, assuming she doesn't skip. She could tell them she was just giving Teller what he wanted, which might even be the way it went down. Besides, don't they teach you anything about legal at college? She was involved. You can't base a case on the testimony of a co-conspirator."

"What about that little girl, the runaway?"

He nodded as he swallowed a large gulp of coffee. Well, first the parents won't let me talk to her. I threatened them with obstruction, and the lawyer laughed. Then I tried begging, 'in the interest of justice,' that kind of shit. Finally, I had to convince them it would be like a part of her recovery. She'd never get past it until she got through it. That they went for. With their attorney present of course.

"I've seen women who killed their children and they weren't as tough as that kid. What do the shrinks call it? Lack of affect? Nothing fucking phased her. She just stuck to the story. She wasn't anywhere near the apartment until after it happened. Never saw a body. If Kyra remembers differently she's 'mistaken.' She doesn't know a Joe Holiday. She's never seen anyone like that. Yeah Lenny told her Ingrid was dead, just like he was telling everyone, and she grabbed the diary, she said because she thought it might be important. Said she was going to hand it over to Peter, because she thought that 'giving it to a reporter would be like giving it to the police.' And the way she remembers it, she handed it to him *before* she got grabbed."

He scooped more food into his mouth and still chewing added. "Surprise, surprise, the mother backs that. My guess is Mom figured out what it was, and *whose* it was and dumped it."

"I'm sorry," Terri said. She asked him about Peter's death. Was he thinking it was anything more than a simple accidental overdose?

"The M.E. said the shit he had on board wasn't anything out of the ordinary. His respiratory system collapsed. That's all. Happens. He got so happy he forgot to breathe."

Terri looked down into her coffee.

Stan touched her arm. "Did I say something?"

Their eyes met, and for a moment she felt an overwhelming tenderness, a sense that here was a man who would always keep her safe.

"It's nothing," she said, then tried to think of something else to ask, break the silence. "What about Moira? Do you think they'll ever find her?"

Moira

Moira sat sipping her coffee on the verandah overlooking the Pacific. She was thinking about her wasted time with Joe and that their relationship had not been a healthy one. She'd been weak, indecisive. But maybe that's how it had been with Robby as well. It was as though she couldn't stay with a man without his shaping her.

"*Más café, señora?*" Mercedes asked.

"*Si, yo quisiera más.*"

Still, she missed his touch sometimes. Like she told Johnny that day when she might have wound up with him, Joe had awakened something.

Moira reached out her hand and touched the fine metal mesh of the screen in front of her. Michael screened it in because she complained about the bugs. But now, it made her feel caged.

She and Joe should never have taken PD with them when they left New York. It had been her idea to take him in case the police started questioning Lenny's friends. Besides, he had some connection with a commune in Oregon. It would be a great place to lay low until the heat died down.

PD hadn't wanted to go, but she convinced him. Told him it would just be a matter of time before the cops came around. She played on his paranoia. Described the subtle forms of psychological torture, the tricks they'd use. Besides, hitting the road would be fun, like they were radicals going underground in the sixties.

They pooled their money and bought some groceries and as much dope as they could for she and Joe to get through. Then they bought their bus tickets and got on Greyhound.

Joe hated Blythedale on sight. It reminded him of a foster home run by Quakers that he'd once been sent to. They were out of drugs and money, so they spent a week in PD's "house," a rusted out trailer, throwing up everything that had ever been inside of them.

PD gave them a bitter herbal blend of valerian root and who knew what else to mellow the withdrawal. He brought a woman who was known on the commune as a healer. She put crystals on their bodies and her own cool hands on Moira's forehead. But when she tried to touch Joe, he'd yelled, "Get her the fuck out of here!"

PD brought them food when they could hold it down.

Once she kicked, Moira started to enjoy herself. She hadn't had a garden since Robby's bust, and found it peaceful to work with the other women. She even milked a cow for the first time since she was a teenager and Robby brought her to the French countryside.

But Joe didn't find the country peaceful. He complained about the outhouses, no hot water, and of course the lack of wages.

"This isn't socialism. It's fuckin slavery."

Then he started to get worried, convinced PD was blabbing about the murder.

"He hasn't said anything," Moira told him.

"If he hasn't, he will. The cops get him, we're dead."

She was in no hurry to leave until the letter arrived at the commune's post office box. Addressed to her as "Maureen Roberts," a name she sometimes used. It was from her father, which didn't make sense. She hadn't told him where she was going. It was a short note:

Sweetheart,

The man you are traveling with is dangerous. He was involved in something in New York. The police may find him very soon. Please take care of yourself and stay safe.

Love,

Daddy

He'd also enclosed two one hundred dollar bills.

She showed Joe the note. That was probably her big mistake. She should have just walked away. They decided to head for California. Moira had friends there who might be able to help. Joe wanted PD to come too.

"I want to keep an eye on him," he said.

They'd saved enough farm credits to barter for another engine for PD's van. They were already in the process of getting it roadworthy. It still leaked oil and couldn't go over 45 on a flat, but they took off.

At the end of the first day, the van died. They managed to pull it over to a trailhead. Joe decided they should head for the woods to spend the night although both she and PD thought it was much too cold. It was late afternoon, not yet dark, but too late in the day and the season to meet other campers on the trail. About a quarter of a mile in, PD stopped to take a leak. Joe came up behind him and hit him in the back of the head with a rock. Then he hit him a couple more times when he was down. He and Moira dragged the body a few feet till they were at a drop-off and they pushed it over.

"That wasn't necessary," she said watching it roll down the hill.

"At least now we don't have to worry about him."

Moira knew that now they'd have a lot more to worry about. But she listened to Joe's plan. First, he thought they should torch the van, get rid of any fingerprints.

"Joe, a fire's going to attract the troopers."

So they decided to throw water over everything and wipe down as much as they could. Then they started walking. They were going to hitch, but not much passed. There was a truck stop a couple of miles down the road with a restaurant, motel, gas and groceries. They checked in.

A few minutes later, Joe was playing with the remote, complaining about the reception.

"I could use a drink." Moira said.

"Want me to go get something?"

"Hmm. I can go, get us something to eat while I'm out."

She took her purse. Forty dollars left from what her father had sent. She walked across the parking lot to the convenience store, and there she found the right man. Not a trucker, just a guy, a salesman with a wedding band, a little overweight, driving a K-car.

"Mister," she said, "do you think you could help get a girl out of a bad situation?"

That got her to San Diego. Then she had to figure out a way to get across the border. She checked out the scene. Weekdays it wasn't too crowded. The Mexicans mostly just asked to see ID. If you were walking in, they might not even ask for that. They didn't expect American citizens would be bringing in contraband. The problem was when you hit the internal border about twenty miles on and they asked for your passport.

She crossed over to Tijuana using her not very convincing fake driver's license. Met a fellow American in a bar. Told him the sad story of how her passport and wallet had been stolen, and she had to get down to Cabo the next day. Her crazy sister was all alone about to have twins. She didn't have time to wait.

He co-owned a restaurant in Camulu. "With a Mexican. Under the water, like they say here."

He knew the border cops. Told her he'd take care of it. "I'll give you a ride. No fuss, no problemo."

She worked at his place a couple of weeks. Long enough to get a little travel money. The guy didn't seem to care much that there was no sister she had to run off to tend. Then she moved on down the coast. Wound up in some hippie beach town. There was a woman staying in the same ramshackle, posada, Rebecca Mills, Canadian, twenty-six, maybe an inch shorter than Moira, a little bigger on top. Similar coloring. and hair. When the opportunity presented itself, Moira lifted her passport, which wouldn't expire until 1996. Nobody ever looked twice at the photo.

She didn't want to chance using it at a border, but it made it easy to get around. She was supposed to carry a tourist card as well, but she'd never been asked for it.

She survived for a while off of the tourist trade. It wasn't something she was proud of. There was, as Robby might have said, no honor to it. The gringos and Europeans were always leaving money around and blaming the locals when it disappeared.

She felt free in a way she hadn't in years. Clean from drugs. She slept with different people, men and women, travelers who didn't want anything more from her than the comfort of her body.

She wound up in Cabo where she met Michael.

He had gray hair and a neatly trimmed salt and pepper beard. A little paunch. Just about right for a man in his early fifties. At first she thought he might have been a retired lawyer or something.

"Toronto?" he'd said. "You don't sound Canadian."

She explained that her mother was from the states and they'd moved to Detroit after the divorce.

She moved in with him that day. Besides the ocean view, there was some land on which she'd started a garden. They even talked about buying horses. They ate out a lot and when they didn't, the maid cooked. There was a satellite dish and a VCR. It wasn't the worst life.

It turned out he *was* retired. But not a lawyer. A cop. San Francisco. Vice. She was sure he must have been dirty. Made a big score before he took his pension. But he never admitted it to her.

She knew it was risky, but she loved the perversity of it. She'd listen to him recount heroic tales of his undercover days.

"It must have been so dangerous, huh?"

"Sweetheart, you can't even imagine."

It was something, and she needed something in her life while she waited for Robby.

Jesus

Jesus sitting on the front stoop, smoking a cigar which Ana won't let him do in the apartment. The smoke is a gift from the landlord, Veroni.

He watches people pass by. *Keeping the streets safe*, he jokes when anyone asks what he's doing. There's a moving van across the street. Two young women stand guard supervising as two men empty out the truck and bring things into the building. The girls are tall and leggy, but lacking asses. Jesus wonders where they are from, probably Minnesota or someplace where they make those American types you see on TV, definitely not New York.

He spots the gnarled form of old lady Sobczak coming up the block pushing a shopping cart filled with clean laundry. He rises and drags the cart up the front steps for her and then into the building.

"Listen, Mrs. S., you leave the cart down here in the hallway. I'll bring it up in a couple of minutes."

She gives him a toothless grin, her skin a wrinkled drape over her skull. She starts her slow climb up to the fifth floor.

Ana, big as a blimp but still so graceful she floats, comes out of their first floor apartment, pushing the stroller with the baby strapped in.

"I'm going shopping," she says. "Watch him, okay?"

"*Claro, mi vida.*"

She laughs. Maybe at his Spanish. What does she want from a *Nuyorican* from the Bronx? He watches her go out the door and down the steps.

His mother, a cynical and embittered old lady, was convinced Ana only wanted him for the citizenship.

He half believed it at first. After all, what could she see in an older man, a burn out, like himself? But it was like his former sponsor once said, "You expect them to see what you were, not what you've become."

It took him a while to realize that Ana liked him *because* he went to church, and didn't drink, and had a job. It didn't matter to her that he wasn't nineteen years old, and couldn't do it three times a night.

He can still hear Sobzcak's footsteps on the stairs. He calculates another half an hour before she reaches her floor, no hurry about the cart. He frees his son from the carriage and carries him out to the stoop where he goes back to his sentry post on the steps with the boy in his lap.

He's going to miss this little life of theirs in the neighborhood – the smell of curry powder on Sixth street where there are at least twenty Indian restaurants and all of them good and cheap, or on a cool night like this one, walking all the way down to Chinatown for take out so hot and spicy that even Ana who throws chili peppers into everything, can't take it.

It was a week ago Veroni stopped by, handed him an envelope with severance pay, told him they were selling the building. The new owners were planning to buy out the tenants so they could gut renovate, wouldn't be needing a super, at least not for a while.

Ana was happy to hear the news. She made him call his uncle who worked as the maintenance manager in a complex in Secaucus, New Jersey, bunch of three story town houses near the stadium. His uncle wanted to retire, move back to Ponce, had said for years he was just waiting for Jesus to take over. Now there was no excuse not to. Job came with a two-bedroom apartment convertible to three, even a yard.

Jesus had his doubts.

He tried to explain to his wife. "You don't know what it's like for me. I need my supports."

"They have meetings there," she said, "and there's buses to the city."

She talked about the little garden they could have, room even for a slide or a swing set.

He'd been in Loisaida for years, in the bad old days on the streets and then an SRO down on Rivington. Last time he looked, that building was being gut renovated too. There was a storefront on B where he used to go to program, now some club.

This was where he'd found himself, where his life began. When his sponsor ,who'd grown up over on Avenue C, learned that Jesus was the son of a super and knew a little about plumbing and electric, he introduced him around, got him day jobs which led to his current position.

As he sits, surveying the world of East 7th Street, he wishes he had the words to explain to Ana, to describe the connection he feels. The neighborhood is like a friend? No, not that. Maybe it's like him – changing, getting better every day. But Ana would reject the idea, point to people losing their leases, small stores closing up replaced by places like the one that only sells overpriced dog treats. Terrible things still happened like that girl who got chopped up by the crazy man or that poor SOB in 5C.

If he dared to actually bring it up again, Ana would tell him the move was all for the good. It wasn't bad luck, but a break, an intervention from the saints or the higher power he called on.

He looks at his son, begins to bounce the boy on his knee, evoking a smile. He imagines him and the new one in a few years playing in a backyard with a swing set, the New York skyline visible but distant beyond a picket fence.

Jesus smiles.

Acknowledgements

An early draft of this novel was written long ago in cabaña overlooking the Pacific at Shambala/Casa de Gloria in Zipolite, Oaxaca. Belated thanks to Gloria and the Shambala family for providing an inspiring setting.

Years later, parts of a revision were showcased on the Authonomy website. I am grateful for the feedback – both critical and encouraging, provided by readers and writers there. Special thanks to JD Revene for his astute beta-reading skills and unremitting but tactful honesty, and to Bradley Wind for designing the Cara de Loca logo and the first edition cover.

Also thanks go to Dan Holloway for bringing together some immensely talented people and forming the *Year Zero Writers Collective*. Without *Year Zero*, I might never have found the courage to go "indie."

Finally, I must acknowledge the contribution of Craig Savel – my partner in crime and all other things – for his patience, encouragement, and belief.

About the Author

Marion Stein is a New York based fiction writer and blogger. You can catch up with her at Marionstein@twitter.com, and on her blog www.marionstein.net. You may also find her work elsewhere on the web and in print.

Other available books by Marion Stein

The Death Trip
Schrodinger's Telephone
Blood Diva (as VM Gautier)